TOO GOOD TO BE TRUE

TOO GOOD TO BE TRUE

Sheila O'Flanagan

headline

First published in 2003
by HEADLINE BOOK PUBLISHING

10 9 8 7 6 5 4 3 2 1

Cataloguing in Publication Data is available
from the British Library

ISBN 0 7472 7297 2 (hardback)
ISBN 0 7472 7000 7 (trade paperback)

Typeset in Galliard by
Palimpsest Book Production Limited,
Polmont, Stirlingshire

Printed and bound in Great Britain by
Clays Ltd, St Ives plc

HEADLINE BOOK PUBLISHING
A division of Hodder Headline
338 Euston Road
London NW1 3BH

www.headline.co.uk
www.hodderheadline.com

Many, many thanks to:

Agent, friend and shoe-freak Carole Blake

Two wonderful editors – Anne Williams who helped to get Carey off the ground and Marion Donaldson who brought her safely in to land

The Headline team

My family and friends

Colm – my all time high

Very special thanks to Lilian Cassin of the Irish Aviation Authority who was so helpful throughout. Any air traffic control mistakes are definitely mine and not hers! My gratitude also to the teams of controllers in Dublin and Shannon who took the time to explain it all to me

And to everyone who reads my books – a million thanks as always

Chapter 1

Clary Sage

An essential oil with a warm, nutty scent, it has euphoric properties which promote a sense of wellbeing

When Carey Browne stepped out onto West 34th Street she stopped in surprise. Not that she should have been surprised, she said to Ben, who was standing beside her holding at least half-a-dozen Macy's bags thanks to her indulgence in a sudden frenzy of last-minute shopping; last night's report from the Weather Channel had shown a shocking weather system heading in from the Midwest and they'd said there was a likelihood of snow on the East Coast. It was just that – despite the bitingly cold morning air which had caused their breath to hang in little puffs in front of them when they left the hotel – there hadn't been any signs of snow as they walked into the store over an hour earlier. Now it was falling in a slow-motion frenzy of heavy white flakes and was at least an inch thick on the sidewalk.

'Sorry,' said Ben, who'd told her that the Weather Channel wasn't always accurate and that January snowstorms often blew themselves out. 'I wanted to be optimistic.'

She linked her arm through his and snuggled closer to his fur-lined leather jacket. 'It doesn't matter,' she told him. But she frowned because if the snow continued falling at this rate their flight was sure to be delayed. She did some mental calculations and hoped that even if they were delayed she'd still manage to get back to Dublin in time for her shift the following day. If the worst came to the worst she could always phone, let them know she'd be late

1

and get someone to cover for her. But she didn't want to phone Ireland because, if she did, she'd have to tell them everything that had happened in the last few days and she wasn't ready to do that yet. She'd hardly got her head around it herself. Besides, she wanted to tell them face to face.

'We'd better leave ourselves a little extra time to get to the airport,' she told Ben as they walked down the street, carrier bags bumping against their legs. 'I've never been here in a snowstorm before but whenever it snows at Dublin there's always problems with people getting delayed.'

'I do my best to be optimistic because you always look on the worst side.' He grinned at her. 'I bet you anything we get away on time.'

'You think?' There was amusement and challenge in her voice.

'Absolutely.'

'How much?'

'Five dollars,' he told her. 'It's all the cash that I've left since you cleaned me out in the store.'

She looked at him penitently but her brown eyes twinkled. 'I couldn't help it. The discounts were so utterly brilliant that those clothes just begged to be bought.'

'I know,' he said. 'But to max out both your credit cards and all of your cash . . .'

'Give me a break!' she cried. 'I didn't do it all today.'

He laughed. 'I know, I know. New York, Las Vegas, New York – what's a girl to do. And,' he added, 'there were some unexpected expenses.'

She flung her arms round him and kissed him on the lips. 'I loved the unexpected expenses,' she murmured. 'And I love, love, love you.'

'I love you too,' he said.

'Sure?' she whispered.

'Sure I'm sure.'

'Certain?'

'I've never been more certain of anything in my life.' He brushed melting snowflakes from the mass of nut-brown corkscrew curls that framed her face and from the pair of tiny, dark-rimmed glasses perched on her nose. 'You're a wonderful woman, and you'll

2

certainly be the best dressed woman in town when we get home if today's spree is anything to go by – what's not to love?'

'I don't want you to think that we've made a terrible mistake,' she told him. 'And I'm sorry about the shopping. Really I am.'

He grinned. 'I don't think that *I've* made a terrible mistake – at least I managed to keep my credit card number to myself!'

'You think?'

'I hope so.'

''Cos if you really loved me you'd definitely give me your credit card number.' She smiled teasingly at him.

'I'm hoping our love transcends mere money,' he told her sternly. 'All the same, I'd better take you away from the temptation of the stores. Besides, we should get a move on if you want to pack and leave earlier than we planned.'

He put his arm round her waist and they hurried back towards Penn Station and their hotel. A whirlpool of people and their luggage took up most of the lobby, getting bigger all the time as more and more of them hurried in from the snow-filled streets, brushing the huge white flakes from their shoulders and stamping their feet with the cold.

Carey looked at the throng. 'Our car had better turn up,' she remarked. 'We haven't a hope in hell of getting a cab with that lot lurking round.'

'You're being pessimistic again,' said Ben cheerfully. 'You don't have to worry – I've got it under control.'

'My hero.' She looked at him in mock-adoration.

'What I haven't got under control is the packing,' he informed her. 'Everything has to be crammed into the cases and it seems to me that we have finite space but infinite purchases to put in it.'

She made another face at him and followed him to the bank of elevators. He pressed the button for the thirty-sixth floor and she leaned against his shoulder as it moved upwards.

'I still can't believe it,' she murmured. She lifted her head and looked into his eyes. 'I believed it when we were in Vegas and when it was all happening, but now, getting ready to go home, it doesn't seem real.'

'It's real all right,' said Ben. 'Don't for one minute think you can get out of it.'

3

'I don't.' She turned to him and kissed him again. 'I don't want to get out of it.'

The elevator stopped on the twenty-first floor but the couple who were waiting decided not to interrupt the pair who were already occupying it. Carey and Ben were too engrossed in their kiss to notice them anyway.

'Have you ever done it in an elevator?' he asked as the doors closed again.

'Nope.'

'Would you like to?'

She giggled. 'Of course I would. But I rather have the feeling we'll be at the thirty-sixth floor before we can really get down to it. Don't you think?'

'Yes,' he admitted. 'Though I can be very quick, you know.'

'I don't know whether that's a good thing or not!' Her chuckle was warm and happy as she nuzzled against his neck.

The elevator stopped and the chime told them that they were at their floor.

'Oh well.' Carey straightened her jacket. 'Another time perhaps.'

'On the plane,' suggested Ben. 'That Mile-High Club thing. Have you ever done that?'

'What kind of sex-life d'you think I've had?' she demanded. 'I went to a convent school, for heaven's sake.'

'Convent girls.' He sighed. 'Always looking so demure in those uniforms. But we all knew what little vixens you were really.'

She shoved him in the small of the back then followed him down the narrow corridor to their room. Ben opened the door and both of them groaned as they looked at their already full luggage.

'We'll never manage to pack this lot in as well,' she wailed as she peered into the Macy's bags. 'Why didn't you stop me?'

'I tried. I tried. But you were like a woman possessed.'

'Rubbish,' she said robustly and stretched out across the bed.

'Don't do that,' said Ben.

'What?'

'Disport yourself like that,' he told her. 'You're taking my mind off the task in hand.'

'Sorry,' she said, though her tone belied her words. 'I suppose

4

I shouldn't take your mind off the task because if we do miss the damned plane I'll be fired when we eventually get home.'

'We won't miss it. It'll leave on time and you won't be fired,' said Ben. 'Anyway, you told me that there's always someone to cover for you.'

'There is,' she told him. 'But I don't want to let them down. It's a team, you know?'

'I know.' He kissed her on the nose. 'It's nice to know that underneath that ditzy exterior is a responsible adult.'

'Oh yeah?'

'Well . . .' Ben laughed and then groaned as she caught him by the waistband of his jeans. 'Even still, we probably don't have time to—'

'Of course we do,' she interrupted him. 'I'm on a roll right now. I don't want it to end.'

'It won't,' he promised her. 'You know it's only just beginning.'

The driver of the limousine which Ben had booked to take them to the airport was making better time than they'd expected. But the snowfall was now even heavier and deep white drifts had piled up at the side of the roads. The driver left the freeway and took a route through the suburbs which, he told them, would get them there faster though Ben looked sceptical.

'I'm not sure I want to get there faster,' murmured Carey. 'This is probably the first and last time I'll ever travel in a limo. The least I can do is enjoy the experience.' She stretched out across the rear seat and put her feet on Ben's lap. 'Thank you for surprising me with this. I thought it was just going to be an ordinary car.' She smiled at him. 'And I know that we should probably be doing all sorts of sexy things back here, but you have me utterly worn out. What would be nice would be a little foot massage. I'm wrecked from all the walking around this morning.'

Ben eased her tan leather boots from her feet and began to rub her soles.

'I just might keep you.' She sighed with pleasure. 'I really might.'

They arrived at the airport with plenty of time to spare. Ben tipped the limo driver lavishly and then followed Carey to check in. According to the clerk, flights were still departing on schedule.

'Haven't heard of any delays yet,' he said cheerfully as he handed them their boarding cards.

'You see?' said Ben. 'No need for all that pessimism earlier. I think that secretly you want to stay a little longer. That's why you're hoping the weather will get worse.'

'Sod off,' she said amiably. 'It's still a five-dollar bet.'

They had coffee and doughnuts then strolled to the gate where a knot of people were already waiting. They sat side by side, Carey skimming through a copy of *Vanity Fair* while Ben read *USA Today*. They both looked up when a small squadron of stewards and stewardesses walked through the gate.

'Hand over the money,' said Ben.

'It has to depart on time,' Carey told him. 'The crew arriving means nothing.'

'That means within fifteen minutes of the time on our ticket, doesn't it?'

She laughed. 'Oh, OK.'

'I'm in the money,' he said, looking at his watch.

Five minutes later they announced the flight. Carey asked the stewardess who was collecting the boarding cards if it was really possible they'd make an on-time departure.

'Of course,' said the woman confidently.

Carey shrugged and followed Ben along the airbridge. Her teeth worried at her lower lip. She really didn't want to miss her shift the following day. The original flight time had scheduled them to arrive at Dublin Airport at six o'clock in the morning. Plenty of time, she'd thought, for her to get home, grab some extra sleep and arrive at the air traffic control centre, where she worked as a controller, by two o'clock. She knew that she could sleep during the flight but it wasn't the same thing. She followed Ben down the aisle and decided that if they were badly delayed she'd get the captain to let Dublin know. He wouldn't mind.

They found their seats on the aircraft and stowed their cabin bag in the overhead bin (plus a stuffed Macy's carrier, the contents of which would simply not fit in the rest of the luggage). Then they settled into their seats and Ben peered out of the window.

A Delta plane had just touched down and was rolling along the runway.

'You see?' said Ben smugly. 'Bet he's on time, no problem.'

Carey shrugged. 'They'll have to de-ice us,' she said. 'That'll take twenty minutes.'

'De-icing time doesn't count,' said Ben. 'Once we've moved from the stand, that counts.'

Carey pursed her lips. 'OK, OK,' she said. 'But only because you blew all your money on that limo.' She made a face at him. 'I loved it, I really did.'

He smiled but then looked at her seriously. 'And I love you.'

'I know,' she whispered. 'I love you too.'

'Ladies and gentlemen, this is the captain.'

They both sat up straight.

'Bad news, I'm afraid. The weather is getting worse, and we have to allow additional time for some aircraft to land before we obtain clearance for departure. We're third in the queue for de-icing at the moment so it looks like we'll be on the stand for a little while longer. Apologies for the delay, we'll keep it as brief as we can.'

Carey turned to Ben triumphantly. 'My five dollars,' she demanded.

'Bloody hell,' he said. 'Are you always going to be right at the last minute?'

'Always,' she said positively.

'Great.' Ben sighed as he handed her the five-dollar bill. 'I'm just beginning to wonder what I've let myself in for.'

An hour later the captain made the announcement that Carey had both anticipated and feared. Due to the heavy snow, the airport had closed. They expected flights to resume again in two to three hours.

'Three hours!' Ben looked at Carey in horror. 'I really don't want to hang around an airport for three more hours.'

'You won't be hanging around the airport,' she told him. 'They won't let us off the plane.'

'You're joking.'

She shook her head. 'Once we're boarded we can't get off again.'

'What about deep vein thrombosis?' demanded Ben. 'I can't sit folded into this seat for an extra three hours.'

Carey grinned. 'That's what you get for being six feet tall,' she told him. 'And you won't get deep vein thrombosis simply by sitting around. I didn't realise you were a hypochondriac!'

'I'm not,' he retorted indignantly. 'Just cramped.'

'I know,' she said. 'I sympathise, I sympathise, I really do. I don't want to sit here either.'

He looked at her. 'What are you going to do about work?' he asked her.

She shrugged. 'Wait and see. I thought of asking them to let Dublin know I'd be late but if we really do depart in three hours I'll still have time.'

'You'll be exhausted,' he told her.

'I'll be fine.'

'Don't you have to be at the peak of physical condition all the time?' he asked. 'After all, people's lives depend on you.'

'Oh shut up.' She grinned at him. 'I'm always in peak physical condition.'

'That's true.' He nodded. 'You've proved it over the last few days. Besides, I thought that from the first moment I saw you.'

'No, you didn't,' she said. 'You thought I was going to throw up.'

'That wasn't the first moment I saw you,' he told her. 'The first moment was in the departure lounge at Dublin. You were reading the newspaper and you looked fantastic. You have a great profile. I only thought you were going to throw up during the flight.'

'I'm still not sure that wasn't an excuse for putting your arm round me,' she said. 'I was never going to throw up.'

'You looked a bit green,' he said. 'Honestly.'

Her eyes sparkled. 'I'm glad I didn't have to go to the bother of being sick to make you put your arm round me.'

'Don't tell me you were faking it?'

'No.' She shook her head. 'I had awful indigestion. But that was all it was.'

'Or an ulcer,' he added.

'Even if I had an ulcer, it would've been worth it,' she told him. 'I don't know what else I could have done to get you to notice me.'

'You didn't need to do anything,' he said. 'I was always going to put my arm round you. Sooner or later.'

She smiled. It was hard to believe that it was less than a week since he'd first put his arm round her. It was already hard to imagine what her life had been like without him.

She hadn't originally intended to go to New York at all. She hadn't even been thinking of time off. But she was due some leave and Gina, her closest friend in the Irish Aviation Authority and with whom she shared a house in Swords, had suggested that Carey see if there were any available seats on a flight to the States because then she could come to the party Ellie Campion was giving in Manhattan. Ellie had been a stewardess for fifteen years but she'd recently met and become engaged to a Wall Street investment banker and was dying to show him off. The Wall Street banker wanted to show Ellie off too and, not having had a social function in his apartment for some time, he was keen to pull out all the stops. So he'd told her to ask as many people as she could.

Carey didn't know many stewardesses, since staff in the Aviation Authority didn't often get to meet people in the airlines themselves, but Ellie and Gina had gone to school together and they occasionally went out with Carey in a threesome – or even a foursome when Finola Hartigan, an air traffic controller like Carey, also came along. Carey hadn't been to New York in seven months even though it was one of her top three shopping destinations. But she hadn't planned anything special for her time off either and the idea of going to NYC for some fun was suddenly very appealing. She'd always known, she told Gina, that Ellie Campion would land someone rich and handsome some day. Ellie was the adman's dream of an air hostess – tall and thin, with honey-gold hair, sapphire-blue eyes and bee-stung lips. Now that she'd landed her banker she was giving up her job and moving to the States to live in his extravagant and phenomenally expensive Upper East Side apartment. And although her wedding would be in Dublin, Ellie wanted everyone to come to the States first. To brag, Gina had told Carey, but they agreed, reluctantly, that Ellie had something worth boasting about. After all, some stewardesses might be content with marrying pop stars or B-list celebrities and getting their names in *Hello!* magazine but Ellie was classier than that. Bill Stannick was worth millions and nobody even knew about it. Much better, Carey said, to be wealthy and not have anyone know about it. Gina had nodded and sighed and looked at the engagement ring on the finger of her left hand. Her fiancé Steve was a really nice guy and she was madly in love with him, but it would've been nice if he had even a tenth of Bill Stannick's money!

Due to the timing of her shifts Carey hadn't been able to fly out with the other girls but she was quite happy to travel on her own. And, even though air travel wasn't everyone's favourite method of transport any more, she still loved it. It was, and always had been, a part of her life.

She'd noticed Ben while they were waiting at the gate. He was the sort of guy you couldn't help noticing – tall, athletic, with a lightly tanned face and fair hair which was in need of a trim. The slightly too-long hair softened his angular features and emphasised his dark-blue eyes. Carey looked away from him before he caught her staring. Anyway, she told herself as she checked her bag to ensure she had some dollars and her credit cards, she wasn't interested in tall, athletic men who were exuding sex-appeal. She wasn't interested in men at all right now. She was taking one of her regular breaks from them, especially ones who were too attractive for everyone else's good.

Much to her surprise (because she normally got the seat next to the overweight man whose girth expanded onto passengers sitting beside him) she found herself sitting next to him on the plane. She didn't usually talk to her fellow travellers but he smiled at her and said hello and offered to put her bag in the overhead bin for her. She thanked him as he squeezed it into the cramped space and smiled when he made a comment about how little room they gave you and how, one day, he'd be able to justify splurging money on the first-class seats. Although not yet, he said regretfully.

'Are you travelling for business or pleasure?' she asked as she fastened her seat belt. 'If it's business you should get your company to pay up the next time, no matter how ridiculously expensive it is.'

'I nearly did once,' he told her. 'I worked for an internet company for a couple of months and we splashed money round like crazy, but the week before I was due to go to LA – very definitely business class, stretch limos laid on at the other end and everything – the outfit that was going to buy us went bust.'

10

'Not good,' she agreed. 'What happened?'

He smiled ruefully. 'Our own company went down in a blaze of glory three months later.'

'So what do you do now?' she asked.

'I run a healthfood store,' he said.

'You look far too healthy to run a healthfood store,' she said in surprise. 'Usually people who are into tofu and vitamin supplements look as if a puff of wind would knock them over.'

'Only if they don't eat properly,' he objected. 'I do. Anyway, I'm not really a nut cutlet and tofu person. I eat meat too. It's not written in stone that if you use herbal remedies you can't enjoy a bit of chicken tikka from time to time.'

'I think it's a load of mumbo jumbo myself,' said Carey robustly. 'All this obsession with organic this and herbal that! And you think that you're being way out by sucking on a chicken wing or something. Nothing I like better than a juicy steak washed down with a pint of red wine.'

He laughed at that but then took a book from his jacket pocket. Clearly, Carey thought, he wasn't the sort of bloke who could take a bit of criticism. Which didn't actually surprise her since most men of her acquaintance had difficulty in accepting criticism. Even when it was justified. She tried to make out the title of his book but couldn't. She pushed her glasses higher to sharpen her vision but he suddenly folded back the pages of the book and hid the cover. Probably a tract about the evils of modern living anyway, she thought. Which meant he wasn't really her type of guy.

She shook her head and reminded herself that she wasn't in the market for chatting to guys, whether they were her type or not. In the past she'd frequently fallen into the trap of chatting to men when her heart was already broken, and it always ended in disaster. Her friends told her that she thought with her heart and not her head, and that she simply rushed in no matter what the consequences. She knew that they were right because the last attractive man she'd gone out with – having met him on the rebound from the not-too-bad but ultimately incompatible James – had turned out to be married with a two-year-old son. Of course she hadn't known about either the wife or the son when she'd started dating him. Or when she'd totally and utterly lost her heart to him. It was only when she realised (after a

11

chance remark from her mother) that he never asked her to his place and that he always had to be somewhere at the most inconvenient times that she became suspicious. And then, of course, he'd rolled out the usual platitudes about Sandra being a great girl but that they'd married too young and it had never really worked out.

Carey gritted her teeth. She wasn't going to think about Peter Furness any more. It had ended three months ago but she still felt raw and hurt whenever she remembered. Which was why she had to avoid situations where she'd talk to a stranger and suddenly think that he was the man she'd been waiting for all her life and then start the whole thing all over again. She needed to give herself a bit of breathing space. The girls, Finola and Gina, had been fully supportive of her stance for about six weeks, but lately had been on at her to get out there and meet someone new. She realised they were concerned that she'd been really rattled by Peter Furness, but somehow she couldn't find the enthusiasm for throwing herself into the dating scene again just yet. Once a fixture at night-clubs and parties, she'd spent a lot of evenings at home on her own in the last few weeks. Anyway, she was tired of meeting guys, thinking that it was going somewhere, finding out that it wasn't, and having to break up with them.

At least she didn't get hurt all the time. She wasn't a complete fool. Sometimes she realised that, despite the fact that the man she was going out with was attractive or solvent or caring or had a good sense of humour, she just didn't like him enough. Gina told her that she was too fussy. Finola said that she enjoyed being single too much, that she set her standards too high. Neither of those things were true, she told herself, as she pushed her wayward curls out of her face and rubbed the bridge of her nose. She just wasn't a very good judge of potential boyfriends.

Oh well, she thought, as she flicked through her magazine without reading it, at least I always realise my terrible mistakes in time. And I might do stupid things sometimes, but I always get over them in the end. Still, she added to herself, it would be nice to get it right just once. To fall for the right bloke at the right time and for him to fall for her too. It was astonishing how it never happened like that.

The plane pushed away from the stand and began to taxi towards the runway. Carey glanced towards the control tower where today

12

Stan Mullary was the ground movements controller. She could picture Stan sitting in his seat, bright green baseball cap backwards on his head, as he ordered the planes around the airport like huge, rumbling chess pieces. Sometimes Carey thought that Stan would really have liked to be a pilot himself. But he always said no, that he'd hate all that palaver with uniforms and starched shirts and peaked caps, and he'd pull his own cap further down on his head and say that air traffic control was a much better job.

She gazed out of the window as they taxied to their position at the end of the runway. At this point she knew that Stan would hand over control of the plane to the air movements controller, Jennifer O'Carroll, who'd clear them for takeoff. According to the pilots, Jennifer had the sexiest voice in air traffic control. A kind of Mariella Frostrup with honey, the British Airways guys told her. Carey knew what they meant. Face to face, Jennifer's voice was lilting and mellow, but the mike added a huskiness that men found incredibly attractive.

'Fortunately they never get to see me,' Jennifer said when they teased her about it. Jennifer herself was short and slightly plump, with cropped red hair and a cheerful face full of freckles.

'The Americans would love you,' Stan often told her. 'A kind of retro-colleen is what you are.'

The engines whined and they began rolling. Carey closed her eyes and yawned as the plane built up momentum. She visualised them in the tower, watching the huge Airbus hurtle down the runway and lift into the air until it reached around 800 feet. At which point the tower lost interest in it completely and passed it over to the control centre where the controllers (younger than most people ever imagined – she was a veteran at thirty-three) plotted their course out of Dublin airspace.

A sharp pain suddenly ripped through her stomach and she winced. She'd eaten a full Irish breakfast while she was hanging round the airport that morning. It had seemed a good idea at the time but sausages, rashers and fried eggs really didn't do her digestion any good at all. She wondered why she did the wrong thing so often when it would be just as easy to do the right thing. Why it was that she ate things that were bad for her, or did things that were stupid, or generally behaved in a

13

silly and possibly juvenile way for someone who was in her thirties. She wondered at what point in her life she'd turn into a grown-up.

The plane had lifted. She felt the jolt as the wheels were retracted and then a sinking feeling in her stomach as they turned westward. Between the air pockets and the indigestion she wondered for a moment if she was going to be sick. She hoped not. It would be totally embarrassing, absolutely humiliating in fact, for Carey Browne to throw up on a flight. She winced again. It was then that she felt his arm round her shoulders.

She opened her eyes abruptly. The fair-haired vegetarian health-freak was smiling at her as he held the tops of her arms.

'What the hell d'you think you're doing?' she demanded.

'Distracting you,' he said.

'From what?'

'From the fact that you're clearly terrified.'

'I'm not terrified.'

'Of course you are,' he said confidently. 'You're about to squeeze that armrest into submission.'

She glanced at her hands. She'd grasped the armrest when her stomach had spasmed. Her knuckles were white. She made an effort to relax them.

'You know, there's really no need to worry,' he said.

'Thanks for your concern.' She removed his arm from her shoulders. 'But I'm fine, honestly.'

'You don't look it,' he told her.

'Listen, Veggie,' she said crossly, 'the only thing that's wrong with me is that I have indigestion from my full fry-up breakfast. Not that you'd know what a fry-up is, but it was absolutely gorgeous and worth every pang.'

He grinned. 'Feisty little thing, aren't you.'

'Would you give it a rest!' She regretted the fact that such a good-looking guy was a total dickhead, but regrettably she'd found that was often the case.

'I'm sorry,' he said. 'I guess I'm teasing you a bit. But I was worried about you.'

She looked at him in silence for a moment. 'Apology accepted,' she said eventually. 'You shouldn't make snap judgements.'

14

'It was based on available information,' he said. 'But I'm prepared to revise it.'

'Revise away,' she said dismissively.

He grinned. 'So perhaps you're really a pilot?'

She shrugged and he suddenly looked aghast.

'Don't tell me you actually *are* a pilot,' he said. 'Please don't tell me that I've insulted one of Ireland's only female 747 captains or something like that. I do have a habit of opening my mouth and putting my foot in it.'

'Relax,' she said. 'I'm not a pilot.' She smiled suddenly and her face lit up. 'Far more important than that! I work in air traffic control.'

'Do you really?' He stared at her and she nodded.

'I've always thought that must be a really cool job,' he said. 'All that peering at radar screens and looking at those dots, knowing that they're actually planes. What do you do?'

'Anything that's necessary,' she told him, 'but because I have an approach rating that's what I do most often. Which means bringing the aircraft in to land basically.'

'You tell them what runway to line up on and all that sort of thing?'

She nodded cheerfully. 'It's great,' she told him. 'All these macho pilot types have to do exactly what I tell them.'

He laughed. 'And do you get off on that?'

'Naturally.' Her smile dimpled her cheeks.

'How many?'

'What?'

'Landings?'

'Oh, it depends,' she said airily. 'The maximum number of movements in an hour should be forty but we can handle whatever they throw at us.'

He looked at her sceptically. 'You're sounding a bit macho yourself.'

'Comes with the territory,' she told him, and then she grimaced as another pain darted through her stomach. 'Actually, sometimes it can get quite stressful but you learn to cope.'

He exhaled. 'Beats organic chips any day.'

She laughed and the pain subsided. 'Depends on what you like doing, I guess.'

15

'Do you work in the control tower?' he asked enviously.

'Sometimes,' she replied. 'Really the tower looks after things on the ground and gives clearance for departing planes. Most of us are actually in the Centre and we don't see the light of day at all, unfortunately.'

He nodded. 'I've seen pictures of them. Little green blobs on the radar screen.'

'That's my life,' she agreed. 'Little green blobs.' She looked at him from beneath her lashes. 'The best video game in the world.'

'You don't think that, do you?' he asked in horror.

'Lighten up,' she said easily. 'Of course not. But you don't think of them as planes full of people either. Just – well, blobs on the screen that you have to move around. Like a video game.'

'Are you ruthless or heartless?' he demanded.

'Neither,' she said with amusement. 'But you can see that it's not exactly part of my job description to be clutching at the armrests in terror.'

'I suppose not,' he said. 'In which case you must have pretty bad indigestion. Sure it isn't an ulcer?'

She shook her head. 'Indigestion.'

'Because like you said, your job is very stressful.'

'Yes and no,' she told him. 'It can be, when it's busy or when there are problems. But the great thing is that when I've finished my shift I can just walk out and go home and I don't have to think of anything. Somebody else deals with the next batch of planes.'

He nodded. 'Nice not to have an in-tray to deal with or anything like that.'

'Exactly,' she said.

'Well, Ms Air Traffic Controller,' said Ben as he sat back in his seat. 'It might be indigestion but it could still be an ulcer, or stress. In which case can I recommend lycopodium.'

'I beg your pardon?'

'Lycopodium is good for mental exhaustion,' he told her. 'Also those who are stressed.'

'I'm not stressed, honestly,' she said. 'I just shouldn't have eaten sausages, rashers, black and white pudding, baked beans and a fried egg before leaving.'

He grimaced. 'Do you eat anything with whole grains in it?'

16

'Afraid not.' She grinned.

'Oh well, it's your stomach to destroy,' he said. 'And you don't really look overweight to me.'

'I have a brilliant metabolism,' she told him. 'Burns off loads of stuff. Besides, most times I eat healthily. More or less.'

'You must do,' he said. 'You've got good skin, great hair and clear eyes.'

She stared at him. 'You make me sound like a spaniel or something,' she told him.

'Sorry.' He was quiet for a moment then turned to her again. 'Why air traffic control?'

'I grew up under the flight path to Dublin Airport,' she told him. 'I always wanted to make sure the planes landed in the right place.'

'Really?'

She nodded. 'And my dad worked at the airport so it was kind of inevitable, I suppose.'

'Are you a family dynasty of controllers?'

'Not really,' said Carey. 'Dad was ground crew until he retired. My older sister worked in one of the airside shops until she got married and had a gaggle of kids.' Her brown eyes twinkled at him. 'But my brother's a pilot.'

'I feel a right thick asking you if you were scared,' he sighed. 'You've probably sat in the cockpit with your brother loads of times.'

'Actually, no,' she admitted. 'Tony's married to an Australian girl and I haven't seen him in a couple of years. He doesn't do commercial flights, he works for a private company in Perth. And controllers don't often get the opportunity to go up front in a plane.'

Ben looked at her. It could all be true, he thought, or she could be making it up just to sound more interesting. She looked far too happy-go-lucky to be an air traffic controller with those mad curls dancing round her face and her lively eyes sparkling at him from behind that cute pair of specs. Air traffic controllers should surely be more serious? His only experience of them was from the movies, where actors like George Kennedy played grizzled, tough guys who had to come through in any crisis. This girl didn't look as though she could chomp on a cigar like George.

She should be the love interest, being rescued rather than doing the rescuing.

His next question was drowned out by the stewardess announcing that they'd start their cabin service shortly. Carey, feeling that she'd done rather more talking than she'd intended, no matter how nice her neighbour might appear, took a fresh magazine out of her bag and began to read. He went back to his book which, she realised, wasn't actually a vegetarian handbook but a John Connolly blood and guts thriller. In her opinion, this showed a secret longing for gore in a far too healthy life but she said nothing and immersed herself in *20 Ways to Get Your Body Ready for Spring*.

But they got chatting again when the meal was served, which was when he told her his name was Ben Russell and that he lived in a modernised two-up, two-down house in Portobello. And that he actually owned the healthfood store he ran as well as two other similar stores in the city. She told him that she hadn't pegged him as a multi-vitamin entrepreneur, more of a shopkeeper. And he laughed and said that there wasn't as much money in it as you'd think but that he was very happy doing what he was doing. Money wasn't everything, he said, which was just as well because he'd lost a fortune on the internet company and now he ploughed most of whatever he made back into the shops.

She warmed to him. He was easy to talk to and easy to get on with. He wasn't as patronising and sexist as she'd originally thought. He talked about the radical change his life had taken when the internet company went bust and he moved into herbal remedies instead. He told her that he was in partnership with his sister, Freya, and that they were trying to get away from health foods and natural remedies as being a goody-goody way of looking after yourself.

'That's why we sell fruit-flavoured condoms,' he remarked, causing her to splutter into her glass of wine. He grinned and confirmed that they were excellent sellers. 'You'd be surprised,' he added, 'how many people ask me if the orange-flavoured ones have Vitamin C added.'

'And do they?' she asked.

He laughed. 'You mean you haven't already tried them?'

She asked him what it had been like when the internet company had gone bust and he told her that it had been the weirdest feeling

18

in the world. One day he was the marketing manager of a company employing a hundred people, the next he had nothing. 'If only the damn takeover had gone through first,' he said gloomily. 'It was worth a fortune. At least then we could have gone bust with some personal cash in the bank!'

'So why did you go into healthfood stores?' she asked.

It had been his sister Freya's idea, he explained. Six years older than him, she'd worked in a bank all her life but had always wanted to do something else. Alternative remedies were an interest of hers. So when she came to him with a business plan which exploited her business knowledge and his marketing expertise, they'd taken their proposal to the bank, succeeded in getting a loan and had taken the plunge together. Now, three years later, things were going really well.

Carey realised she was enjoying the sound of his gravelly voice as he chatted to her, and the way his bondi-blue eyes lit up with animation when he spoke of things he was interested in, as well as the way he listened when she spoke of things that interested her. Their interests were very similar. They both liked action movies, loved Italian food, agreed that Barcelona was probably the most beautiful city in the world – and neither of them could stand opera. Quite suddenly she understood what people meant when they talked of meeting someone whom they felt they'd known all their lives.

For the first time ever she was disappointed that the trip across the Atlantic didn't take longer.

'D'you need me to hold your hand?' Ben asked as the captain announced that there were fifteen minutes to landing. 'In case you're really a sales rep for a sheep dip company or something, and everything you've told me is a complete lie and you are, actually, secretly terrified.'

'No,' she said, her voice brimming with laughter, and then she mentally kicked herself for not saying yes. And then she told herself that she was right to say no because she was definitely still hurting from the Peter Furness episode and she was better off not getting involved with anyone, no matter how quickly they made a transatlantic flight pass by. Just for once, she reminded herself, learn your lesson. Don't fall for someone on the rebound.

They didn't talk as the plane descended through the wispy white clouds that hung over JFK. When they landed it was as though the previous six-and-a-half hours hadn't even happened. Ben was extra polite as he took his bag from the overhead locker. She smiled at him in the way that strangers smile when they're forced to acknowledge each other, while realising with a pang that the enforced intimacy of their journey had come to an end. But maybe it was just as well, Carey thought. She wasn't ready to lose her heart again, she really wasn't. Peter Furness's betrayal had shaken her more than she'd realised.

'Maybe I'll see you on another trip to New York,' said Ben as they waited to disembark. 'I'll definitely think about you whenever I'm flying, though. I'll be wondering if you're the one putting us into some crazy holding pattern over the Bay.'

'I doubt that I'll be back in New York any time soon,' she told him. 'I'm here for a party.' She looked at him quizzically and spoke impulsively. 'You wouldn't like to come, would you?' After the words were out she wished she hadn't said anything. But he was looking back at her, his eyes bright and interested.

'What kind of party?'

She shrugged. 'You don't have to come, of course you don't. It's just – well, you said you were here to see your US suppliers, and I thought you might be bored . . .' Her voice trailed off. She wasn't usually so tongue-tied. Everyone knew her as decisive and determined. 'A friend of mine is getting married. She's having a bit of a do in her soon-to-be-husband's totally awesome apartment.'

'I'd love to come,' said Ben. 'Of course I get bored when I come here. There's only so much you can say about Vitamin E supplements. And I've never been in a totally awesome New York apartment before!'

She smiled. 'Where are you staying?'

'The Pennsylvania. Not flashy but OK.'

'You're only a couple of blocks from me,' she told him. 'I'm in the New Yorker.'

'Is this party tonight?' he asked. 'I'm supposed to be having dinner with some people, but . . .'

She shook her head. 'Tomorrow. It'll give you time to get over your meetings and your dinner.'

'OK,' he said. 'Will I meet you at your hotel?'

'Great.'

'How are you getting into the city now?' he asked.

'Oh, the bus,' she told him. 'I'm travelling light and it leaves me near the station.'

'Share a cab?' suggested Ben.

She smiled. 'I'd love to.'

In the cab, the intimacy was restored. Once again, Carey felt as though she'd known Ben for years instead of hours. Even when they lapsed into silence she didn't feel uncomfortable in his company. She simply gazed out of the window and watched as the Manhattan skyline grew ever closer.

She was tempted to ask him into the hotel but she knew that the New Yorker didn't have a bar. So she simply said that she'd see him the next day and he said fine. They looked at each other uncertainly for a moment, then she smiled at him and walked through the revolving doors without looking back.

Chapter 2

Jasmine Absolute

This oil is sensual and luxuriant; it is also relaxing and uplifting

Carey's fond reminiscing about her first meeting with Ben was interrupted by another announcement from the captain. Despite his desire for a speedy departure, JFK remained closed and the snow was still falling, although not as heavily as earlier. But they weren't going anywhere in a hurry. The cabin staff came along the aisles offering orange juice and peanuts. Carey and Ben both took the juice but refused the nuts. She looked at her watch.

'Worried?' he asked.

'Not yet. My shift starts at two. As long as we get back before then it's fine.'

'You'll be exhausted,' he said.

She shrugged. 'I'll get some sleep. I wish we'd managed to get upgraded, though; it'd be nice to be able to stretch out.'

'Prop your pillow against my shoulder,' Ben said. 'You might as well try for some shuteye now.'

She smiled and did as he suggested even though she wasn't tired yet. But she was accustomed to falling asleep at will and it wasn't long before she'd nodded off. It seemed only moments later that she was woken by another announcement. She blinked and glanced at her watch to discover that she'd slept for three-quarters of an hour as the captain told them that the airport had finally been re-opened and that they would shortly be ready for de-icing. A murmur of anticipation and relief ran through the cabin as they were eventually pushed back from the terminal building and the de-icing of the plane began.

She closed her eyes to blot out the sight of the workers hosing the thick coating of snow from the wings and allowed her mind to drift back to the night of Ellie's party. The night of her first date with Ben. She'd intended to wear her one and only posh frock to the party – a plain black silk sheath which looked well no matter what the occasion. But now that Ben was coming too it seemed drab and boring. She tried to tell herself that this was a one-off, that she wasn't going to get involved with him and that she needed space and time. Rushing into a new relationship wasn't on her agenda so whatever dress she wore was irrelevant.

But even though she told herself all these things, she still wanted to look good. In fact, she wanted to look fantastic. She wanted to wear something that would make him be glad he was with her. Something that said sophisticated but charming. A somewhat demanding task, she realised, as she stood in the Bloomingdale's changing room and looked at her lanky body and almost non-existent chest in the long mirror in front of her. Carey desperately wished that she had some curves to fill the slinky dress she was trying on, that her bones weren't so big, that her knees didn't look so damned knobbly and that her feet were smaller and narrower. The sales assistant who looked in to see how she was doing tried to tell her that nobody had boobs any more – hadn't she seen the pictures of Sarah Jessica Parker or Gwyneth Paltrow lately – but Carey wasn't convinced. She longed for a cleavage. A natural cleavage, not one manufactured by Berlei and cotton wool.

Eventually though, she succeeded in buying a cocktail dress in vibrant purple which showed off her creamy skin and dark brown eyes to perfection. Although the neckline was low it didn't make her look as flat-chested as some dresses. It also showed off rather more flesh than she'd originally anticipated but the assistant told her that it was breathtaking.

Carey agreed, but she wasn't quite sure how her friends, who were accustomed to seeing her in either the black dress or a pair of black leather trousers, would react to the wisp of purple. Nor she was sure how the clean-living and organic Ben would react to going out with someone who considered it OK to wear a dress which was nothing more than a chiffon hanky. Yet it was undoubtedly breathtaking.

23

And with the expensive high-heeled shoes that she'd also bought it made her look very, very sexy.

Which was exactly what Ben said when they arrived at Ellie's and she slid out of her navy wool coat. And what Ellie said when she greeted Carey with her newly acquired Manhattan air-kiss. Ellie's glance had flickered appreciatively over Ben and then she ushered them further into the apartment where a throng of friends was already gathered. Carey had forgotten that outside Ireland eight o'clock means eight o'clock, and that by arriving at half-past, she and Ben were almost the last to show.

Suddenly, though, she was caught in the middle of the throng and people were asking her about her devastatingly attractive new man and murmuring that he was absolutely gorgeous and wasn't she the clever one to have picked him up. How long had she known him and why had she kept him a secret?

'Well, we know why!' Gina grinned at her as they looked at Ben talking to Ellie's fiancé, the investment banker. 'I wouldn't let him loose in a room of single women if I were you, Carey.'

'He's rather lovely, isn't he,' she said diffidently. 'Just as well you and Finola are already hitched.'

'He's walking sex,' said Bernice Taylor. 'And *I'm* not hitched. How on earth did you manage to snare him?'

When they heard that she'd met him in the plane on the way over there were shrieks of astonishment which turned to nods of understanding.

'You always manage something like this, don't you?' said Gina. 'Carey Browne, the lightning rod for the unexpected! Things just fall into your lap and you end up doing everything without thinking.'

'I certainly don't do things without thinking, as you know perfectly well,' Carey retorted. 'And he didn't fall into my lap.'

'Looks like he might want to.' Gina grinned knowingly at her. 'But you know what I mean, Carey. You rush in where angels fear to tread and all that sort of thing. It doesn't matter whether it's men or it's something else. You were the one who bought a king-size bed for the house without wondering how on earth it was going to fit in that cell they call a bedroom. You were first up for the Karaoke night at Christmas . . .'

'OK, OK.' Carey nudged her. 'I don't hang around, I know that.'

24

'You were right not to hang around with him,' said Anna Irwin. 'I'd snap him up in an instant myself given half the chance.'

'Is that a warning?' asked Carey.

'Could be, girl,' said Anna. 'Could be.'

Then Ben walked over to her and asked to be introduced to her friends. Carey was astonished at the amount of eyelash fluttering that went on among them, particularly in the case of Gina, who was engaged to Steve, and Finola who'd been living with her boyfriend for the past two years.

'So it's true,' said Ben. 'You guys are all in the airline industry?'

'Carey and I are both controllers.' Finola flicked her jet-black hair from her forehead and tucked it behind her ears, showing off dangling amber earrings which emphasised her long, slender neck. 'Helping to keep the skies safe and all that sort of thing. Gina works in admin.'

'I do things like buy them new computer equipment,' said Gina. 'When they complain that the state-of-the-art stuff they already have isn't good enough.' She tucked her arm in Ben's and smiled at him. 'Doesn't it do your heart good to know that whenever you're in a plane you've got a gang like us looking after your best interests?'

'Is air traffic control totally run by women?' he asked.

'No.' Carey sighed. 'Naturally we will take over one day but at the moment we're probably outnumbered five to one.'

'Any George Kennedys?' asked Ben.

'Pardon?' Finola looked at him in puzzlement and he explained his movie-generated knowledge of anything to do with airlines.

Finola laughed. 'I think George was always the plane's engineer, wasn't he? And surely you'll concede that Carey, Gina and me are a bit better-looking than him in a crisis?'

'That wouldn't be hard,' said Ben, amid chuckles from the assembled group. 'What about the rest of you, what do you do?'

Anna and Bernice were both stewardesses with Aer Lingus. They regaled him with stories of passengers from hell which had him vowing to be on his best behaviour any time he flew in the future. Both girls promised to look out for him on their flights since both of them covered the New York route.

'Ellie might be disappointed she hitched herself to Bill before she met you,' suggested Anna mischievously as she caught her friend looking over at them.

'I don't think so,' said Ben. 'He was telling me how much he was worth. I'm afraid that I pale in comparison with him.'

'Not from where I'm standing,' murmured Finola.

Carey looked at her friend in astonishment and annoyance. She couldn't believe that Finola was coming on so heavy to Ben. But Finola was a terrible flirt if her own boyfriend wasn't around. Even, sometimes, when he was.

'Pity Dennis couldn't come along tonight,' she said to Finola. 'Or will he make it later?'

'No.' Finola shook her head. 'He's in Bermuda.' She turned to Ben. 'He's a pilot too. Works for one of the American airlines.'

'Finola's been living with him for two years,' said Carey.

'Must be difficult for you if he spends a lot of time in places like Bermuda,' said Ben.

'Not really,' said Finola. 'It works for us. And he always comes home to me so I guess we're doing something right.'

'Gina's engaged,' said Carey.

Ben looked at her and smiled. Then he turned to Gina. 'When's the wedding?'

'God knows,' she told him. 'Now that I've met you . . .'

He laughed. 'Don't break up with your boyfriend on my account,' he told her. 'I'm a serial womaniser.'

'All to the good.' Gina chuckled. 'We can have a great time and nobody will worry about it.' Then she turned to Carey and put her arm round her while Ben took the opportunity to have his wine glass refilled. 'Don't look like that, Browne, I'm only pulling your leg.'

'Looks to me like you were trying to pull more than that,' muttered Carey.

'Sorry.' Gina looked contrite. 'We were teasing, honestly. It's just that you took us by surprise. We set out for a celebratory girls' peek at Ellie's place and you turn up with the Incredible Hunk. How d'you always manage to do things like this?'

'I don't,' Carey protested. 'And what about my last so-called Hunk? Married with a kid!'

'Don't get upset,' said Finola. 'I'm sorry too. I didn't realise you actually cared about this bloke.'

'I *don't* care,' said Carey. 'How could I care? I've only just met him. And it's a one-night kind of thing. But it'd be nice to know that you guys weren't circling like vultures.'

Anna and Bernice laughed.

'Those two might not be vultures but we could be,' said Anna. 'Let us know if it lasts longer than a night, Carey. If not, he's fair game.'

'Who's fair game?' Ben turned back to them.

'You are,' said Carey. She smiled at him. 'Come on, let's look around a little more.'

'Are you really?'

Ben returned Carey's gaze in puzzlement as she asked him the question. She'd led him through the apartment and they were now standing on the huge balcony which overlooked Central Park while the lights of the Manhattan buildings chequered the darkness.

'Really what?' he asked.

'A serial womaniser,' she said. 'You told Gina that's what you were.'

He laughed and his breath clouded in the cold night air.

'I don't know,' he said. 'I've done the long relationships and the shorter ones. But your friends were terrorising me and I thought it might be a good idea to let them know that I wouldn't be a decent prospect in the going-out stakes.'

'I couldn't believe them,' said Carey. 'I mean, Gina and Finola are both seriously, seriously attached! Admittedly Anna and Bernice are a different kettle of fish, but . . .'

'Actually, I'm not,' said Ben.

'Not?'

'Come on, Carey. I don't want to be a serial womaniser – not really. I want what everyone wants. To meet the right person, to marry them, to live happily ever after.'

'And you think that it's possible?' she asked.

'You have to hope, don't you?'

She shivered in the sudden gust of wind that blew across them. Ben put his arm round her shoulder. She leaned closer to him and then, before she realised it, they were kissing each other, inhaling each other's scent, twining together in the freezing air. She could

27

feel her body trembling and she didn't know whether it was because of the cold or because she was in his arms and because it felt so perfect.

She broke away from him but he kept his arms linked behind her back. His blue eyes looked darker in the subdued lighting of the balcony.

'My God,' he breathed slowly. 'I never realised it could be like this.'

'What?' Her own voice was shaky.

'A kiss.'

She smiled slightly. 'I'm sure you've had much better kisses.'

'No,' he said. 'I've had longer kisses. And kisses with girls I've known for ages. But I've never kissed anyone like you before.'

She didn't want him to say things like this. Things he couldn't possibly mean. She didn't want her one-night stand to be infused with a whole heap of sentiment that wouldn't mean anything in the cold light of day.

He held her tightly. 'Do you believe in love at first sight?' he asked.

'No,' said Carey firmly. 'But I believe in lust at first sight.'

He laughed. 'And dare I hope you feel any lust for me right now?'

'Oh yes.' She leaned forward until her head was resting on his shoulder. 'I absolutely do.'

'Would you like to leave this party?'

He felt her nod her head but it was a couple of minutes before either of them moved. Then they left the party together, much to the disappointment of her friends who'd wanted to talk to him again.

As a one-night stand it was phenomenal. Carey felt a thrill of illicit pleasure when they took a cab back to his hotel and hurried up to the room. The pleasure was heightened as he slid her chiffon dress from her shoulders, slowly peeling the fabric from her body, his hands sliding along the silkiness of her skin, bringing her to an intensity of desire that she hadn't realised she could ever feel. And then the pleasure was shared as he made love to her slowly and easily as though they had made love together a thousand times before but with all of the passion that the first time together brings. She felt as though she was part of him and he was part of her. She felt as though she never wanted to let him go.

Afterwards, as they lay side by side in the darkness, he whispered, 'Marry me,' and she turned towards him and gazed into his eyes. And she knew, without a shadow of a doubt, that the only answer she could give was 'yes'.

She hadn't, of course, initially realised that he meant get married that week, nor even that he was 100 per cent serious. But when she woke up beside him, her hair a tumbled mess of wayward curls and her eyes panda-smudged with mascara, he was already on the phone to a travel agent and booking tickets to Las Vegas.

'We might have to get it notarised or something when we go back to Ireland,' he told her, 'but I've booked us into the Chapel of Everlasting Love for four o'clock tomorrow afternoon.'

She stared at him wordlessly.

'Unless,' he added, 'you think that this is too sudden.' He laughed, but his expression was troubled. 'It *is* too sudden, isn't it? I know it is. I'm being incredibly stupid to assume . . . I'm sorry. It's just that I've never, ever felt like this before. Last night – last night was perfection. I can't allow perfection to escape, I just can't. I didn't think it would happen. I wasn't expecting it to happen. But it did. You felt it too. I know you did.' He ran his fingers through his hair so that it stood up in corn-coloured spikes. 'I don't want to let you out of my sight. And I don't want anyone else to have you. I knew it from the moment I saw you last night. I knew it even before that – maybe I even knew it on the plane. But at the party I was talking to loads of people and all I could think of was being alone with you. Your friends were chatting me up and I could only think of you. I wanted to make love to you right there, on the balcony of someone else's apartment. Nothing like this has ever happened to me before, Carey. I don't want to lose the feeling. I don't want to lose you.'

'I've never felt this way before either,' she told him. 'I want to marry you too, Ben.'

'But do you want to marry me tomorrow?' He looked at her ruefully. 'You probably want to go home and get engaged and have a big do back in Dublin like any normal girl dreams of. Like your friends. You don't want to get married in some awful clapboard chapel on Las Vegas Boulevard with nobody you know to see it and with hundreds of other couples queuing up behind! I'm being thoughtless and selfish. I'm sorry.'

'No,' she said. 'You're not being thoughtless and selfish. You're being perfect. I want to marry you in the Chapel of Everlasting Love, despite the incredibly tacky name, and I want to marry you tomorrow. I never dreamed of the big do back in Dublin that you're talking about. I hate all that sort of thing, always have. I want something that's just for us.' She shrugged. 'And why wait? I know that you're exactly the right person for me. I knew it the moment you put your arm round me in the plane. I love you and I want us to be married for the rest of our lives.'

He kissed her. She kissed him. And she knew that even if she was rushing in, this time it was right to rush.

'Good news, ladies and gentlemen,' said the captain. 'We've been given permission to start our engines and we should be on our way very shortly.'

There was a murmur of exhausted approval from the passengers. Ben turned to Carey who'd sat up at the announcement.

'Are you worried?' he asked.

'No,' she said as she looked at her watch. 'We'll get there with a bit of time to spare.'

'I don't mean about getting to work on time,' he said. 'I mean about going home. About telling everyone what we've done.'

She looked at her thin gold wedding band and smiled at him. 'I'm not in the slightest bit worried about it,' she said. 'Why should I be?'

He shrugged. 'I know you said that you wanted to marry me straight away, and I know we had a great time in Vegas – but do you regret it?'

She laughed. 'We've been married less than a week and you're asking me if I regret it already? Give me a break!' Her eyes sparkled. 'Though I suppose if I did we could pop back to Reno and get a quickie divorce.'

'It's just – I rushed you into it, Carey. I didn't mean to but I did.'

'You didn't rush me into anything,' she assured him. 'Except my dress at the hotel.'

30

'We only had the Chapel of Everlasting Love for thirty minutes,' Ben reminded her. 'Our time was ticking on. I was afraid you were stalling.'

'I wasn't stalling.' She giggled. 'My zip got stuck, if you recall.'

He reached into his jacket pocket and took out a photograph. It was of the two of them, standing outside the white wooden chapel, rice in their hair as they emerged into the scorching sun. Carey had bought a short white dress and had pulled her curls up high onto her head, securing them with a mother-of-pearl comb. She'd exchanged her glasses for contacts and her brown eyes looked warm and happy. Ben was wearing a rented tux, a red carnation in his lapel. He was grinning widely at the camera.

'You clean up well,' she told him as they looked at the photograph together. 'In fact, you look good enough to eat.'

'You looked mighty fine yourself,' he said.

She kissed him. The plane began to taxi to the runway. They were still kissing as it took off on its journey to Dublin and still kissing by the time they'd reached their cruising altitude. And neither of them wanted to break free, even though Carey murmured that she really had to get some sleep.

She slept for most of the journey. She had never felt so secure before, so right with one person. It was as though her entire life had suddenly clicked into place, as though she'd found a new meaning in everything she did. She hadn't expected to feel like this. She hadn't known what true love really meant. She'd thought she'd experienced it before – with Ray and with Seamus, with Frank and with James and even, at first, with the traitorous Peter Furness. She'd been convinced that it was the real thing with Peter. But it wasn't. It was nothing like the real thing. Nothing like the contentment she'd unexpectedly found with a man she hadn't even known existed a week earlier. And, although the sex was unbelievably good, it was the feeling of contentment that was the most important thing. The feeling that she'd found someone who already knew what she was thinking and who already knew what she was going to say. The person who loved her just as much when she was shapelessly wrapped up in her navy-blue coat, blue scarf and blue hat as when she was lying naked on his bed wearing nothing more than her pearl earrings. (And who loved her naked because she really wasn't sure that, with her body, being naked was the best way for her to turn on a prospective lover anyway.)

Despite the fact that all of her friends used to tease her for losing her heart so quickly, Carey knew that this was different. This was for ever. And love at first sight really happened.

Chapter 3

Rosemary

An invigorating herb which promotes mental stimulation and helps muscle fatigue

By the time the return flight to Dublin finally landed and they retrieved their luggage, it was eleven o'clock. Ben pushed the trolley through the baggage hall and into the arrivals area and then stopped.

'What now?' he asked.

'I guess I'll go home,' said Carey. 'Have a shower, change and then come back for my shift.'

'Home being the house you share in Swords?'

'At this point, yes.' She squeezed his arm. 'Home will change but not until after my shift.'

'I understand.' He began to push the trolley again. 'Will you have time to pack all your stuff before going to work?'

'I doubt it,' she said cheerfully. 'I'm a hoarder, unfortunately. I hope you have plenty of space. I'll do my best though.'

'My house is small.' Ben looked worried. 'How much have you got?'

'Don't panic,' said Carey. 'I'll do some pruning. It's time I got rid of some stuff anyway.' She walked quickly to keep up with him.

'You don't have to throw out things you want just because of me,' said Ben.

'I won't do anything just because of you!' She grinned at him. 'Though it's so weird, isn't it? When I left here last week everything was normal. Now it's changed. I can't quite get my head round it.'

33

'Can't you?' He looked at her anxiously. 'You're still OK about all this, aren't you?'

'Sure,' she said confidently. 'It's just – well, I hadn't given much thought to the practicalities, that's all. Packing my stuff. Moving out.' She made a face. 'Moving to the southside. I'm a northsider, Ben – we don't cross the river.'

'Well, I'm a southsider and neither do we.' He grinned at her. 'And since I actually own my house – or at least since I'm the one with the mortgage – and you're only renting, it does make sense for us to live in Portobello.'

'I know that,' said Carey. 'It's just that moving southside is like – like emigrating.'

'Oh, for heaven's sake!' But he smiled. 'It's not such a big deal.'

'I know it's silly,' she said. 'But I can't help it.' Then she glanced at her watch. 'Anyway we don't have time to argue about it right now. Come on, let's grab a couple of taxis and get on with it.'

The queue for the taxis was unexpectedly short. Carey opened the door of the third cab that arrived and looked at Ben. 'I'll call you when I'm finished,' she said.

'I'd better give you my mobile number,' he told her.

'God, yes!' She looked surprised. 'I didn't think of that. I feel as if your number's somehow automatically stored on my phone.'

'Well, it's not. Here you are.' He handed her a business card. It was white with a border of intertwining green leaves. His name was embossed on it, along with the title *Managing Director, Herbal Matters* and his phone numbers.

'This is beyond freaky,' she said as she slid the card into the pocket of her jeans. 'I'm putting my husband's business card away because otherwise I don't know how to contact him!'

He laughed then leaned towards her and kissed her. 'See you later, Mrs Russell,' he said.

'See you later.' She kissed him again and then got into the car.

She told the driver where she was going and then turned to look out of the rear window. Ben was getting into the next taxi. She closed her eyes, suddenly tired despite having slept through most of the flight. She'd woken as they'd begun their final approach and, as always, had visualised them as they appeared on the radar in the control centre, a green blip with their call sign and altitude beside it. She could hear the controller giving instructions to the pilot, see the blip vector along the runway until finally it disappeared as it was handed over to ground control again. Ben had watched her as she rubbed the sleep from her eyes and told her he was glad that he wasn't on any plane under her control that afternoon.

She'd be fine when she'd had her shower and washed her hair. She was more dehydrated than tired really, because she hadn't drunk as much liquid as she normally would on a long flight since she'd needed to sleep. A pint of water would sort her out. She yawned and stretched her arms out in front of her as the taxi driver drew up outside the two-bedroomed house with its tiny front garden. She paid him, then hefted her bags out of the boot.

Gina was out. Because she worked in the office, Gina kept normal hours. It was a pity, thought Carey, because it would have been nice to have been able to tell her friend about Ben before she arrived in for her shift. She pursed her lips as she thought of Gina's reaction. She'd be stunned. Shocked. And maybe she'd also be annoyed that Carey hadn't said anything before now. Carey hadn't been in touch with Gina since the night of Ellie's party. She'd told her friend that she'd probably stay in New York for a day or two, or possibly come back to Ireland and spend a few days with another friend who lived in Shannon. So Gina wouldn't have been put out by the fact that she hadn't spoken to her since last week. But when she learned of Carey's marriage, when she found out how it had all happened, she probably wouldn't even believe her. She'd have to believe her, thought Carey as she rubbed her wedding ring, when she saw all her stuff packed and ready to go.

She walked into her small bedroom and pulled open the curtains. Clothes and books and CDs were piled high on every surface. There were more piles of stuff downstairs. Carey loved shopping even though she invariably bought jeans and jumpers because they covered her body the best. Her weakness, though, was shoes. She had boxes and boxes of shoes in all sorts of shapes. Some were expensive and bought for style rather than comfort. They were in the car-to-bar pile – shoes that could only be worn if she didn't have to walk anywhere. Some were chain-store shoes – bought because they were such good value that she couldn't say no. Some shoes hadn't even been worn yet. She grimaced. Ben would have a fit when he saw her shoe collection. In addition to the ones she'd bought to go with the purple dress for Ellie's party and her flimsy wedding dress in Vegas, she'd acquired another three pairs in New York, but he'd assumed that was because she was capitalising on the sales.

Yawning and feeling grubby, Carey peeled off her clothes and walked into the bathroom. She switched on the electric shower and scrubbed her body with an exfoliant cream. By the time she stepped out from under the hot water she was glowing and refreshed. She dried her hair, pulled on a pair of black jeans and a black roll-neck jumper and slid into her most comfortable ankle boots. Then she rubbed tinted moisturiser onto her face and lip gloss on her lips. She never wore anything else by way of make-up in work: when you were shut in a windowless room with a dozen or so people whose job was to stare at a radar screen, there didn't seem to be much point. Then she went downstairs and made herself a cup of strong coffee. She drank the coffee in three gulps, reapplied her lip gloss and went out to her car.

Her heart was beating rapidly as she drove to the airport. She pulled into the car park in front of the control centre and walked through the blue gates that surrounded the prefabricated concrete building. The first thing people would say to her was, 'How was the holiday? Any news?' and she knew she'd have to tell them about her marriage straight away. But it already seemed as though it had happened to someone else, as though the last few days were a dream. She found it difficult to believe that she'd actually done it: she'd married Ben Russell, a man she hardly knew, and now she was officially his wife.

'Hi, Carey.' Tim Benson, the security guard, greeted her as she pushed open the entrance door.

'Hi, Tim.' She stood hesitantly in the reception area for a moment. She was early and wasn't quite ready to go into the centre yet and face everyone. Instead, she decided to go to the Piggery (as the kitchen was known) and make herself another cup of coffee.

'Carey!' The door opened and Gina stepped into reception. 'I was looking out for you. How are you? How was the holiday?'

'I'm great, Gina,' said Carey. 'The break was fantastic.'

'Did you see any more of that handsome hunk?' asked her friend. 'My God, Carey, he was one of your best yet. Really attractive. I know we teased you about him, but Finola and I said afterwards that he was dead gorgeous. If it all goes belly-up with the love of my life, I might just fight you for him.' She grinned. 'Did you see him again, or was it really just a one-night stand?'

Carey moistened her lips. 'Not exactly,' she said.

'Not exactly?' Gina beamed at her. 'Oh, tell us – what happened? Did he stay for a few more days in New York? Or did you come home with him?'

'Sort of. And yes,' said Carey.

Gina frowned. 'Sort of?'

'We went to Las Vegas,' said Carey.

'Las Vegas!' Gina laughed. 'What did you do? Gamble your hard-earned savings away? Or rush into some tacky church and get married!'

'Yes,' said Carey.

'Yes?' repeated Gina.

'Yes, we rushed into a tacky church and got married. Only it wasn't actually tacky, it was really very nice. They treated us well, didn't rush us or anything.'

'You're joking.' Gina stared at her.

The other girl shook her head. 'No, I'm not.'

'You *must* be joking!' Gina looked down at Carey's left hand and then grabbed it. 'Oh, come on, Browne, I know you. You're pulling my leg.' She laughed. 'You really had me going there for a minute, but don't tell me that's a real wedding ring on your finger.'

'It's a real wedding ring on my finger,' said Carey. 'And my name's Russell now.'

'No!'

'Yes.'

'Oh my God.' Gina covered her mouth with her hand. 'I don't believe it. I just don't believe it. You *married* him?'

'Married who?' Trevor Hughes walked up to them. 'Hi, Carey, how was the holiday?'

'She got married,' said Gina.

'What!' Trevor's tone was as shocked as Gina's.

'She got married,' repeated Gina. 'To a bloke she met on the plane on the way over.'

Trevor laughed. 'She's having you on.'

37

'I'm not having anyone on.' Carey had expected this sort of reaction but it was difficult all the same. 'It's perfectly true. I met a guy and I married him. No big deal.'

'Carey Browne! It's a huge deal!' cried Gina.

'Carey *Russell*,' Carey corrected her.

'I think it's a great idea,' said Trevor. 'No messing about. No romantic nights out while you try to pluck up the courage to talk about it. Just meet, make love and get married. Perfect.'

'Well, yes,' said Gina. 'Except you haven't the faintest idea who you're marrying.'

'Thanks,' said Carey shortly.

'Oh, Carey, sorry. I didn't mean – you know what I meant.'

'You met him,' said Carey. 'You know what he's like. You know why I married him.'

'No,' said Gina. 'Actually I don't. He's gorgeous, I'll give you that, and he seemed really nice and amusing and all that – but I don't know him. And surely you don't really know him either.'

'I know him enough,' said Carey steadily.

'If it's all right by you, then it's all right by me,' Trevor told her staunchly.

'And me too,' said Gina hastily.

'Come on, let's have a celebratory coffee.' Trevor looked at his watch. 'Twenty minutes before the best team in the world takes over the airspace. Let's let them know all about it.'

She followed him to the Piggery where some of the team were already drinking tea and coffee. Trevor pushed open the door and announced that Carey had some big news to impart. Once again, she found it difficult to speak. She cleared her throat.

'I just thought I'd let you all know that I got married last week,' she said diffidently. 'In the States.'

'In Vegas,' supplied Trevor.

'To whom?' asked Conor Reid as he tore open a packet of chocolate chip cookies. 'I thought you broke up with that guy you were going out with. Did you patch things up?'

'Of course not,' said Carey. 'There wasn't anything *to* patch up. No, this bloke is different.'

'This sounds fantastic,' said Elena Travers. 'Where did you meet him, Carey? Have you known him for long?'

38

'For a few hours,' said Trevor. 'She met him on the plane on the way over to the States.'

'Carey?'

Although Elena was the one who said her name questioningly, Carey felt six pairs of eyes staring at her. She shrugged.

'You know me,' she told them. 'Good at making quick decisions.'

'Well, absolutely.' Richard Purcell looked at her searchingly. 'This seems to have been a *very* quick decision.'

'Love at first sight,' said Carey lightly.

'There you go!' Trevor laughed. 'It really happens.'

'It's unbelievable,' said Elena. 'Tell us about him, Carey. What does he do? Is he Irish? American?'

She felt better as she talked about Ben. Suddenly he became a real person again and not just the man she'd met and married without thinking about it. She told them about his time in the internet company and setting up the healthfood shops with his sister and, as she spoke, she felt a warm glow of closeness to him.

'And you're madly in love,' said Elena.

'Yes,' said Carey simply. 'I really and truly am.'

'Then I wish you all the best in the world.' Elena kissed her on the cheek. Suddenly they were all clustering around her, wishing her well, telling her that they hoped she'd be very happy.

And she felt good about it all over again.

Ben stood in his living room and scratched his head. The pale February light filtered through the narrow front window and picked out the dust on the floor. At least, it picked out the dust on what part of the floor he could see. Right now, most of it was covered in boxes.

He'd bought his house in Portobello while he was still working for the internet company. At that time he'd also bought a Saab convertible, a Yamaha jet-ski, a flatscreen TV which hung on the wall, a customised sound system with Bose speakers, an ultra-slim Rado watch plus an assortment of electronic organisers and must-have gadgets, most of which he'd never bothered to use. After the company's collapse he hadn't been able to keep up the repayments on the car, the jet-ski or the TV. At least the sound system and the watch were his since he'd bought them outright. And, even though he'd had to negotiate a mortgage holiday with his bank when times were particularly tough, he'd managed to hang on to his house.

He'd fallen in love with it when he'd first seen it because it was an absolutely perfect bachelor pad. The previous owner, an architect – it was always architects who bought small houses close to the city, renovated them and sold them for a small fortune – had gutted it completely. Downstairs now consisted of an open-plan kitchen and living area with matt white walls; the original floorboards had been sanded and varnished. Upstairs, the two medium-sized bedrooms had been altered so that there was one main room and a tiny guest room. The architect had taken the bath out of the small bathroom and replaced it with a shower so that there was more space. He'd originally intended to convert the attic area too, which would have made everything seem much bigger, but hadn't quite got round to it before deciding to emigrate to the South of France and do up an old farmhouse instead.

Ben had made an offer for the house straight away and had then been forced to raise it when someone else had bid higher. But he'd been quite determined to get it and, even though he knew he was paying over the top, it was worth it to own such a lovely home with the added bonus of its being a five-minute stroll along the canal to his office.

Of course, when the company went belly up the perfect location of the house was irrelevant. At first Ben hadn't worried, there were plenty of jobs out there and he was well qualified, but he suddenly realised that the sort of job he wanted didn't seem to exist any more. And eventually he began to re-think his career and his future. At which point the repossessions had started.

He didn't mind the loss of some things. He'd hardly ever used the jet-ski – he'd only bought it because at the time everyone in the company was buying one. He'd been sorry to see the TV go, but he'd replaced it with a 19-inch set which took up a lot less space. And he was heartbroken when he had to hand back the keys to the Saab. But, in the end, none of it really mattered as long as he kept the house.

But now . . . he looked round him. Since he'd gone into business with Freya he'd used his home as extra office space. They had an office above their shop in Rathmines which was only a short walk away, but he did more work at home than he ever did there. Half of the living area was taken up with his computer, paperwork and boxes of samples. The spare bedroom was also packed with samples and additional supplies. He hadn't really noticed, over the past couple of years, that his home had almost completely been taken over by his business.

There'd never been much furniture in it to start with, partly because there just wasn't room and partly because Ben had no interest in buying it anyway, but he suddenly wondered how Carey would feel when she turned up only to realise that there were two armchairs but no sofa, that the one table was a small gate-leg affair in the kitchen area and that he'd never bothered to buy wardrobes but had simply hung his clothes on a pair of chrome rails which Freya had bought for him from Habitat.

He looked at his watch. He'd have to phone Freya soon and tell her that he was back. And then he'd have to tell her about Carey. He rubbed his face with his hands at the prospect. He knew that his sister would think he'd done something incredibly stupid. Freya was always telling him that he'd done incredibly stupid things – it was part of her role as his big sister, the girl who had practically raised him even before his mother and father had died.

He hadn't spoken to Freya since he'd met Carey. He'd sent her an e-mail from New York, simply telling her that he was staying on for a few extra days and that he'd contact her when he got back. He'd known that it would puzzle but not worry her. At heart she always thought of him as slightly unpredictable, even though he'd been extremely hardworking and predictable about the shops. But, for him, disappearing for a few days was more in character than out of character. He'd originally intended to say something in the message about researching some new type of remedies but he simply couldn't lie to her. So he said nothing.

He'd call her soon, he promised himself, but first he would have to tidy the place up a bit. It was unbelievably messy. The trouble was, he thought as he surveyed the room, he needed everything that was here.

In the end he filled two black refuse-sacks with rubbish in addition to packing his green paper-recycling bin to the brim. And that was just with stuff from downstairs. He hadn't even begun on the spare

41

bedroom. He filled the kettle to make some coffee then flopped into one of the biscuit-coloured armchairs and closed his eyes.

Two hours later, he woke up. Of course, he told himself as he jerked into consciousness, he was totally jet-lagged. Unlike Carey he hadn't managed to sleep on the plane although he'd drifted in and out of wakefulness. But he couldn't completely switch off like her. He'd been astonished at the way she'd fallen asleep so easily.

She'd undoubtedly be tired when she got home tonight, he thought tenderly. Her shift ended at ten o'clock but she'd be able to sleep late the next morning because the rostering system meant that the following day she didn't start until nine in the evening although it meant working through the night until six the next morning. Ben scratched his head. It was a while since he'd gone out with anyone who worked really strange hours, although in his time with the internet company his main girlfriend, a web designer, had worked crazy shifts, often sleeping in the office overnight. He'd get used to it, he supposed. He worked some pretty odd hours himself sometimes.

Now he was hungry and restless. He decided to walk to Rathmines, grab something to eat and then call into the shop. There was a chance that Freya would be there, which would mean he could break his news to her straight away. And afterwards he could come back to the house and tidy up the bedroom. He wasn't looking forward to doing it. He knew that girls were fussy when it came to hanging up their clothes and finding places for their myriad pots of face-cream and make-up. He hadn't noticed Carey bothering much with all that while they were away, but she was bound to have more stuff at home. They all did. Even the web designer had kept a bag piled with potions in the office.

He hopped under the shower for a couple of minutes to freshen up, then got dressed and went outside. It was already getting dark and the late-afternoon air carried a winter chill. He walked briskly along the canal then turned onto the Rathmines Road. After a cup of soup and portion of bread from the nearby deli, which warmed him up and staved off the pangs of real hunger, he continued down the road to the shop.

As always when he stood outside *Herbal Matters*, he felt a glow of pride and satisfaction. This was something that he'd built up himself, that he'd worked hard to achieve. With a little help from Freya, of course.

The shop looked exactly like a regular chemist. Ben believed it was important to look like a mainstream shop instead of a niche store. He wanted people who wouldn't normally think about herbal remedies and supplements to feel as though they were taken as seriously in *Herbal Matters* as they were in their local pharmacy. So, like the latter, they also had a display of shampoos and make-up, cottonwool and bits and pieces. In their case, though, everything was made from natural ingredients. Sometimes people came into the shop without realising its speciality nature but very often they left with a natural remedy for their sore throat or bruised arm or feeling of general exhaustion.

Ben pushed open the door and was greeted by a waft of warm air. He flexed his cold fingers with relief.

'Hi, Susie.' He smiled at the girl behind the cosmetics counter. 'How're you?'

'Ben!' She beamed at him in return. 'I'm great. How was the trip to the States?'

'Very interesting,' he told her. 'I've ordered more of that lip balm you said that everyone liked and they're doing a range of it with enhanced sun protection. Not that you'd actually need it today.' He glanced out of the window and made a face.

'No,' said Susie, 'but it'll be an excellent seller in the summer. That whole range just walks out of the shop, it's brilliant. And the new cotton-rich shampoo is doing really well too.'

'So sales last week were good?'

She nodded. 'Absolutely.'

'Thank God for that.' He smiled. 'Is Freya about?'

'Yes, she arrived a few minutes ago. She's in the office.'

'I'd better go up and talk to her,' said Ben. 'I'm sure she'll have a few things to say about my extended trip abroad.'

'Why?' asked Susie. 'You were paying for it, after all.'

Ben laughed and walked through the shop to the narrow stairs at the back which led up to the office area. He pushed open the door marked *Private* and walked in. His sister was sitting behind the grey steel desk, her eyes focused on the computer screen in front of her, her long blonde hair caught back from her face with a wooden clip.

'Hello, there,' said Ben.

'Hi,' she said, without looking up at him. 'Hang on a minute, I'm just updating this.' Her fingers flew over the keyboard for a moment and then she leaned back in the chair and supported the back of her neck with her hands. 'So you finally decided to come home. That was nice of you.'

'Tsk, tsk,' he said. 'You sound a bit peeved.'

'I am,' she told him. 'You leave here for a two-day meeting with clients and disappear for almost a week. The only communication I get from you is a very brief e-mail telling me that you'll be back soon. If you were an employee I'd fire you.'

He grinned. 'But I'm not an employee, I'm the Managing Director. So you can't fire me.'

'*Joint* Managing Director,' she corrected him. 'And I could organise a boardroom coup! However, since you haven't had any holidays in about two years I suppose I can forgive you. What were you up to? Anything exciting?'

'Well, yes, actually,' he said awkwardly. 'I got married.'

Shock flowed from Freya like a physical force. She sat up straight in the chair and stared at him.

'You what?' she asked eventually.

'Got married.' He extended his hand and showed her the ring on his finger. 'Till death us do part and all that.'

'Ben Russell, you're having me on.'

'No,' he said. 'I truly did the deed.'

'How?' she asked. 'To whom? Why?'

'In a chapel,' he replied. 'To a girl called Carey. Because I love her.'

'I don't know anyone called Carey,' said Freya accusingly. 'You never mentioned her before. And what about Leah?'

'I never mentioned her before because I've only just met her,' said Ben.

Freya got up from the chair and perched on the corner of the desk. 'You've only just met her?' she repeated. 'You've only just met her and you married her?'

'Why not?' asked Ben. 'I love her.' He put his hand into his pocket and took out the photos of their wedding day. He handed them to Freya who looked through them wordlessly. When she'd finished she went through them all over again.

'You actually did this?'

'Proof positive,' said Ben.

'Why didn't you tell me before now?'

'I didn't have time.'

'You could have made time.'

'We were in a time bubble,' Ben told her. 'Nobody existed but ourselves.'

'Oh, come on.' She looked at him irritably. 'That's bullshit.'

'No,' he said. 'We were together. Nothing else mattered.'

'For fuck's sake, Ben!' Now her blue eyes were angry. 'You went off and got married to a perfect stranger and you think that nothing else matters?'

'At the time nothing else did. Of course other things matter. Now that we're home we have to get on with life. But I love her, Freya. I really do. And that's all that really counts, isn't it?' He looked at his sister defiantly.

She picked up the photos again. 'The Church of Everlasting Love?'

'It's in Las Vegas,' said Ben. 'Actually it was a lot nicer than you'd think. They were really good to us. Afterwards we went over to Caesar's Palace for a meal.'

'Oh my God.'

'And it was great. At the ceremony the pastor spoke very thoughtfully, not at all schmaltzy. And when we got to Caesar's there were other people who'd just got married too and it was all great fun.'

'Great fun,' repeated Freya faintly.

'Absolutely,' said Ben.

'And who is this girl exactly?' asked Freya.

'I told you. Her name's Carey, she has a sister and a brother and she works at the airport.'

'How old is she?' Freya peered at the photo. 'She's not some flighty teenager, is she?'

'Come on, Freya.' He smiled at her. 'You can see that Carey's not a teenager. She's not some silly gullible girl that I picked up—'

'I'm more concerned with you being the silly gullible bloke,' interrupted Freya.

'She's a very lovely, very intelligent woman in her early thirties,' said Ben. 'She's a mature person with a responsible job.'

'She's not lovely,' said Freya dismissively. 'Look at her, Ben. All arms and legs. She hasn't got a pair of boobs to bless herself with despite wearing a dress which appears to be slashed to her navel.'

'That's enough.' Suddenly Ben was annoyed with his sister. 'You don't have to slag her off, just because you haven't vetted her first.'

'I don't need to vet your girlfriends,' said Freya acidly. 'I just thought it'd be nice to meet your future wife before you actually married her.'

'Why?' asked Ben.

'Because – because that's what people do!' cried Freya. 'Oh Ben, I'm not trying to say that you were wrong to marry her. How can I say that when I don't even know her? But even you have to admit that meeting her and marrying her in a couple of days is sheer madness. What happened anyway?'

Ben explained about sitting beside Carey on the plane and her invitation to the party and their sudden realisation that they wanted to be with each other for ever.

'But, Ben . . .' Freya stared at him in amazement. 'She's not even your type of girl.'

'What d'you mean "not my type"?'

'Her looks, her job, her lifestyle . . . she's not like anyone you ever went out with before. She's not in the slightest bit like Leah.'

'Yes, well.' Ben looked stonily at his sister. 'Maybe that's why I married her and not Leah.'

The phone rang and both of them jumped. Freya picked it up. Her glance flickered towards Ben as she listened to the caller.

'Actually, yes, and we were just talking about you,' she said. 'I'm sure he does want to speak to you.' She held the receiver out to her brother. 'Leah.'

Chapter 4

Rose Absolute

A floral oil with a delicate perfume

Carey stood in the Piggery sipping a cup of coffee. She was on the first break of her shift and she was glad to have a few minutes to herself. Fog in London that morning had delayed a whole heap of flights and every single pilot wanted their particular plane to be given an early slot for landing. She knew that the pilots were under pressure to keep to their timetables, but on days like today it was impossible. Peeling the paper from a Cadbury's Snack she began to nibble the chocolate from around the biscuit. She'd swallowed the last bite when Chris Brady walked in.

'So, Carey Browne, what's all this about rushing off to get married?' Chris poured himself some coffee and looked at her enquiringly. 'And why didn't you tell me you were thinking about it?'

Chris was one of the longest serving members of the team. Carey had worked with him when she'd first started in air traffic control and, of all the people she worked with, she respected Chris the most.

'It was a love at first sight sort of thing,' she explained. 'I didn't tell anyone I was thinking of it because I didn't know I was thinking of it myself. I was only supposed to be going to New York for a party!'

'Some party.' Chris pulled up a chair. 'What happened to make you run off with him?'

'I didn't run off with him,' Carey said patiently. 'When we left the party I spent the night with him and afterwards he asked me to marry him. So I did.'

47

'Wow.' Chris leaned back in his chair. 'The sex must've been good.'

She made a face at him. 'The sex was brilliant,' she allowed. 'But it wasn't – *isn't* – just about sex, Chris. I love him. It's that simple.'

'And what does your family have to say about it?'

'Nothing yet,' said Carey. 'I only got back a couple of hours before my shift. I haven't had time to tell them yet.'

Chris laughed. 'We normally have engagement parties and pre-wedding drinks and all that sort of stuff. I'm not sure what we'll have for you, Carey.'

'Nothing,' she said. 'You know, Chris, I was never into the whole wedding thing. My sister Sylvia made such a bloody fuss over hers – it was lace this and satin that and music and menus and God knows what from morning till night every single day of her engagement. So I'm quite happy to have given it all a miss, to tell you the truth.'

'I thought you were only a kid when your sister got married.'

'I was thirteen. I saw enough to put me off completely.'

'You still could've come home and done it,' Chris said gently. 'You didn't have to rush into it.'

'Look, Chris, you're my friend and I really like you. Always have. But it's none of your business how I chose to get married.' Carey crumpled the gold foil from her biscuit into a little ball and threw it at the wastepaper bin where it bounced harmlessly off the side and onto the floor. Chris leaned over and put it in the bin.

'I'm sorry,' he said. 'I guess I was concerned.'

'Too late to be concerned!' She grinned at him in forgiveness and waved her left hand in front of him. 'I've done the deed and I have to live with it.'

As she finished the sentence the door opened again and some of the administrative staff walked in.

'Carey!' cried Laura Sullivan. 'What's the story, girl? I hear you've been tripping up the aisle.'

'True,' said Carey.

'You dark horse,' said Laura. 'Let's see your ring.'

'It's only a plain band. Nothing special.'

'Aren't you the brave one all the same?' Deirdre Quinn smiled knowingly at her. 'Keeping him under your hat, were you?'

'She didn't even know him,' said Laura. 'At least, that's what Gina

48

told me. Jesus, Carey, are you not afraid he'll turn out to be an axe murderer or something?'

Carey laughed. 'More likely *he* should be afraid.'

'True,' conceded Laura. 'Everyone knows you've got a bit of a temper. Remember that time you threw a cup at Elena?'

'That was an accident,' protested Carey.

'Accident my foot.' Deirdre sat down and put her hands round a mug of tea. 'So, come on then. Give us the gory details from the horse's mouth.'

Chris stood up. 'I'll be getting back,' he said. 'I'll talk to you later, Browne.'

'I'll be back in a minute myself,' she told him. 'And it's Russell now, Chris. Carey Russell.'

'You're not going anywhere before you tell us all about the wedding,' Laura insisted. 'I've always wondered what Vegas was like.'

'It's different,' Carey admitted. 'But nice.'

'Photos?' asked Deirdre.

Carey nodded. 'In my bag. I left it inside.'

'For God's sake!' Laura sighed. 'I'll really only believe it when I see the photos.'

'Oh, come on.' Carey grinned. 'Don't I look like an old married woman to you yet?'

Laura tilted her head to one side and scrutinised Carey. 'Maybe you do,' she said. 'Or maybe you just look like a person that's had a massive improvement in her sex-life lately.'

'Laura Sullivan!' But Carey couldn't help laughing. She was still chuckling as she made her way back to her radar screen.

Ben Russell sat in the café and waited for Leah. He hadn't told her about his marriage on the phone despite Freya's dark looks and her constant pointing at the third finger of his left hand. His conversation with Leah had been stilted and unpromising and, in the end, he'd told her that he had a bit of news but he really needed to see her and so would she like to meet for a drink.

In fact, the very last thing Ben wanted was to see Leah Ryder. But he knew that he couldn't have told her about Carey with Freya listening to his every word, and he also knew that he had to tell

Leah about his marriage in person and as soon as possible. It was only fair, but he wasn't looking forward to it.

Tipping a sachet of brown sugar into his latte, he stirred it slowly. He didn't usually take sugar in coffee but very occasionally he needed the sweetness it provided. This was one of those occasions. He looked at his watch – she'd be here any minute. Leah was never late. His glance flickered towards the door of the café as it opened. He'd known it would be her, and he was right. She stepped inside and shook the raindrops from her bright red umbrella. Then she looked across the room and saw him and her mouth broke into a smile.

She was beautiful when she smiled. In fact, thought Ben, as she walked over to him, she was always beautiful. She was the most beautiful girl he'd met in his life. And everyone else thought so too. Leah was small, barely five feet tall. Her face was heart-shaped and her skin flawless. Her features bore the traces of an Asian origin that had been diluted over two generations: her grandmother was Japanese, born in Osaka. She'd married an Englishman – practically unheard of in those days – and had moved to London. Her daughter, Leah's mother, had married an Irishman and moved to Dublin. Leah was Irish. She'd been born in Dublin and had lived here all her life but there was a fragility about her that few Dublin girls possessed.

She waved as she threaded her way through the too-close-together tables. Her hair, long and straight, fell in a black sheet down her back. She was wearing a quilted jacket in the same shade of red as her umbrella over a royal-blue cotton dress. The colour brightened up the dull and steamy café. But then, thought Ben, Leah had a way of brightening up a place even if she was wearing nothing but black.

He'd met her three years ago, just after he'd opened the second shop with Freya. She'd come in a couple of days after it had opened and had asked him for an essential oil which he didn't have on display. He frowned as he tried to remember what it was. Patchouli, he thought. Or maybe sandalwood. Whatever it was, he'd known at the time that they did have it but he didn't know why it wasn't on display. So he'd offered to check out the storage area and find it for her.

It had taken ages. He'd been convinced that she'd be gone when he finally found it (he was almost sure it was patchouli) but she was still waiting for him, standing patiently beside the counter, dressed that day in a red and white houndstooth check skirt and a plain red

T-shirt. He'd learned, afterwards, that red was her favourite colour. It was certainly her best colour. It brought out the raven blackness of her hair, the tinted ivory of her skin and the darkness of her eyes. The same colour eyes as Carey, he thought suddenly. The colour of bitter chocolate.

Leah was a beautician. She worked in an exclusive salon near Ailesbury Road which was frequented by the wives and daughters of diplomats and very successful businessmen. Leah had a deft touch with make-up but her speciality was massage. Ben learned this because he'd been so attracted to her that he'd asked her all about herself and had then wondered, aloud, whether or not men ever came to her salon for massage.

'Of course,' she said. 'Men are as stressed as women.'

'More so, probably,' Ben mused and Leah had laughed and said no, that women's lives were a million times more stressful than men's but that he was welcome to book himself in for a massage if he thought he needed it.

Eventually he had made a booking, but he'd asked her out first. He said that it would be wrong of him to book in for treatment under false pretences. She said that she was glad, since it would be wrong of her to give him a massage under false pretences too. But there was no pretence in the way that they felt about each other. Ben fell in love with Leah. Leah fell in love with Ben. And Freya was delighted that her brother who, up to now (in her opinion) had gone out with very unsuitable girls, had found someone as intelligent and as caring as Leah. Freya had gone to the beauty salon for a makeover a couple of weeks after Ben and Leah had started dating, which was how she knew that Leah was intelligent and caring and how Ben discovered that Leah did wonderful things with make-up.

They'd gone out together for a year. Ben wasn't sure how or when things had started to go wrong between them. He didn't know whether or not it was the night that he went round to her apartment and was greeted, as usual, by the scent of jasmine and lavender from the floating candles that she always lit and which, being truthful, he didn't really like; he didn't know whether or not it was the day that she laughed at a joke which he simply didn't get; he didn't even know whether or not it was the day she accused him of not caring about her enough because he'd insisted on going

51

to a football match with his friend, Phil, instead of going shopping with her as he'd originally promised. He couldn't put his finger on the moment that their relationship had begun to change, but what he did know was that, much as he cared for Leah, he had stopped loving her.

There had been low-key arguments, then hostile silences, then fully-fledged rows and they'd stopped seeing each other although Freya still went to the beauty salon for treatments and remained friendly with his ex-girlfriend. She kept him in touch with what Leah was doing and how Leah was getting on, and Ben had been pleased (although slightly jealous) when Freya came into the office one day and told him that Leah had a new boyfriend – a property developer who owned a string of apartments in the city and who drove a Saab turbo. Afterwards Ben wasn't sure whether he was jealous about the fact that the property developer was going out with Leah or whether it was because the man was driving the make of car that Ben had lost to repossession. Then one night Leah had called him to say that she'd split up with the property developer but he was supposed to have accompanied her to a formal dinner that evening – was there any chance that Ben, as an old friend, could help her out and come along?

He sighed deeply as he remembered. Sometimes he wished that he'd said no. He'd wanted to say no but he hadn't because there was a part of him which had been quietly triumphant that the property developer and his damned Saab hadn't been enough for Leah and so he'd said yes. He hadn't expected to have a good time – he'd been sure that Leah would shoot plenty of barbed comments in his direction about their failed relationship, but she hadn't and they'd spent a really enjoyable evening together which made him wonder why on earth they'd split up in the first place. They began to see each other again although more occasionally than in the past. They told each other that it wasn't an exclusive thing, that they were friends who helped each other out, that it wasn't a boyfriend-girlfriend type of relationship. Sometimes they didn't see each other for weeks because one or the other of them had met someone new. Once, Ben had been convinced that Leah had found someone really important because she hadn't contacted him in over two months. But she'd phoned again, telling him that it hadn't worked out, and he'd called round to her with a box of Belgian chocolates and a bottle of champagne. And he'd spent the night with her. In the last couple of months he'd been the one to meet new people, although the latest – a flirtation with a sales rep from a multi-vitamin company – had been a mere two-night stand which had left him feeling vaguely dissatisfied with the way he was living his life. He'd rung Leah to talk to her about it and had ended up in her apartment – and in her bed again – only this time she'd provided the champagne.

That had been the night before he'd gone to New York.

'Ben, sweetheart, it's lovely to see you again so soon.' Ben was jerked back to the present as Leah pulled out the wooden chair and sat opposite him. 'How was the Big Apple?'

'Big,' he said.

'And your meetings? Everything go well for you?'

'Yes,' he said.

'You sounded very mysterious on the phone,' she said. 'I felt quite excited at coming here to see you. What's the news that you had to tell me in person?' She flicked back her river of hair, suddenly reminding him of Carey's friend, Finola, who'd done exactly the same thing at Ellie's party.

He took a deep breath. 'I met someone in New York,' he said. 'On the way to New York actually.'

'Someone?' She raised her thin black eyebrows questioningly.

'A girl,' said Ben.

'Oh, Ben.' She pouted. 'Not another one. You know that I'm getting tired of being your old friend in between all the girls that you go out with and get messed up over.'

'Hopefully I won't get messed up over this one,' he said. 'I married her.'

'Pardon?' She pushed her hair behind her ears and leaned forward. 'I don't think I quite got that.'

'I married her,' he said again.

'Married?' she repeated.

'Yes,' he said. 'Married.'

She stared at him. Actually, he thought, her eyes weren't exactly the same colour as Carey's. Leah's were definitely the colour of dark chocolate but Carey's were more of a milk chocolate shade. Although maybe it was emotion that was darkening Leah's now.

'And why did you marry her?' she asked finally. 'Is it some kind of joke? Is she American? Do you want to live in America and get American citizenship?'

'Don't be silly, Leah,' he said mildly.

'It's not me who's being silly,' she snapped. 'Honestly, Ben, what were you thinking of? You said you met her – did you know her already? Is she one of your former cast-offs?'

'No.' Ben kept his voice calm. 'She was a girl I met on the plane.'

'Are you out of your fucking mind?' The words were louder than she'd intended and people at the nearby tables glanced in their direction. Ben studiously avoided looking back and instead kept his eyes fixed on Leah.

'You know, it'd be really nice if at some point someone didn't say that to me,' Ben remarked. 'Freya used a similar expression and it's getting boring.'

'I'm not surprised she used a similar expression,' said Leah angrily. 'Ben, this is crazy. You've married someone you don't even know!' Her voice rose again and this time Ben was sure that everyone in the café had heard.

'I had to tell you in person because we've always been friends,' he said. 'I didn't feel it was something I could say over the phone.'

'Friends!' She stared at him. 'Friends! We were fucking lovers, you bastard.'

'Leah, please.' He could see that the two women at the table beside them had abandoned any pretence of not listening and were openly staring at them, their cream buns forgotten as they waited in anticipation for what might come next.

'Please what?' she asked. 'Please sleep with me on Tuesday and please say nothing when I turn up married a few days later?'

'Leah, I didn't plan to get married.'

'Oh great, that makes it all OK then.'

'You and me, we were friends. We—'

'Oh, what planet are you on, Ben Russell? Friends, my arse! We went out together for a year. You got a fit of nerves because I started talking about the future and you began to pick fights with me. We

54

split up but you couldn't stay away from me. And because I loved you, because I was prepared to give you the time and space which I thought you might need, I went along with your "occasional" dates. You think that I was happy with that? You think I didn't want more? You think that there wasn't a time when I didn't cry about the fact that you would willingly sleep with me but you wouldn't ever tell me that you loved me?'

'Leah—'

'Don't.' Her voice trembled with fury. 'Don't even speak to me. You tell me that you want to meet me and you bring me to this place to tell me that it's over between us because you've got married to someone else – and I'm supposed to be OK with this?'

'I didn't think you'd mind. You've had other relationships, haven't you?'

'I was trying to make you jealous, you insensitive shit!'

'You don't mean that,' said Ben. 'You cried when you split up with the property bloke. You cried on my shoulder and you told me that he'd been the best thing that had ever happened to you.'

'But he wasn't you,' said Leah. 'And it was you I wanted.'

'We fought all the time,' said Ben.

'So what?' Leah's eyes flashed at him. 'We always ended up in the sack afterwards, didn't we? Is that all I ever was to you, Ben Russell? A good lay when there wasn't anyone else available?'

'Of course not,' said Ben miserably. 'Oh Leah, I don't want to hurt you.'

'A bit late for that, isn't it?'

'I'm sorry,' he said. 'I really am.'

'Sorry isn't good enough.'

'Leah, we were friends,' he said. 'Sure, we slept together but it wasn't – we didn't—'

'*You* didn't,' she hissed. 'Whatever it was, *you* didn't. I loved you, Ben. I was waiting for you. And you've betrayed me. Just like all men betray good women in the end.' She stood up, her eyes blazing with fury. 'I don't know what sort of game you think you're playing at but I can tell you one thing and that's nobody, not even you, treats Leah Ryder like this. Nobody. So you'd better fucking watch out, Mr Just Got Married, because if you think that I'm finished with you, you have another think

55

coming.' She turned and stormed out of the café, slamming the door behind her.

The café had gone silent. Ben picked up another sachet of sugar and emptied it into his cold coffee. He looked up as he raised the glass cup to his lips to find twenty pairs of eyes fixed on him. He knew that if he was in a movie he'd be able to say something witty and amusing to shrug off the incident. But he wasn't. And he couldn't.

He put down the coffee without drinking it and hurried out into the rain.

Chapter 5

Niaouli

A clearing oil particularly useful for problem skin

Once her shift was finished, Carey didn't hang around. She hurried to her trusty Audi A3, took out her mobile and dialled Ben's number. He answered on the second ring. 'Hello,' she said. 'I'm just about to head home and pick up my stuff. I should be with you soon.'

'Good,' said Ben. 'I've missed you.'

'I've missed you too,' said Carey, although she hadn't really had time to miss him while she was working. But now, hearing his voice, she wanted desperately to be with him again.

'I've cleared some space for all your gear,' he told her. 'It wasn't easy. I didn't realise how much of a slob I was.'

'You're not a slob,' she said. 'I didn't see any evidence of slobbish behaviour when we were in New York.'

'I was on my best behaviour then,' he said. 'Now that I'm home I'll revert to type again.'

'Oh God!' She giggled. 'Two slobs together. I didn't realise what I was signing up for.'

'Hurry home,' said Ben. 'So's you can find out.'

'I'll be as quick as I can,' she assured him.

The porch light was on when she arrived back at the house in Swords fifteen minutes later. As she opened the front door she heard the sound of the TV and looked into the living room where Gina was sprawled on the sofa.

'Welcome home.' Gina sat up. 'Even if it's for the last time.'

Carey slung her bag onto the nearest armchair and flopped onto the sofa beside her friend. 'I'm knackered,' she confessed. 'And I still have to get loads of my things together to go across town.'

Gina looked at her sympathetically. 'I know,' she said. 'That's why I did a bit of packing for you.'

'Really?'

Gina nodded. 'I bunged your clothes into all of the available cases and kitbags. You can give my cases back to me whenever you feel like it. I don't have any holidays planned so I don't need them any time soon.'

'Oh, thanks Gina, that was really decent of you.' Carey stretched her legs out in front of her and wiggled her toes. 'I feel so exhausted all of a sudden and I really wasn't looking forward to packing clothes. I put as much of my other stuff in boxes as I could.'

'What'll he say when he sees your shoe collection?' asked Gina. 'Men are never entirely understanding of that kind of thing.'

Carey laughed. 'I haven't told him. I'm not going to take them all tonight. This morning he spent ages telling me that his house is really small. D'you think he's trying to hint at something?'

'Definitely.' Gina nodded. 'Would you like a cup of tea or coffee before you head off?'

'Love one,' said Carey. 'But you don't have to make it for me – I'll do it.'

'No bother.' Gina got up. 'You sit there and chill out for a bit.'

Carey ignored her. She followed Gina into the kitchen and sat on the edge of the table while her friend spooned coffee into two huge white mugs which had their names printed on them.

'I didn't mean to do this,' said Carey. 'It just happened.'

'It seems such a drastic step.' Gina screwed the lid back onto the coffee jar. 'I mean, I know he's wonderful, Carey, and I can quite see how you fell for him. I'm just a bit worried that it was so damn sudden.'

'I can't explain it,' said Carey. 'I really can't. You know, he asked me if I believed in love at first sight and I said no but – oh, Gina – there was a spark straight away. Even on the plane when it was kind of prickly and we weren't sure whether or not we were getting on. And when we disembarked and he started to walk away, I felt gutted. Then, at Ellie's party . . .' Her voice trailed off. 'Gina, it was magic. Absolute magic.'

'Lucky cow.' Gina poured boiling water into the mugs.

'You have it too,' Carey pointed out. 'You're engaged, for heaven's sake. You're getting married next year.'

'I know, I know,' said Gina. 'And I'm madly in love, don't think that I'm not. But you have to admit that the way you've done it – well, it's out of the ordinary to say the least. With me and Steve, yes, there was the attraction, yes, there was the excitement and yes, there was the one perfect night too. It's just – we're friends too, Carey. You and Ben can't be friends yet.'

'Yes, we are,' said Carey fiercely. 'We've been together a week. We know lots of things about each other – everything there is to know. Everything that matters. After Ellie's party, after we made love, we talked for hours. About everything. We like the same kind of things – actually, we discovered that on the plane! His favourite food is Italian too. He supports Chelsea Football Club. His parents died when he was young. He works with his sister, they're really close.'

'Too close?' asked Gina. 'Is she a kind of mother influence on him or anything?'

'I don't think so,' replied Carey. 'Although she brought him up – their parents weren't very child-oriented, according to Ben – so I suppose it's a bit different from the usual brother-sister thing. He didn't contact her to tell her about getting married. I think he would've done if there was some sort of issue there.' She sipped her coffee. 'I love him, Gina. I know it's mad and crazy and sort of unbelievable but I love him.'

'As I said, lucky cow.'

'But I'm sorry to be moving out from here.' She looked round the kitchen. 'I've enjoyed living with you. I'll keep paying rent until you get someone else.'

'No need to worry about that,' said Gina. 'Rachel Hickey is moving in next week.'

'That was quick.' Carey looked surprised.

'The lease on her place comes up at the end of the month,' explained Gina. 'She'd been asking round in case anyone knew of a house-share or a flat-share. So it's worked out really well.'

'I'm glad,' said Carey.

'So I'll get by even though you've deserted me.' Gina grinned at her friend. 'I'll miss you, though. It's been fun.'

'I know.' Carey drained her mug. 'But I suppose it's time for me to turn into a happily married woman with a place of her own.'

'I'm glad for you,' said Gina gently. 'Especially after that whole Peter Furness thing.'

'I'm not marrying Ben on the rebound,' Carey retorted.

'I never said you were.' Gina shook her head. 'I'm just pleased you're over it.'

'Couldn't be more over it,' Carey told her as she looked at her wedding ring. 'Couldn't be more over it if I tried.'

Later that evening, Gina helped Carey to pile her stuff into the Audi. The car was already overflowing with boxes of tissues, numerous bags of liquorice allsorts and other sweets, a variety of road maps, a selection of gossip magazines and a few pairs of shoes. Carey regarded her car as an extension of her home. Gina stood at the end of the driveway and waved until her friend was out of view. Then she bit her lip, walked back into the house and locked the door behind her.

It took Carey half an hour to get to Portobello and another five minutes to find Ben's street. As she pulled up outside the redbrick house and switched off the engine, the front door opened and Ben stood in the doorway. Carey pushed open the car door and tumbled out.

He put his arms around her and kissed her deeply on the lips. 'It's been hell without you,' he told her as they eventually separated.

'And without you.' She kept her arms twined round his neck. 'Everyone thinks I'm crazy, you know.'

'Why?'

'They reckon we could've had the great sex without having to get married.'

'Did you tell them that the great sex was only part of it?'

She nodded. 'But I don't think they believed me.'

'Probably 'cos it's such a great part of it. Come on.' He undid her arms and suddenly picked her up. She squealed with surprise.

'I'm carrying you over the threshold, you idiot,' he informed her. 'Stop kicking and screaming as though I'm trying to kidnap you.'

'Sorry.' She laughed. 'I didn't realise.'

He manoeuvred her through the narrow doorway and into his living room. Then he set her down. She looked round her and smiled.

'It's lovely,' she said.

'It took me all day to get it lovely,' he confessed. 'When I got home I realised that it was a nightmare. Books everywhere. Papers everywhere. Invoices all over the place . . .'

'I wouldn't have cared,' she told him. 'It's not the house I fell in love with, it's you.'

'Oh, Carey.' He drew her towards him again. 'I can't believe how lucky I am. A week ago – a week ago I thought I was happy – and now I realise that I was only living.'

'You say such amazing things.' She kissed him. 'And you do such amazing things too.' She wriggled with delight as his hand slid beneath her black jumper. 'I wonder,' she added, 'if there'll ever be a time when I won't want to make love to you the minute I see you.'

'I hope not,' he responded as he unclipped her bra with one hand. 'It'd be such a waste of a good body!'

They made love standing up. It was a necessity, Ben murmured as he entered her, because the armchairs weren't comfortable enough and he didn't have a sofa yet.

She almost fell asleep in one of the uncomfortable armchairs, but Ben didn't let her; he made her wake up again and help him carry her cases and boxes into the house. 'It's not that bad,' he said as he looked at the pile. 'Although why do you have ten pairs of shoes in individual boxes?'

'Actually I've a few more than that,' she confessed. 'I didn't want to terrorise you by bringing them all together. I've a bit of a shoe weakness, you see.'

'How many pairs?' he asked.

'Oh, thirty, forty.' She tried to look nonchalant.

'You're joking!'

'No,' she said. 'But it's my only weakness. Honestly. All my clothes are here and they'll hardly take up any space in your wardrobe.'

'I don't have a wardrobe,' he told her. 'Chrome rails.'

61

'Even better,' she said robustly. 'You can definitely squash things onto chrome rails.'

'You're mad, you know.' He grinned at her.

'I'm bloody exhausted.' She yawned. 'My shift wasn't the busiest but I had to keep my concentration going. And now it's deserting me.'

'Poor thing.' He hugged her. 'Come on. Let's leave this stuff and go to bed.'

She nodded and followed him up the stairs. Ben's king-sized bed took up most of the room but it looked soft and inviting.

'D'you mind if I don't do anything very sexy and first-night in our home together and just fall asleep?' she asked.

'Given that we did the first-night stuff downstairs I guess I can put up with it.' Ben grinned. 'But I'll expect full service tomorrow.'

Carey yawned again. 'Don't worry. I'll get home just in time to wake you up in the nicest way possible.' She threw her clothes into a heap in the corner of the room and crawled into the bed. Ben did the same. They burrowed beneath the duvet and he put his arms round her.

'How did your friends in work react when you told them?' he asked.

'Shock.' Carey snuggled closer to him. 'They thought I was mad. Can't blame them, I suppose, but they don't know you.' She kissed his chest. 'How about you? Did you tell anyone yet?'

'My sister, of course,' replied Ben. 'And she was pretty shocked too.'

'I suppose that's what everyone will be,' murmured Carey. 'We'll be a kind of ten-day wonder for a while but it'll die down. I'll have to tell my family tomorrow. I suppose I'll get even more shock and horror from them. How shocked was Freya?'

'Very,' admitted Ben. 'She thought that maybe I was a gullible bloke who'd been snapped up by some opportunistic girl.'

'Are you that good a catch?' asked Carey.

'Freya obviously thinks so.' He laughed shortly. 'But she's biased. She believes that one day we'll sell the health stores for a fortune and become incredibly rich. I've told her often enough that I've been down that road before and that wealth is transitory, but she doesn't quite believe me.'

'I wonder will she like me when she meets me.' Carey's voice was very sleepy.

'Of course she will,' said Ben. He lay silently for a few minutes with his eyes closed and listened to his wife's steady breathing. 'There is something else I have to tell you about.'

'Mm?'

'I had to tell one of my old girlfriends about you.' He opened his eyes again and glanced at Carey. She didn't move. 'Carey?' he whispered.

There was no reply. He stared at her for a moment then kissed her gently on her forehead and lay down again. He fell asleep almost immediately.

In his dreams Leah was standing beside him. She was dressed in a long white gown and carrying a bouquet of deep red roses. More roses were twisted through her black hair, splashes of colour against its darkness.

'I love you,' he told her. 'I really do. But I'm married already.'

'Nonsense.' Leah handed him the bouquet. 'Nothing we can't deal with.' Then she walked across the room and shoved Carey out of the window which had suddenly appeared. She turned to Ben.

'There,' she told him. 'Problem solved.'

Carey slept through Ben's departure for work the following morning and he didn't try to wake her. He left her huddled beneath the duvet with only the top of her curls showing and he made himself promise not to wake her by phoning her. He was amazed at her capacity for sleep although she'd told him that she could just as easily go for hours without any. She'd trained her body to sleep when the opportunity was there, she'd told him, and to stay awake when it had to be awake.

She woke at nine o'clock feeling totally refreshed. She sat up in the bed and stretched. Then she shivered because the house was chilly. She got out of bed, pulled on the jumper she'd been wearing the previous day, and went downstairs.

He'd left a note propped up against the coffee-pot on the kitchen table. *Hadn't the heart to wake you*, it said. *Call me when you emerge into the land of the living. I love you even more today. xxx Ben.*

He was such a cute man, she thought, as she peered inside the huge American-style fridge that took up far too much space in the kitchen. Cute and desirable and a real softie. A real softie who had an oversized fridge and no food. There was a Bio-Activa natural yoghurt a day past its sell-by date on the third shelf, a jar of olives on the second and a low-fat dairy spread in one of the containers on the door. She wrinkled up her nose and hoped that the lack of food was due to the fact that he'd been away for a while. She had slightly better luck with the cupboard beside the fridge which contained dozens of healthfood snack bars and six different jars of dried fruits. The breadbin, on the grey Velstone worktop, held a wholewheat brown loaf.

She filled the kettle and rummaged round some more until she found a jar of coffee. Lucky I like black coffee in the mornings, she thought, as she smeared the dairy spread onto the brown bread. She helped herself to a few dried apricots and chewed on them while she walked around the kitchen and waited for the kettle to boil. He might have tidied up but there were still a lot of papers lying round the place. She looked at articles downloaded from the net on the benefits of different natural therapies, disregarded a pile of brown envelopes which were clearly bills, flicked through half-a-dozen postcards from a variety of places, all from someone called Phil who was having a great time, and finally glanced at a notepad covered in scribbled messages, the clearest of which said cryptically, *LR 7.00. Don't forget BC.* She replaced the notepad, guilty at reading messages that weren't for her no matter what they were about.

It felt strange to think that this was her house too now and that some time soon her messages and postcards and bills would be fighting for space on the counter. She checked out the contents of some more cupboards then made her coffee and drank it as she walked into the living room. She turned on Ben's hi-fi system and listened to 98FM as she investigated her surroundings some more.

The house was essentially male, she thought. There were no real concessions to anything other than utility. He was right about the armchairs, they were stylish but not comfortable, and the lack of a sofa to sprawl on was a big disadvantage. She didn't mind the ascetic look but she thought that she'd like a little more cosiness.

64

She shivered and got up again. The controls for the central heating were in the hallway. From the panel she could see that the heat was set to come on at seven every morning and go off at eight-thirty. She pressed the over-ride switch and smiled as it gurgled into life again.

Her plan for the day was to drive to Swords and pick up the rest of her things. She'd pencilled in a possible visit to her parents' house on the way home but she wasn't sure about that yet. She wanted to have everything (shoes included) put away safely before Ben got home again and she had a horrible feeling that if she called in to see her mother and father it'd be hours before she'd get out of the house. She wasn't sure what type of hours Ben worked. She assumed that, since he was a part-owner of the business, his working life was flexible but busy. That was OK by her. She'd always hated the idea of a nine to five job, which was why she loved her shiftwork so much, even though it had occasionally messed up her social life in the past.

She went back upstairs and took her phone out of her bag. She'd forgotten to save Ben's mobile number on it but she still had his business card. She rang the number but got his message minder. So she rang the business number beneath it.

'*Herbal Matters*, Freya speaking.'

Carey held the phone from her ear and looked at it in surprise. She hadn't expected anyone but Ben to answer although when she thought about it, there was no reason why she should have assumed this. She wasn't really ready to talk to the sister yet. Even though Ben had told her quite a bit about Freya, Carey felt that she'd rather meet the woman before chatting to her on the phone. But she couldn't hang up. That'd be silly.

'Hello, Freya,' she said. 'This is Carey.'

'Oh. Carey. The new wife.' Freya's voice was clipped and Carey winced. Don't tell me that she disapproves of me already, she thought. Not when she hasn't met me. That's not fair.

'Yes,' said Carey. 'I'm sorry, I didn't expect to reach you when I dialled this number. It's a little odd to talk to you out of the blue like this.'

'Not at all,' said Freya briskly. 'I'm sure we'll meet soon – I'm looking forward to it. I told my brother that he was a bit mad marrying someone he'd just met but I'm sure he knows what he's doing.'

'Oh, I think so,' said Carey brightly. 'Is he there?'

'He had to go and meet a supplier,' said Freya. 'Can I give him a message?'

'Just tell him that I've gone to Swords to get the rest of my things,' said Carey. 'And I'll see him later.'

'Sure,' said Freya.

'I love him,' Carey told her. 'It's not some crazy stupid thing we've done.'

'I'm sure it's not.'

'We clicked, you know. Straight away.'

'Look, he's my brother not my child,' said Freya. 'It's really up to him what he does.' The conversation lapsed into an uncomfortable silence.

'I just get this feeling that you – you don't approve,' said Carey eventually.

'I can't approve or disapprove,' said Freya. 'It's not up to me.'

'I'm a bit nervous about things because I know that you're Ben's only family.' Carey knew she was babbling now. 'I don't want you to think that we did this without thinking.'

'There are lots of people in Ben's life besides me,' said Freya. 'He doesn't have to ask my permission to get married, you know. I'm his sister and I work with him. That's as far as it goes.'

Carey frowned. She wished Freya sounded friendlier. But maybe the other girl was still in shock.

'Don't judge me.' Her voice was suddenly sharp. 'Don't get all sorts of preconceived notions, that's all.'

'Don't worry,' said Freya. 'I won't.'

'And you'll tell him I called?'

'Of course,' said Freya. 'And I hope we get to meet soon.'

'I'm sure we will,' said Carey and hung up.

She had a shower, got dressed and then drove to her old house to retrieve the rest of her belongings. She'd just stashed them all in the boot and the back seat of the car when her mobile rang.

'Hi,' said Ben. 'How're you?'

'Oh, fine,' she told him. 'I've got all my stuff and I'll be bringing it back to the house shortly.'

'Home,' he corrected. 'You'll be bringing it home.'

She laughed. 'Of course. I was kind of thinking of dropping in to see my parents on the way back, only I'm afraid I won't get to leave their house until I'm due to be in work! And I'm not sure that I have the strength to persuade any more people that neither of us are crazy teenagers who got married on a whim.'

'I know what you mean,' said Ben. 'Freya told me you called.'

'She doesn't like me,' said Carey.

'She doesn't even know you.'

'I'm aware of that,' said Carey. 'That's why she doesn't like me.'

'Don't worry, she'll love you when she meets you,' said Ben. 'How could she not?'

'Very easily,' Carey said gloomily. 'I suppose I can understand it. People don't really like these kind of surprises, do they? After all, they think they know you and then you go and do something totally unexpected and it throws them.'

'So you're expecting a hostile reception at your folks'?' surmised Ben.

'Actually no.' Carey laughed suddenly. 'They hated my last boyfriend, so anyone else would be an improvement.'

'Who was your last boyfriend?' asked Ben.

'His name was James.' Carey didn't want to talk about Peter. She didn't consider Peter to have qualified as a boyfriend. Besides, he'd never met her parents.

'Why did they hate him?'

'For the same reason they hated most of my boyfriends,' Carey said. 'He just wasn't good enough.'

'God.' Ben exhaled. 'They'll think the same about me.'

'Oh no,' she said. 'He wasn't good enough and he was afraid of flying. He had no chance really.'

'At least I make up some ground on that score,' said Ben in relief. 'I'll be home by six o'clock this evening. That should give you plenty of time to chew the fat with the family and still get back to Portobello in time to have my dinner on the table.'

Carey chuckled. 'You should be so lucky. There isn't a scrap of food in the house.'

'I know,' said Ben. 'I was really busy before going to the States and I ate loads of takeaways.'

'I'll try to do some shopping before I get home but I'm not promising anything.'

'Fair enough,' said Ben.

'See you later.' Carey made a kissing noise down the phone.

'God, woman, you nearly deafened me!' But he made a kissing noise back.

She grinned as she put down the phone and started the car. Whenever she spoke to other people about Ben she felt pressurised simply because they were so surprised. But when she talked to him everything was perfect again.

She looked at her watch. She'd have to go and face her parents. It wasn't something she could really put off. She switched on the ignition and pulled out of the driveway. Ten minutes later she drew up outside her family home. She glanced upwards at an Aer Lingus 737 on its final approach (Runway Two Eight brought it directly over their house) and then pushed open the garden gate.

'Hello, stranger.' Carey's mother opened the door before she had a chance to ring the bell. She pecked her daughter on both cheeks and ushered her into the house. 'I saw your car pull up,' she told Carey as she led the way into the warm and welcoming kitchen. 'To what do we owe the pleasure?'

'This and that.' Carey sat down at the table and smiled at her mother.

Maude Browne was a sensationally good-looking woman even at sixty-eight. Her skin, while obviously not wrinkle-free, was still smooth and the fine lines of her face added character. Like her daughter, her eyes were dark brown and her hair, although now totally grey, was lustrous and healthy. Unlike Carey's hair, though, it was wavy rather than curly and Maude kept it long, pinning it up on the back of her head to accentuate her slender neck. Whenever Carey looked at her mother she wondered how it was that such an elegant woman had produced such an ungainly daughter.

'So.' Maude filled the kettle and looked at Carey. 'What do you have to tell me?'

'Why do I have to tell you anything?'

Maude raised an eyebrow. 'Come on, honey,' she said. 'I know you. You only ever call here when you've got a crisis brewing.'

'I haven't got a crisis brewing,' said Carey crossly. 'Honestly, Mum, just because I'm not here every minute of every day . . .'

'Relax, relax,' said Maude easily. 'I was only teasing you.' Her eyes searched Carey's face. 'But there is something, isn't there?' She looked worried for a moment. 'It's not that man again, is it?'

'No, it's not Peter,' said Carey. The back of her throat was dry. 'Look, I don't want you to blow a fuse or anything but it's just that – there is someone else. Someone wonderful. I met him on the way to New York.' She swallowed. 'I married him.'

The kettle boiled and clicked itself off. Maude tipped some tea into a china pot and poured boiling water over it. Then she turned to Carey.

'Are you out of your mind?' she asked conversationally.

'God Almighty!' cried Carey. 'Just for once can't someone say anything other than ask me if I'm out of my mind? No, I'm not. I met someone. I love him. I married him.'

'But Carey.' Maude's eyes were wide as she looked at her daughter. 'Only two weeks ago you were in floods of tears at this very table over the married man.'

'I know I was,' said Carey hotly. 'You should be glad that I found someone else.'

'I'd be glad if I thought you'd found someone and were starting a nice new relationship,' said Maud. 'But getting married . . . How? Why? Where?'

'In Vegas,' said Carey mutinously.

'Oh, Carey!'

'I love him.' She felt hot tears pricking at the back of her eyes and blinked a couple of times so that they wouldn't fall.

Maude sat down at the table and rubbed her forehead. 'What am I going to do with you?' she asked.

'Don't talk to me like that,' snapped Carey. 'As though I'm a child.'

'You don't think that what you've done is very, very childish?' asked her mother.

'No, I don't,' retorted Carey. 'I think I've done exactly what I wanted to do most in the world. Marry a man I love and who loves me too.'

'I'm not going to talk to you as though you were a child,' said

Maude, 'but can I remind you that you fall in love at least twice every year and that if that other man had said he was leaving his wife and toddler and getting a divorce you would've married him?'

'No, I wouldn't,' said Carey.

'You waltzed in here before Christmas and told me that you'd met the most wonderful man in the world,' Maude reminded her. 'You said that he was the best thing that had ever happened to you. You told us that you thought this was *it*. Remember?'

'Yes, but—'

'So what's different this time?'

'Ben wasn't married and he is now,' said Carey.

'Oh, God.' Maude sighed. 'Is this a valid wedding?'

'Yes.'

'So you can't just get an easy divorce?'

'I don't want an easy divorce!' cried Carey. 'And I came here to share my happiness with you, not to be lectured.'

'I don't mean to lecture you,' said Maude. 'Honestly I don't. But – oh Carey, I want you to be happy. And I'm terribly afraid that you're going to be hurt all over again.'

'I won't be hurt,' said Carey. She leaned down and picked up her bag. 'I brought photographs to show you.'

Maude looked at the shining gold ring on Carey's left hand as she took the photographs from her. She studied them carefully.

'He's very attractive,' she said finally.

'I know,' said Carey.

'Tell me about him.'

So Carey told her about the plane journey and about the party – although she clearly didn't go into details about the wonderful sex that she'd shared with Ben. And she told Maude about his healthfood stores and the house in Portobello and his experience with the internet company. While she spoke Maude watched her, noticing the flush in her cheeks and the defiant sparkle in her eyes.

'And you think that marrying him was the only thing you could do?' she asked finally.

'It was so right,' said Carey. 'I know it's not really how you'd like things to have happened but it was how I wanted it and how he wanted it. And I wouldn't change a thing.'

'There isn't anything else I can say.' Maude got up and put her arms round her daughter's shoulders. 'I really and truly hope you'll be very happy. And I hope you'll bring him over very soon. I can't believe that I have another son-in-law.'

'Of course I'll bring him to visit soon,' said Carey.

'You haven't met his family yet either?'

'Well, as I told you, there's only his sister. I spoke to her on the phone this morning.'

'And what did she sound like?'

Carey grinned at her mother. 'Much as I guess you'd sound like if Ben rang you up out of the blue.'

'That friendly, huh?'

'A few degrees above icy,' admitted Carey.

'You've made it very difficult for yourselves,' said Maude. 'You know, you could've come home and got married.'

'I know, I know.' Carey sighed. 'But you've got to understand how we felt.'

'I understand it,' said Maude. 'I just don't know whether or not giving in to it was your brightest ever idea.'

'It was,' Carey promised her. 'It absolutely was.'

'Your dad'll have a fit.'

'Oh well, you know Dad, he has fits about everything,' said Carey easily.

'As for Sylvia!'

'She won't want to believe that her baby sister finally took the plunge,' grinned Carey. 'You do know, don't you, that it was Sylvia's wedding that put me off the idea for so long?'

Maude laughed. 'It was a lovely wedding,' she said. 'And it *was* twenty years ago, for heaven's sake!'

'I know,' said Carey darkly. 'But you can get very scarred at thirteen.'

Maude laughed again. 'Don't say that in front of Sylvia.'

'She knows.'

'I suppose you're right.' Maude picked up the photographs again. 'He is very attractive,' she repeated.

'I know.' Carey's eyes twinkled. 'You don't think I'd pick on an unattractive one, do you?'

'I guess not.'

71

'Everything will be fine, I promise you,' Carey said gently. 'And when you meet him you'll understand.'

'I hope so,' said Maude.

'I know so,' said Carey.

She felt light-hearted as she drove back to Portobello. She'd hoped that her mother would be supportive yet had been nervous about telling her. But Maude, as always, had taken things in her stride – even though her crack about a divorce wasn't very nice. Carey offered a brief prayer of thanks for having an understanding parent. She also knew that Maude would break the news to her father in such a way as to make it all seem perfectly reasonable. Arthur was much less able to deal with family crises than Maude. Not that this was a crisis, of course, thought Carey. But her dad was perfectly capable of seeing it like that.

Her phone began to chirp and she answered it on her handsfree set. 'Hello,' she said brightly.

'It's me. I need to talk to you. I need to meet you.'

She felt her throat go dry and she gripped the steering wheel tightly. 'That's not really possible,' she said.

'Oh, come on, Carey.' Peter Furness spoke determinedly. 'I know I did things to hurt you, and I'm sorry about that, I truly am. I didn't realise how much you meant to me.'

'It's irrelevant,' said Carey. 'It's in the past.'

'Not to me.'

'Look—'

'No, listen,' said Peter quickly. 'We do need to talk. Things have changed. Changed a lot. I need to see you.'

'I told you the last time we met,' she said firmly, 'we've nothing to talk about. I don't want to see you, Peter. I can't.'

'Things have changed,' he said again. 'Think about it. I'll call you.'

'No, don't!' she cried. 'Things have changed for me too.'

But he'd already broken the connection.

Chapter 6

Linden Blossom Absolute

This is a luxurious oil with an unusual scent which helps relaxation

At six o'clock on the Friday of the week they came home, Ben propped his legs on the desk in his tiny office and leaned backwards in his chair, his eyes closed. He supposed it was partly still jet-lag that had him so tired, but he knew that the sense of weariness also came from adapting himself to having someone else living in his house. He hadn't quite accustomed himself to the times Carey was there and the times she wasn't. Today's shift didn't start until ten o'clock in the evening and he wanted to get home before she left for the airport, even though he normally went for a drink after work on Fridays with Freya to discuss the week's business. He still wanted to chat to Freya – his sister had been aloof since the news of his marriage and Ben understood that she was hurt by the unexpectedness of it all and the fact that he hadn't confided in her before coming home. She still had to meet Carey too. The timing of both Carey's shifts and Freya's own schedule had made it difficult so far. Ben wanted the two women to meet properly so that they could get to know and like each other in a relaxed situation, not on an evening when one of them was more focused on work than on finding common ground.

Ben was hoping that they might get to meet at the weekend. Unusually, as Carey had pointed out to him, she had both Saturday and Sunday off and although Ben had originally dreamed of them having two blissful days alone together, he now thought that it might be a good idea to invite Freya to dinner so that his sister and his wife could spend some time together.

Of course, that would mean tidying up a bit first. He'd never been the tidiest of people himself but since Carey had moved in, almost every available space was taken up with clutter. God, he thought, but she had an immense number of jumpers and trousers, most of which appeared identical. And as for the shoes! He'd counted forty boxes in addition to the ten she'd brought the first night and yet, as far as he could tell, she'd worn the same pair of boots into work every day that week. He yawned widely and then opened his eyes. Freya was standing in front of the desk looking at him.

'I didn't hear you come in,' he said as he took his feet down from the desk.

'I thought you were asleep,' she told him. 'Married life exhausting, is it?'

He rubbed his eyes. 'This week has been exhausting. *Irish Tatler* were on about doing a piece on the Drumcondra store and I thought their reporter was dropping by yesterday afternoon, which is why I went over there. But we'd got our wires crossed and they weren't due till today – only, of course, I already had meetings set up . . . nothing disastrous, but you know how it is when you're rushing round. I had to do some crazy re-jigging and the last person to call this afternoon was Stephen Fuller. I hate him being last, it's so hard to get rid of him!'

Freya smiled sympathetically. 'Never mind,' she said. 'You can go home, put your feet up and Carey will mop your fevered brow.'

He laughed. 'As if! Well, she might for a while, I guess, but she's due in work at ten.' He looked apologetically at Freya. 'Which is why I'd better skip our drink this evening.'

'Fine by me,' said Freya airily. 'I wasn't expecting you to come with me. I'm meeting someone anyway.'

'Oh.'

'But I really have to meet Carey too. It's nearly a week and she must be due some time off by now.'

'This weekend,' confirmed Ben. 'I thought perhaps you might like to come to dinner tomorrow night.' As he issued the invitation he hoped that Carey wouldn't mind. He hadn't discussed it with her yet but he knew that she expected to see Freya soon and Saturday was as good a day as any.

'I'm going to the trade fair in Galway tomorrow,' said Freya dryly. 'She's not the only one to work all hours.'

He made a face. 'I'd forgotten all about that.'

'I know. Your mind is clearly on other things'

'I'm jet-lagged,' he told her. 'I'll have my brain in gear by next week, I promise. Maybe you'd like to call round on Sunday instead?'

'You'd better talk it over with her first, don't you think?'

'I'll check with her and call you,' said Ben. 'I know she wants to meet you as much as you want to meet her.'

Freya looked at him in silence for a moment and then she smiled. 'Actually I was thinking,' she said, 'that it might be a good idea if you had an event.'

'What sort of event?' he asked tiredly. 'We did a lot of that sort of thing last year, didn't we, when we were promoting that herbal boost stuff. I know it was very successful but I think you need to have a product to hang it on and—'

'Not that sort of an event, you dope,' she interrupted him. 'You and Carey.'

He frowned. 'What d'you mean?'

'You are so dense!' She sighed. 'A party, a drinks reception – something to mark the fact that you're married.' She shrugged. 'It just seems like a good idea. So many of your friends don't even know that you're married yet.'

Ben nodded thoughtfully. 'Maybe. Carey and I haven't talked about it really.'

'It'd be a way that we could all get to meet her,' said Freya.

'Well, with luck you'll meet her at the weekend.'

'Sure. But other people want to meet her too. The staff, and Brian. And I'm sure your friends would like to see her.'

Ben didn't tell her that Carey was – as she'd told him herself with a hint of surprise in her voice – more nervous than she'd expected about meeting his friends. And that she was actually very nervous about meeting Freya.

Holding a party might be a good idea, he conceded as he mulled over the thought a little more. He still hadn't told any of his mates at

75

the football club where he played in a local league, nor had he phoned Phil, his closest friend, with the news yet or even spoken of it to any of the reps who had called in to see him during the week. The only person he'd told was Leah and, of course, she'd blown a gasket. But then he should have expected that. His ex-girlfriend's mood-swings were wild and her temper explosive. But it rarely lasted. And, despite what she'd said to him in her flash of anger, Ben was certain that she had never seriously expected them to get married. It wasn't a topic they'd even discussed.

Watching him, Freya noticed the changes in his expressions as the different thoughts ran through his head.

'So what d'you think?' she asked.

'It's a good idea,' he decided. 'But I'll have to talk to Carey about it.'

'Of course,' said Freya. 'And I want to do it for you.'

'What d'you mean?'

'My wedding present,' explained Freya. 'I'd like to organise the party for you.'

Ben stared at her. 'Why?' he asked.

She shrugged. 'Whenever we have events for the shop you do everything. I thought it'd be nice if I did this for you.'

'It's a lovely idea,' he said warmly. 'Thanks.'

'So you just leave it all to me,' she said. 'I'll do up a guest list, you can check it over but don't even attempt to get involved.'

'OK.' He grinned at her. 'Who are you meeting?'

'What?'

'Who are you meeting tonight? You said "someone". Not Brian?'

'You think just because you've rushed off and met someone new I'm likely to do the same thing?' Freya smiled as she sat on the wooden chair in front of his desk. 'Brian and I have a good relationship. I'm not going to wreck it by doing something as crazy as you.'

'You still think I'm crazy?'

She sighed. 'I don't know. How can I tell until I've met her?'

'I'm lucky,' he said fiercely. 'I never wanted to be married before. Never.'

'Not even to Leah?'

'Especially not to Leah,' said Ben. 'Strange as it may seem to you,

76

Freya, because I know you're good friends with her – marrying her was the last thing on my mind.'

'That's not what she thought,' commented Freya.

'Maybe not.' The memory of his last meeting with Leah was still fresh in Ben's mind. 'But she'll understand, given a bit of time. And I honestly don't think she really wanted to marry me. She was just put out that someone else did.'

'Are you sure?'

'Who can ever be sure about Leah,' he said irritably.

'All right, all right.' Freya shrugged. 'I'm not trying to fight her corner, you know. It's a bit late for that anyway.'

'Yes, it is.'

'So perhaps I'll finally get to meet Carey on Sunday?' said Freya.

Ben nodded.

'Call me and let me know.'

He nodded again.

'Goodnight,' said Freya.

'Goodnight.' He picked up his battered briefcase and walked out of the office.

Carey was curled up in one of the armchairs when he came in, her eyes tightly closed. She opened them and smiled as he leaned down to kiss her hard on her luscious, pouting lips.

'How was your day?' she murmured as he nuzzled against the base of her throat.

'Awful,' he told her. 'Busy, boring, complicated . . . I couldn't wait to get home to you.'

'And I couldn't wait for you to get here.' She pulled him closer to her and slid her hand beneath his shirt.

'Here or upstairs?' he asked.

'Here,' she whispered fiercely. 'I can't wait for upstairs.'

Lying on the floor, she grasped the legs of the uncomfortable armchair as he entered her, glad that it was good for something, for giving her the leverage to push herself towards him so that he was deeper inside her than ever before. She cried out as his movements became ever more urgent and then she wrapped her arms around him and hugged him fiercely to her. He gasped and thrust again and then

77

the two of them lay motionless beside each other on the floor.

'I never believed it could be like this,' he said eventually as he kissed her gently on the cheek. 'I never knew that it could be so mind-blowingly wonderful. I've had some good lays in my life, but you're the best.'

'A good lay!' Her eyes glittered as she looked at him. 'I was rather hoping I was more than that.'

'You are,' he said. 'Of course you are. I love you, Carey. That's what makes the difference.'

'I know.' She cuddled into the crook of his arm even though the wooden floor was now killing her back. 'Uncomplicated sex is great fun, but loving the person makes it a whole heap better.'

'I love it being complicated,' he told her.

'Will there ever be a time you don't love me?' Her voice was serious.

'No,' he said simply. 'There won't.'

Freya Russell walked into the bar and looked round her. Already it was filling up with the after-work crowd and the students from the college across the road. Friday nights, she thought. When everyone goes out looking for a good time and hopes against hope that they'll find it.

Ben and she would sometimes joke about the Friday-night crowds – the crush of singletons thinking that things would be better if only they found the perfect partner; the couples in varying states of their relationships, from those who couldn't keep their hands off each other to those who couldn't think of anything to say to each other any more; the contented men and women who knew that they had found someone but who were now having a good time on their own . . . Ben always said that, with Freya, he didn't have to look like one of the desperate singletons and Freya told Ben that at least she had found someone, even if they'd got to the stage of not talking to each other very much. But different, she'd say, from the bored couples together simply because they hadn't managed to find the courage to split up. Brian and she didn't need to constantly communicate with each other by talking. They knew how they felt. Ben would laugh at that because he often called his sister's boyfriend 'boring Brian'. Brian worked in the bank where Freya had once worked too. He was, she told him, extremely good at his job and took it seriously. And she'd punch Ben playfully on the shoulder and tell him that, despite how well the shops were doing, he didn't always take things seriously enough.

But he had now, she acknowledged, as she scanned the throng of people again. He'd taken things so bloody seriously that he'd married a girl whom no one knew and who sounded the complete opposite of anyone he'd ever gone out with before. The complete opposite of Leah, in fact.

She spotted Leah now, sitting in the corner of the bar, a bottle of lemon Bacardi Breezer in front of her. The younger girl looked miserable, thought Freya, and she bit her lip. How could he possibly think that marriage had never been on the agenda?

'Hi, Leah.' She pushed her way past an unnatural blonde who was wearing too much make-up and too few clothes and sat down beside Ben's ex-girlfriend.

Leah turned her bitter-chocolate eyes to her. 'Hello, Freya.'

'Want a drink?' Freya opened her bag and rummaged for her purse.

'No,' said Leah. 'I've just got one.'

'I'll be back in a second.' Freya knew it was pointless waiting for someone to take an order. She went up to the bar and returned with a gin and tonic. Then she settled herself beside Leah again.

'So how've you been?' she asked.

'Do you really have to ask?' Leah's voice held an undercurrent of anger.

'I guess not.'

'You know I met him?'

'Yes.' Freya nodded. 'He told me.'

'He said that we were just good friends.' Leah chugged back half the bottle of alcohol. 'Good friends, Freya! After all we went through together.'

Freya looked at her sympathetically. 'I know.'

'We weren't just good friends,' said Leah scathingly. 'God, Freya, you know how I would've done anything for him. I thought he felt the same.'

79

'So did I,' admitted Freya. 'When you two got back together I thought it was just a matter of time before you got married.'

'I don't know what I thought,' said Leah. 'But it wasn't that he'd sleep with me one night and turn up with a wife a week later.'

Freya grimaced.

'Maybe we wouldn't have worked out,' said Leah. 'I know we were on-off a lot. But – but how could he do this to me, Freya? How could he humiliate me like this?'

'I don't think he meant to humiliate you,' said Freya. 'And he hasn't, Leah. Not really.'

'You don't think it's humiliating to be dumped for someone he doesn't even know? On-off it might have been but it was nearly four years!'

'I'm sorry,' said Freya. 'I really am. This girl has obviously entranced him.'

'What's she like?' asked Leah.

'I haven't a clue,' Freya replied. 'She works in the airport, shiftwork, we haven't managed to get together. Not that I really want to, other than to see what she's like. I know it sounds old fashioned but I really don't approve of what he's done.'

'She must be a real looker then,' said Leah.

'Actually no,' Freya told her. 'He showed me photos. She's nothing to write home about at all. Masses of curls and a lanky body.'

Leah twisted a lock of her own gleaming tresses around her middle finger. 'Then she must be great in bed.'

'Leah!'

'Sorry.' The girl made a face. 'But what else is there?'

'You're right, I suppose.'

'I lost my temper with him, you know, when he told me. I screamed and shouted at him in the café.'

'He didn't tell me that.' Freya smiled at Leah. 'But you were probably right.'

'D'you think it'll last?'

Freya sighed. 'I find it hard to believe,' she said. 'And I don't relish picking up the pieces when it's over.'

'And I don't know whether I want to be around to help pick up the pieces either,' said Leah as she looked into her glass.

The two women sat in silence for a while then Freya went to the bar and brought back another couple of drinks.

'I have to tell you something,' she said as she set the drinks on the table. 'I've offered to host a party for them.'

'What?' Leah looked at her in astonishment.

'Well, I thought that they needed to do something to prove to everyone that they're married, and I thought the best way of doing it was to have some kind of do, you know. Family and friends, that sort of thing. So I offered to organise it.'

Leah's eyes darkened further.

'I can't pretend it hasn't happened, Leah. I have to acknowledge that they're married even if the whole thing is utterly ridiculous.'

'And they've said yes?'

'I only suggested it to Ben today. But he seems happy with the idea.'

Leah picked at the Barcardi Breezer label. 'Are you going to invite me?'

'Do you think that's a good idea?' asked Freya. 'Let's face it, you'll hardly want to see him and this girl together.'

'Oh, but I do.' Leah nodded. 'I want to see what the usurper is like.'

'I couldn't tell him to his face that he's a shit,' said Freya. 'But I think he's been a bloody bastard about this, Leah. Even though I want to understand him.'

Leah tucked her straight black hair behind her ears. 'Aren't they all?' Her smile wobbled.

'You won't say anything awful to him at the party, will you?' Freya looked at Leah in sudden panic. 'When you lost your temper with him, you didn't turn into a bunny boiler, did you?'

'Glenn Close had the right idea,' muttered Leah. 'But I won't cause a scene if that's what you're afraid of, Freya. You're my friend and I wouldn't do that to you.'

'Thanks,' said Freya. She got up and ordered another round of drinks. The two girls sat in a companionable silence. This was why she liked Leah so much, Freya mused as she sipped her gin and tonic; she was easy to be with. She was a friend. Freya thought it was important to be friends with Ben's girlfriends, but Leah was the only one she'd ever really got on with.

'What did Brian think about Ben's marriage?' asked Leah suddenly.

'I think it terrified him,' Freya chuckled. 'He keeps looking at me as though he expects me to demand a huge engagement ring and an immediate date for the wedding.'

Leah laughed shakily. 'And will you?'

'Do you think it's a character flaw in the Russells?' she asked. 'Until Ben's sudden rush up the aisle, neither he nor I were much into the marriage thing.'

'It's strange,' mused Leah. 'You'd think that because you didn't have much of a family life yourselves that you'd actually both be the opposite.'

'Maybe,' said Freya, 'but I never felt much like marrying anyone. I've always been . . .' Her voice trailed off and she swirled her drink in front of her. 'I suppose I've been afraid that they'll leave me. Maybe it is a throwback to Mam and Dad and the fact that their dying left us on our own, I don't know. But I've always been happiest by myself.'

'And Brian?' asked Leah.

'It suits him.' Freya shrugged. 'He has someone to go with him to all his banking functions but he doesn't have to worry about being home at six o'clock every evening for a quiz on how his day's been.'

'Haven't you ever wanted children?'

Freya frowned. 'Sometimes,' she admitted. 'Sometimes I want them so much I could cry. And yet the feeling passes and I remember that they're hard work and that I'm getting a bit on the old side to have them in the first place. So I can't really say it's a big thing for me any more.'

'I thought about getting pregnant once,' admitted Leah. 'I thought it might be the thing to finally push Ben into making a commitment to me. But then I decided against it.'

Freya looked horrified. 'I didn't realise you'd had those kind of thoughts.'

'Only once,' sighed Leah. 'After all, I did have other boyfriends besides Ben. It's just – well, I thought he might be the one, that's all.'

'You'll get over him,' said Freya comfortingly. 'You did it before and you'll do it again.'

'How will you feel?' asked Leah. 'If and when his marriage to this woman breaks up?'

'Sorry for him, I guess. Even though he doesn't deserve it.'

'I'll feel sorry for him too,' said Leah. 'It's not nice coming down to earth with a bump, is it?'

Chapter 7

Pine

A stimulating oil with a fresh, sharp scent

The green light of the radar swept across the screen as Carey spoke into her headset. 'Shamrock 119, Dublin, good morning. Identified on handover.' She rubbed the base of her spine which ached. Since she rarely felt sore from sitting at her suite she rather felt that it had something to do with having had some wonderful sex with Ben on the floor at home over twelve hours ago. She adjusted her mike and continued to speak to the descending aircraft. 'Your position is thirty-three miles east of Dublin, number one, straight in.' She followed the blip of the plane on her screen as it approached the airport. 'ILS approach Runway Two Eight. Descend three thousand feet.'

The pilot's voice crackled in her ear. 'Dublin, Shamrock 119. Good morning. Continue descent till three thousand feet.'

She watched the screen as the plane's altitude decreased and he lined up to the westerly Runway Two Eight which was Dublin's most commonly used runway. 'Shamrock 119, Dublin,' she said. 'Descend two thousand feet. Turn left heading two hundred and fifty degrees. Establish localiser Runway Two Eight. Report established.'

The pilot repeated her instructions and confirmed that he was established on the runway's localiser.

'Eight miles from touchdown,' she told him. 'Cleared ILS approach Runway Two Eight. Contact tower, 118.7. Goodbye.'

'Roger,' said the pilot cheerfully and Carey knew that he was probably finished work for the day too. 'Tower, 118.7. Cheerio.'

She looked up and smiled at Andrew Murphy who was taking over from her and who'd been standing behind her watching the Aer Lingus flight make its approach. Carey didn't know who'd originally decided to call all Aer Lingus flights Shamrock but that's how they were known. The same as all British Airways flights were known as Speedbird. She liked the nicknames. It made it all a little more personal.

'How're things?' asked Andrew as he plugged in his own set of headphones.

'Quiet enough,' she told him. 'One slightly bumpy ride for a charter flight bringing back some supporters from the football match. No drunken brawls on board but the pilot was apparently getting a bit concerned about the dancing in the aisles when they should've been strapped in.'

Andrew laughed. 'We won, didn't we?'

'Did we?' Carey hadn't the slightest interest in football and hadn't been aware, until one of the other controllers had told her, that Ireland had been playing Spain in Barcelona's Nou Camp stadium. It was a match from which Ireland had desperately needed the points but wasn't expected to win. Unusually for the Irish team (which was known for giving away goals at the last minute), they'd scored in the dying seconds of the match to notch up a 2–1 victory over their Spanish rivals. There had been quite a few flights laden with happy supporters on their way back to Dublin from Barcelona during the night.

Carey stood up and stretched. Her back was definitely sore; she wondered should she visit the chiropractor. Then she grinned to herself as she imagined telling him why she thought it hurt. Maybe not, she decided as she picked up her bag. Some things were better left unsaid.

She hurried out of the building and towards her car. It was still bitterly cold and she pulled up the collar of her suede jacket. The idea of sliding into a bed warmed by Ben's body was very appealing. She flung her bag onto the back seat and almost immediately retrieved it as her mobile rang. She looked at the caller ID warily. Whenever it rang now she was expecting it to be Peter Furness because she knew that he was a persistent man. Besides, he'd sounded so desperate that she couldn't imagine he wouldn't call back. There was a certain pleasure in knowing that the man who had hurt her so much wanted to see her again, but she didn't want to see him. Peter's time had gone; he was too late. But it wasn't Peter this time, it was Gina who'd hit Carey's speed-dial number by mistake.

'No problem,' Carey assured her when Gina apologised. 'See you soon.' She put the phone on the passenger seat then switched on the ignition and drove out of the car park.

She still hadn't got used to heading south to the city instead of north to Swords. She yawned as she turned onto the motorway and wondered how on earth she was going to persuade Ben to move from Portobello to the northside. She wasn't a southsider at heart. She couldn't imagine herself on the wrong side of the river for the rest of her life. Of course, she thought guiltily, Ben might feel the same way. The side of the river where you lived was an important issue for many Dubliners. She hoped Ben was more flexible about it than she seemed to be.

The house was in darkness as she let herself in. She closed the front door as quietly as she could and slid her boots off her feet before tiptoeing up the stairs. When she pushed open the bedroom door, her husband was asleep, buried beneath the heavy duvet and snoring gently. She smiled to herself and went into the bathroom. It was cold in the house. She got undressed and into bed as quickly as possible.

'Uh!' Ben grunted as she snuggled into him. 'You're freezing.'

'Cold outside,' she whispered.

'Cold inside too,' he complained. 'You could've warmed your hands. And your feet,' he yelped as she put them on his legs.

'Sorry.' But her tone wasn't in the slightest bit penitent.

'Come here.' He turned towards her and drew her to him. 'I'm sharing my body warmth with you because I love you. But just this once.'

'Thanks,' she murmured sleepily. 'I'll warm them up first the next time.'

'It's OK,' he said. 'I like warming you up really.'

She giggled.

'Busy night?' he asked.

'Sort of.'

'You didn't allow any planes to plough into the runway?'

86

'No,' she yawned widely.

'That's my girl,' he said as he cradled her in his arms.

He realised that she was asleep. But what with her cold hands and cold feet, he was now thoroughly awake himself. He wondered whether one day he'd mind that she might come home cold and tired and wake him up. He didn't think so.

She woke to the enticing aroma of sizzling sausage and bacon. She blinked a couple of times and looked at the bedside clock. It was nearly one in the afternoon. She'd had five hours' sleep. Not quite enough, she thought, but since she had the day off it didn't really matter. She got out of bed and pulled her dressing gown around her.

'Good afternoon.' Ben was turning sausages on the grill as she walked into the kitchen. 'How're you?'

'Great.' She leaned her head on his shoulder. 'And what are you doing?'

'Brunch,' he told her. 'Thought you might appreciate a cooked brekkie. You were a block of ice when you got home.'

'I know.' She wrinkled up her nose. 'I'm a cold extremities kind of girl. Sorry.'

'Oh, that's all right.' He wasn't going to tell her that he hadn't been able to get to sleep after she'd come home. In fact, he'd been up since nine and had done a lot of paperwork for the shops.

'Surely this is totally against your principles,' she said. 'I'd have thought that massive fry-ups were anathema to healthfood freaks.'

'I told you before but you don't want to believe me.' He smiled as he cracked an egg on the side of the pan. 'I'm not a healthfood freak. The shops are a business, not my mission in life, though I do like to eat healthily if I can. But I also succumb from time to time.'

'I didn't buy any of this stuff yesterday.' She watched him crack a second egg.

'I know,' he said. 'I nipped down to the shops earlier and bought it.'

'You really are a marvel.' She grinned at him then kissed him on the ear.

'That's me,' he told her. 'Now make yourself useful, woman, and get some plates out of the cupboard.'

As she sat at the table and pulled her plate towards her, Carey suddenly shivered involuntarily.

'You OK?' asked Ben.

'Sure.' She smiled wryly. 'Someone walking over my grave.'

He laughed and she cut one of her sausages into bite-sized pieces, but she felt as though something had darkened the morning. She really wasn't sure what.

'We didn't really get the chance to chat last night,' said Ben. 'And I wanted to talk to you.'

She looked at him in frozen horror. They'd only been married for two weeks. Surely it was a bit early for him to need to talk to her?

'What about?' she asked faintly.

'Doing something,' he replied. 'To celebrate our marriage.'

She released her breath slowly. It was OK, after all. The feeling of dread lifted. 'What sort of something?'

'A party, get-together . . .' He shrugged. 'I'm not exactly certain.'

'It's a good idea,' said Carey. 'People at work have been on at me to have a booze-up or something but I've put them off.'

'I was thinking of something a little more upmarket than a booze-up,' said Ben a trifle haughtily.

Carey laughed. 'Us air-traffic people aren't exactly upmarket. Certainly not as upmarket as you health-freak types.'

'Sorry,' said Ben. 'That sounded a bit naff, didn't it?'

'A bit.' She dipped a slice of sausage into her egg and watched as the bright yellow yolk spilled over the white and onto the cobalt-blue plate.

'Freya has offered to do it for us,' said Ben.

'What?' She looked up at him, the egg-coated sausage on the end of her fork.

'That's what I wanted to talk about,' explained Ben. 'She suggested it yesterday. Said that she wanted to organise it as our wedding present.'

'Oh.' Carey popped the sausage into her mouth and chewed it slowly.

'I told her we'd be delighted.'

88

'Did you?'

'Aren't we?' he asked.

Carey put her knife and fork on the plate. 'Maybe.'

'Look, I know she hasn't exactly fallen over herself with good wishes up till now,' said Ben, 'but I can understand that. She was shocked. But now she's had a bit of time to consider it she realises how happy you've made me and she wants to welcome you into the family.' He made a face. 'Mind you, it's only a family of two so it's not exactly a big welcome.'

'I haven't even met her yet.' Suddenly Carey wasn't hungry any more. She pushed her plate to one side and rested her chin on her hands.

'That was the other thing,' said Ben. 'I asked her if she'd like to come to dinner tomorrow evening. I know your shifts meant it was difficult this week and she's away in Galway today so she can't come tonight, but we're not doing anything tomorrow and though I'd like to have you all to myself, I guess we can't be alone for ever!'

Carey bit her lip as she looked at him.

'What's the problem?' he asked.

'It's just that – well, my parents asked us over to lunch tomorrow and I said yes.' Her expression was apologetic. 'They're dying to meet you and I didn't think you'd mind. I really don't think we'd be up to having Freya round by the time we got home again and I don't want to meet her if I'm not at my best.'

'Shit,' he said.

'Look, I'll try and arrange something with Freya next week,' said Carey. 'She won't mind waiting a little longer, will she?'

'I guess not.' But Ben looked put out.

'Tell me more about her,' said Carey. 'When we talked about things in the States we only talked about ourselves. We didn't go into much detail about our families. Go into detail now.'

'She's the best sister anyone could have,' said Ben warmly. 'I was only seven when my dad died. She was thirteen. I was distraught, my mother was – disconnected. Freya kept me going.' He leaned back in his chair and closed his eyes. 'After Dad died, Mum was different. She didn't get the same fun out of life any more. She died of heart trouble a few years later but, you know, I think it was more of a broken heart, Carey. She never really got over it. She went through the motions, that's all. I probably should've been a wild child after Dad died but I wasn't. I was a quiet kind of kid. I stayed quiet. Sometimes I think that when my mother died I could've become someone much darker, but Freya helped again. She'd just turned twenty-one, she was working in the bank – a clerical job, nothing special. But she looked after me the whole time. I owe her. Lots.'

'Why didn't she get married herself?' asked Carey. 'She's a good bit older than you, isn't she?'

Ben shrugged. 'She'll be forty this year. I don't know why she didn't get married. She's been going out with this guy, Brian, for years. I asked her once. She just said it wasn't for her.'

'I'm afraid she'll resent me,' said Carey. 'I felt that from her when I talked to her.'

'Don't be silly,' Ben said. 'You only spoke to her for a couple of seconds. When you meet her, it'll be so different. She's a great person, Carey. Really great.'

'Yeah.' Carey's grimace was hidden by her cupped hands. 'So what does she have planned for us?'

'A party, I guess,' said Ben. 'She's really good at that sort of thing. Well . . .' he scratched the back of his head. 'I'm probably better at conceptualising it. I do it for the shops. But she's the organiser, she gets things done. If she says we'll have a great party then that's what we'll have.'

'I'm not sure about it, that's all,' said Carey doubtfully. 'I mean, I do like parties, of course, but I don't like wedding pala-ver. Half the reason we got married in Vegas was to avoid the fuss.'

'I thought we got married there because we couldn't wait.'

'That too,' said Carey hastily. 'But not having a big bash was a bit of a bonus.'

'Do you want me to tell her not to bother?' asked Ben.

'God, no!' Carey looked horrified. 'No, absolutely not. I'm sure you're right, it'll be great.'

'It will. I promise.'

'In that case I'm really looking forward to it,' she said brightly.

'So what about tomorrow then?' asked Ben. 'My induction into your family?'

'It'll be very informal,' Carey assured him. 'Mum's fine, Dad can

90

be a bit crotchety but he's good at heart. My sister and brother-in-law will be there, too, plus some or all of their kids.'

'How many kids?' asked Ben.

'Four,' said Carey. 'There's Jeanne, who's seventeen and, like, totally cool.' She laughed. 'Then Donny who's sixteen and thinks all girls are sex objects. Zac is . . .' she frowned '. . . nearly fifteen, I think. And Nadia's twelve.'

'And they'll all be at lunch?' Ben sounded panicked. 'I don't think I've ever met that number of people from the one family before.'

'You'll be fine,' Carey assured him. 'And they'll love you, honestly they will.'

He breathed out. 'I hope so.'

'Of course they will.' She got up and kissed him. 'I love you, don't I? So will they.'

Freya Russell sat in the living room of her two-bedroomed apartment in Rathgar. People who'd never been there before were always surprised when they first stepped inside. They expected a place that reflected her character, cool and distant, and they were always astonished to find that the walls were painted in dramatic shades of purples and pinks, while her voile curtains were vivid blocks of orange and her bright green sofa was piled high with yellow sequinned cushions. Brian had once told her that it was like an Eastern bazaar and Freya replied that she liked Eastern bazaars.

In contrast to the colour and warmth indoors, the bare branches of the chestnut trees swayed and creaked outside her window. During the summer she liked to leave the balcony doors open so that she could feel the warmth of the summer breezes and hear the rustle of the leaves. But in the winter even the lightest breeze was cold and the trees looked menacing rather than soothing.

She looked at the guest-list in front of her. The people she'd planned to invite to what she'd termed the Ben and Carey extravaganza were mainly friends of both her brother and herself. Many of them were business friends but she'd also remembered to include Ben's football friends and his mate, Phil. She wished there were more people she could put in the 'family' column which was on one side of the A4 sheet she was using, but both her mother and father had been only children. It was why, she supposed, her mother had been so devastated when her father died.

Ben hadn't told her much about Carey's family so she knew she'd have to ask him who to invite. Maybe there was a clatter of them, she thought glumly, a clatter of noisy, gregarious people with whom she'd find nothing in common. She didn't know exactly why she felt she'd have nothing in common with the Brownes but she just sensed that they'd be a struggle to get on with. She picked up her ballpoint and wrote *Browne Family* on the paper.

Her glance flickered over the 'friends' column again. The last name on the list was Leah Ryder's. She chewed on the end of the biro as she looked at it. She hadn't been talking to Leah since the evening they'd met in the bar and had rather more drinks than they'd intended. Afterwards they'd gone for a Chinese meal and had spent the whole time wondering whether or not men were worth the effort. Freya had told Leah that she'd always thought Ben would be worth the effort. Her brother was a decent person, a good bloke. Except that he'd clearly lost his marbles.

And then Leah had said that she'd always be friends with Freya because Freya was kind and understanding and knew how she felt despite having a total shit for a brother.

And Freya said that she didn't know whether or not she wanted Ben's marriage to break up, because surely her brother would be devastated if that happened – but didn't Leah think it was almost inevitable?

'Absolutely,' Leah murmured drunkenly. 'I want to go to the celebration wedding party, though, Freya. I definitely have to go to the party.'

In their alcohol-induced haze it seemed perfectly reasonable that Leah should come to the party. But now Freya was having doubts. She trusted Leah not to do anything stupid but she wasn't sure that having a new wife and an ex-lover in the same room was a good idea. Yet Leah had phoned her after their drinks together and told her that she was really looking forward to coming. It'd be good for her, she told Freya, to see Ben and his wife together. Help her to accept it. Freya had agreed but she still wasn't certain that it would be good for anyone.

She sighed deeply and looked at the list again.

'How's it going?'

She looked up as Brian let himself into the apartment. He'd stayed the night last night and had gone to the shops to buy the papers.

'Not bad.' She turned her face up towards him for a kiss. 'Working on the guest-list.'

Brian peered over her shoulders and massaged them gently while she sighed with pleasure.

'Robert Kingsley.' He groaned. 'Why are you asking that bore?'

'He does business with us,' said Freya sternly. 'I know he's investment banking's answer to the Sandman, but I can't leave him out.'

'Browne family?' he asked. 'How many?'

'I don't know,' said Freya. 'I was thinking that maybe I'd ask *her* about them.'

'Ask who?'

'You know,' said Freya crossly. 'Carey.'

'You really don't like her, do you?'

'How can I like or dislike her when I haven't even met the woman yet? When she couldn't even be bothered to make an effort to see me?'

'Aren't you being a little unfair?' Brian stopped rubbing her shoulders and perched on the arm of the sofa. 'It's not her fault that you haven't met. You make snap decisions about people, Freya.'

'No, I don't,' said Freya. 'I knew you for a long time before I decided you were good enough to go out with.'

'Gosh, thanks!'

'I'm sorry.' She looked up at him. 'I didn't mean it to sound like that.'

'Have you decided on a date yet?' asked Brian, looking at her guest-list again. 'Because if you want me to book Oleg's I'll have to let them know pretty soon.'

'As soon as I can manage,' said Freya. 'Ben's giving me her shifts so that I can have it on a night when she doesn't have to be in work the next morning. I don't want to be responsible for her having aircraft landing on the M50 or whatever might happen if she's too hungover to do her job properly.'

Brian nodded. 'And before then you'll have debriefed her about her family?'

93

Freya looked at him. 'Are you taking the piss?'

'A little,' he admitted as he scanned through the list and then stabbed his finger at Leah's name. 'Have you lost your marbles? What's *she* doing on the list? D'you want a riot?'

'Why shouldn't she come? asked Freya. 'She's my friend too.'

'Oh, come on.' Brian stared at her. 'She's Ben's ex-girlfriend – the girl he's been trying to dump for a year. You really think it's a good idea to ask her to his wedding party?'

'He hasn't been trying to dump her for a year,' said Freya. 'He was sleeping with her, for God's sake. That's not exactly the way you go about dumping someone.'

'He might have been sleeping with her but he never loved her,' Brian said.

'Don't be ridiculous,' said Freya. 'He was crazy about her.'

'He was crazy about the massages,' agreed Brian. 'But there wasn't the faintest chance of him marrying her.'

'My brother isn't that shallow,' snapped Freya.

'Of course not,' said Brian hastily. 'But you've got it all wrong about him and Leah. She was good company, that's all.'

'How can you say that when they spent nights together?' demanded Freya.

'So what?' Brian shrugged.

'You're all the same!' Freya looked at him in disgust. 'Once you're getting it you don't give a toss about how the girl feels.'

'Don't be so bloody stupid—'

'And don't talk to me like that!' cried Freya.

Brian threw the newspapers he'd still been holding onto the coffee-table in front of them. 'You know, you can be a real pain in the arse sometimes,' he said angrily. 'You just don't have a clue.'

'What's that supposed to mean?' Freya's eyes, bright blue like her brother's, glittered.

'People aren't like your business,' he told her. 'Life isn't some kind of management project. Everyone won't do exactly what you want them to when you want them to.'

'I'm not expecting them to,' said Freya.

'You're expecting that flaky girl to mingle with a wedding party for the bloke she's obsessed over,' said Brian.

'Leah isn't obsessed,' Freya objected. 'She was hurt, of course she was, when she heard about Ben's marriage. She was shocked too. But, like she said to me the other night, she accepts that it's over. She's coming for closure reasons.'

'Freya, how thick can you get?' demanded Brian. 'If the girl is that upset she should stay away. Even you can't possibly believe that if she thought Ben was going to marry her – which I'm pretty sure was on her agenda – she'd have a good time seeing him with his new wife!'

'I told you, she's OK with the whole thing,' said Freya. 'She'll be fine.'

'I still can't believe you're thinking of asking her.' Brian shook his head. 'It's just asking for trouble, Freya.'

'I can't ignore her,' said Freya obstinately. 'Besides, she wants to come.'

'You've told her about it already?' Brian looked shocked.

'Yes. I met her for a drink and we talked. She said she'd like to come along.'

'I bet.'

'Oh, for God's sake!' Freya looked at him angrily. 'You haven't a clue what you're talking about. Leah's a lovely person and she isn't going to cause a fuss. You're just trying to make trouble when there isn't any.'

'If you believe that you believe anything,' Brian snorted.

'Why don't you just fuck off home and let me get on with it?' Freya bent her head over her list again.

Brian stood in the middle of the room and looked at her. 'I thought we were going to go to the movies.'

'No,' said Freya. 'I'm not in the mood now.'

'Fine.' His voice hardened. 'I'll go if that's what you want.'

'It'd be better,' she said.

'Do you want me to call you later?'

'No,' said Freya again. 'I'll be busy.'

Brian banged the apartment door as he left. Freya sat and stared at the bare chestnut trees as they swayed in front of the window, then she crumpled up the guest-list and threw it into the bin.

Chapter 8

Basil

A fortifying herb oil with a spicy, warm aroma

Ben drove to Maude and Arthur's in a small van emblazoned with the *Herbal Matters* logo.

'I didn't bother replacing my car when they repossessed the Saab,' he told Carey as she removed a selection of brochures on homoeopathic remedies from the passenger seat before climbing in. 'Anyway, this is fine for getting round the place.'

Carey fastened the seat belt and decided that traffic looked slightly different from the vantage point of a higher seat.

'I've never actually been in a van before,' she said. 'Though I was once in a 747 simulator.'

'Show-off!' But he grinned as he put the van into gear.

Carey hoped that her family would like him. How could they not, she'd asked herself over and over again the previous night as she lay awake in bed while Ben slept beside her. But her father was such a difficult man and her mother – well, Maude would be polite, she was always polite, but she could do politeness with effervescent sincerity or with all the warmth of cut-glass crystal. As for Sylvia . . . Carey screwed up her nose at the thought of her sister and how she'd react to meeting her new brother-in-law.

Carey could never figure out how it had been decided in the Browne household that Sylvia's eventual partner would be perfection personified while she, Carey, would simply have a succession of ever more unsuitable boyfriends, all of whom would be compared unfavourably to John Lynch. But that was what had happened. Sylvia was a stable kind of person, placid and undemanding who'd always seemed to attract marriage-minded men. Carey had never been placid. And she usually attracted the kind of men who just wanted to have fun. Nevertheless, her place in the Hall of Fame of totally unsuitable people ever to get married had probably been assured when she'd kicked up such a fuss at Sylvia's wedding by refusing to wear the sugar-pink confection that her sister had demanded of her as a bridesmaid. She'd warned Sylvia over and over that she wasn't going to end up like a fairy on top of the Christmas tree but her sister simply wouldn't listen.

The worst of it all, Carey mused, was that she did like to dress up occasionally. But after the fuss of Sylvia's wedding she'd felt that – where her family was concerned in any event – she could never be seen to wear anything that looked even vaguely feminine or had the merest hint of pink. Today she was wearing a pair of rust-coloured trousers and a cream jumper teamed with one of the four pairs of shoes she'd bought in New York. She shook her head ruefully. Twenty years later she still had the scars! And Sylvia had never really forgiven her.

'You OK?' Ben broke in on her thoughts.

'Fine,' she said.

'I'm nervous,' he told her.

She giggled. 'They'll love you. Really they will.'

'I thought you said they'd probably hate me.'

'Oh, one or the other.' She squeezed his arm gently. 'Opposite sides of the same coin, aren't they?'

'God, I hope not.'

They continued the journey in companionable silence. Carey wondered whether this was what Sylvia felt with John. This oneness that she'd never experienced with anyone else before. She knew that Sylvia and John had probably discussed her sudden marriage and had doubtless come to the conclusion that it was doomed from the start. Sylvia had probably discussed it with Maude too, over-excited and shrieking at the madness of it all. But what did Sylvia know about it? Actually, Carey conceded after a moment's thought, she must know something. After all, Sylvia's marriage had lasted for twenty years despite the fact that she didn't have a bridesmaid in half of the photographs!

'Left here,' she told Ben, suddenly realising that they'd reached the turn-off for her parents' house. 'Then left again when you get to the little crossroads.'

He followed her instructions and a couple of minutes later they pulled up outside Arthur and Maude's whitewashed dormer bungalow.

Ben stepped out of the van and looked at Carey in surprise. 'It's the country,' he told her.

She giggled. 'Not exactly. It's only a mile to the motorway.'

'But there are fields around your house!'

'They can't build more houses here,' she told him, 'because of the noise from the planes.'

'It's lovely.' He gazed at the garden full of blue and white winter flowers, small ornamental trees and surrounded by a glossy green box hedge.

'They'll be pleased to hear you say that. And tell Mum that you like the pyracantha growing up the walls. She planted that when Sylvia was five.'

'Right.' Ben nodded and followed Carey up the pathway.

'Hello, darling!' Maude opened the door before she had a chance to ring the bell. 'We saw you pull up.'

'Hi, Mum.' Carey kissed Maude on the cheek then moved away. 'This is Ben.'

'Ben.' Maude stretched out her hand and he took it firmly.

'Nice to meet you, Mrs Browne,' he said.

'Oh, Maude, please.' She made a face at him. 'Mrs anything sounds so old, doesn't it? Do come in. Arthur's in the living room.'

Carey realised that she was holding her breath as she walked through the house. When she pushed open the door of the living room, she saw her father standing at the window, gazing out of the back garden. He was a tall, thin man and Ben immediately saw where Carey's gangly genes had come from.

'Hi, Dad,' she said brightly. 'It's us.'

'So I gathered.' Arthur Browne turned towards them. 'About time you came to visit and brought your husband to meet us.'

Carey smiled edgily. She wasn't sure about the tone of her father's voice. Not entirely censorious but not entirely welcoming either. His angular face was expressionless.

'This is Ben,' she said.

'Obviously.' Arthur looked at Ben appraisingly over the gold rims of his square-cut glasses which were perched on the end of his long nose. 'Did you coerce her or did she coerce you?'

'Neither,' said Ben pleasantly. 'We met, we fell in love, we married.'

'Quick worker, aren't you?'

'Dad!'

'It was rather sudden, I know,' said Ben. 'But just because we did it quickly doesn't mean that we don't love each other.'

'Now,' said Arthur. 'What about later though?'

'We'll love each other just as much at six o'clock tonight,' said Carey tartly.

'Watch your tongue, missy,' said Arthur.

She felt Ben tense beside her and she reached for his hand. He twined his fingers around hers and squeezed them.

'Arthur, don't be so rude,' said Maude cheerfully. 'They're married and there's nothing you can do about it. It's up to them to make it work, and I'm sure they will.'

She smiled at Carey and at Ben but Carey could see that her smile didn't quite reach her eyes. She felt herself begin to tremble. Ben squeezed her fingers again and she moved closer to him.

'Are Sylvia and John coming to lunch too?' she asked her mother brightly.

'Of course,' said Maude. 'And Jeanne and Donny and Zac and Nadia.'

'A full turn-out.' Carey grinned. 'Sylvia's marshalled the troops.'

'We love having Sylvia's family for lunch,' said Arthur. 'Very well-behaved children.'

'Arthur, don't be such a liar,' said Maude. 'You know perfectly well that we hardly ever see any of them these days. And you used to think that Donny and Zac were spawn of the devil.'

Carey giggled and Ben smiled. Arthur looked at Maude crossly. But she held his look and suddenly he sighed.

'I admit they weren't always the best,' said Arthur, 'but she's brought them up well. They try.' He looked at Ben. 'You planning to have a family with my daughter?'

'Dad!' Carey hoped she wouldn't have to spend the whole

99

afternoon trying to deflect some of her father's more intrusive questions. It was a habit of his that had always annoyed her – he felt he was perfectly justified in asking anybody absolutely anything.

'We haven't discussed it in great detail yet,' replied Ben calmly. 'But it may well be on the agenda at some point.'

'You'll have to make her give up that job of hers if she gets pregnant,' said Arthur. 'No life for a married woman. I always said so. No life for a woman at all.'

'Dad, if you're going to spend the entire day picking on me then we're going home,' Carey snapped. 'You know that I love my work and that – like with almost any other job on the whole damned planet – women are just as good if not better at it than men. So don't start all of this chauvinist crap. I'm not in the mood.'

'All I—'

'Arthur.' Maude interrupted him firmly. 'That's enough. Carey and Ben are here for a family lunch, not an inquisition.' She cocked her head. 'And I think that's the doorbell. Be a pet and answer it.'

'Thanks,' said Carey shortly as her father left the room.

'He cares about you, darling,' said Maude. 'As I do. He only wants you to be happy.'

'On his terms,' muttered Carey, but she didn't have time to say anything else as the sunlit room suddenly filled up with people all talking at the same time and all looking at Ben with undisguised interest.

'I suppose congratulations are in order!'

Ben watched as a tall woman put her arms round Carey and hugged her. She then stood back and looked at her while still holding her shoulders. If there'd been any other candidate in the room he wouldn't have been sure that this was Carey's older sister, Sylvia. Although there was a superficial resemblance, Sylvia wasn't in the least bit like her. She had shoulder-length dark hair, but it was perfectly straight and as unlike Carey's unruly mop of curls as it was possible to be. Her face was softer than her sister's, her cheekbones less pronounced and her lips slightly fuller. The resemblance was more to Maude than to Arthur, thought Ben as he studied her. She wore perfectly tailored charcoal grey trousers with a gold chain at the waist and a white silk blouse. A dusty pink scarf hung loosely round her neck.

'Hey, Carey, absolutely cool.'

The girl who stood to one side looked much more like his wife. She was tall too, but with the same long arms and legs as Carey and curls which were almost as unkempt. Her denim jeans had fashionable rips at the knees and the thighs, and her tartan T-shirt sported a label that said *Never Be Bored*.

'Thanks, Jeanne,' said Carey.

'Have you photos?' asked Sylvia. 'We want to see the proof.'

'Here's the proof.' Carey removed her sister's hands from her shoulders. 'This is my husband, Ben.'

'So this is the man.' Sylvia looked at him in the same appraising way as Arthur. 'Well, honeybunch, I can see how you fell for him. Quite the handsome hunk.'

'Don't call me that,' said Carey. 'And I didn't fall for him because he was a handsome hunk although clearly that was a major plus.'

'She fell for me because of my mind.' Ben extended his hand. 'Nice to meet you. Sylvia, I presume.'

'And impeccable manners too.' Sylvia winked at Carey. 'You are the lucky one.'

'Show us your ring?' The youngest female in the room was Sylvia's twelve-year-old daughter Nadia – another one with tumbling curls. 'I want to see your ring.'

Carey showed Nadia the plain gold hoop – which clearly disappointed the younger girl – while Ben was greeted by Sylvia's husband, John, and their two sons, Donny and Zac.

'It's not always this mad here,' John told him. 'But you and Carey sure did fire up the family by getting hitched like that.'

'In retrospect maybe we should've come home and done it here,' admitted Ben. 'But it seemed so right at the time.'

'I'm never getting married,' said Donny. 'Why confine yourself to one woman when there are so many in the world?'

'Absolutely,' said Zac.

Ben grinned at them. Arthur came over to the men and offered them a drink. Ben accepted a can of Guinness despite the fact that he hated the iconic black stout.

'He's gorgeous, isn't he?' Jeanne was looking at Ben even though she was talking to Carey.

101

'Oh, for heaven's sake, Jeanne, get a grip,' said her mother. 'He's just a man.'

'I know,' said Jeanne. 'But he's a great-looking man. I think you've done really well for yourself, Carey.'

'Thank you.' Carey grinned. 'I do too.'

'Wouldn't it have been better to have waited till you got home before marrying him?' Sylvia suggested.

'Why?' asked Jeanne. 'There's such a thing as love at first sight you know, Mum.'

'Rubbish,' said Sylvia firmly. 'And you needn't get ideas, Jeanne Lynch, that the first spotty bloke you decide is gorgeous is the one you're going to marry.'

'Oh, grow up, Mum.' Jeanne looked at her wearily. 'I've had boyfriends. So has Carey. Lots more than me, I expect. She didn't marry the first. Neither did I.'

Carey giggled and Sylvia looked annoyed. 'That's not what I meant,' she told Jeanne. 'As well you know.'

'I think you made a great choice,' said Jeanne. 'And it was a great idea too. Away from all the hustle and bustle of this family.'

'What d'you mean by that?' asked her mother.

'Just that it was nice for Carey to get married without all the fuss,' said Jeanne.

'You're just like her.' Sylvia sounded disgusted as she looked at her daughter. 'I don't know why.'

'Yes, you do,' said Jeanne, and Carey felt a sudden tension between mother and daughter.

'You'll probably change your mind loads of times about the bloke you might want to marry and the way you do it,' she told Jeanne cheerfully. 'God knows, I nearly got hitched to other men before. It was just that something held me back.'

'I'm glad to hear that!' Ben had come up behind them and now put his arm round Carey's waist. 'I'd hate to think I missed out because you were too hasty.'

'Tell us about yourself,' said Sylvia. 'I find it impossible to take on board the fact that I suddenly have a brother-in-law. I'd like to know all about you.'

'Ben can tell us about himself over lunch,' Maude announced. 'Come on, everyone. Into the dining room.'

When Carey was a child the dining room had only been used for important occasions like Christmas and Easter and their birthdays. The rest of the time the family had eaten in the big south-facing kitchen which was a much more relaxed eating place. As far as Carey knew, her parents still didn't use the dining room very much. She wished they weren't using it today. It was darker than the kitchen and made her feel uncomfortable. The décor and furnishing were old fashioned and intimidating.

Maude had extended the rosewood table to accommodate all of them and had laid the places with the silverware that also only came out for important occasions as well as the olive green placemats that were hardly ever used either.

'Soup to start.' Maude carried in a tureen. 'It's been so cold that I thought you'd like something warming to get you going.'

She began to ladle her home-made vegetable soup into the bowls in front of them, and Carey felt her mouth begin to water. Her mother was a damned good cook and, except for Ben's breakfast fry-up the previous morning, they hadn't had any home-cooked food all week. Nice though Marks & Spencer or Tesco ready-meals could be, Carey didn't feel they qualified as home cooking.

'Come on, Ben.' Sylvia looked at him expectantly. 'We're ready to hear all about you.'

Carey listened as he told them what they wanted to hear. He didn't gloss over his life, he spoke in detail about the loss of his parents, Freya's part in his upbringing, the collapse of the internet company and the success of the healthfood stores. By the time he'd finished speaking, Carey herself knew more about him than she'd ever done before.

'So how does your sister feel about the marriage?' asked John. 'Was she as surprised as us?'

'Oh, I'm sure she was.' Ben nodded. 'But I'm glad to say that she's organising a reception for us very soon. The invitations will be sent out shortly.'

'A reception!' Sylvia's eyes glittered as she looked at Carey. 'I thought you got married in Las Vegas because you didn't want a reception!'

'This is different,' said Carey.

'I don't see how.'

Carey ignored her and turned instead to Jeanne. 'How about you, god-daughter?' she asked. 'Any men on your horizon?'

'Not as good-looking as yours.' Jeanne giggled. 'They're all so juvenile at my age.'

Ben laughed and Donny looked at his sister in annoyance.

'I'm not juvenile,' he said.

'Come on!' Jeanne shook her head. 'You know that teenage boys are a mass of testosterone. You only think of one thing.'

'Maybe the blokes you hang round with only think of one thing,' said Donny spiritedly. 'Not all of us are so one-dimensional.'

'So your two dimensions are Manchester United and Caitlin Hegarty.' Jeanne chuckled.

'Caitlin Hegarty?' Sylvia looked at her son in surprise. 'Who's Caitlin Hegarty?'

'Top totty,' sniggered Zac.

'Zac Lynch!' John exclaimed. 'We do *not* use those sorts of expressions in our house.'

'I'm only stating a fact,' said Zac. 'You haven't seen her yet, Dad.'

Carey was relieved that the focus of the discussion had switched away from her and Ben. She reached under the table and slid her hand onto his thigh. His hand closed over hers and held it tightly.

She felt safe with him. Protected and cherished in a way that she'd never felt before. In the past she'd been intimidated by John and Sylvia and their noisy family. She loved them, of course, but their whole way of life was completely beyond her. She'd never been very good at joining in their family spats. And when she did, she always seemed to get it wrong. But now, no matter what else was going on around her, it seemed that with Ben at her side she could deal with it.

For the rest of the meal the conversation was more general. John talked about the attic conversion they were getting done, Sylvia gave them an update on the furniture restoration classes she was attending on Wednesday evenings. Zac and Donny argued the relative merits of Manchester United and Leeds while Jeanne complained about the workload for her exams and Nadia talked about her selection as the lead in the school play.

When they'd finished eating Carey helped her mother to clear the table and then filled the sink with hot water for the washing-up.

'You should get a dishwasher,' she observed as she stacked the plates beside the sink.

'Don't need one,' Maude told her. 'It's usually just your dad and me and all we really generate are cups. I never meant to turn into a tea-swilling old woman but that's what I've become.'

'We won't consider you old until you've passed your seventieth birthday.' Sylvia walked into the room. 'And even then you're far too much the glamorous granny to think of you as old. But you've done great work here in feeding the masses, so why don't you go in and sit down and leave Carey and me to deal with this.'

'It's fine.'

'Go in and sit down.' Carey echoed Sylvia's words.

Maude looked at both of them and shrugged her shoulders. Then she joined the others in the living room.

'He's nice,' said Sylvia as Carey began to immerse the dishes in the soapy water.

'Thanks.'

'He's nice but you hardly know him,' said Sylvia. 'You haven't even met his sister yet and by all accounts she's been the big influence on his life.'

'I didn't marry his sister,' said Carey spiritedly.

'No, but—'

'I don't want to hear it.'

'You've got to be realistic.' Sylvia took a plate out of her sister's hand and began to dry it.

'I am being realistic,' said Carey. 'It's not as though I was a silly twenty year old who didn't know what she was doing. I'm a lot older than you were when you married John. I remember Aunt Evelyn saying that you were terribly young to get married but you seem to have lasted the pace.'

'Did Evelyn really say that?' asked Sylvia.

Carey nodded. 'And there's no reason that me and Ben won't last either.'

'It just seems a very radical way of getting out of the dress thing,' said Sylvia.

'You'll never forgive me for not liking that bridesmaid's dress, will you?' demanded Carey. 'It was so long ago.'

'It was my wedding day,' said Sylvia shortly. 'A bride gets what she wants on her wedding day. That's the rule. And I wanted you looking pretty and feminine just for once.'

'The dress looked horrific on me,' said Carey. 'I never minded looking feminine though I always preferred being comfortable. But that dress was awful.'

'It was the eighties,' protested Sylvia. 'Everything was awful in the eighties.'

Carey giggled and Sylvia smiled wryly.

'I wish you all the luck in the world,' said Sylvia eventually. 'I really do.'

'Thanks.'

'But if there's a problem . . .'

'There won't be,' Carey interrupted.

'I know we're not the closest of people,' her sister continued. 'You got on miles better with Tony than you ever did with me. It was probably the age thing. But, Carey, if you need to talk any time . . .'

'I'll keep it in mind,' said Carey. 'Really I will.'

It was after six by the time they left Arthur and Maude's. Carey sighed with relief as she waved goodbye through the van window and then settled back in the seat.

'It wasn't that bad,' said Ben. 'They're nice, your family.'

'Sometimes,' said Carey. 'But Mum and Dad can be so nosy. So can Sylvia. John's OK, although I never talk to him that much and the kids are a hoot. But en masse they can all be a bit intimidating.'

'It was new to me,' admitted Ben. 'But I'll get used to it.'

'We won't be going over there every Sunday!' Carey sounded horrified and Ben laughed.

'Of course not. But I can deal with them whenever I meet them.'

'Were you nervous?' asked Carey.

'Of course I was,' said Ben. 'I was afraid they wouldn't like me.'

She leaned her head against his shoulder. 'I was afraid they

106

wouldn't like you either,' she admitted. 'Though I couldn't see why. You're eminently likeable.'

'Loveable even?' suggested Ben.

'Absolutely.'

'So now the only thing is for you to meet Freya,' he said. 'And then we'll have our reception and just get down to day-to-day sort of stuff.'

'I'm looking forward to that,' said Carey.

'Day-to-day sort of stuff?'

She nodded. 'I'm tired of feeling like a news item,' she told him. 'I thought that we'd come back and that everyone would be amazed, but that it would only last for a day or two. It seems to be going on for ever!'

'That's why the party is a good idea,' said Ben. 'Everyone can get together and talk about how surprising it all was and that'll sort them out.'

'You think?'

'Sure,' he said. 'And I'm always right.'

Carey laughed. 'I thought I was the one that was always right.'

'We'll split it,' said Ben comfortably.

A message alert sounded on her mobile phone, breaking the easy silence that had fallen on them. She dug into her bag and retrieved it.

'Hv 2 tlk,' said Peter's message.

'Ntg 2 tlk abt,' she replied.

'Pls. Not long.' She glanced at Ben who wasn't taking any notice of her. 'Why?' She pressed the keys quickly.

'Just need 2 c u.'

She chewed her bottom lip. 'OK,' she sent eventually. 'Will call u to arrange. Bi.'

Then she switched off the phone and put it back into her bag.

107

Chapter 9

May Chang

A fruit oil which is sweet but with astringent properties

Her shift the next day was another one which began at two o'clock in the afternoon. She got up at the same time as Ben, had breakfast with him – brown bread and coffee – and then ran herself a bath when he left. She dumped half a bottle of Body Shop bath salts into the extra-hot water and then lowered herself cautiously in. She could feel her skin tingle with the heat but she didn't care, she liked hot, hot baths. Strands of curls toppled from the casual knot on the top of her head and dangled in front of her face. She lay back in the bath and closed her eyes.

Peter Furness. She hadn't been able to stop thinking about him since his phone call and messages. Ben had commented on the fact that she'd been unusually quiet the previous night but had put it down to having had lunch with her family. It had probably been a bit difficult for her, he surmised, and she didn't let on that, difficult though she had found it, it was nothing in comparison to hearing from Peter Furness again. And seeing the anxious, almost pleading tone to his message. He'd never pleaded with her before. He'd been cooler with her than many of her other boyfriends but somehow she'd enjoyed that. It was only after she realised that he was married that she understood his coolness and the reason why he had sometimes called her at the last minute to change their plans. She felt a trickle of sweat slide down her cheek and she exhaled slowly, blowing it away.

She didn't want to meet Peter Furness. There was nothing left to

108

say to him. She'd said it all the night they split up. He'd said it all too. At least, she thought he had. He'd cried too, which had made her feel better, even though she was unsure whether he was crying because they weren't going to see each other any more, or because his idyll with two women was over.

They'd agreed that he couldn't leave Sandra and Aaron. It was important that he give it another try. It wasn't that he didn't love Sandra – he did. But he had never felt the level of passion for her that he felt for Carey. He'd loved her and he'd married her because he'd thought that this was it. With Carey he knew that it could be so much more.

She stretched her arm over the side of the bath and reached for a sponge on the nearby ledge. She soaked the sponge and then dribbled the hot water over her face. He'd broken her heart, she remembered. She had been so much in love with him.

But not in the way she loved Ben. Not with the joyful, careless sense of elation that she felt whenever she was with him. Not with the same depth of emotion either. She'd been in love with Peter Furness but she loved Ben. She wasn't entirely sure in her own mind what the difference was, but she knew that there was a difference. Her future was with Ben and not with Peter. She was *married* to Ben, for heaven's sake! And Peter was married to Sandra. If their marriage wasn't perfect, that wasn't *her* fault. She was married to Ben and it was up to her to keep things as perfect as they could possibly be. And that she intended to do. It wasn't often that perfection came along.

She laughed suddenly. She was so used to being tense about her relationships, so used to worrying about whether her boyfriend of the moment would dump her for someone else that she hadn't yet adapted to the security of being married. She was looking for trouble where none existed. She was over-dramatising. Sylvia often gave out to her for being overly dramatic. Probably, Sylvia surmised, because she had to be cool and unfazed when she was at work. So that when she was away from the studied calm of air traffic control she lost the plot completely. Carey knew that Sylvia was partly right. All controllers were a bit crazy. It came with the territory.

She rubbed the sponge over her body and then pulled the plug out of the bath. Then she switched on the electric shower and

109

washed her hair, grimacing as she got shampoo into her eyes and splashing water around the bathroom as she reached for her towel. When eventually she got dressed and dried her hair she took out her mobile and dialled Peter's number.

He answered on the second ring. 'Hi,' he said.

'Where are you?'

Peter was a company rep for a supplier of gym equipment. He spent most of his day on the road although his physique was almost as good as anyone who spent a lot of time working out. Which was one of the things that had attracted Carey's attention when she'd (literally) bumped into him at a music festival. She'd allowed him to buy her replacement drinks for the ones he'd caused her to spill and she'd enjoyed his company as they tried to talk over the sound of rock bands who took themselves too seriously. They'd left before the concert was over and gone for something to eat in a place where they could actually hear each other speak. The thing about Peter, as she'd told Gina afterwards, was that he might be built like a minor Adonis but he was actually very sensitive and understanding. Much, much later Gina told her that married men looking for someone else generally were.

'Clonee,' said Peter. 'My next call is in Castleknock.'

'What do you want to talk about?' she asked.

'Can we meet?'

'I don't want to meet with you, Peter.'

'Come on, Carey. I wouldn't ask if it wasn't important.'

'It's not important to me,' she told him simply.

'Well, it is to me,' he said urgently.

She knew she should just tell him that she was married, and that nothing he had to say could be as important as that, but she wasn't able to.

'What time's your shift?' he asked.

'Two,' said Carey.

'Meet me at twelve,' he said. 'Eddie Rocket's in Swords.'

'Look, Peter—'

'Carey, I really need to talk with you. Just do it.'

She sighed. 'OK.'

'Great.' She could hear the relief in his voice. 'I'll be there.'

She was five minutes late arriving at the hamburger joint. She was

110

never usually late and, when it came to her dates with Peter, she'd nearly always been early. No, she amended, as she pushed open the glass door, she'd been on time. He was the late one.

But not today. He was already sitting in a booth looking at the menu. Not that he needed to. They'd often met at the restaurant before and they always had the same thing.

'Hi.' His grey-green eyes lit up as she slid onto the seat opposite him. 'How're you doing?'

'I'm fine,' she said.

'It's great to see you again. You wouldn't believe how much I've missed you.'

'Wouldn't I?' she asked. She kept her hands folded on her lap, out of sight.

'No,' said Peter. 'You wouldn't.' He leaned towards her and kissed her on the cheek.

'I missed you at first,' she told him. 'But not recently.'

He raised his eyebrows. 'New boyfriend?' His tone indicated that he didn't believe she'd found someone to replace him yet.

'New husband,' she said baldly, and put her hands on the table.

He looked at the thin gold band on her finger and then at her. 'You're joking.'

'No.'

'Christ, Carey, tell me that you're having me on.'

'No,' she said again.

'Because it's only three months since we split up.'

'Nearly four,' she said.

'You cried and told me you'd never find someone like me.'

'I didn't,' she said. 'I found someone who wasn't married.'

Peter flinched. 'I see.'

'And he's all the things I ever wanted in a husband so I married him,' said Carey.

'You met him and married him in the space of nearly four months.' Peter laughed shortly. 'Quick work for someone who told me I'd broken her heart.'

'You did break my heart,' she said fiercely. 'You broke my heart because you let me fall in love with you and you never told me you were married.'

'I know what happened was wrong,' said Peter. 'I didn't expect

111

you to fall in love with me. I didn't expect to fall in love with you either.'

'You didn't fall in love with me,' she told him. 'You had a bit of a romance with me. That's totally different.'

'Of course I fell in love with you,' Peter said angrily. 'Why the hell did you think I broke it off?'

There was a sudden silence between them. As she sat and stared at him a waitress arrived at their table and put a plain burger in front of her and one smothered in tomato relish in front of Peter. Then she placed a bowl of chilli fries between them.

'You ordered for both of us?' Carey looked at him quizzically.

'I guessed your order wouldn't have changed,' he said. 'But maybe I was wrong.'

Carey shrugged.

'Tell me about this man of yours,' said Peter.

'Nothing to tell.' Carey didn't want to talk about Ben. 'We met, we married. I love him.'

'Carey, you can't possibly love him,' said Peter. 'You hardly know him.'

'I loved you when I hardly knew you,' she said. 'I loved you because I thought that you were a caring, decent man, because you treated me so differently from anyone else in the past, but I didn't know you had a wife and a kid waiting for you at home, did I?'

'Not any more,' said Peter blankly.

'What?' She stared at him.

'Sandra and I have split up.'

'Oh.' She mouthed the word but no sound came out.

'You didn't believe me when I told you that our marriage was in trouble, did you? You thought I was spinning you a line. But I wasn't. We married too young and we didn't love each other enough and neither of us was the person we thought.'

'I'm sorry,' said Carey.

'I did my best to patch things up,' he said. 'Even though I was more devastated over losing you than anything else. But I gave it another go and I really tried. I even bought her flowers.' He laughed cynically. 'I suppose buying the flowers was a sure sign that it was never going to work. Then one day she told me that she didn't love me any more.'

112

'Just like that?'

He nodded. 'She said that I'd changed. She'd changed. That I bored her.'

Carey looked at him sympathetically.

'She said that she'd thought we were right for each other but she knew that we weren't. And that she'd wanted us to stay together because of Aaron, but that she'd found someone else.'

'What!'

'Yes.' Peter shrugged. 'All the times that I thought she was at her bloody bridge session she was meeting him. Marty. He's a fucking computer technician.'

'I'm sorry, Peter. I really am.'

'Yeah, well.' Peter took a chip from the bowl and shoved it into the sauce. 'She's left me and she's living with him.'

'What about Aaron?'

'She's taken him with her.'

'But . . .' Carey looked at him in astonishment. 'Surely she can't just do that. Surely she has to ask for custody. Surely—'

'I don't care.' Peter interrupted her. 'Well, that's not strictly true, of course I care. I'm making sure I see him as often as I can. But even I can see that Aaron is better off with her than with me. I'm on the road a lot. I make a decent living, but the geek earns much more than me. He's got a house in Blanchardstown which he already owns. She's happy as a pig in shit.'

Carey heard the bitterness in his voice even though he tried to hide it.

'Is it my fault?' she asked. 'If you hadn't been with me . . .'

'You were the only thing that kept me going,' he said. 'From the moment I met you at that stupid festival . . . I only went because the company was a sponsor, I wasn't looking for someone . . .' His voice trailed off. 'I love you, Carey. I loved you then and I love you now.'

'You were looking for someone and I was available and I was stupid,' said Carey. 'I thought it was love but it wasn't, Peter. It was – oh, I don't know. A rush of emotion maybe.'

'And you think what you've got with this bloke is different?' he asked scathingly.

'Of course,' she said vehemently. 'I do love him. That's why I married him.'

113

'If you hadn't met him . . .' said Peter. 'If he didn't exist and I was talking to you now . . .'

'I wish things were different,' Carey said. 'I really do.' She stared at her untouched burger for a moment and then looked up at him again. 'No, I don't,' she amended. 'Ben is good for me. We're good for each other. I'm happy I met him and I'm happy I married him. And I'm sorry that things haven't worked out between you and Sandra, but it's got nothing to do with me any more.'

'You and me – we were good friends,' said Peter. 'It wasn't just a flash of something, Carey.' He reached across the table and took her hand in the way he'd done so many times before. She bit her lip and said nothing. Eventually she slid her hand away from his.

'We can still be good friends,' he said.

'No,' she said. 'We can't. We were friends while we loved each other. I don't love you any more, Peter. And you don't love me.'

'Of course I do,' he said. 'I never stopped loving you.'

'I haven't got time for this.' Carey stood up. 'I have to get to work. I'm sorry things haven't worked out for you, Peter, but there's nothing I can do about it. I'm living a different life now. And I'm happy. I don't want to see you again.'

'Sure,' said Peter. 'I understand.'

'So don't call me or anything because I won't take your calls.'

'Yeah, fine,' he said.

'Goodbye.' She turned away from him.

'Carey?'

'What?'

'You were the best thing that came into my life.'

She shook her head and walked out of the restaurant.

Freya tapped perfunctorily on the door of Ben's tiny office and walked in. 'How'd it go this morning?' she asked.

'Good,' he said. 'The magazine is going to do a feature on alternative remedies and we'll be their main source. Good publicity, free advertising.'

'Great.' She sat on the edge of his desk and handed him a sheet of paper. 'Run your eagle eye over this, will you?'

'What is it?' he asked as he took it.

'The guest-list,' she told him.

'For the reception?'

'Clearly.' She looked at him as though he were stupid. 'What other kind of guest-list is there?'

'Could've been something to do with that health-drink promotion,' he said. He looked at the paper. 'Thursday week?'

She shrugged. 'Friday would've been better, of course. But this Friday is too soon and she isn't off for another Friday or Saturday for ages. So that was the next best option.'

'Oleg's?' He looked up at her enquiringly.

'A customer of the bank,' she said. 'Brian knows the owner well. They lent money for it. Restaurant, night-club. Very trendy.'

'Rathgar,' said Ben. 'A bit out of the way.'

'Out of the way?' She looked at him in amazement. 'It's very convenient.'

'Not for Carey's family and friends,' said Ben. 'Most of them will be coming from Swords and Portmarnock on the other side of the city.'

'Oh, it's not that far,' said Freya dismissively. 'They should be glad to hit some southside civilisation.'

'Don't say things like that in front of them,' warned Ben. 'I'm sure it wouldn't go down too well.'

'Teach your granny to suck eggs,' said Freya. 'That list OK?'

Ben nodded.

'I'll need the addresses for your mates in the soccer club,' said Freya. 'For the invitations.'

Ben tapped on his computer keyboard and the printer rattled into life. 'There you go.'

'Thanks,' she said. 'I'll get them done up today and send them tomorrow.'

'You're a gem,' said Ben. 'You really are.'

'I know.' She grinned at him. 'But I guess my brother only gets married once . . .' Her voice trailed off.

'Absolutely,' he told her.

'And how's it going?'

'Great,' he said. 'You'll love her, Freya. You really will.'

'I'd assumed she'd make time to meet me before the party,' said Freya dryly. 'But now I think I'd prefer to see her then. Makes it all the more exciting.'

Ben laughed. 'She's nervous about meeting you. She's afraid you won't like her.'

'Her folks liked you, didn't they?'

'Ah, yes.' He laughed again. 'But that was me!'

'True,' said Freya.

'What about you?' asked Ben.

'Pardon?'

'You. You and Brian. Wouldn't you think of tying the knot?'

'Why?' she asked. 'We're perfectly happy the way we are. There's far too much pressure put on people to be madly in love with someone. Or to be with the same person for ever.'

'Do you think I'm crazy?' asked Ben.

Freya sighed. 'I don't know,' she said eventually. 'I really did think you'd marry Leah if you were going to marry anyone.'

'Sometimes I did too,' said Ben.

'I'd better get on with this.' She stood up and walked to the door. 'It'll be a great party.'

'I hope so,' said Ben. He returned his attention to the printout he'd been studying before she interrupted him.

Freya went back to her office and closed the door behind her. She put the invitation list on her desk and stared at it. Then she wrote Leah Ryder's name in block capitals at the bottom. She'd promised an invitation to Leah and she wasn't going to back down on that promise. But she knew, deep down, that Brian had a point when he'd said that inviting her was asking for trouble. What if she got horribly drunk and started shouting accusations at Ben? What if she had a blazing row with him and Carey got involved? Freya felt herself grow hot as she visualised the two girls going hell for leather at each other over the baked Alaska that she'd ordered to take the place of a wedding cake.

She pushed the sheet of paper across the desk. It was all Brian's fault for making her think like this. If he hadn't stuck his nose in then she wouldn't have worried about Leah because she was Leah's friend, she'd known her for a long time and she was almost certain that the other girl wouldn't do anything to upset her. But now she was nervous because of Brian. Brian who normally rang her up and apologised after every argument (even ones instigated by her) but who hadn't made contact since walking out of her apartment on

Saturday. She supposed she couldn't really blame him, she'd been rude and irritable, but just because she hadn't begged him to stay didn't mean she didn't want to hear from him again. They usually spent weekends together and it had been strange to have had the whole day to herself yesterday without him. She hadn't even been able to drop in on Ben because he, of course, had been at the Browne family lunch.

She tapped her teeth with her pen as she recalled him phoning her and telling her that she couldn't come to dinner with them as he'd originally hoped because Carey had agreed to show him off to her family instead. And the wretched girl hadn't been available any day during the week to meet – something to do with switching a shift with one of her colleagues or some equally lame excuse – which only confirmed Freya's suspicions that Carey was trying to avoid her. Afraid, thought Freya grimly, that she'd see right through her. The girl had clearly reckoned on Ben as great husband material and had snapped him up before his brains had a chance to out-think his balls. And now Carey was trying to envelop Ben into her family and drive a wedge between him and the people who really cared for him. Well, as far as Freya was concerned, that just wasn't going to happen.

She wondered how he really felt about Carey's family. She couldn't imagine sitting down at the table with an assortment of nephews or nieces, brothers- or sisters-in-law. She supposed there'd be lots of shouting and bickering and people trying to get their own points of view across. That's how big family dinners were always portrayed in films. And there'd usually be some gigantic argument which ended up with someone storming off. Well, that was taking things a bit far, she knew. The storming off was part of the movie thing. But the shouting, arguing and bickering – they were all family things, weren't they? She sighed deeply. It was hard to tell. Even when their parents had been alive, family meals in the Russell house were quiet affairs. The only proper family meal had been on Sundays and then Charles Russell had retreated behind the *Sunday Times* while Gail dealt with the children.

She reached out and pulled the invitation-list to her again. Given that the party was being held in Oleg's and that Brian had been the one to arrange the venue she knew that she would have to call him. She didn't want to contact his friend without some kind of notice.

117

Brian wasn't at his desk so she left a message on his voice mail. She hated leaving voice-mail messages so it sounded clipped and cool.

'Can you call me?' she said. 'I need to talk to you about meeting Oleg for this stupid wedding party. I'm in the office all day. Thanks.'

Chapter 10

Lavender

*Blends well with other oils and is very versatile, being both relaxing
and rejuvenating*

The apartment where Leah Ryder lived was in a five-storey block
which had been built in the late sixties. This meant that, even
though she rented a studio, it was reasonably spacious. When Leah
had moved in a couple of years earlier she'd immediately stripped
away the hideous multi-coloured swirling wallpaper that had made
her feel as though she was on some wild drugs trip, invested in some
deep-pile rugs to cover the plain grey carpet and repainted the walls in
soft cream. Then she'd hung them with huge copies of her favourite
Japanese silk paintings. She'd consulted her feng shui book before
rearranging the furniture, bought a handprinted screen to separate
the sleeping and living areas and had invested in hundreds of scented
candles which she dotted around the apartment in clusters of deep
and vibrant colour. She also had an assortment of unscented ones;
thin and tapered in wide dishes filled with fine sand, fat and chunky
embossed with Japanese calligraphy and pale pink floating shapes
which were in a patterned bowl on the black lacquered table.

Now, on the evening of Ben and Carey's wedding party, she
walked around the apartment and lit all thirty of her jasmine candles,
including the one decorated with the Japanese symbol for good luck.
Her heart was hammering in her chest and her hands trembled. She
took the invitation from the glass-topped table then sat in her soft
and squashy maroon armchair and drew her legs beneath her.

Ben and Carey just got married, she read as she clenched her teeth.

119

We'd like you to celebrate with us. Oleg's, Rathgar, Friday 14th, 7.30 p.m. RSVP. The replies were to be sent to Freya either by phone, e-mail or post. Leah had sent her acceptance to Freya's e-mail address almost straight away and since then had thought of nothing else. She couldn't wait to see Ben's wife. She couldn't wait to see the woman who, one day, would leave him.

She tore at the corner of the invitation. She'd been anticipating tonight for ages, telling herself that she was going to look so gorgeous and so sexy that Ben would be shocked into realising what he'd given up. Part of her wanted to ruin the night because she really did want to humiliate Ben in the way that he'd humiliated her. But if she did that she'd also ruin her friendship with Freya and she didn't want that to happen. And she might generate sympathy for Carey, which was out of the question. Yet how could she go and smile and pretend that none of it mattered to her? He'd treated her so badly, sleeping with her, pretending that he cared about her when all he wanted was to find any other woman to marry! It wasn't fair. It wasn't right. And he should suffer for it.

The trick would be to find the right time to make him suffer the most.

Freya was waiting for Brian to pick her up. They were going to Oleg's early to make sure that everything was perfect. When she'd spoken to Ben on the phone earlier he'd told her not to fuss about it all, that he and Carey would come early themselves if she liked and she'd snapped at him and told him that she was organising the bloody event and that he was to have nothing to do with it other than turn up! And that they weren't to be early or fashionably late, simply on time. At which he'd uncharacteristically snapped back at her and said that it was all her idea and that he'd gone along with it but now he wished he hadn't because Carey was having some kind of crisis in the bathroom and it really wasn't worth all the goddamned effort, was it? After all, he said furiously, this was exactly the kind of thing they'd been hoping to avoid by getting married in Las Vegas! And she'd retorted that this was rubbish, since they'd obviously just rushed off and got married without thinking of anything at all.

The whole conversation had left her absolutely reeling and shaking with rage so that she'd managed to smudge mascara all over her carefully powdered eyelids, necessitating a complete re-do which had left her running late. But even though she was late Brian was even later and, as she looked at her watch, she was giving him five more minutes and then she was leaving because she really couldn't be doing with the tension of hanging around waiting for him.

Things were still not going smoothly with Brian. When he'd eventually responded to the message she'd left on his voice mail his tone was cool and unfriendly – totally unBrianlike, in fact. The best thing about Brian, the thing that had kept them together for so long, had been his willingness to shrug off any disagreements between them and act as though nothing had even happened. Only this time he hadn't done that and she knew that there was an undercurrent but she didn't know how to deal with it. Brian was supposed to be the easy part of her life, she told herself as she checked her hair in the mirror for the tenth time. He was her rock, the person she depended on, and she didn't want that to change.

She didn't want it to change at all. She wanted to hold on to things exactly as they were. And yet now, with Ben getting married and other people raising their eyebrows at her – a sort of middle-aged spinster if you wanted to be old fashioned about it – she was beginning to wonder what exactly she was holding on to. She shook her head. She wasn't going to let her thoughts stray down those paths. She did know what she was holding on to. She was holding on to her carefully constructed and very happy life.

She'd just glanced at her watch again when the buzzer sounded. About bloody time, she thought, as she picked up her bag and closed the door behind her.

'Do you think I look like the mother of the bride?' asked Maude as she walked into the bedroom in her stockinged feet.

'You *are* the mother of the bride,' said Arthur.

'I'm not.' Maude stuck another clip in her hair. 'I'm the mother of the married woman and I don't want to look too frothy.'

'You never look frothy,' said Arthur. 'You look elegant.'

'Thank you.' Maude beamed at him. 'You know, sometimes – very occasionally, obviously – you say the nicest things to me.'

'Don't start with all this romantic guff now,' Arthur grunted. 'I

121

don't need to say romantic things to you, woman. Sure you know them all already.'

'It's nice to hear them just the same,' said Maude.

'What is it with you females?' asked her husband. 'No matter that we've been married for more than forty years, you still want romance?'

'Of course.' Maude turned from the full-length mirror in which she'd been surveying her appearance. 'I can still feel romantic, can't I? Even though I might look more like a date with destiny than Destiny's Child.'

'Who's Destiny's Child?' asked Arthur. 'Do I know her?'

'They're a group,' said Maude. 'Actually, they could be any kind of group for all I know, but they're one that Nadia used to like. In fact, I suppose by now they've broken up and have started pursuing their solo careers as serious artistes.'

Arthur laughed. 'You're mad, you know that?'

'I always want to be a bit mad,' said Maude. 'At least that way I know that I'm still young at heart despite what the exterior shows.'

'The exterior looks damn good to me,' said Arthur.

'Really?'

'Really.' He put his hands on Maude's shoulder and drew her towards him. 'I just hope that Carey is as lucky as I've been. Even though I've no hope that she will be.'

'I hope she's as lucky as me.' Maude kissed Arthur on the lips. 'Do we have time for this?' she whispered as he began to unzip her salmon-pink dress.

'Of course,' he told her. 'Besides, I need to check out everything you're wearing. Make sure that you look good from the bottom up.'

'Arthur!' But Maude giggled as she lay on the bed while her husband removed his carefully pressed jacket and trousers. 'I love you,' she added as he joined her.

'I love you too,' said Arthur. 'I love you more now than I did when I first married you. And if that's not romantic enough for you, you can just divorce me!'

'I have to get into the bathroom!' Nadia Lynch thumped on the door and stamped her foot.

'I'm not finished yet,' called Jeanne. 'Go away.'

'You've been in there for about three hours,' complained Nadia. 'It's not fair. I have to get ready too, you know.'

'What getting ready do you need to do?' asked Jeanne scornfully. 'You've washed your face, haven't you?'

'You think you're the only one in this house who wants to look nice,' cried Nadia. 'I'm entitled to look nice, too. I'm going to tell Mum that you won't let me in.'

'Oh, don't be so childish!'

'I'm going to tell her. And,' added Nadia grimly, 'I'm going to tell her that you took her Age-Defying Mask face capsule things – and that really expensive body spray that Dad bought her for her birthday.'

'You are such a pain.' Jeanne flung the bathroom door open so that it banged off the wall and the handle took a lump out of the plaster. 'Now look what you've made me do.'

'I didn't make you do anything,' said Nadia. 'And you'd better hurry up and get her make-up back into her room 'cos she'll be up shortly.'

'You're a complete bitch,' muttered Jeanne. 'You really are.'

'I've a good teacher.' Nadia stuck her tongue out at her sister before closing the bathroom door and locking it firmly behind her.

Jeanne walked along the landing and slipped into her parents' room. She replaced Sylvia's beauty products on the dressing-table and managed to get out just as her mother started up the stairs.

'You look lovely,' said Sylvia as she caught sight of her elder daughter whose hours in the bathroom really had resulted in a pretty good make-up job. 'Although you know what your dad thinks about those studs.'

'It's just stuck on,' said Jeanne. She wrinkled her nose. 'And I like it.'

Sylvia shook her head. 'I hate it,' she told Jeanne. 'But I suppose that's a good thing, is it?'

Jeanne giggled. 'At least I didn't get it pierced,' she said. 'Amanda Robinson did, plus she got some kind of infection and—'

'Don't tell me,' Sylvia shuddered. 'I haven't the stomach for it. What have you decided to wear tonight?'

'You saw what I'm wearing,' said Jeanne. 'The blue skirt I bought last week.'

Sylvia winced. 'I was rather hoping you'd have decided against it by now.'

'Why? It's lovely.'

'It barely covers your bum,' said Sylvia.

'Grow up, Mum,' said Jeanne. 'I'll be wearing my opaque black tights and my blue boots. You won't see anything.'

Sylvia sighed. 'And what top?'

'White,' Jeanne told her. 'With little blue spots. Very chaste.'

'I just hope your dad thinks so too,' said Sylvia.

'I wonder what Carey'll be wearing,' mused Jeanne. 'I think it's great what she did.'

'So I gathered.'

'Well, saves so much hassle, doesn't it,' said Jeanne cheerfully. 'None of that usual wedding lark.'

'You'll probably want it yourself one day,' said Sylvia.

Jeanne laughed. 'I'm not like you, Mum. I don't want a fuss.'

'Everyone wants a fuss,' said Sylvia. 'Some people just get theirs differently from others, that's all.'

Carey stood in the bedroom wearing nothing but her black bra and thong. Although everyone said that once you managed to wear thongs for a fortnight you never went back to ordinary knickers, Carey never felt properly dressed in a thong. But she'd decided to wear the purple hanky dress that she'd worn the night of Ellie's party in Manhattan and it was the kind of dress that, she felt, expected the wearer to be sporting a thong rather than a pair of serviceable high-legs. Still, it was a great dress and it was her romantic dress, since it was the first dress that Ben had seen her in.

She turned round as he opened the bedroom door.

'Oh.' He looked at her and smiled. 'That's it, is it?'

She laughed. 'It'd certainly get them talking but no, I will put on a bit more.'

'Why are you wearing black underwear?' he asked. 'Won't it show?'

'What d'you mean?' She looked at him in puzzlement. 'It didn't before, did it?'

'But you weren't wearing white then,' said Ben.

'What?' Her face was even more perplexed.

'Under your wedding dress,' he said. 'It seems a bit strange to wear black under your white dress.'

'I wasn't going to wear my white dress,' she told him. 'I was going to wear the purple.'

'Oh, but Carey, you have to wear the white!' Ben looked horrified. 'It was your wedding dress after all and this is our wedding party.'

'Ben, it's a party,' said Carey. 'I know it's to celebrate our marriage but you can't, by any stretch of the imagination, call it a wedding party.'

'Everyone's calling it a wedding party,' said Ben.

'*Freya's* calling it a wedding party,' amended Carey.

Ben shrugged. 'OK – well, yes. But I feel it's a wedding party too.'

'You were yelling at her earlier,' said Carey. 'As far as I can recall, you told her that it wasn't a big wedding thing and that she should just cop on to herself.'

'I shouldn't have yelled at her,' Ben said. 'She's done her best for us. And I know I said that we hadn't wanted it or anything but – oh, she's done it now and I want to make sure it goes well. I'm sure you do too.'

Carey sat on the edge of the bed. 'To be honest, I don't give a toss,' she said. 'I told you before and I meant it – this kind of thing just isn't me. People are either wedding people or they're not. I'm not.'

'I know. I understand all that,' said Ben. 'But it's only one night and it seems mad not to wear the dress.'

'Ben, it's a trashy white dress!' cried Carey. 'And it might have looked OK in the Chapel of Everlasting Love in the heat of the desert but it'll look cheap and tawdry in Dublin where it's currently a degree below freezing.'

'I thought it was lovely,' said Ben in a low voice.

She sighed deeply. 'Don't you think the purple dress is nicer?'

'But it's not the wedding dress.'

'If that's what you want.' She unhooked her bra and threw it onto the bed.

'Not if you're going to get into a temper over it,' said Ben. 'Look, if you feel better wearing the purple then wear the purple. I just thought that you'd be wearing the white, that's all. I don't care what you wear, Carey. I really don't.'

'Yes, you do,' she said. 'You want me to look bridal.'

'I just think you should look bridal tonight,' he told her. 'But not if you don't want to.'

'I'll wear the white.' She pulled off the thong and flung it into the laundry basket. 'If I wear the white I can wear my favourite knickers.' She stood naked in front of the open wardrobe contemplating her collection of shoe boxes. 'But I was going to wear my purple boots with the other dress. I hardly ever get a chance to put them on. I don't have good white-dress shoes.'

'You must have,' said Ben. 'You lied about your shoes. You have fifty-two pairs. I counted them last week.'

'Not all shoes,' she said carelessly. 'Some of them are sandals, some are boots.'

'Splitting hairs,' said Ben.

She hunkered down and looked at the boxes. Her hair tumbled across her naked back, reminding Ben of Old Master portraits of Venus. Although, he admitted, Carey was too bony to be Venus.

'I suppose I can wear these again, too!' She removed a pair of ultra-high-heeled transparent sandals with a little white bow on the Perspex uppers which she'd bought in Vegas.

'You'll freeze,' said Ben.

'I'll freeze anyway,' said Carey. 'Might as well go down fighting.' She slid her feet into them. 'What d'you think?'

Ben couldn't say anything. He was wondering what incredible stroke of luck had helped him to meet and to marry a girl who would stand in front of him naked except for a pair of incredibly sexy shoes and a silver pendant round her neck.

'Come here,' he said as he held his arms out to her.

'Oh, no.' She shook her head. 'We're running late as it is – spilling relaxing sea salts all over a damp bathroom floor didn't do anything for my timekeeping! And I'm not going to have your sister saying that I didn't turn up on time.'

'Everyone knows that the bride is always late,' said Ben.

'I told you already.' She reached out and grabbed her dressing-gown. 'I'm not a bride. It's not a wedding reception. It's just a party.'

126

'It's *our* party,' said Ben.

'Yeah, well – in that case you'd better get ready too,' said Carey as she slid a pair of silver hoops into her ears. 'Because the groom is never late, is he? And Freya'll have your guts for garters if you are.'

Chapter 11

Cypress

An oil with a woody fragrance and a natural astringent

Oleg's Bar and Restaurant took up the basement and ground-floor levels of a renovated Georgian house on the Rathgar Road. Huge scarlet ribbons were tied around carefully cultivated bay trees lining either side of the gravel pathway that led to the house. Warm lights shining through the sash windows added to an almost festive atmosphere courtesy of the frost that had tipped the grass a glittering silvery white.

Freya and Brian were greeted by Colman Murphy, who'd come up with the idea for Oleg's after spending a few months in Russia. Colman's partner, Dimitri, was the chef while Colman looked after everything else.

'So there's no Oleg at all?' Freya sounded disappointed.

Colman grinned. 'Nope. We just thought it sounded sharper than "Dimitri's".'

'It's very impressive.' She looked around the bar area which was decorated in deep reds and greens and hung with huge gilt mirrors and heavily brocaded swatches of silk and velvet. 'Very Russian.'

'That's the idea,' said Colman. 'It's great in the winter. I'm not so sure how we'll do during the summer.' He looked nervously at Brian. 'I shouldn't have said that in front of my banker, should I?'

Brian shrugged. 'Your projections look good. And if it all goes horribly wrong we'll simply close you down and repossess the mirrors.'

Freya laughed. 'Actually, I'd love one of those mirrors.'

'Not first thing in the morning,' Colman assured her. 'They have a habit of magnifying every little blemish.' He took her coat and hung it on the rack in the corner of the room. 'Can I get you a drink?' he asked. 'Obviously vodka is our speciality. You can have lemon or strawberry or blackcurrant – a whole range of flavoured ones.'

'Would you mind if I had a white wine?' asked Freya. 'I don't want to rush into spirits just yet.'

'I'll have an honest to goodness plain vodka with tonic,' said Brian.

'Excellent.' Colman went to get the drinks while Freya sat down on one of the quilted banquettes which lined the walls. After a moment Brian sat beside her. He said nothing. He hadn't, in fact, said anything much to her at all so far this evening.

'I'm sorry,' said Freya eventually.

'Sorry?' Brian turned to look at her.

'For annoying you. For snapping at you last week.'

'I'm used to it,' said Brian.

'Are you?' asked Freya. 'In that case, why did you get so annoyed with me?'

'Just because I'm used to it doesn't mean I like it,' Brian told her. 'I've better things to do with my life than be snapped at.'

'I know,' said Freya contritely. 'I guess I was worried about tonight.'

'Is Leah coming?' asked Brian.

'She accepted the invitation,' Freya said. 'But I haven't been talking to her so I'm not certain.'

'Everything will be fine,' said Brian. 'And even if it isn't, it's not your problem.'

'It will be if Leah does something terrible.' Freya worried at the edge of her jacket. 'You were right. I shouldn't have asked her.'

'I doubt that she'll do anything too terrible,' said Brian. 'Don't get uptight, Freya. It'll be a great party.'

'I hope so,' said Freya, 'because I insisted on it. I know that *she* wasn't too keen.'

'She?' Brian smiled at her.

'The wife,' said Freya dismissively. She looked up as Colman returned bearing their drinks on a highly polished silver salver. 'Thanks.'

129

'You've got to be more welcoming to her,' said Brian. 'I don't see why you dislike her so much. You don't know her.'

'That's why I dislike her,' admitted Freya. 'I know it's silly.'

'Very silly,' said Brian. 'But I forgive you.'

Freya was surprised at how relieved she suddenly felt. She leaned against Brian's broad shoulder and sighed. He was a decent man, she thought. She was lucky to have him in her life. She sat up abruptly as she heard more people arrive.

They were members of Carey's air traffic control team, shivering in the cold night air and jostling for position in front of the gas-effect fire in the huge marble fireplace at the far end of the room. Freya instantly forgot who was who but it didn't matter because they chatted to each other and happily knocked back the shots of vodka that Colman began to hand round. Then some people from the bank arrived, followed by the staff from the healthfood stores. The buzz of conversation filled the air as more and more people arrived. Freya wondered about the wisdom of having so much vodka on tap. As far as she could see, the entire air traffic control team were well on the way to being totally out of their heads and Brian, who'd had another couple of shots, was grinning foolishly at everyone. She hoped that Ben and Carey would arrive before all their guests were too drunk to recognise them.

She hadn't long to wait. Five minutes later she saw her brother come in the door, followed by a gangly woman with a headful of curls held in place by a pearled comb and wearing an extremely short white dress which plunged dramatically at the neckline. She must be absolutely freezing, thought Freya, as she pushed her way through the throng to greet them.

'Hello, sis!' Ben beamed at her. 'We didn't think there'd be such a crowd here already. It's great, isn't it?' His beam grew even wider as he pulled Carey closer to him. 'And this is her! This is Mrs Russell. Carey, Freya. Freya, Carey.'

Carey smiled at Ben's sister while she took in the other woman's expensively tailored mauve suit, trimmed with black fur at the sleeves. Freya's hair, fair as Ben's although, thought Carey, not entirely natural in its golden hue, was swept back smoothly from her face and secured by a small velvet clip. She looked chillingly elegant and her smile, though friendly, wasn't particularly warm.

130

'It's lovely to meet you finally,' said Carey uncertainly.

'You too,' said Freya. 'I've heard a lot about you.'

'I'm sure.'

They looked at each other awkwardly for a moment then Freya smiled again and hugged Carey very briefly. 'Welcome to the family,' she said. 'I have to tell you I'm still in shock about it.'

'So am I,' said Ben cheerfully. 'But we've managed to survive the first couple of weeks so I think we've made a good start.'

'You made a good choice, Ben,' said Brian. He, too, hugged Carey although his embrace was much firmer than Freya's. 'She's an absolute dote.'

'Dote?' Carey smiled up at him. 'I don't think so.'

'Oh, you are,' said Brian. 'I love the comb in your hair.'

'Do you?' She patted it doubtfully. 'It's what I wore with this totally unsuitable dress when we got married.'

'It's very – pretty,' said Freya unconvincingly.

'It's not really,' said Carey, 'but it was fine in Vegas. Besides . . .' she shot a sideways look at Ben, 'if I'd worn the dress I originally intended, we would have clashed. It's almost the exact same shade as your lovely suit.'

'My favourite colour.' Freya patted her sleeve.

'Mine too,' said Carey.

'Something in common already.' Brian laughed.

Colman appeared with his tray full of vodkas.

'Great,' said Carey and knocked back a shot. 'I needed that. It's freezing outside. Honestly, the last few weeks have been so unseasonably cold . . . oh!' She broke off as she saw her parents arrive. 'It's Mum and Dad. I'd better say hello.'

'She's very – vibrant,' said Freya to Ben as Carey went over to Maude and Arthur.

Ben chuckled. 'She's a livewire, all right,' he said. 'Just what I need. Someone to make me get up and go all the time.'

'So are her friends.' Freya nodded to where the air traffic control crowd were laughing uproariously.

'Probably something to do with the job,' said Ben. 'They're letting off steam, I guess.'

'She's older than I thought,' Brian remarked. 'From what Freya said, I got the impression she was barely out of her teens.'

131

Ben frowned. 'She's the same age as me,' he told Brian. 'And she might be a livewire but she's totally clued in.'

'Of course she is,' said Freya hastily. 'I can't wait to meet her family.'

'They're nice,' said Ben. 'D'you know, I suddenly realised tonight that they're kind of my family too. It's a strange sensation. A few weeks ago it was just you, me and Auntie Moira who isn't really an aunt and who doesn't recognise us any more anyway. Now I have sisters-in-law, brothers-in-law and a whole selection of nieces and nephews.'

'Big families are totally overrated,' said Freya.

'I don't know,' said Brian. 'It must be nice to be part of a whole group of people who look out for each other.'

'I didn't mean . . .' Freya shook her head. 'Oh, it doesn't matter. Let's get another drink.'

'That's what you got married in!' Sylvia looked at Carey in shock. 'It's very—'

'Trailer-trash,' supplied Carey.

'Not at all,' Jeanne disagreed. 'I like it, I really do.'

'Except I can't wear a bra with it,' said Carey, 'and it makes me feel as though I might hit people with my excuse for boobs if I turn round too quickly.'

Nadia giggled.

'So you'd better watch out, Ms Lynch,' Carey warned her. 'Or I'll have your eye out with my left one before you know where you are!'

'What did Mum think?' asked Sylvia.

'The same as you. But actually this dress was very appropriate in the desert.'

'Well, I think it's lovely,' Jeanne repeated.

'Thank you,' Carey told her. 'And you're looking pretty good yourself. I like the skirt.'

'Mum thinks it's too short.'

'You don't, Syl, do you?'

'It *is* a bit on the short side,' said Sylvia.

'You sound like our own mum!' Carey laughed.

'You'll sound like it too when you have kids of your own,' said Sylvia tartly.

Carey looked shocked. 'That's not on our agenda. Not by a long chalk.'

'Not at all?' asked Nadia. 'Don't you want any children, Carey?'

'To be honest, I haven't thought about it very much,' said Carey. 'Ben and I haven't talked about it much either.' She grinned. 'We haven't talked about it at all.'

'I guess there's a lot of things you haven't got round to talking about yet,' said Sylvia dryly.

'I guess there are,' said Carey and went to join the air traffic control crew.

'There you are!' cried Gina drunkenly. 'And looking every inch the blushing bride.'

'Hardly blushing in that outfit,' said Finola. 'Carey, you are such a bitch to have married that gorgeous, gorgeous man without giving me the opportunity to make a play. Seeing him again makes me realise what I let you get away with.'

'I thought we agreed before, that owing to your own attached state you didn't really need to make any kind of play for anyone else,' said Carey.

'I know.' Finola sighed dramatically. 'But he's such a hunk.'

'He's not that much of a hunk,' said Carey irritably.

'Oh, he is!' cried Gina.

'This is a great party, Browne,' said Chris Brady. 'Even if we had to traipse across the city to get here.'

'Ben's sister chose the venue,' Carey told him. 'She did everything.'

'That's the frosty woman in purple, isn't it?' asked Elena. 'She welcomed us on the way in but I could see she was looking at us as though we were potential gatecrashers.'

'I don't blame her if you all arrived at the same time and took up your drinking positions.' Carey grinned. 'She'll think that all we ever do is roar, shout and get drunk.'

'We're not making that much noise,' protested Gina, 'although we're all probably drunk. That guy's handing out vodka like it's going out of fashion. And it seems churlish to refuse!'

'I've never known you to refuse a drink in your life,' said Carey. 'Anyway, Elena, you're right about her being a bit frosty. This is the

133

first time I've met her and she's managing to make me feel like a naughty child.'

'Who gives a stuff what she's like?' Finola made a face. 'You've done the deed, Browne, you've captured the man and there's nothing she can do about it.'

'Which means, as I've told you enough times already, that my name's Russell now.'

'You know, I'm kind of surprised you changed you name.' Richard Purcell looked at Carey quizzically. 'I always thought you were one of those feminist-type women.'

'What exactly is a feminist-type woman?' demanded Carey.

'You are,' said Richard. 'Tough as old boots.'

'Thanks,' said Carey.

'You're welcome.'

'So why the name change?'

'Why not?' she asked. 'I might be tough as old boots but I don't mind admitting that I'm Ben's wife.'

'That's so romantic.' Gina looked blearily at her friend. 'It really is.'

'Maybe,' said Carey. 'Or maybe it's just plain daft.'

'Ladies and gentlemen!' Colman's raised voice caught everyone's attention and the hum of conversation died down. 'Ladies and gentlemen, food is now being served. Could I ask you all to make your way upstairs as quickly as possible. And could I ask Ben and Carey to wait until everyone has gone up before they join you.'

'Bloody hell,' muttered Carey. 'I hope he hasn't got something awful in store.'

'We probably have to shower you with rice,' said Gina.

'It was precisely to avoid this kind of palaver that I married Ben in the States,' said Carey grimly.

'Don't be ridiculous.' Gina giggled. 'It was because you wanted to make sure that the erotic sex you were having was quite, quite legal.'

Carey stood beside Ben as they watched everyone troop out of the basement bar and up the stairs. He put his arm round her shoulder.

'Having a good time?' he asked.

'Sort of,' she replied. 'I like parties but I hate being the centre of attention at one. And I really would've preferred a few drinks in the pub to all this. I didn't realise that your sister had gone to so much trouble.'

'I know.' Ben frowned. 'It must be costing her a fortune. I can't possibly let her pay for it all.'

Carey nodded. 'I'd feel bad about that too. Didn't you tell her that a few ham sandwiches in the local would be enough?'

'She never listens to me,' said Ben resignedly. 'Not when she has her heart set on something.'

'I don't know why she had her heart set on this,' Carey said. 'Ben, I know she's your sister and you love her, but I still don't think she likes me very much.'

'Of course she does,' said Ben.

'She doesn't really know me yet, I suppose.' Carey sighed.

'She was shocked at first but she's come round,' said Ben comfortably. 'I bet you'll be friends in no time. You're quite alike in lots of ways, you know.'

'Are we?' Care looked horrified.

'Absolutely.' Ben hadn't seen the expression on her face. 'You're both determined sort of people.'

'We both like purple and mauve,' added Carey.

'What?' He looked at her.

'Freya's suit. It's exactly the same colour as the dress I was going to wear. Did you know that?'

'It's a similar colour,' agreed Ben.

'And did you know she'd be wearing it?' asked Carey. 'Is that why you didn't want me to wear mine?'

'Of course not.' Ben looked surprised. 'I've never seen that suit on her before. And I told you why I wanted you to wear that dress – it's your wedding dress.' He sighed. 'I get the feeling you're mad at me over it and I don't want you to be. I didn't mean to upset you. But if you're upset I don't really know why.'

'It doesn't matter.' Carey squeezed his arm. 'I'm being silly. Forget it.'

Colman arrived then and led them up the stairs and into the restaurant; it was also decorated in reds and greens, and an enormous crystal chandelier reflected multicoloured diamonds of light across the room. Because of the high ceilings the mirrors were even bigger than downstairs and, at the far end of the room, an enormous oil painting of the ill-fated Romanov family hung over another huge marble fireplace. A long table was piled high with colourful and appetising buffet food.

'Welcome, welcome!' It was Dimitri, the chef, who smiled as they stepped into the room. He presented them with bread and salt which, he told them, was traditional in Russian weddings. 'You must both take a bite,' he said, 'at the same time. Whoever takes the larger bite wears the trousers in the family.'

The assembled crowd laughed as they took the bread.

'No cheating!' called Jeanne Lynch.

'Go for it, Ben!' yelled the crowd from his football team.

'Come on, Carey Browne!' cried Gina. 'Give it your best, woman!'

They both bit into the bread and pulled at it with their teeth. White crumbs fell onto the deep green carpet.

'And the winner is . . .' Dimitri looked at the bread. 'The husband, of course!'

A wild roar went up from the football team, matched by a groan from the air traffic controllers.

'It's OK,' said Carey, batting her eyelashes at Ben. 'He can wear the trousers. I'll just make the decisions.'

Everyone laughed and then began to chant for Ben to make a speech.

'Not a speech,' he groaned. 'I'm useless at speeches.'

'Oh go on, Ben,' said Brian. 'It's the least you can do.'

Ben sighed then wrapped his fingers round Carey's.

'Brief, brief speech,' he told them. 'As you all know, Carey and I didn't need to spend a lot of time getting to know each other before we got married.'

The crowd laughed.

'Sometimes there *is* such a thing as love at first sight,' he said. 'And that's exactly what—' He broke off for a second as a movement at the edge of the throng caught his eye, then he recovered. 'That's exactly what we found. So I'm really glad I met her and I'm really glad I married her and I'm delighted you all joined us tonight.'

Everyone clapped furiously.

'And a special thanks to my wonderful sister, Freya, for organising everything. She's one in a million.'

More clapping as people broke into groups and began to form a queue at the laden buffet table while Russian music filled the air.

'You OK?' asked Carey.

'Fine, fine,' said Ben. 'I just saw someone I need to have a word with.'

Leah had arrived just as Ben and Carey were going upstairs. She'd waited for a moment and then followed them, slipping into the restaurant as he began his speech. He looked pale, she thought, and more tired than she'd seen him in a long time. Maybe it was the strain of the evening. Or maybe – she gritted her teeth – maybe it was all the sex he was having with the incredibly gawky-looking girl beside him. But as she watched Carey she exhaled slowly with relief. It couldn't be the sex, it just couldn't. She'd thought that Ben might have been ensnared by a gorgeous Jennifer Lopez lookalike who had enchanted him with her wonderful body and her equally wonderful technique in bed. But Ben's wife wasn't in the least bit attractive and Leah wasn't ready to believe that she was some kind of expert between the sheets. In fact she couldn't, for the life of her, see what had attracted Ben so much that he'd done the silliest thing in his life and married the wretched woman. She flicked back her mane of glossy black hair and waited for him to come to her. Which, she was pleased to see, didn't take long. She saw him mutter to the girl and then make his way towards her.

'Hello, Ben,' she said. 'Great party.'

'What are you doing here?' he asked sharply.

'I'm a guest,' she said. 'Freya invited me.'

'Freya did?' He looked shocked. 'Why? And why did you come, Leah?'

'You're afraid I'll make a scene?' Her lips twitched.

'You made one the last time we met,' he reminded her.

She shrugged. 'I'm sorry about that. I was upset.'

'And being here won't upset you?'

She shrugged again. 'Don't be silly. I came because I was curious to see her, that's all. And because I'm still Freya's friend. I want to still be yours too.'

'You do?' He looked at her in surprise. 'As far as I recall, your last words were something about making me suffer.'

'Look, Ben, let's be grown-up about it. I was very annoyed with you. And, I have to admit, hurt. After all, you slept with me the night before you went to the States. And while I accept that it wasn't a declaration of undying love or anything, I didn't quite expect that the next time I saw you you'd be married to someone else.'

'I understand,' said Ben uncomfortably. 'I really do, Leah.' He rubbed his hand through his shock of blond hair. 'I didn't intend to hurt you. You know I wouldn't have done that on purpose, don't you? It was just – when I met her, I couldn't think of anything or anyone else.'

'You've fallen hard, haven't you?' asked Leah.

'I guess so.' He grinned. 'I'm happy with her, I really am.'

'And you were never happy with me?'

'Oh God, Leah, you know that's not true. I had great times with you. I cared about you – still care about you – very much. But it was never a marrying thing, was it? For either of us.'

She smiled shortly. 'Clearly not.'

'I don't know if men and women stay friends when one of them marries someone else,' said Ben, 'but I'll always think of you as a friend, Leah. Despite the fact that you scared the life out of me in the café.'

'That's fine by me.' She kissed him lightly on the cheek then rubbed the spot where her cherry-red lipstick had stained it.

'It's a wonderful party,' Maude told Carey as she tucked into a plate piled with smoked salmon which was her favourite food. 'I didn't realise it was going to be such a big do.'

'Neither did I,' admitted Carey.

'But it's worth it,' said Maude. 'And Ben's sister seems to be a lovely girl.'

'You think so?'

Maude arched an eyebrow. 'You don't?'

'I don't really know her yet,' Carey said. 'I think she's still put out about the whole thing.'

'Carey, darling, everyone's still put out about the whole thing,' said Maude. 'I don't think you realise how disconcerting it was for us all to have you come home and calmly announce you were married.'

'Maybe not,' said Carey. 'I'm sorry if I upset you.'

'Oh, at my age nothing much upsets me any more,' Maude told her. 'When you get older you can't help feeling that people get far too upset about trivial things.'

Carey laughed. 'I'm glad that my getting married has bounced into the area of a trivial thing.'

'You know what I mean.' Maude made a face at her daugher. 'Anyway, if you're happy, I'm happy.'

'Oh, I'm happy,' said Carey as she scanned the crowd to see where Ben was. 'I'm really and truly happy.'

She didn't recognise the girl in the scarlet dress who was talking so intently to Ben. Clearly, thought Carey, they knew each other well because their conversation was animated and their body language was familiar. Then she saw the girl kiss Ben proprietorially on the cheek and, even more proprietorially, wipe the mark of her lipstick from his face. Carey felt her stomach contract. There was too much familiarity there, too much ease with each other. And the girl in the red dress was much too beautiful to be left alone with her brand-new husband.

She walked across the room. The girl noticed her first.

'You must be Carey,' she said. 'I'm Leah.'

'Hi,' said Carey. 'Nice to meet you.'

'I've known Leah for years,' said Ben casually.

They've slept with each other, Carey realised. Her stomach contracted again.

'I'm glad you could come along,' she said.

'It's a big crowd.' Leah shook her head so that the sheet of raven-black hair fell across her face. She smoothed it back again. 'I always feel intimidated in big crowds,' she added. 'Must be because I'm so small.'

'I don't mind crowds myself.' Carey stood up straight in her high-heeled transparent sandals so that she towered over Leah. 'Probably because I can see over them.'

Leah's laugh was soft. 'You're actually quite different from how I imagined,' she said.

139

'How did you imagine me?' asked Carey. 'How did Ben describe me? When did he describe me?'

'Actually he didn't,' said Leah. 'But he told me that he was crazy about you.'

'That's good to hear,' said Carey.

'I am crazy about you,' interjected Ben. 'You know that. Would you like something else to eat, Carey?'

'No, thanks.' She shook her head. 'I thought it'd be much better fun to get the low-down from your old girlfriends.'

'Not girlfriend,' said Ben hastily. 'Not as such.'

'Oh, Ben.' Leah put her hand on his shoulder just as Phil, Ben's best friend from the football team, arrived over. 'I do so love being your cast-off.'

Carey welcomed Phil's interruption. Ben had introduced Phil to her earlier and they'd hit it off instantly. Obviously, she thought now, as she watched Phil carefully push his way between Ben and Leah, he knew the score with Ben's cast-off girlfriend and he was trying to help them all out. Which was pretty decent of him, she decided. Sometimes women didn't give men enough credit for being decent. She stood beside them for a couple of minutes as Phil deftly worked the conversation round to the latest standings in the Premiership then slipped unobtrusively out of the dining room and back downstairs to the bar.

'Hi there.' Freya was standing at the polished counter sipping a glass of white wine.

'Hello,' said Carey.

'Having a good time?' asked Freya.

'Of course,' said Carey.

They stared at each other in silence for a moment then Carey ordered a strawberry vodka. 'I'll have a hangover,' she told Freya ruefully.

'I'm glad that you or your colleagues aren't working tomorrow,' said Freya. 'I can't honestly think that the skies would be very safe after all the vodka consumption.'

Carey frowned but said nothing.

'It was a joke,' Freya said eventually.

'Oh good,' said Carey. 'I wasn't sure.'

'I'm sorry we didn't get to meet before now,' said Freya after another awkward silence. 'I would've liked to get to know you a little before tonight.'

'You were busy,' said Carey. 'And my shifts didn't help. Anyway, I feel I know you already. Ben talks about you a lot. You're obviously very important to him.'

Freya shrugged. 'We were very much on our own after our parents died,' she told Carey. 'I suppose it's made the bond quite strong.'

'He said you went to work to keep things going even though you wanted to go to college.'

'Actually, I don't know whether I wanted to go to college or not,' admitted Freya. 'But I certainly didn't want us to be in a bad situation financially and my parents hadn't really made enough provision for us. Things were different twenty-five years ago. People weren't as clued in about money matters as they are now.'

'He owes you a lot,' said Carey.

'He's my brother. What else would I do but look out for him?'

'And now?' asked Carey.

'What d'you mean?'

'Do you feel that you didn't look out for him recently? That because he married me the way he did you've failed somehow?'

This was so exactly what Freya felt that she was unable to answer.

'I love him,' said Carey. 'I know it seems hard to imagine but I care about him as much as you.'

Freya smiled slightly. 'I suppose you do. It's just that – I've known him my whole life and I'm finding it hard to adjust to the fact that someone who's only known him for a few weeks is now more important to him.'

'I understand,' said Carey. 'I really do.'

'I don't want to seem unfeeling or judgmental,' Freya said next, 'but I find it hard to believe that this will work.'

'Because I don't live up to your expectations?' asked Carey.

'Because I don't believe in love at first sight,' said Freya. 'It doesn't happen that way.'

'I didn't think so either,' Carey told her. 'But then I met Ben.'

'He's never done anything like this before,' said Freya.

Carey laughed. 'I hope not!'

'You know what I mean.' Freya's voice was cool again. 'He usually takes ages about making up his mind. Weighs up all the pros and cons. He doesn't rush into things.'

'I do love him,' repeated Carey. 'He loves me too, Freya. I know he does. And I know we can make it work.'

'I hope you're right,' said Freya.

'Tell me about the girlfriend.' Carey adjusted the pearl comb in her curls.

Freya frowned.

'I've met her,' Carey added. 'Short. Black hair. Absolutely stunning.'

'I'm sorry about Leah.' Freya sounded genuinely contrite. 'It's my fault that she's here. She's my friend too and I invited her. It was stupid.'

'How serious was it?' asked Carey.

Freya looked uncomfortable. 'I thought it was more serious than he did,' she told her. 'And so did Leah. But Brian told me that it wasn't serious at all. At least not as far as Ben was concerned.'

'They were together for a long time?'

'On and off,' said Freya.

'Are you being diplomatic?' asked Carey.

'No.' Freya sighed deeply. 'It was an off and on thing but I suppose most of us thought it would end up being on. And I was surprised it didn't and – I have to tell you – disappointed.'

Carey swallowed hard. 'Thanks for being so honest with me.'

'I didn't want to like you,' said Freya. 'Because of how he married you and because of Leah too.'

'There's no need to be too honest,' Carey tried to joke.

'But I know why he fell for you,' said Freya. 'You're very different – from Leah and from me. And I suppose that's what attracted him.'

'You think the attraction will wear off?' asked Carey edgily.

'Not necessarily,' said Freya. 'I don't suppose that has to happen. I just . . .' Her voice trailed off and she looked up as Sylvia and John approached them.

'Hi,' said Carey brightly, both annoyed and relieved at their arrival. 'Have you met? This is Ben's sister, Freya.'

She chatted with them for a few minutes then disappeared in search of the Ladies. She wanted to be on her own for a while. She felt raw from her encounter with Freya, who clearly believed that Ben had made the biggest mistake of his life. Did everyone, she wondered as she pushed open the door. Were they all waiting for her to fail?

The rest area was as ornate as everywhere else. Carey sat down in a gilt and maroon velvet chair and closed her eyes. What was the real story about the ex-girlfriend? she asked herself. It was clear from her conversation with Freya that Leah had been an important fixture in Ben's life. But it was over. So why had she come tonight? Carey knew that, no matter how terrible she'd feel about her ex-boyfriend getting married to someone else, she wouldn't turn up at the wedding. It was ridiculous. Unless she planned to create a scene.

Carey opened her eyes again. If Leah created a scene it would be Leah who'd look foolish. She didn't think that the beautiful girl with the raven hair was a fool. Maybe she'd come simply because she was curious. Even so . . . Carey shook her head. She'd done some stupid things over men in her past but she'd never chased one who'd broken up with her. Well, almost never. There had been the incident with Michael O'Dowd where she'd rung his mobile thirty times the day after he'd told her that it was over between them. And she'd waited for him outside the office building where he worked one afternoon simply to see him again and try to make him change his mind. But she wouldn't have gone anywhere he might be with a new girlfriend. Would she? She nibbled at her fingernail as she thought of driving past Peter Furness's house in Castleknock the day after he'd admitted that he was married. She'd done it in the hope of seeing Sandra Furness, just to know what she looked like. Maybe it was the same thing.

No it wasn't, she told herself as she took an emery board out of her bag and began to repair the damage to the nail she'd bitten. She hadn't tried to meet Sandra. Hadn't gone places where both of them might be. She'd broken it off with Peter herself and, despite his efforts to get back with her, she hadn't succumbed. So she was very, very different from Leah.

The door of the Ladies opened. Carey slid the emery board back into her bag and took out a lipstick.

'Hello again,' said Leah. 'Escaping for a bit of peace and quiet?'

'Just doing a touch-up,' said Carey as she daubed frosted pink over her lips and wondered how it was that she had known that the person coming into the Ladies would be Ben's ex-girlfriend.

143

'I wish I could wear those pastel colours.' Leah sighed. 'But they're far too insipid on me. That's why I stick to reds.'

'They suit you,' said Carey.

'Thanks.' Leah took a brush out of her black leather bag and began to run it through her hair. 'I like bold colours myself. I think that if I ever do get married I'll wear scarlet.'

'I'm sure it'd be very appropriate,' said Carey.

'Are you?' Leah put her brush on the table. 'Why?'

'I think you're a scarlet sort of person,' said Carey.

'Not a flimsy white dress sort of person like you?'

Carey glanced down at her white dress. 'This was bought for Las Vegas,' she said. 'It's not exactly what I'd wear here but Ben wanted me to.'

'Oh, Ben!' Leah laughed. 'He's persuasive when he wants to be.'

'Yes,' said Carey, 'he is.' She replaced her lipstick in her bag and looked at Leah in the mirror. 'So how long have you known him?'

'Ages.' Leah shrugged dismissively.

'And the two of you slept together?' Carey was pleased to see Leah's cheeks flush.

'Naturally,' she replied. 'Strangely, though, we were sleeping together when he married you.'

Carey's heart thudded in her chest. In fact, she could feel the drum of the beat in her head too and a hollow sensation in the pit of her stomach.

'Obviously not at the exact time,' she said calmly.

'Obviously. But I wasn't aware that he was going to America to find a wife when he'd just left my bed.' Leah's voice was clipped.

'Shit happens.' Carey took out her mascara but replaced it when she realised that her hand was shaking far too much to apply it. Instead she sprayed herself liberally with the latest Giorgio Armani perfume she'd bought in New York.

'And it doesn't bother you?' asked Leah.

'What?'

'That he was sleeping with me before he found you?'

'I was sleeping with someone before I met him,' said Carey.

'Oh?'

'It wasn't as though I was hanging around waiting for him to show

144

up.' Carey sprayed the perfume again so that the air was laden with the sweet-smelling scent. 'I've had lots of relationships. I guess if you meet someone and marry them as quickly as Ben and I did, there's bound to be a few people who are put out about it. I'm sorry if you were.'

'Not put out,' said Leah. 'Just surprised. And concerned.'

'Concerned?'

'For you,' said Leah sweetly. 'After all, if he could dump me so easily, where does that leave you?'

'Still married to him.' Carey dropped the perfume bottle back into her bag. 'I intend to make it work.'

'I'm sure you'll do your best,' said Leah. 'And I don't mean to be nasty, it's just that when your boyfriend comes home married to someone else it does alter your view of him somewhat.'

'I can imagine.' Carey was astonished at how even her voice was when she felt as though she were about to collapse.

'I'll always be friends with Freya,' said Leah. 'And, now that I've forgiven him, Ben too. I practise alternative therapies. They often recommend me to customers of their shops. And, of course, I've given both of them stress massages from time to time.'

Carey held her bag tightly. 'I'm sure I'll manage to de-stress Ben now. But I'm glad that you'll still be friends with Freya.'

Leah turned from the mirror and faced Carey directly. 'Do you really think your marriage will last?'

'Why on earth shouldn't it?' Carey asked.

'He's not the settling down sort,' said Leah. 'He's the love 'em and leave 'em type.'

'Maybe with you.' Carey opened the door of the Ladies. 'But certainly not with me.'

Chapter 12

Kanuka

A foliage oil with a fresh, bracing scent

Ben ordered a beer from the barman at Oleg's and gratefully took a large gulp. Vodka and wine were all very well, he thought, but both made him thirsty. Besides, he wasn't really a spirits drinker; he'd only downed a couple of shots to get into the party mood. He looked across the crowd to see how Carey was getting on but he couldn't find her. He hoped she was having a good time. It had occurred to him, as they'd been biting on the bread earlier, that Freya had really taken over the entire event and had forced them into the kind of party that he knew she herself enjoyed. She loved themed nights, quite often held them to promote different products in the shops. But he'd known all week that Carey wasn't looking forward to it, and it suddenly seemed unfair that she'd had to go through it simply because Freya had thought it was a good idea.

'You're looking a bit morose for someone who's married a fine-looking woman!' Brian Hayes stood beside Ben.

'Not at all,' said Ben genially. 'Just stepping back from the mayhem a little.'

'It's fairly buzzing all right.' Brian glanced to where the air traffic control people and the football team were engaged in animated debate which involved a great deal of shouting and laughter.

'Is Freya enjoying herself?' asked Ben.

'Oh, you know Freya.' Brian grinned at him. 'Once she's organising things she's as happy as a pig in the proverbial.'

'That's what I thought,' said Ben.

'You didn't want her to do all this?'

'We weren't expecting quite so much of a do,' said Ben, 'but I should've guessed, knowing my sister.'

'She means well,' said Brian.

'People who mean well usually drive everyone else up the wall,' Ben told him. 'They have you doing all sorts of things that you never wanted to, simply to keep them happy.'

'Freya's not that bad,' said Brian mildly.

'Not usually,' agreed Ben, 'but she got a bee in her bonnet about this party and I wish she hadn't invited quite so many people.'

'I see Leah is here.'

Ben glanced at Brian but the other man's face was expressionless.

'You can imagine what I thought when I heard she was invited,' said Ben eventually. 'I really don't know what Freya was thinking of, and I sure as hell don't know what Leah was thinking of to accept.'

'She probably wanted to see her replacement,' said Brian.

'I wish everyone didn't talk about Leah as though we were a permanent fixture and Carey came in and jostled her out of the way,' complained Ben. 'Leah was a friend and I know we had an on-off thing going but I was never going to bloody well marry her.'

'I know that and you know that, but it's not what Freya thought,' said Brian.

'You talked about it with her?'

'Of course we did.' Brian laughed. 'She'll talk about anyone's marriage except her own.'

Ben drained his glass and ordered another beer for himself and one for Brian. 'Do you want to marry my sister?' he asked Brian when the fresh drinks were placed on the counter.

'I've thought about it,' said Brian, 'but she seems to have a thing about losing her independence. Mind you, she used to say that she didn't want to get married because she was afraid it'd put pressure on you.'

'What?' Ben looked surprised. 'She told me that she couldn't be bothered. Or words to that effect,' he added, noticing the slightly hurt expression on Brian's face.

Brian shrugged. 'She thought that you'd feel left out,' he explained. 'She'd have a family and you wouldn't.'

'That's complete horseshit,' said Ben. 'Why on earth would I feel like that?'

'Oh Ben, she worries about you all the time!'

'That's ridiculous,' said Ben.

'Yes, I know, but that's Freya for you.' Brian put his arm on the other man's shoulder. 'Looking out for her baby brother.'

'Her baby brother is thirty-three years old and can look after himself,' snapped Ben.

Brian laughed. 'I know. And you'll have to do a bit of looking out for yourself right now.'

'What d'you mean?'

'I mean that Ex-girlfriend Number One is making her way towards us and she has the kind of gleam in her eye that means she wants to talk to you.'

'Bloody hell.' Ben finished his beer. 'I've talked to her already tonight and I really don't want to do it again. Actually,' he confided, 'I talked to her before tonight. Met her after we came back from the States. She threw a complete wobbler and told me that I couldn't treat her like this and that I'd be sorry.'

'Fuck.'

'My sentiments exactly,' said Ben.

'You think she might try to cut your balls off or something?'

Ben paled. 'Surely not.'

'You'll find out soon enough.' Brian stood to one side as Leah joined them. 'Hi, Leah,' he said casually. 'Having a good time?'

'Surprisingly so.' She smiled sweetly at Brian and then took Ben's arm. 'Come on, Ben. Spend a few minutes with me.'

Ben grimaced as Brian drew his fingers slowly across his throat and walked off in search of Freya.

'You look worried.' Leah laughed and leaned closer to him. He caught the familiar scent of her perfume, a white musk which she usually wore.

'Why did you come?' he asked.

'You asked me that already,' she reminded him. 'And I gave you the very plausible and accurate answer that I was curious to see the woman you married. I wouldn't have been human if I wasn't curious.' She looked at him quizzically. 'Are you still afraid I'll make a scene?'

148

'Not really.' He shook his head. 'Sorry, Leah. I'm feeling a bit distracted right now. It's been a hectic day, I've had too much to drink and I guess I'm just being stupid.'

'That's all right.' Her soft hair brushed against his face. 'All of us say stupid things from time to time. Do stupid things too.'

'Stop analysing me.' He leaned his head against the wall.

'I can't help it,' she said. 'I know you so well, you see. And I can tell that you're stressed out right now. I'm not surprised. Getting married is really high on the stress-o-meter, you know.'

'Getting married wasn't stressful,' said Ben. 'Being married is.'

'Is it?' Leah looked at him with interest.

'You have to get used to someone's ways,' he said. 'You're not on your own any more. So that can be stressful. And tonight – tonight is unexpectedly stressful.'

'Why?'

'Neither of us were mad about the idea of a party,' said Ben, 'and Carey was nervous about meeting Freya. She doesn't think my sister likes her very much.'

'Freya just feels left out,' said Leah loyally. 'I don't blame her.'

'Neither do I,' said Ben. 'But she'll have to get used to it.'

'So will I.' Leah brushed her hair from her eyes. 'I have to apologise to you again, Ben, for the coffee shop. I don't know what came over me. I was in shock myself.'

'It's OK.' He smiled at her. 'I understand. Although I'm not sure the people in the café ever will.'

'Friends?' asked Leah.

'Of course friends,' said Ben.

'Good.' She tilted her mouth towards his so that it was almost inevitable that they kissed. He could taste the cherry lipstick on her lips. She touched the side of his face and drew him closer to her. He felt the heat of her body through her red silk dress. It was amazing, he thought, how different the kiss of two women could be. It was amazing how different the feel of them could be, the scent of them could be. Yet both of them were good at kissing. Both of them seemed to know what he liked. Gently, he pushed her away from him and she smiled up at him, her hands still resting on his shoulders.

'Friends,' she whispered again.

Ben wiped the cherry lipstick from his mouth and nodded word-lessly.

Carey's arms were turning an interesting shade of mottled blue. She knew that coming outside in sub-zero temperatures had been extremely silly but she'd been so shaken after her encounter with Leah that she hadn't been able to remain in the restaurant. So she'd walked down the gravel pathway and out onto the main street where she'd stood shivering in the icy wind while she tried to get things into perspective. She told herself that it didn't matter how Leah felt about Ben, it was how Ben felt about Carey herself and their marriage that was important. It didn't matter that Leah and Ben had slept together – given that they'd been in a relationship it'd be more worrying if they hadn't. It mattered a bit that they'd still been in that relationship, sleeping together, when she'd first met Ben. It worried her that he hadn't said anything about it because it reminded her, uncomfortably, of how Peter Furness hadn't said anything about Sandra when she'd first met him. But this was different. Ben and Leah weren't married and Ben was perfectly entitled to dump her and marry whoever he wanted. Even if to the objective observer that did seem a bit callous. She didn't like to think of Ben as callous. She liked to think of him as perfect.

Well, nobody's perfect, she thought as she turned back towards the restaurant. We all make mistakes. It's how we get on with the rest of our lives that matters. Suddenly she jumped in shock as a figure moved out of the shadows at the gateway and into her path.

'Jesus Christ,' she gasped. 'You scared me half to death, lurking in the bushes like that! What d'you think you're doing?'

'I'm sorry.'

'Sorry? You're out of your mind. What the hell are you doing here?'

Peter Furness shrugged. 'I'm not sure, to tell you the truth. I think I came because I didn't quite believe you.'

'How did you even know where I'd be?' demanded Carey. 'And why didn't you contact me some other time? Are you crazy?'

'I know it's a bit crazy,' admitted Peter. 'It was Gina who told me. I phoned her after we met. I asked her how serious this thing between you and your – Ben – actually was.'

'Pretty damn serious, obviously,' snapped Carey. 'I did explain to you, didn't I, that we're married? I mean, I thought I made that perfectly clear. I used the word "married", didn't I? What other proof did you need?'

'I know, I know,' he said helplessly. 'And I'm sorry, it was just that I couldn't believe it. After all we'd been through together and then finally I'm in a position to . . . and I thought that if I came, if I saw you . . . I'm shattered, Carey. Truly shattered.'

'I don't care how you are,' said Carey hotly. 'I can't *believe* that Gina didn't tell me you called. Did she know you were going to turn up here tonight?'

'Of course not,' said Peter. 'When I phoned she said, very scathingly, that you were lucky that you'd found someone great and that you were celebrating it in a flash Russian restaurant in Rathgar this Thursday. So it wasn't exactly difficult to work it out.'

'And what did you intend to do?' The initial shock of seeing Peter had made Carey forget about the cold but now she shivered suddenly and rubbed her arms to warm them up.

'I don't know,' said Peter. 'I just wanted to talk to you.' He shook his head. 'I wasn't thinking straight.'

'Well, you've talked to me now,' said Carey abruptly. 'And there's nothing else to say.'

'I had to let you know how I felt. How I still feel.'

'Cut the crap,' she said. 'You always had a great line in crap.'

'And you always had a great way of putting me down,' said Peter.

'Not enough.' Carey's teeth chattered and she rubbed her arms more vigorously.

Peter stared at her as though he'd only just realised that she was outside in a dress that had no thermal qualities whatsoever. He frowned.

'What are you doing out here anyway instead of being inside cutting your cake or whatever it is you do? You're freezing.' He reached out to her and put his hands on her shoulders. Then he began to rub her arms very quickly.

'I'm OK,' she said irritably. 'You don't have to do that.'

'You should be inside.'

'I came out for some air,' she told him. 'There's a lot of people in there.'

151

'And are they all delighted at your marriage and wishing you well?'

'Yes,' she said firmly.

'Even your family?' asked Peter.

'Naturally,' she said.

'I never got to meet your family.'

'Of course you didn't,' she said nastily. 'You had one of your own to worry about.'

'Carey, I know you don't think much of me because I kept Sandra and Aaron a secret. It wasn't something I meant to do. It just happened. When I met you . . .'

'I don't want to hear it.' Her voice trembled. 'I told you before, you broke my heart. And now it's perfectly mended and I don't want you breaking it again.'

'You think I might?' he asked softly. 'In the right circumstances?'

'No, I fucking don't!' Suddenly she was angry again. 'And I don't want you here. I don't want to see you ever again. I don't want to hear from you again. I don't want you messing up my life any more than you messed it up already.'

'I'm sorry.' He'd stopped rubbing her arms now but he still had his hands on her shoulders. 'I never meant to hurt you. I never meant for any of it to happen, Carey. I really and truly didn't.'

'It's all right.' She closed her eyes. 'Forget it.' She opened her eyes again. 'Forget me.'

He looked at her. 'I'll never forget you,' he said and kissed her on the lips.

Ben downed a strawberry-flavoured vodka as Carey walked back into the restaurant, her arms wrapped tightly across her body. He moved towards her but was stopped by the touch of Leah's hand on his shoulder.

'You deserted me,' she said.

'What?' He didn't look at her, his eyes were fixed on Carey.

'You kissed me and walked off.'

Ben looked away from Carey and round at Leah. 'Look, Leah, I don't have time to—'

'I'm not asking you to spend the entire evening with me,' she said.

'I just wish you didn't always rush away when you've had intimate contact with me.'

'Sorry?' He blinked.

'You know, when we slept together you'd always get up early the next morning because you were rushing to be somewhere else. And this evening, even though our kiss was one between friends, you rushed off like a scalded cat.'

'Leah, I'm sorry. I didn't mean to make you feel abandoned or anything but—'

'Oh, I'm used to that.' Her eyes twinkled and she rested her head on his chest. 'However, since you've got other women on your mind tonight I'll forgive you.'

Ben felt as though he was in an alternate reality. He could hear Leah's voice, soft and beguiling as always, talking to him as though they were still a couple, he could smell her perfume and feel her against him, but he was still watching Carey who, having seen him and Leah together, had changed direction and was now striding towards the stairs.

'I have to talk to Carey.' He stepped backwards.

'I know,' she said, 'and you're right. New wives are so much more important than old friends.'

'Don't give me grief, Leah,' said Ben. 'I'm not in the mood for more grief right now.'

She raised an eyebrow in silent query as she watched him walk quickly after his wife.

This time Carey locked herself into one of the cubicles in the Ladies. She was both freezing and boiling – cold from being outside, flushed from her encounter with Peter Furness and hot with rage at having walked into the restaurant to see Leah Ryder with her head resting on Ben's chest. The whole night was taking on the disjointed atmosphere of a Brian de Palma movie. She'd thought about walking over to Ben and Leah and landing a punch on the girl's face when she'd seen them together, but she found it difficult to concentrate on her anger with her husband and his ex-girlfriend when she herself was still reeling with the shock of Peter's appearance. She couldn't quite believe that he'd shown up although it was, perhaps, just as well that she'd met him outside. All

153

she'd needed to really wreck her evening was for him to have come into the restaurant and create a scene. Maybe he could've rested his head on *her* chest. But that was the difference, she thought, as she opened the small window at the back of the cubicle to let in some fresh air. Peter wasn't the male equivalent of Leah. Peter was, essentially, a nice bloke. A lying, cheating, married nice bloke.

'He's lucky the new wife didn't see him.' The words, spoken by a man, floated faintly in through the open window and Carey stiffened.

'How could you resist that though, Paul?' another male voice asked. 'Leah always knows how to get her man.'

'Maybe he thinks he can get away with it. Thinks they're all like Leah and don't mind his bit of offside whenever he likes.'

'He's playing with fire.'

'You know what he's like, Dave. The ultimate commitment-shy bloke. Gets a nose-bleed if he thinks it's getting too serious.'

'Which is why this marriage thing surprises me.'

'Me too. She must be incredibly hot between the sheets!'

'That won't last. Sadly, it never does. And then what – back to Leah again?'

'She knows she only has to snap her fingers and he'll come running. He's fixated on her no matter what he thinks.'

'Shouldn't have married someone else in that case. Kind of complicates things, doesn't it?'

'He probably had a skinful of drink and thought it was a good idea.' Paul chortled.

'But he'll be sorry. That Ryder girl's far too dangerous and the other one – well, I don't know her but she'll have to be easy going. And somehow I don't think she is.'

Carey practically had to lean out of the window to listen over the sound of running water. 'Bit more feisty than the blonde he dumped last time, all right.'

'Maybe you're right and she's sensational in bed. Although if she was he'd hardly be having another go at Leah, would he?'

'He obviously can't help himself.'

'He's a fool.'

'He sure is.' Paul's laugh was harsh. 'If the new one ever finds out that he was practically shagging his ex-bird at the party she'll have his fucking balls for breakfast!'

Carey sat on the toilet seat and buried her head in her hands as she replayed the men's words over again. She felt like someone who'd switched on a video halfway through the movie. Everyone else knew the plot but not her. Suddenly she realised that she had no idea what Ben Russell was really like, no idea about his life before he'd met her, no idea about the people who really mattered to him. Although, from what she'd just heard, that didn't make much difference because nobody (except perhaps the cool and distant Freya) really mattered to him at all. No wonder everyone was so surprised at their marriage. It seemed that Ben really was the serial womaniser he'd denied being in New York. Not only that but he was a serial womaniser who kept going back to the same woman. The woman who had turned up at his wedding party in a scarlet dress and glossy red lipstick and who, according to his friends, he'd been practically shagging here in the restaurant! She made a face. It sounded totally disgusting.

She shivered as she thought of how much she'd enjoyed making love to Ben, how she'd thought of it as more than sex, how she'd felt loved and cherished by him in a way that she'd never experienced before. But now it seemed as though she was just a quick shag too. One that had got a little bit too serious though because he'd dragged her off to Vegas to get married. Why on earth, she wondered miserably, had he wanted to marry her? Was that something he tried on a regular basis too? Asked girls to marry him after he'd made love to them so that they didn't realise they were one in a line of sexual conquests? Only usually he didn't have to deliver on the promises because usually he wasn't a few hours away from a city with a line in tacky wedding chapels and ten-minute wedding ceremonies. She groaned. She'd been a fool, just like everyone said. And her marriage would fail, just like everyone expected. Because it wasn't a marriage at all. It was a one-night stand that had accidentally stretched to more than a week. But that was all. It wasn't love. How could it be? You had to know someone to love them.

She bit her lip. Maybe he'd married her because, out of all the girls he'd broken up with Leah to be with, she'd been more of a challenge for him. Now, back in Ireland, perhaps he'd realised that sex with her wasn't as exciting as sex with Leah. Maybe that's why

155

he'd been, in the words of his friends, practically shagging her at the party. To find out who was better.

Oh God, she thought, as she rubbed at her eyes and smudged her mascara. What have I done by marrying him? Why on earth did I think it might work out?

'She was always quite mad.'

Sylvia and Freya were sitting in the upstairs dining room sharing a bottle of Pinot Noir. They'd exchanged the raucousness of the downstairs bar for the serenity of the deserted dining room and they were unexpectedly enjoying each other's company.

'In what way mad?' Freya asked Sylvia.

'A bit of a tomboy. Very stubborn. Headstrong too. Carey's the kind of girl that if you tell her not to do something she'll immediately do it just to see why you said no.'

Freya nodded in understanding. 'And do you think that has something to do with why she married my brother?'

'I've no idea why she married your brother.' Sylvia swirled the wine around the wide glass. 'She was always the non-marrying type. Hated anything to do with weddings. Called it unnecessary fuss and bother.'

'So this Vegas thing doesn't really surprise you?'

'Actually it does,' said Sylvia. 'I could understand her going there to marry someone she knew but someone she's only just met . . . no offence, Freya, but he could be violent or an alcoholic or anything.'

'He's not,' said Freya shortly. 'He's one of the nicest blokes you could meet.'

'I wasn't talking about him specifically,' Sylvia assured her. 'I just meant – well . . .'

'I know what you meant,' said Freya. 'I feel the same about your sister.'

'Even though she's mad she's a really good person,' said Sylvia hastily. 'And I'm sure she'll work very hard at the marriage.'

Freya sighed. 'I wish I could feel confident about it,' she said, 'but it's damn hard to think of one good thing—' She broke off as the dining-room door was pushed open and Carey almost fell inside.

'Carey!' Sylvia stood up hurriedly and knocked over her glass of wine. A purple-red stain spread across the white linen tablecloth. 'Are you OK?'

'I'm f-fine.' Carey's teeth were chattering. 'I went outside for some f-fresh air, but now I c-can't seem to w-warm up.'

'You went out? In that dress?' Freya looked at her in amazement. 'I'm surprised you didn't turn into a block of ice straight away.'

'What are you doing up here?' asked Sylvia. 'Where's Ben?'

'I d-don't know,' said Carey. 'I came up for some peace and quiet.'

'Peace and quiet!' Sylvia couldn't hide her astonishment. 'What d'you want peace and quiet for? I thought you liked a good party.'

'I do,' said Carey, finally managing to stop her chattering teeth. 'I was just sick of talking to people.'

The dining-room door burst open again and this time Ben stepped into the room. 'There you are,' he said to Carey.

'Here I am,' she said.

The two of them stared at each other while Freya and Sylvia looked on.

'I was wondering if you wanted to dance with me,' said Ben.

'With you?' Carey's voice was strained. 'Not just yet.'

'Oh, come on, Carey!' cried Sylvia. 'It's about time you and Ben put on a bit of a show for everyone.'

'I'm sure we've already done that,' said Ben tightly.

Carey frowned.

'But maybe you're right,' he said. 'We're the star attractions, after all.'

'Are we?' asked Carey.

'Sure you are,' said Sylvia.

'Is everything all right?' asked Freya.

'Yes,' said Ben and Carey simultaneously.

'Because you both seem a bit weird,' she told them.

'Hardly surprising,' said Carey. 'It's been a weird time for us.'

'Very,' agreed Ben.

'But we'll go downstairs again,' said Carey.

'Have you warmed up?' Sylvia looked at her sister curiously. 'What possessed you to go outside on a night like tonight?'

'Maybe she was bored with my company,' said Ben.

Carey threw him a sideways look but said nothing.

157

'Have you two had a row?' demanded Freya.

'No, we haven't,' said Ben decisively. 'Come on, Carey, let's go downstairs again.' He grabbed her cold hand and dragged her out of the room leaving Freya and Sylvia staring at each other.

'What was all that about?' asked Sylvia.

'Beats me.' Freya shook her head. 'There's something definitely askew, isn't there?'

'The whole damn thing is askew.' Sylvia sighed. 'But I hope it doesn't all unravel tonight. You've done such a marvellous job, Freya, it'd be a shame if they went and ruined it.'

'By what? Breaking up?' asked Freya.

'God, no.' Sylvia looked at her in horror. 'D'you think . . . ?'

'I've absolutely no idea,' Freya answered. 'But if they got married after spending a night together or something, I guess there's no reason for them not to divorce after a stupid row.'

'I hope not,' said Sylvia. 'I always knew there'd be problems though.'

'You know what the problem is?' Freya looked at Sylvia. 'They're both headstrong and stubborn.'

'You've realised that about my sister already?' Sylvia laughed.

'And I've always known it about my brother.'

'It should make for an explosive match.'

'Maybe it already has,' said Freya darkly.

Chapter 13

Citronella

A very stimulating and powerful grass oil

'Let go of my hand,' muttered Carey as Ben tugged her down the stairs.

'No,' he said. 'You're my wife.'

'Wife,' she hissed. 'Not chattel.'

'I know that.'

She glanced at him but he wasn't looking at her. She didn't know what was the matter with him, what was making him so angry. She was the one who should be annoyed, she told herself; she was the one who'd been forced outside by the words of his fucking ex-girlfriend with whom, apparently, he was still having some kind of relationship. She was the one who'd just listened to a potted history of his sexual conquests and she was the one who, belatedly, was realising that the reason his friends were so shocked about their marriage was that they knew him too well to believe that it would ever last. She was a flash in the pan. Or a grope in the dark. It was obvious that everyone believed that Leah was the real long-term partner and that she, Carey, was just the result of a stupid impulse on Ben's part. She wished she knew just what it was that Leah possessed that kept him coming back. Then she shook herself mentally because it was perfectly obvious what the attraction was; it was all in Leah's small but sensuous body and the languid way she moved across a room, and the fire in her bitter-chocolate eyes. There was no other attraction, Carey told herself furiously. It was nothing but sex.

And then she remembered that the first blaze of attraction between

159

herself and Ben had been all about sex too, and she wanted to scream because she'd thought it was different with them. Only now, having listened to the people who knew Ben well, she acknowledged that she'd been wrong. Until then she'd been so sure of herself and Ben, despite the uneasiness that Leah had caused. She'd told Peter that she was sure, she'd told him that she wanted him to forget her and never contact her again because she was ready to work at it with Ben. But he wasn't ready to work at it with her. Maybe he just wanted them both, because there Leah was again at the bottom of the stairs, looking up at them. Carey clenched her fist. Perhaps if she cracked the bitch in the jaw this time it might change things a bit.

'Hi, Ben and Carey.' Her voice was honey-sweet. 'I thought I'd head home, I've a busy day tomorrow. So I just want to wish you both the best in the world.'

Carey kept her fist clenched as Ben let go of her other hand.

'Thanks for coming,' he said to Leah. 'How are you getting home? D'you want me to order a cab?'

Leah shook her head. 'I already did. It's waiting for me outside.' She leaned towards Ben and kissed him on the cheek. 'May you always be happy,' she told him. 'I wish that with all my heart.'

Carey gritted her teeth. Leah leaned towards her and, even though Carey moved her face to one side, Leah still managed to brush her cheek. 'I wish you everything you deserve,' she told Carey softly. 'Absolutely everything.'

Ben glanced at Carey and then looked back to Leah. 'I'll walk you to the cab,' he said.

Leah shook her head. 'No need,' she said. Then she smiled brightly. 'Maybe Carey'd like to walk to the cab with me.'

'No, I wouldn't,' said Carey.

'Carey!' Ben looked at her in annoyance. 'There's no need to be rude.'

'I think your wife's feeling a bit threatened.' Leah smiled. 'Though she doesn't need to feel that way. After all, even though I gave you my nicest kiss, Ben, it didn't make any difference.'

'I heard.' Carey looked at both of them and watched Ben's jaw tighten. 'Although I thought it was a bit more than a kiss.'

'It was a farewell sort of kiss,' said Leah. 'We definitely came up for air.'

160

'I hope you enjoyed it, Ben,' said Carey.

'I'm sure that's not something that worries you over-much,' he replied tartly.

'Actually . . .'

'We're all grown-ups, after all,' he said.

'I'd better go,' said Leah. 'Nobody need walk me to the cab.'

'No,' said Carey. 'I will. I want to make sure you actually leave.'

Leah turned away while Carey followed her.

'You're a complete cow, you know,' said Carey as they walked outside. 'You don't want me and Ben to be together.'

'Of course I don't,' said Leah. 'He's my boyfriend.'

'He's my damn husband,' snapped Carey. 'And you'd better remember that.'

'Oh, he's reminded me of it over and over,' said Leah.

'Good.'

'The problem for him is that this time he isn't sure I'll be around when it all goes horribly wrong.' Leah got into the taxi and smiled at her. 'Bye, Carey. Nice to have met you.'

The worst part was, thought Carey miserably as she trudged back up the gravel path, that as far as she was concerned, it had already gone horribly wrong. But she was damned if she was going to give the Leah bitch the satisfaction of knowing that tonight.

The first person Carey met when she came inside again was Maude. Her mother beamed and embraced her and Carey realised that Maude had clearly sampled rather too many of the fruit-flavoured vodka shots.

'This is a wonderful party,' mumbled Maude as she rested her head on Carey's shoulder. 'But we're going to go now. I'm feeling really, really tired.'

'I'm glad you had a good time,' said Carey tautly.

'Oh, I did.' Maude raised her head to look at Carey. 'Me and your dad both. And everyone else. It was fun. We haven't done anything that was really fun in ages.'

'Freya'll be pleased you thought it was fun.'

Maude beamed again. 'I told her that she was more than welcome to visit us any time. She's a bit shy, I think. I was so worried, you

161

know, about what you'd done. But he's lovely, he really is. You couldn't have done better.'

'Couldn't I?' asked Carey.

'Absolutely not. And I'm delighted that you've socked that married man in the eye, so to speak, and that you've found the right person.'

'You think I've found the right person then?'

'Absolutely,' said Maude confidently.

Carey did her best to smile at her mother as her father came over to them and told them that John was ready to go.

'I didn't realise that John had driven you over tonight,' said Carey. 'I thought you'd taken a cab.'

'We did to get here,' said Arthur, 'but John said he'd drive us back. He doesn't drink much so he didn't mind staying on the dry tonight.'

'He's a nice man too,' said Maude dreamily. 'Both my girls have married nice men.'

'Tipsy.' Arthur mouthed the words at Carey.

'Everything all right?' John Lynch appeared beside them, the keys to his MPV in his hand. 'You ready to go, Maude?'

'Well, you know, it's been such a lovely evening I kind of hate to leave,' said Maude. 'But I suppose I'm not as young as I once was.' She made a face. 'Who cares about that really? It's how you feel inside that counts, isn't it?' She hiccoughed gently and Arthur laughed.

'I'll tell you how you'll feel inside tomorrow.' He put his arm round his wife. 'You'll feel sorry that you sampled so many vodkas.'

'Probably,' murmured Maude, 'but it was worth it. The last few years we haven't made much of an effort, have we, Arthur? We've done old people things. We've sat in the garden and sipped glasses of wine like a couple of decaying antiques. I'd forgotten about going out.'

'Look what you've started, Carey!' John laughed. 'There'll be no stopping her now.'

Carey smiled faintly as her eyes scanned the crowded room. Ben was now talking to Brian Hayes. Laughing with Brian Hayes, she noticed, and she wondered if they were laughing because Ben had told him that, as well as being married to Carey, he was having a

162

bit on the side with Leah. As per usual, apparently. And maybe the bit on the side would suddenly become something else so that one day Ben and Leah would be having a full-blown affair and she'd be like Sandra Furness, waiting in the evening for the man she thought she loved to come home but knowing that he'd found happiness somewhere else.

People don't allow their fucking exes to come to parties, she told herself. It doesn't matter who they are. It doesn't matter what kind of pretend good reasons there are. Leah shouldn't have been here and he shouldn't have let her come. If he really loved me, if he intended it to be for ever, he'd have kicked her out the minute he saw her. Just like she'd got rid of Peter Furness.

'Ready to go yet?' Sylvia, her family in tow, put her arm on John's shoulder. He nodded.

'Just getting Maude and Arthur organised,' he said.

'You OK?' Sylvia looked at Carey searchingly.

'Yes,' answered Carey shortly.

'Sure?'

'Of course.'

Sylvia frowned. 'There wasn't any trouble . . .'

'I'm fine, Syl,' Carey interrupted her. 'Don't nag, for God's sake.'

'OK, OK, keep your hair on.'

'Carey, I had the most wonderful time,' Jeanne told her.

'I saw you talking to one of the blokes from the football team.' Carey's voice was bright and brittle. 'You seem to have made a hit.'

'Don't be silly.' Jeanne blushed. 'He was nice, though.'

'The football team!' Sylvia looked at her daughter. 'Surely he's too old for you.'

'Don't be so stupid, Mum,' said Jeanne. 'He's only nineteen. Ben is the old fogey on the football team. Him and Phil. Everyone else is miles younger.' She grinned at her mother. 'I might start supporting them. They usually play on Saturday morning.'

'Where?' asked Sylvia.

'Depends on the match,' said Jeanne, 'but they train in Coolock. That's not too far away from us really. If Dad would let me have the car . . .'

'No,' said John. 'And Dad wants you and the rest to get into the car now. It's late.'

'I got his phone number,' Jeanne whispered to Carey as she kissed her goodbye. 'His name's Gary.'

'Come on, Jeanne, let's go,' said John as his daughter looked round the room in the hope of seeing Gary again. 'We're leaving now.'

'Thanks for coming,' said Carey.

'You and Ben must visit us soon,' Sylvia told her.

'Sure.'

She followed them to the door and waved goodbye. She felt as though her smile was cemented onto her face as she turned back into Oleg's. The party was still in full swing but all she wanted to do was curl up in a corner and cry. This was the worst party she'd ever been at and it was supposed to be celebrating her wedding. But how could she celebrate her wedding when she knew that it was all a sham? Her husband didn't really give a damn about her. Only she didn't know him well enough to have realised that. This was why people didn't meet other people on planes and get married to them a couple of days later. Because they could turn out to be unfaithful shits.

She saw Ben say something to Brian Hayes and walk towards her. Her heart began to hammer in her chest and she could feel adrenaline surge through her body. And then Freya stopped Ben and spoke to him and he turned back towards the bar.

'Yo! Browne!!' Gina grabbed her by the arm. 'You're looking a little left out over there. Come on, get down and boogie with your mates.'

'I don't feel like boogie-ing,' said Carey tiredly.

'Don't tell me you're starting to flag,' protested Gina. 'Come on, we're going to do some Russian dancing!'

Carey allowed herself to be dragged into the group where Conor Reid and Chris Brady were desperately trying a Cossack-type dance but failing miserably so that they ended up lying on the floor. She couldn't help smiling at their antics but it seemed as though all of these things were happening to another person. Right now she was so confused that she didn't know whether she should be celebrating or not. Maybe she should be celebrating the fact that she'd found out about Ben now. Maybe she should be celebrating the fact that she could get out of this marriage with some dignity if she did it straight away.

Am I really such an idiot that I didn't see what he was like, she wondered bleakly. Is there something about me that invites my own personal black cloud to accompany me, no matter where I go and no matter what I do? Why is it that everyone else seems to have perfectly satisfactory relationships while I mess it up at every available opportunity?

The worst part was that everyone now seemed to think that she and Ben were absolutely made for each other even though they'd been so sceptical before.

'Come on, Carey, you have a go!' Suddenly they were pushing her into the centre of their circle and clapping their hands and expecting her to dance.

'I can't,' she said.

'You must.' Chris looked at her sternly. 'I'm the most senior member of your team and I'm ordering you to dance.'

'Not in these shoes,' she said.

'Take them off,' said Gina.

Carey sighed deeply then took off her high-heeled Perspex shoes and crossed her arms in front of her body. She began kicking her legs Cossack-style as the group whooped and cheered and applauded loudly. She managed to stay upright for almost thirty seconds before collapsing on the floor to roars of encouragement from her friends.

'Way to go, Browne!' yelled Finola. 'Best effort yet.'

'And what a sight!' cried Conor.

'Thanks,' gasped Carey as she lay on her back and looked at the faces grinning down at her.

'Want a hand?' Ben reached out for her and hauled her to her feet. 'You might want to rearrange your clothes first,' he said as she looked for her shoes.

'Oh!' Carey gasped as she realised that her exertions had twisted her trailer-trash white dress around and that her right boob (such as it was, she thought dolefully) was totally uncovered.

'Maybe it's time for us to go,' said Ben.

'I'm having fun,' said Carey as she pulled her dress back into position. 'I thought you were too.'

'Carey—'

'I'm going to have another drink with my friends and then maybe I'll go. I don't know yet.'

'Don't be silly,' he said.

'Silly?' she hissed. 'I don't think that when they're giving the awards for silliness at this event that it'll be me who's getting first prize.' She turned back to her group of friends. 'Come on,' she said. 'I want to see if anyone can beat that!'

It was another hour before the party broke up, by which time Carey had a raging headache and Gina had fallen asleep on one of the velvet banquettes.

'See you the day after tomorrow,' she said as Conor, supporting Gina, kissed her goodbye.

'We had a great time,' Conor said. 'And I really and truly hope you'll be very happy. It was about time you found the right man, Browne.'

'Russell,' said Carey blankly. 'It's supposed to be Russell now.'

Freya, Brian and Ben were thanking Colman and Dimitri when she went over to them.

'Ready?' asked Ben shortly.

She nodded and then rubbed her temple as her headache bounced around her head.

'Come on then.' He took her by the arm. 'Freya and Brian want a quick word with Colman. Let's leave them to it.'

'Thanks, Freya.' She was finding it difficult to talk now. 'Thanks, Brian, I really like you. And thanks for a great party, Colman.'

'Come on,' said Ben again. 'You don't have to thank everyone a thousand times.'

'I haven't,' she said irritably. 'I thanked them once. You should thank people. It's polite.'

'Freya, I'll see you soon,' said Ben. 'I think I'd better get her home.'

'Don't talk about me as though I was a naughty kid,' snapped Carey.

Ben shrugged, made a face at his sister, and propelled Carey out of the bar.

'There's something wrong,' said Freya to Brian as soon as they'd left.

'What?'

'Ben and Carey. Something happened.'

166

'I know,' said Brian. 'Ben kissed Leah earlier. A rather more than friendly kiss,' he added.

'No!' Freya's voice was a horrified squeak.

'Yes,' said Brian. 'I saw them.'

'Oh my God,' said Freya slowly. 'Did Carey see them?'

Brian shook his head. 'She wasn't around. But she found out about it.'

'How?'

'Leah told her.'

'Oh my God,' said Freya again. 'I don't believe you.'

'It was all in some jokey kind of way,' said Brian.

'Which was the joke?' demanded Freya. 'Ben and Leah kissing or Leah telling Carey?'

'Leah telling Carey,' said Brian. 'She told her when she was saying goodbye.'

'And why were they kissing?'

Brian sighed. 'According to Ben it just happened.'

'Oh, for crying out loud!' Freya pushed her hand through her hair so that it suddenly lost its careful styling and fell untidily around her face. 'What was he thinking of?'

'These things happen,' said Brian. 'They'll sort it out.'

'These things do *not* just happen!' cried Freya. 'Brian, I can tell you now that I wouldn't sort out my husband snogging ex-girlfriends without a hell of a row.'

Brian grinned. 'I know.'

'I can't believe it,' said Freya. 'Leah promised she wouldn't do anything and—'

'I told you it was asking for trouble, inviting her.'

'Don't do the "I told you so" routine with me,' said Freya. 'I already admitted earlier that it was a mistake.'

'OK, OK.' Brian shrugged.

'Sorry.' Freya shook her head. 'I didn't mean to snap at you. I just don't believe that they're married less than a month and already Ben's going around kissing other women. Poor Carey.'

'So you've changed your tune about her?' asked Brian.

'She's not exactly my sort of girl,' said Freya, 'but she doesn't deserve to be sandbagged at her own wedding party.'

'What about Leah?' asked Brian.

'What about her?'

'She was the one you felt sorry for. What d'you think of her now?'

'I don't know.' Freya sighed. 'I did – *do* – like Leah. I know she does odd things from time to time but she's like family. And, as everyone points out, it's not as though Ben and I had a huge family to start with.'

'It might come down to choices in the end,' Brian told her. 'Between family and friends.'

'Oh bloody hell,' snapped Freya. 'How could he have been so damned stupid?'

'You're always telling me that men are stupid,' said Brian. 'All he's done is to prove your point.'

Tiny white flakes of snow began to fall as Ben and Carey stood on the pavement and tried to hail a taxi to take them to Portobello. Carey scrunched and unscrunched her toes in an effort to keep her feet warm but they were already freezing.

'Let's walk,' said Ben. 'I'll keep watching for a cab.'

'I can't walk in these shoes,' said Carey tonelessly. 'They're from my car-to-bar pile. They're not made for walking. They're made for standing.'

'You'll be warmer if we walk.'

She shook off Ben's supporting arm as she took tentative footsteps on the slippery ground. Their progress was so slow she was beginning to think that they'd be lucky to get to the house before daybreak when a cab finally responded to Ben's wave and pulled in beside them. She fell thankfully into the back seat and wedged herself against the door.

'Do you want me to apologise to you?' Ben asked curtly after he gave directions to the driver.

'Apologise to me?'

'For Leah.'

'I don't want to talk to you at all,' said Carey.

'Why?'

'Because you obviously had a much, much deeper relationship with her than you ever told me about. Everyone says so,' said Carey. 'She hates me and she thinks I've stolen you from her and part of me can't blame her.'

'Everyone is wrong about her and me,' said Ben. 'And she doesn't hate you.'

'Oh, don't give me that.' Carey snorted. 'She warned me off in the loo before you and she got into whatever clinch you got into.'

'It wasn't a clinch,' said Ben. 'It was . . . it was a kiss but she kissed me, I didn't kiss her.'

'Surely you can do better than that!'

'And no matter who kissed who it wasn't important,' he said. 'Look, I was going out with her. I came home married. She's got a right to be upset.'

'Maybe,' said Carey. 'But she doesn't have a right to act as though you never got married at all! She should just fuck right off and leave us alone. Although perhaps the reason she doesn't is that you don't want her to.'

'You can't just cut people out of your life,' said Ben. 'Something you probably already know. And she's been part of my life for a long time.'

'Then why didn't you marry *her*?' demanded Carey. 'God knows, you seem to have had plenty of opportunity.'

'I didn't love her enough to marry her,' said Ben.

'But you did love her?'

'Don't start,' he said. 'Don't do this girlie thing about degrees of love and who's more important than who. Just don't.'

'OK,' said Carey, and she sat back in the seat. 'I won't say another word.'

They passed the remainder of the short journey in silence. The driver gave Ben a sympathetic look as Carey got out of the cab and stalked up to the front door. Her fingers trembled as she tried to put the key in the lock.

'Let me,' said Ben.

'I can do it,' she snapped. 'I'm not helpless, you know.'

'I never said . . . oh, I don't care any more!'

He waited until she eventually got the front door open and followed her inside. She kicked off the Perspex shoes and went into the kitchen, where she opened the fridge and took out a bottle of sparkling water. Her fingers trembled as she tried to unscrew the top and it took her ages to open it. She drank the water in three large gulps as she listened to the thud of Ben's footsteps on the stairs.

169

She knew that she was still angry and still upset. But more than that she was scared. Scared that she'd made a monumental mistake in marrying a man she didn't even know. Scared that his friends were right about him. She wasn't sure how she should tackle this, what she should say. But she knew that she wanted to sort things out tonight.

She waited until her breathing had calmed down and the trembling in her hands had eased a little before she followed Ben upstairs. He was lying in bed, his clothes a jumble on the floor.

'Ben,' she said sharply. 'Are you awake?'

The sigh from beneath the covers was gargantuan. 'I'm tired.'

'We have to talk about this.'

'No, we don't.' His words were muffled by the sheets.

'We do, Ben. This is a major problem.'

'Oh, for God's sake!' He pushed the bedclothes down and looked at her. 'What is it with women? Why do you all overreact so bloody much? You want to fight with me, box me into a corner, get me to admit to something that's not true. I'm not trying to figure out everything about your past and I don't need you trying to over-analyse mine. I didn't think you were like this, Carey. I thought you had more sense than stupid women who spend their lives obsessing about the tone of voice that their boyfriends use to them. I thought you were different.'

'Different in that I don't care if you start getting down to it with an ex-girlfriend?' demanded Carey. 'Different in that it might not bother me that you'd only just left her bed before you hopped into mine? That kind of different?'

'And I suppose you led this life of perfect purity before you met me?' said Ben. 'I suppose there's nobody in your past who might come crawling out of the woodwork and up the garden path?'

Carey looked at him in horrified silence. Peter Furness, she thought. Had he seen her with Peter Furness? Did he know that she'd met him for lunch? Was he thinking the same kind of thing about her and Peter as she was thinking about him and Leah?

'I had a boyfriend before you,' she said. 'Peter. But we'd split up long before I went to New York. It's over between us. Completely over. And I didn't invite him to our wedding party. Of course,' she added, 'I didn't get the chance because your bloody sister did the guest-list and I'm sure she was only allowing exes from one side of the family.'

'You told me about someone called James,' said Ben. 'You never mentioned anyone called Peter.'

Carey winced. She'd forgotten her original decision not to tell him about Peter.

'But if this non-person Peter had been at the party you wouldn't have kissed him either?' continued Ben.

He couldn't have seen us together, thought Carey miserably. Nobody saw us together. It would've been impossible because we were hidden by the huge lilac bush near the gate. And even if Ben had somehow seen her kiss with Peter Furness he could hardly get upset about it. It had been a totally different sort of kiss to his clinch with Leah. She knew it had. It had been a farewell kiss and Ben's had been something else entirely. So she wasn't going to give him the satisfaction of even talking about Peter.

'He wasn't at the party so it's a hypothetical question,' she said eventually.

'Fine,' said Ben. 'Let's ignore the fact that you've just lied to me.'

'I haven't.'

'I saw you. You went outside to meet him. And you've lied about it. But you're the one trying to make me appear in the wrong,' said Ben. 'Don't even try to pretend it didn't happen. I saw you. I assumed the man in question was probably your last boyfriend. James, as you'd told me. But, hey – James, Peter – who cares.'

Carey felt as though he'd hit her with a brick. She rubbed her hands over her eyes and smudged her mascara across her cheeks.

'He turned up. There was nothing I could do. I went outside after a particularly horrible encounter with your ex-fucking-girlfriend because I couldn't bear to be in the same building as her.'

'And he just happened to be there?'

'Lame as it sounds, yes.'

'So it's OK for you to have a perfectly good reason for meeting and kissing an ex-boyfriend – and for lying about it – but not for me to kiss Leah and tell the truth about it.'

'It depends on the type of kiss,' said Carey furiously. 'And from all accounts yours was a very different type of kiss.'

171

'You're being silly.'

'No, I'm not.'

'You want to make me appear as some kind of sex maniac.'

'Your so-called friends think you are.'

'Which friends?'

She said nothing. She wasn't going to tell him about the overheard conversation. It would be too humiliating.

'What are you then?' she asked instead.

'An ordinary bloke who's had too much to drink and who wants to get to sleep and would it be too fucking much to ask you to shut up right now?'

'Yes, it bloody would!' cried Carey. 'I don't believe what I'm hearing.'

'And I didn't believe what I was seeing when you decided to display your boobs for all and sundry,' said Ben. 'But I didn't throw a complete wobbler about it.'

'Oh!' Carey realised that she had actually just stamped her foot. She'd always believed that it was just a turn of phrase but she was so angry that that was exactly what she'd just done. 'You're utterly impossible! I can't believe I married you.'

'I can't believe I let you,' muttered Ben and then pulled the covers over his head again.

She stared at his inert body beneath the sheets and realised that she was literally shaking with rage. She picked up Ben's shoe from beside the foot of the bed and threw it at him.

'What the hell are you doing?' He sat up.

'You're a pig!' she cried. 'You don't care about me. Your friends knew what they were talking about. You never cared about me.'

'Damn right,' yelled Ben. 'You sure hid your true colours in New York.'

'Not as well as you hid yours.' She picked up the second shoe and aimed it at him. Ben ducked and it hit the wall behind his head, leaving a black mark on the white paint.

'You need therapy,' said Ben coolly.

'Therapy wouldn't even help you!' cried Carey.

'Stop throwing things round the place, get into bed and shut up.'

'No.' Carey was too angry to consider sleeping. She stomped out of the bedroom and slammed the door closed behind her.

Ben snorted and pulled the duvet over his head again.

Freya sighed with relief as she and Brian walked into her apartment. She'd left the heat on while they were out and it was blissfully warm.

'Would you like a coffee?' she asked.

He shook his head. 'I don't need the caffeine to fight with the alcohol,' he said. 'Let's just get into bed.'

He ambled into the bedroom and got undressed while Freya removed her make-up in the bathroom. By the time she joined him in the bedroom Brian was asleep. Although he lay on his back he didn't snore and Freya (remembering that her mother had always complained about her father's snoring) mentally congratulated herself on finding a non-snoring man. Although he's not mine, she murmured, as she slid into bed beside him. I'm not his and he's not mine. Though you'd never guess it, she mused. We're as bad as any old married couple with him falling asleep before I even get into bed. Not to mention the fact that we don't make love every single time he stays here. Surely we should be gagging for it every night? Brian rolled over and Freya turned with him so that his back spooned into her front. She put her arm round him and held him closer. There was more to love than having sex every night. And yet . . .

She'd always thought that there was more to Ben and Leah's relationship than the fact that they slept together. Even after their break-ups and subsequent relationships she'd always felt that they'd get back with each other because what kept them together was greater than the brief thrill of something new. Whenever she talked about Leah to Ben he referred to her proprietorially, as though he was simply biding time before marrying her. And then he'd gone off and married someone else instead. Even if he had subsequently done something extremely stupid and kissed Leah again.

Freya felt an uncomfortable rush of perspiration envelop her as she thought of Brian dumping her to marry someone else. She'd been going out with him for three years and it was supposed to be an exclusive relationship, but what if it wasn't? What if he secretly hungered after whatever it was that Ben had hungered after? What if he left her?

The prickles of sweat were at the roots of her hair. How would I

173

feel, she asked herself, if Brian went off and married someone else? Someone who wasn't as argumentative and picky and irritating as she was. Freya knew that she was all these things, because both Brian and Ben had told her that in the past. And she knew that she liked to do things her own way and have plenty of time to herself and that she wasn't as bubbly and outgoing as Carey seemed to be. Or as beautiful and sensuous as Leah either. So why, she wondered, did Brian stay with her? Simply because finding someone else would be too much trouble? And what if he suddenly decided that he wanted children? She bit her lip. The only time the subject of children had come up he'd seemed uncomfortable about it and she'd been dismissive anyway. But what if he now felt ready for a family? She shuddered. She wasn't sure about children and she knew that it would be more difficult for her to conceive given her age. Not only her age, she reminded herself. Her damned hit and miss cycle wouldn't help either. Thinking of her irregular cycle made her realise that she was late again this month. In fact, she realised, her eyes snapping open, she was very late. She felt herself begin to sweat again.

Not pregnant, she thought wildly. That would be too much. That might actually frighten him away because, sure as fertilised eggs were fertilised eggs, he wouldn't want to be confronted by an unplanned pregnancy. Brian, the banker, planned everything with total precision. So if she announced that she was up the spout he'd probably bolt, leaving her aged forty and a single first-time mother!

She crept out of the bed and into the bathroom. Despite the fact that she reckoned she was one of the most infertile women on the planet she had a pregnancy testing kit. Just in case. As far as she was concerned, the kit was a far more effective talisman against getting pregnant than any real method of contraception. She knew that the middle of the night when her alcohol content was high wasn't the ideal time to do the test. But according to the indicator she wasn't pregnant. Deep down she'd known that she wasn't, but she wondered if it mightn't be a good idea to have a check-up to see whether or not she was so run down that her cycle was getting even worse. She didn't feel run down and she took supplements to keep herself fit, but running the shops was stressful and the last few weeks had been the most stressful of all.

174

She got into bed again and this time Brian turned to her and put his arm round her.

'Are you all right?' he asked.

'I thought you were asleep,' she whispered.

'I dozed off,' he admitted. 'I didn't mean to. I wanted to be awake when you got into bed and then when you got out again I realised that I'd been sleeping. Sorry.'

'It doesn't matter.' She snuggled closer to him.

'It does,' said Brian. 'We can't talk when I'm asleep.'

'What d'you want to talk about?' she asked.

'I was thinking this evening,' said Brian.

'Man thinks!' Freya giggled. 'Headline news.'

'Shut up.' He pulled her closer to him. 'I was thinking when I saw Ben and Carey together that it was something we should do.'

'Have a row?' asked Freya.

'No.' Brian laughed. 'Get married.'

'What?' Freya sat upright in the bed.

'Come back to me.' He pulled her gently down until her forehead was touching his. 'I think we should get married.'

'Why?' she asked.

'Because it's a statement,' said Brian. 'Because I love you, Freya. I've got to admit that I've enjoyed our life together until now but tonight – well, I felt there should be something more. I want people to know that we're a couple.'

'People do know we're a couple. And I told Ben we were happy the way we were,' she said.

'When?'

'When he asked me if we'd ever think of getting married.'

'He asked me that too,' said Brian.

'And you said?'

'That you didn't like talking about it.'

'I couldn't see the point.'

'But there is a point,' said Brian. 'I want people to know how much I love you. I want us to be together every night, not just at weekends. I want us to be a family.'

'I never knew you felt like that.' She kissed him gently on the lips and he pulled her tighter to him so that their bodies touched in all the right places. He stroked the inside of her thighs until

175

she moaned with pleasure and then he slid into her, easily and smoothly, beginning an easy rhythm which she matched. And as their lovemaking grew more intense she knew beyond a shadow of a doubt that she loved him more than she'd ever loved anyone, and that being with him was the most important thing in her life. And, she told herself, it was good to know that they could still have knock-out sex together. Even if they were as comfortable as an old married couple already.

Chapter 14

Cardamom

Good for fighting fatigue, this oil is warm and spicy

C arey handed over the Lufthansa evening flight to the tower and turned her attention to the Iberia craft which was fourteen miles from touchdown and next in line to land. She rubbed her eyes. Two days after the party she still had a thumping headache and a churning feeling in her stomach. She blinked, looked at the radar screen again and frowned.

'Iberia 543, Dublin, fourteen miles from touchdown, descend two thousand feet. Report indicated airspeed.'

'Dublin, Iberia 543, descend two thousand feet. Indicated airspeed two hundred and twenty knots.'

Carey rubbed her eyes again. The damn Iberia plane was in danger of catching the Lufthansa flight in front of it. She spoke into the mike, her voice calm. 'Iberia 543, Dublin, roger. Reduce speed to one hundred and eighty knots.'

The pilot acknowledged and Carey flexed her fingers as she watched the plane slow down on the radar. But she already knew it wasn't enough.

'Iberia 543, Dublin. You're catching the number one. Reduce now to one hundred and sixty knots.'

'Dublin, Iberia 543, roger. Reducing now to one hundred and sixty knots.'

Carey watched the blips. The minimum separation distance between aircraft was five miles. She had to maintain this separation until touchdown. At this rate, she knew she wouldn't. 'Iberia 543,

Dublin. Report visual with the number one traffic – six miles ahead.'

'Dublin, Iberia 543. Negative visual contact.'

She realised that she was holding her breath but when she spoke again the tone of her voice was unchanged. 'Iberia 543, Dublin, roger. Reduce immediately to minimum approach speed.'

The pilot's tone was equally calm. 'Iberia 543, Dublin, roger. Reducing to minimum approach speed.'

Fuck, she thought, as she watched the radar. Fuck, fuck, fuck.

'Iberia 543, Dublin, you're still closing too quickly on the number one traffic. I'll have to break you off the approach. Turn right heading 010, climb three thousand feet.'

'Dublin, Iberia 543, roger, turn right heading 010, climb three thousand feet.'

She'd laughingly told Ben that she got off on pilots having to do what she told them but this was different. This was her making a complete fuck-up of a straightforward approach simply because she hadn't been concentrating enough. And she hadn't been concentrating enough, because how could she concentrate on anything other than the fact that somehow she and Ben hadn't managed to speak civilly to each other since Thursday. Because her mind wasn't on her job she now had a possibly irate flight crew and a definitely shaken set of passengers who certainly wouldn't have enjoyed a sudden swoop back into the air when they'd been expecting to touch down. It was the first time ever that she'd let her personal life interfere with her work.

She rescheduled the Iberia behind an incoming Aer Lingus flight and this time the approach was perfect. But Finola, who was doing area control and who had realised that Carey had broken off an approach, looked across at her.

'Everything all right?' she asked.

Carey nodded. 'I'm going to take a break,' she said. 'I have a headache.'

The situation with the Iberia flight had made it worse. She waited until Patrick Carragher was ready to take over from her and then trudged to the Piggery. The error had been stupid and basic. Not dangerous, because she'd had time and options. It was part of her job to make time and options so that mistakes didn't turn into anything worse. But it wasn't a mistake that she should have made. Breaking off an approach was an admission of bad control, an admission that she'd failed in what she'd set out to do – and Carey hated failure.

I should be getting used to it, she thought savagely, as she filled her mug with boiling water and dropped a tea bag on top of it. I'm a failure at loads of things. Certainly everything to do with my personal life. I've failed to become a normal person who can have normal relationships with other normal people. And I've failed miserably, utterly and totally, with my marriage. She held the hot cup against her forehead as she thought about her marriage. She'd been trying desperately not to think about it for the past four hours.

After she'd stormed out of the bedroom she'd made herself a cup of coffee, the result of which was to make her feel even more jumpy. She'd sat in the kitchen and wondered whether she was more annoyed with Ben because he'd kissed Leah or because he'd been so blasé about it. And she wondered whether her anger was unjustified because it had been stoked by hearing the half-cut conversation of his mates. All the same, how could he have simply gone to bed and not talked about it? In New York they'd talked all the time, about lots of things. Although obviously not enough about their previous relationships. They'd made a pact (how bloody silly and childish was that, Carey wondered) not to discuss their past partners because Ben had said that nothing in the past mattered. He was wrong. The past always matters. After the party he'd simply refused to discuss anything further with her, had burrowed down under the duvet and clammed up. Guilt, she'd decided. Guilt at loving Leah instead of her. Guilt at having married her. Guilt at just about everything. When, eventually, she'd felt her eyes begin to droop with tiredness, she'd tiptoed up the stairs and, still wearing her white dress, she'd lain down on the bed and fallen asleep.

She didn't wake up until the afternoon (with a filthy hangover and a mouth that tasted of stable scrapings) and Ben had already gone out. He'd left a note on the kitchen table to say that he was at the shop but probably in meetings all day. When he hadn't arrived home by eight in the evening she'd called his mobile and been diverted to his mailbox. She hadn't bothered leaving a message.

It was ten in the evening by the time he got back and, when she'd asked him, tightly, where he'd been he responded that she wasn't his minder and that just because they were married it didn't mean they were chained together. Carey had a horrible feeling in the pit of her stomach that he'd been with Leah. Yet she was reluctant to say anything that might provoke another row and he didn't offer anything else by way of explanation but had sat in the other uncomfortable armchair and had opened the newspaper. She wanted to clear the air, tell him that maybe she'd overreacted the other night, but point out to him that any girl is entitled to overreact when her husband's ex-girlfriend turns up at their wedding party and tries to get off with him again. Especially an ex-girlfriend as gorgeous as Leah. And she wanted to tell him, too, that she regretted having kissed – if you could call it that – Peter Furness too, and for not telling him about it straight away. But she thought that by making the first move she'd appear weak. After all, it was Ben who was really in the wrong.

So she remained silent while he read the newspaper and she said nothing when he eventually folded the paper and told her that he was tired and was going to bed.

She wasn't certain whether he was asleep or not when she went up herself a short time later but he lay on his side, turned away from her, and didn't budge when she got in beside him. She lay in silent fury until she finally fell asleep and then woke up when he got out of bed that morning. She waited for half a minute then followed him downstairs.

'Why are we fighting?' she asked as he filled the kettle.

'I'm not fighting,' he said.

'Of course you are.'

He shrugged. 'I'm giving you time to come to your senses.'

'What?'

'Because you've clearly lost them.'

'For God's sake, it wasn't me who invited a maniac to the party.'

'Nor me.'

'It wasn't me who spent more time wrapped around old lovers.'

'No?'

'No!' she cried.

'So we're conveniently forgetting your bloke.'

'I told you,' she said. 'He showed up. I asked him to leave.'

'Very nicely,' said Ben.

180

'It was nothing.'

'The same kind of nothing as me and Leah?'

'Yes. No. Mine really *was* nothing.'

'So if we take a different attitude then there's no problem at all.' Ben slammed a mug down on the table, shovelled a huge spoonful of coffee into it and poured on the almost boiling water. 'You check out your old boyfriend, I have a brief flirtation with my old girlfriend. Where's the big deal?'

'Oh come on!' She couldn't help yelling at him. 'Take this seriously.'

'I am taking it seriously.' He stirred the coffee vigorously and liquid slopped over the side of the mug and onto the table. 'But I just reckon that we might as well leave it as two wrongs not making a right.'

'Oh, Ben . . .' She was close to tears but didn't know whether they were of rage or unhappiness.

'Look,' he said. 'I was as honest with you as I could be, but you wouldn't have said a word about Peter if I hadn't asked you. If anyone's in the wrong, you are.'

'No,' she said. 'I told him never to see me again. You'll keep on seeing that bitch-woman.'

'Of course I won't. And she's not a bitch-woman.'

'Huh!'

'Carey, you're blowing things so out of proportion as to be unreal. I didn't realise how fucking stupid you were.'

'Don't call me stupid.'

'I'm not staying to listen to any more of this,' he told her. 'I'm playing football today. I'll see you later.' And he dumped the remainder of his coffee into the sink before picking up the kitbag from the kitchen floor and walking out of the house.

She'd shaken with rage after he'd left. She'd spent most of the day shaking with rage. But right now she simply felt sick. Sick that she'd let her feelings interfere with the one thing that she was really good at, the one thing at which she wasn't a failure. Today she'd done something she hadn't ever let happen, even in her early days with an approach rating. Everyone would know about it because the tower would have been ready for the Iberia flight and Finola, as the area

181

controller, had to accept it back under her responsibility until it made the final approach again. But if she hadn't broken off the Iberia approach and hadn't maintained the separation then she'd have had to do a Mandatory Occurrence Reporting form with all the questions that would entail and the horrible black mark on her file. She sighed deeply and took a sip of tea which she immediately vomited into the sink.

'Are you OK?' Finola walked into the Piggery as Carey turned on the cold tap.

'Upset stomach.'

'I wasn't that great yesterday myself,' Finola comforted her. 'Though I'd have thought you'd be over the strawberry-, raspberry- and orange-flavour vodkas by now.'

Carey smiled wanly. 'You'd think. I must be getting old.'

'Nothing else the matter?'

'No,' said Carey.

'You seem a bit distracted today.'

'Maybe I should've stayed out sick.'

Finola grinned. She knew that Carey never stayed out sick. 'You're not pregnant or anything, are you?'

Carey thought she might vomit again at the thought. 'I hope not. I doubt it.' Then she looked ruefully at Finola. 'Well, if I was, the poor thing will be pickled by now anyway.'

'Hopefully not.' Finola laughed.

'Hopefully not pickled or not pregnant?'

'Whichever you prefer,' said Finola.

'Hopefully not pregnant,' said Carey definitely. She took some Nurofen out of her bag and swallowed them. 'But if I am, I guess these'll finish off the poor sucker altogether.'

'You're not pregnant,' said Finola. 'You're just alcoholically poisoned.'

'I must be,' said Carey. 'At the very least.'

The rest of her shift passed without incident and she was able to keep herself together and thoughts of Ben out of her mind. As she drove back to Portobello she rehearsed what she would say to him. She was going to tell him about hearing the guys talking and how much what they'd said had upset her. She was going to explain her doubts

182

about him and their relationship and ask him to understand why she felt as though she was suddenly living with a stranger. And she was going to apologise. She was going to explain, without shouting, about her relationship with Peter Furness. She was going to be as understanding as she possibly could about Leah. She would do all this without yelling at him or provoking another argument. There was no point, she told herself as she waited impatiently at the traffic-lights, in writing off her entire life just because both of them had been pig-headed and foolish. Besides, he'd probably been telling the truth about the kiss. The Leah bitch could have wrapped herself around him and given him very little option. 'Well, OK,' she muttered under her breath, 'he had the option of throwing her across the room, but maybe not under the circumstances.'

She pulled up outside the house and got out of the car. 'No more misery,' she said out loud. 'Positive thinking, positive action, get things back on track. I married him because I love him. He's still the same person I fell in love with. I can fix this because I love him. Everything else is just incidental. What his friends said doesn't matter. They don't really know him at all. He's not that sort of person, I know he's not. I wouldn't have married him if he was.'

But Ben was out. She glanced at her watch to check the time. It was ten-thirty. Where the hell was he? All of the old doubts flooded her mind again. She walked into the kitchen. The message indicator was blinking on the machine.

'Hi, Ben, it's me, Leah. How are you? Look, just wondered if you had time to meet me for a chat? Love you. Give me a call.'

Carey just about made it to the sink before she threw up again.

She didn't have room in her car for all her things. When the boot was jammed she piled as much as she could into the back seat and the passenger seat, but there wasn't enough space for her fifty-two shoe boxes. What the hell, she thought. Maybe she needed to rebuild her shoe collection. She wouldn't miss the ones she was leaving behind. Ben could throw them out if he wanted. She regretted leaving the orange Prada mules but they were very much the season before last and she could manage without them. And she was sorry about abandoning the gorgeous soft leather sandals she'd bought in Milan but the heels needed to be redone on them and she'd never got

183

round to it. She left the Perspex high heels in the middle of the bed. She didn't regret leaving them behind at all.

When she saw the flashing blue light of the police car she panicked and worried that they'd pull her over for not being able to see out of her rear window. But the car sped past her and she breathed a sigh of relief. It would have capped a truly horrible day, she thought, if she'd been pulled over by the cops for driving without due care. Although she wasn't exactly sure what the bookable offence was for driving with thirty-nine boxes of shoes and the entire contents of your life in a silver Audi A3.

She still had a set of keys to the house she'd shared with Gina but she rang the doorbell instead. It was answered by Gina's new house-mate, the tousled-haired Rachel Hickey, who'd clearly got out of bed to answer it.

'I'm sorry,' said Carey. 'I didn't mean to wake you up.'

'What's wrong?' Rachel peered at her sleepily. 'It's nearly mid-night.'

'I know,' said Carey. 'I wondered if I could bunk on the sofa for the night.'

Rachel opened her eyes wide. 'On the sofa? What happened? What's the matter?'

'Anything wrong, Rachel?' Gina walked down the stairs and stopped in amazement as she saw Carey on the doorstep. 'Browne! What are you doing here?'

'Reclaiming my surname and borrowing your sofa,' she said with false brightness.

'What?' Gina stared at her. 'What are you on about?'

'You all kept calling me Browne even though I changed my name.' Carey couldn't quite keep the tremble out of her voice. 'But you were right. I was wrong.' A tear slid from her eye and rolled slowly down her cheek. 'I've been an idiot, Gina. A complete idiot.'

'Come in.' Gina almost dragged her into the hallway. 'What's wrong, Carey? Tell me.'

'He doesn't love me.' Suddenly the tears were streaming down her face and there was nothing she could do to stop them. 'He doesn't love me and he probably never loved me and it was only bloody sex after all.'

'Oh, Carey!' Gina put her arm round her friend's thin shoulders. 'He does love you, I'm sure he does.'

'If he loved me, then why were all his pals laughing and joking about the fact that he might have a bit of rough and tumble with other women but he always goes back to Leah. And why did he practically make love to the bitch on the night of our wedding party?' Carey scrabbled fruitlessly in her pocket for a tissue and finally took the piece of kitchen roll that Rachel handed her.

'He didn't!' exclaimed Gina. 'He couldn't have.'

'He did.' Carey gulped. 'We argued about it like crazy. And I think he's spent the last couple of days with her too. I hardly saw him yesterday, he came home really late. And he went playing football this morning but he wasn't home when I got back. So where the hell is he?'

'Did you ring him to find out?' asked Gina.

'I didn't need too.' Carey blew her nose noisily. 'There was a fucking message on the answering machine from the bitch.'

'Oh, Carey!' This time it was Rachel who put her arm round her. 'What a complete and utter bastard.'

'I didn't think he was,' Carey sobbed. 'I really didn't. I thought this was the real thing. I'm a fucking idiot. I wouldn't recognise the real thing if it walked through the door carrying a placard.'

'Maybe there's some explanation.' Gina sounded doubtful.

'The explanation is that he did something really daft by marrying me when he's clearly still in love with that bitch Leah.'

'But why would he marry you if he was still in love with her?' asked Gina. 'It doesn't make sense.'

'Because he's as much of an idiot as me,' cried Carey. 'Both of us thought we were made for each other but clearly it was just being away and great sex and all of the kind of things that happen on holiday romances, only I didn't realise it was a holiday romance because it was New York and five degrees below.'

'Perhaps you just need to talk things through,' suggested Rachel.

'I wanted to bloody well talk things through,' said Carey. 'I was all ready to. I'd decided what I was going to say. I was going to be calm and sensible and forgiving. But he wasn't there. And I wasn't going to hang around because he's fucked with me for too long already.'

She took another piece of kitchen towel from Rachel and blew her

185

nose noisily. 'I nearly had a loss of separation today because of him,' she said. 'I wasn't thinking straight. Me! I always think straight, you know that, Gina. I had to break off an Iberia approach because I was worried about my love-life. Nobody has ever made me do something like that before. Not even Peter Furness. And God knows, I was pretty cut up about him . . .' Her voice trailed off. She hadn't told Gina about Peter's arrival at Oleg's and Ben's reaction to that. But Peter was irrelevant in the whole thing. It was Leah who was the real problem.

'I'm so sorry,' said Gina sincerely. 'You both seemed in love. Really you did. And your party was great.'

'Great for him,' sniffed Carey. 'He was obviously thinking of shagging both of us.'

'Oh Carey, I don't think so.' Gina shook her head. 'He's not that sort of person.'

'Well, if he's not, why am I here?' asked Carey blankly and Gina couldn't think of a single word to say.

Chapter 15

Coriander

Spicy but sweet, this is a stimulating oil which helps combat lethargy

Carey had never slept on the sofa before. Other people had, of course – friends who'd crashed out at their place, boyfriends who hadn't quite made it to the sharing the bedroom stage yet, or even boyfriends with whom there'd been a row and who were thrown out of the bedroom but not the house. She hadn't realised how uncomfortable the sofa was – it was too short to stretch out on completely and too narrow to roll over with ease. She was totally unable to sleep so that when her phone rang at eight o'clock she jumped on it straight away.

'What's all this about?' asked Ben.

'I thought I made it perfectly clear,' she said.

'You made it perfectly clear that you're acting like a child,' he told her.

'I'm not.'

'Yes, you are. Normal people work things out. They don't go running off at the first sign of trouble.'

'I wanted to work things out but you didn't give me much option, did you?'

'Of course I did.'

'No, you didn't. You argued with me and you went off to football and God only knows where afterwards – probably to that cow since you can't seem to keep your hands off her – and you didn't give me a chance.'

'I see from the letter that chances aren't high on the agenda.'

'What's the point?' she asked wearily. 'It was a mistake. All of it.'

'And you discovered that when? After you made out with your ex-boyfriend?'

'No, after you practically shagged your ex-girlfriend in front of everyone,' she snapped. She rubbed her forehead. She couldn't believe that they were fighting again. She'd written the letter so that they wouldn't fight again:

Dear Ben,

We had a great time in the States but it's obvious that what worked over there just isn't working here. We didn't think about things enough before we got married and we certainly didn't think about the effect it would have on everyone back home. I like you very much but if I live with you any longer I'll end up hating you. I've never rowed so much with anyone in my life before. So the best thing is to call it a day before we get ourselves in any deeper. I'll check out the divorce situation – maybe we can get the marriage annulled or something. But there's no point in sticking together. Besides, you're a southsider and I'm not. I have too much stuff for your house. Anything I left behind you can throw out. Sorry I messed up your life. I hope you and Leah will be really happy together. I hate the bitch but I'm sure she has some good qualities.

Sincerely,

Carey Browne

She'd had to start over a couple of times because her tears had dripped onto the page and smudged the words. The finished note had been stain-free.

'What was wrong with my letter?' she asked. 'I thought it was sensible.'

'You want a divorce?'

'It's best, isn't it? You're obviously still besotted by that bitch-woman. I can't see that we have much of a chance under the circumstances.'

'Look, Carey, let me explain to you about Leah.'

'I don't want to hear some stupid explanation about how you've been friends for years!' snapped Carey, suddenly aware that Rachel and Gina had woken up and were standing in the doorway. 'And I don't want to hear about how snogging the face off her while your hands were planted firmly on her ripe little buttocks at our wedding party was just a companionable gesture on your part.'

'OK, that never happened,' cried Ben. 'Think about the kiss you had with your ex-boyfriend. That's what it was like. And did I scream and yell at you and start throwing shoes at you over it? No, I didn't.'

'You fight differently,' said Carey.

'Leah's a close family friend and she might have her faults – yes, she does have her faults – but I can't just close the door on her.'

'Because you always go running back.'

'Pardon?'

'That's what she told me. That's what everyone thinks! You love 'em and leave 'em. You have loads of girlfriends but then you always go back to her. What would make it different this time? Nothing!'

'I'm sorry,' said Ben. 'I told you I was sorry. You never apologised for the Peter bloke.'

'I wasn't still sleeping with him when I met you. You were still sleeping with her. You didn't tell me anything at all about her when you asked me to marry you.'

'That was a mistake.'

'You're damned right it was a mistake,' cried Carey. 'The whole fucking thing was a mistake – and you know the worst part of it all is that everyone I know is going to look at me and say "I told you so!"'

'The worst part of it is that you're behaving like an idiot,' said Ben.

At this, Carey felt her composure begin to slip and tears well up. Gina, watching her, rushed across the room and grabbed the mobile phone.

'Fuck off out of her life, you miserable bastard!' she yelled and pressed the end button. She looked at Carey. 'Are you all right?' she asked.

Carey stared at the silent mobile phone. 'I think so,' she said eventually.

She wanted to be left alone but Gina and Rachel didn't let her out of their sight. They made her eat breakfast even though she wasn't hungry and they made her watch TV with them for the rest of the

189

day even though she hadn't a clue what she was actually watching. And they plied her with stories of what shits men were, and why they weren't worth the tears, and how it was better that she find out about him now rather than later. And then Gina said, once again, that she hadn't thought he was like that but maybe all those good-looking blokes were the same, and perhaps it was just as well she was engaged to a plug-ugly like Steve. Carey was grateful for their concern but she pretended that she was out for the count on Monday morning when she heard them having breakfast in case they started sympathising with her again. She pulled the spare duvet they'd given her over her head because she really didn't want to talk about it any more. And then, after they'd gone to work, she finally fell into a deeper sleep than she'd imagined possible and didn't wake up until after midday.

For a moment she forgot that she was on the sofa in Gina's house and she reached out for Ben to pull him close to her. When she realised he wasn't there she had to fight to hold back the tears that threatened to fall again. She couldn't believe that reaching for him had become so automatic so quickly. Nor could she believe how empty she felt now that it was over. She tried not to remember the warmth of his arm around her as they stood on Ellie's balcony their first night together; or his boyish grin when she appeared at the Chapel of Everlasting Love in her trailer-trash dress or even the way he'd carried her multiple bags of Macy's shopping through the snow-filled streets of New York. She didn't want to remember the things about him that she'd loved so much when none of it had meant anything to him.

She rubbed her eyes then got up. After a searingly hot shower in which the sting of the shampoo in her eyes made them water again, she dried her hair and then dressed in the most stylish pair of trousers she could find, a plum-coloured cashmere jumper and a pair of soft black leather boots she'd bought in Paris. She wasn't going to look pale and drawn and victimised simply because her marriage had gone down the toilet. She wasn't after sympathy and understanding. Maude had always told her that it was important to look good if you wanted to feel good. Carey hadn't taken her words to heart in the same way as Sylvia had but she knew that her mother was right. If she dressed the way she felt now – sad and tired, despite the unexpected

190

sleep – she'd continue to feel sad and tired. This way she could show her best face to the world. Not that anyone could see her face when it was hidden by her shock of hair which so badly needed to be cut. She spent ages combing it back, trying to pin it close to her head and keep the riot of curls under control. She was going to go shopping and then she was going to go to work, and she was going to forget all about Ben Russell and his stupid girlfriend and his chilly sister, and get on with her own life again. And the next time she met someone on a plane she wouldn't exchange a single word with them.

She was halfway through her shift when the pilot of the incoming British Airways flight radioed that his cabin crew suspected that one of the passengers was having a heart attack and he needed a priority approach. She looked at the pattern of aircraft on her radar. The flight was due in third. She couldn't slot it into the next approach, the first aircraft was too close to the airport for that, but she could make it second.

'Ryanair 168, Dublin,' she told the aircraft which had previously been scheduled second. 'You're now number three for approach due to aircraft with medical emergency. Turn right heading three hundred and sixty. Stop descent four thousand feet.'

'Dublin, Ryanair 168, roger. Turn right heading three hundred and sixty. Stop descent four thousand feet.'

Carey then advised the tower and the station manager about the emergency so that relevant people – especially the ambulance crew – would know what was happening while she ensured that the first aircraft was established on the airport's localiser and ready to land.

'Speedbird 156, Dublin,' she said to the pilot with the emergency on board. 'The ambulance has been called and will be awaiting your arrival on stand. Please advise the seat number of the sick passenger.'

She waited for his response. In the meantime her headphone crackled.

'Shamrock, 156, Dublin roger. Eight miles from touchdown. Cleared ILS approach Runway Two Eight. Contact tower 188.6. Bye.'

At least that was the first aircraft out of the way, she thought. Her headphone crackled again and she adjusted it. Loose connection, she thought. Must get a new set.

'Dublin, Speedbird 156, the patient is in seat 11C.'

Jennifer O'Carroll was in the tower. Carey let her know the seat row number and then turned her attention to the Ryanair plane which had been shifted back in the landing order. She could bring him a little lower and a little closer now, keeping him to the east of the airfield. He acknowledged her instructions to descend to 3,000 feet and turn.

'Dublin, Speedbird 156, now established on localiser.'

Excellent, she thought. 'Speedbird 156, Dublin, roger. Nine miles from touchdown. Cleared ILS approach Runway Two Eight.'

'Dublin, Speedbird 156. Tower 118.6. Bye. Thanks for all your help.'

'You're welcome,' said Carey. 'I hope it works out OK.'

She thought, briefly, of the sick passenger and crossed her fingers for him or her. Then she got on with the business of doing what she was good at. The only thing she was good at. Landing planes.

Ben was having a nightmare day. On the list of bad days he'd ever had, this was in pole position. He couldn't think of a single thing that had gone right, starting with rereading Carey's note which he'd retrieved from the bin where he'd thrown it after talking to her on Sunday. He'd been shocked when he first read it when he got home on Saturday night. He'd been wary about going home, not wanting to face another row with her. He hated rows and only knew one approach – shout back louder. It had worked for his father; his mother always clammed up whenever Charles raised his voice. It had worked with Leah too although they'd rarely had the kind of slanging match he'd had with Carey. But whenever they'd argued and he raised his voice, she'd instantly cave in and wrap her arms round him allowing her perfumed hair to sweep across his face. He knew where he was when he rowed with Leah. But not with Carey. And he'd believed that he was better off out of the house until both of them cooled down. He wasn't sure what he'd expected when he slid the key into the lock but it hadn't been her clearly unhappy but very definite letter. Still clutching it he'd gone upstairs and seen the Perspex shoes sitting on the bed and the white dress still hanging on the chrome rail. He'd been furious with her then and had considered putting her stuff into a black refuse-sack and throwing it into the skip at the end of the road. But he didn't. He went to bed and slept fitfully. So when he woke up, still tired, the shoes were on the floor beside the bed, the dress beside them where he'd flung it in a fit of rage.

He'd called her as soon as he woke and she'd been angry and then that horrible friend of hers had told him to fuck off and he'd waited for Carey to ring him back and apologise but she hadn't. He considered that she had as much apologising as him to do. He'd seen her talking to that bloke and he'd seen the intimacy of the fleeting kiss between them and he'd waited for her to tell him about it but she hadn't and he'd had to confront her with it. Still angry, he'd gone out and bought the papers and spent the entire day in the pub – something he'd never done in his life before. It had been after six when he'd arrived home again and he'd simply passed out in the uncomfortable armchair so that when he woke up that morning, every bone in his body ached.

It was then that he'd noticed the message light blinking on his machine and hit play. The most recent message was from Freya, telling him about a meeting she was going to. But the message before that was the one from Leah asking him to ring her and he'd erased it before finding out when she'd actually called. He was uncomfortably sure that if Carey had listened to it that there was no way she'd believe that his relationship with Leah was over. Right then, he wasn't sure about it himself.

He'd been due to open the Drumcondra shop that morning but had got stuck behind a jack-knifed lorry on Camden Street and the ensuing gridlock made him almost an hour late. The knock-on effect was that he'd spent the day rushing round the store trying to catch up with himself and failing miserably. Because he hadn't been in time to re-stock some of the shelves, he couldn't find all the things that the customers wanted; he managed to lose a raft of brochures on a new vitamin tablet which they were promoting heavily and which had an entry form for a very popular competition; he snapped at Laura, the sales assistant, dropped a glass jar containing bronzing beads on the floor and faxed three incorrect orders to one of their suppliers.

Now, back in Rathmines, he closed the door of his office and stared unseeingly at the graphs on the computer screen in front of him.

'What?' He looked up as the door opened and Freya walked in.

'That's a lovely way to talk,' she said as she perched herself on the corner of his desk.

'Shut up, Freya.' He scrolled down the screen. 'I'm not in the mood.'

'No, I guess not,' she said.

'And why do you guess that?' he asked.

'Only I believe that there's trouble in Paradise.'

'What?' He looked up at her.

'Brian told me,' she said.

'Told you what?'

'Oh, for God's sake, Ben, he told me about you and Leah and the fact that Carey found out that the two of you had been kissing and canoodling at Oleg's. What the hell did you think you were doing?'

'Bet he didn't tell you that Carey slipped outside to meet her old boyfriend and was kissing him too?'

'Ben!' Freya stared at him. 'You're joking.'

'Why should I be joking? Why should it be believable that I jumped on Leah but not believable that Carey jumped on someone else?'

'She didn't, did she?'

'I saw her.'

'Is that why she came rushing into the dining room that night?' asked Freya. 'I knew there was something wrong, but Brian told me about you and I supposed that was it.'

'It seems that both of us had unfinished business in our past,' said Ben.

'And now what?' asked Freya.

'I don't know,' said Ben. 'She's moved out.'

'Oh Ben, no!'

'Freya, she can't stand the sight of me and, to be honest, I'm not too fond of her right now either. You were right about the whole thing. I was stupid to think it would work. Surely it's better that we cut our losses now than wait and make things worse.'

'I guess so, but . . .'

'Don't tell me you liked her.' He laughed bitterly. 'You didn't want to know her at first.'

194

'It's not a question of liking or disliking her,' said Freya. 'It's just – it's a mess, Ben. An absolute mess.'

'I know,' he said. 'It's the way I am. Hopeless.'

'You're not hopeless.'

'Must be.' He shrugged. 'Certainly I'm not good with women, am I?'

'Other than Leah.'

'You see?' He shrugged again. 'It always comes back to Leah. Which should suit you, Freya, since you're her friend.'

'I'm your sister,' said Freya. 'And your happiness is more important to me than Leah's.'

'How sweet.'

'Ben Russell, don't sound so – so childish.'

'Sorry,' said Ben. 'I've a lot on my mind.'

'Don't you want to work it out?' asked Freya. 'With Carey?'

He shook his head. 'She said it was great in New York but awful once we got home. She was right. It was a stupid, stupid thing and I don't know how we could possibly have imagined it'd work.'

'Maybe . . .'

'Maybe nothing,' said Ben. 'In fantasy land, marrying someone you don't know might end happily ever after. But not in real life. In real life it's messy and horrible and the sooner we get it over with the better.'

'But Ben, you can't just give up—'

'She's given up,' said Ben starkly. 'She thinks it was all a terrible mistake and she's probably right.' He smiled lopsidedly at Freya. 'Everyone who thought it was a terrible mistake was right. Maybe I was just being pig-headed in thinking that everyone else was wrong.'

'Oh, Ben.' Freya put her arms around him.

'OK, OK.' His voice was muffled. 'I know you care but you're smothering me.'

'If there's anything I can do,' she said as she released her hold.

'Don't worry. I'll let you know.'

Although she wanted to tell Ben about Brian's marriage proposal, Freya didn't think that this would be a good time. Instead she picked up a sales report and looked through it, then she read and re-read leaflets about a new herbal ice gel until finally Ben asked her if she wouldn't mind leaving his office because he was trying to get some work done.

'Why work now?' asked Freya. 'You surely can't be in the mood.'

'What else would I do?' Ben hit the save button on his computer. 'The alternative is sitting at home and contemplating what kind of idiot I've been.'

'I suppose so,' said Freya. 'Only, Ben – yes, you were an idiot but – well, at least you did it.'

'What d'you mean?'

'You met this girl and you fell for her and you married her, and OK it was mad and crazy, but maybe sometimes we all need to be mad and crazy.'

'The trouble with that,' said Ben as he opened a new file, 'is that at some point you have to deal with the consequences of the craziness.'

'I can't help blaming myself,' said Freya.

'Why?'

'I tried to bring you up kind of sensible,' she said. 'Maybe I overdid it. Maybe that's why you did something mad when you got out of my sight.'

He laughed. 'I've been to the States loads of times and never done anything worse than smoke a joint,' he told her. 'I think the problem is that, intrinsically, the Russells aren't exactly mad and crazy people.'

'Maybe.'

'Freya, you did a really good job with me,' he said. 'You were the best sister a bloke could have. If you start blaming yourself then I'll probably end up in therapy for years with the guilt.'

Freya laughed.

'Go home,' Ben told her. 'I want to stay here for a while.'

'Are you sure?'

'Absolutely,' he said as he scrolled down the page and found the stock number he'd been looking for. 'Absolutely.'

Carey stayed with Gina and Rachel for a week before making up her mind. She'd thought long and hard about it the previous evening while she was idly turning the property pages in the newspaper, the

196

pictures blurred because of the tears that welled up when she was least expecting them. She was going to buy a place of her own. She was going to be a proper, independent woman living on her own for the first time in her life.

She'd first considered it as she'd listened to the hum of conversation between Gina and Rachel in the kitchen during the week, aware that the two girls were keeping their voices low so as not to disturb her. She didn't want to stay and mess up their house-share. She didn't even want to do the house-share thing with anyone any more. She was thirty-three years old and it was time for her to take charge of her life. Obviously she thought she'd taken charge of her life when she'd married Ben, but that had clearly been her letting him take charge of it. And, she muttered to herself as she tidied away the duvet and pillow, like all men he'd messed it up beyond belief. Worse even than Peter Furness because this time she'd said the words, she'd told him how much she loved him, she'd really and truly believed in him. None of them were worth believing in. Ever.

She switched on her mobile and waited for a moment in case there was a message alert. She'd half expected one the day after she'd spoken to Ben but he'd clearly taken her (supported by Gina) at her word. Despite the vague hope that lingered at the back of her mind and that she simply couldn't get rid of completely, she knew he wasn't going to contact her. He was obviously going to contact his solicitor instead. She stood undecidedly in the hallway, her finger hovering over Ben's speed-dial number on her phone. Then she shook her head and shoved the phone firmly back into her bag before going out and closing the door behind her.

The development on the outskirts of Swords village had been under construction for quite some time and she'd been aware of it over the past year. It was a mixture of houses and apartments built around either grassed areas or cobbled courtyards. She'd even talked to Gina about buying a place there when the signs had first gone up. But she simply hadn't bothered because making decisions about buying houses or apartments was something that real grown-ups did and she'd never really felt like a grown-up before. She wondered why she suddenly felt grown-up now.

The woman in the sales office was brisk and businesslike. She was the epitome of everything Carey thought a strong woman should be – charcoal-grey trouser suit, sleek black hair, perfectly made-up face. She looked competent. She asked Carey what kind of property she was interested in and then brought her to see the show apartments although, she added as she opened the door, they would be selling these very soon too because almost every property in the development had now been purchased and they didn't need the show apartments any more.

Carey stepped inside the first one and looked around. There was no doubt that the apartment was very well finished and had everything she could possibly want. Underfloor heating, the saleswoman told her, which maximised space. Fitted oven and hob. Fridge-freezer. Washer-dryer. Power shower. Carey walked through the living area and opened the doors onto the small west-facing wooden balcony. The courtyard was divided up by planted areas containing evergreen shrubs and sapling trees which, Carey imagined, would look lovely in a few years' time although, right now, they still looked freshly planted and somewhat uneasy with their surroundings. She turned back into the apartment again and wondered whether she'd feel at ease living here herself. Quite suddenly she thought of Ben's quirky house on the wrong side of the city where she hadn't had the chance to feel at home, and she had to swallow hard to stop the tears forming in her eyes.

She walked out of the apartment and across the hallway to a second one with a slightly different layout. There was someone else looking over it too; as she walked in she could hear the saleswoman giving her efficient pitch about the great location, the proximity to the motorways and the airport, the wonderful open spaces within the development . . . I almost believe her myself, thought Carey, as she walked into the kitchen.

'Carey!' The other viewer had turned as she entered and looked at her in total shock.

'You again.' She was totally shocked herself. How come he kept turning up like this?

'You know each other?' The saleswoman smiled brightly.

'Yes,' said Peter. 'What are you doing here, Carey?'

'Same as you, I suppose,' said Carey. 'Looking.'

The saleswoman slipped out of the apartment and left them alone.

'You've persuaded him to move to the northside?' Peter smiled faintly at her.

She said nothing.

'Sandra and I are selling the house,' he continued. 'We got a really good offer. I didn't think she'd sell, I thought she'd insist on me buying her out, but herself and the whizz-kid are moving away.'

'Moving away?' Carey's eyes widened. 'Where to?'

'Scotland,' said Peter in disgust. 'Apparently he's been offered a three-year contract with a firm there for some ridiculous amount of money and he's asked her to go with him. They'll be heading off at the end of the summer. She doesn't want the hassle of the house.'

'What about Aaron?'

'She's taking my son with her too,' said Peter.

'But surely she can't just do that.' Carey looked aghast. 'There are laws, you know. You could stop her.'

'What's the point?' Peter shrugged helplessly. 'I'd spend a fortune on lawyers, she'd hate me and Aaron would probably end up hating me too. I don't want my visits to him to be marred by fighting with Sandra. If I let her go – well, that way we stay civil, don't we?'

'Oh, Peter.' Carey had to fight the urge to put her arms round him. 'I'm so sorry.'

'I'll get to see him,' said Peter wryly. 'I'll visit him and he can come to me too.' He looked round the apartment. 'That's why I want to get a decent place. So that he has somewhere nice to stay. So that he doesn't think I don't care.'

'You're a nice man, Peter Furness,' said Carey.

'That's what you once thought,' he said. 'But you changed your mind.'

'Not everything you did was nice,' she amended. 'You went out with me and you let me think that you were a single bloke and I don't know when you would've told me if I hadn't asked. And you turned up at my party and scared the living daylights out of me.'

'I'm sorry,' said Peter. 'I know it was wrong. I couldn't help it.' He sighed. 'Anyway, what does it matter now. You've done your thing and I'm – well, I'll get it all back together. Eventually.'

Carey swallowed. 'My thing didn't exactly work out like I expected,' she said.

'Oh?'

199

'In fact, it didn't work out at all.'

He stared at her. 'How exactly hasn't it worked out?'

'We've split up.'

'Already!'

She nodded.

'Carey, not that I don't think this is a good thing, but why?'

'Complicated,' she said.

He looked anxious. 'Was I to blame?' he asked. 'Did he see you talking to me? Did it cause trouble?'

'Not as much trouble as his relationship with his ex-girlfriend,' said Carey.

'Bloody hell.' Peter exhaled. 'I never realised exactly how fast you moved, Browne. Married and separated within a month!'

'OK, Peter, can you not make me feel even more of an idiot than I do already?'

'I'm sorry,' he said. 'I didn't mean to make you feel anything. But surely it's a good thing?'

'Maybe.' She bit her lip. 'Right now I don't really know.' A tear slid down her cheek. She hadn't intended to cry. She sniffed and wiped it away while Peter watched her speculatively.

'So why are you here?' he asked.

'I'm going to buy a place of my own,' she said. 'I've had it with relationships for a while. I'm obviously not destined for the right sort of one.'

'Oh, honey.' He put his arm around her shoulders and hugged her. 'Don't be silly.'

She allowed herself to lean against his body. He held her a little tighter.

'I'm not ready to start seeing people again.' She moved out of his hold. 'Just in case you had some mad notion about you and me.'

He looked abashed. 'Do you still care about him?' he asked. 'Your husband?'

'Right now I don't have a clue how I feel about him,' she said honestly. 'But I sure as hell know that I'll never trust him again.'

Things had worked out better than she expected, thought Carey as she drove to the airport for her shift later that night. After wandering round the apartments in the new development she'd had a word with the saleswoman, who'd given her a price for the first show apartment she'd seen. The price sounded fairly reasonable for a place that was carpeted and furnished (though the furnishing was somewhat sparse; 'minimalist' was the word the saleswoman used) and was ready to move into. It would probably be at least six weeks before all the paperwork was done on their side, the saleswoman said, which had left Carey chewing her lip and wondering where she could stay in the meantime. There was no way she could spend all that time with Gina and Rachel, and her only other alternative was moving back in with her parents – which, as far as she was concerned, was no alternative at all. She hadn't told them she'd left Ben yet. She didn't have the emotional strength to go through it all again.

Then Peter Furness, who'd waited outside while she dealt with the saleswoman, had asked her about her plans and she'd told him that she was buying one of the show apartments but had some problems about where to live in the meantime because there was no way anyone would rent her a place for less than two months.

'Stay with me,' he suggested. 'My house sale isn't due to be completed until the end of April at the earliest.'

'I couldn't do that,' she said. 'No way.'

'Why not?' he asked. 'I've a spare room and it would be nice to have some company.'

She shook her head and told him that she didn't think it was a good idea. And then he said that they were both in a similar position and that it was stupid to let past history get in the way of a sensible arrangement and that, even though he still found her very attractive, he wouldn't so much as look in her direction if she didn't want him to.

'I don't want anyone looking in my direction right now,' she told him bitterly. 'Not you, not Ben, not anyone.'

He said he understood perfectly and that she wasn't to feel under any pressure, but that this was a good solution to her problem and it was the least he could do seeing as he had – according to her – previously broken her heart. And treated her badly, though he hadn't intended to and he was really and truly sorry about that. And maybe he'd even been partly to blame for her current problems, having kissed her outside Oleg's.

'Oh shut up,' she said eventually and then agreed to stay with him.

Gina had looked at her in absolute horror when she'd told her.

'Let me get this straight,' she said. 'You're planning to move in with the man with whom you had a torrid relationship but who conveniently forgot to mention to you that he was, in fact, married with a kid. And you're leaving your husband of less than a month to do it.'

'You're twisting it round,' Carey said. 'I'm staying in Peter's house, sure – but I'm insisting on paying rent, not moving in with him the way you mean. And I'd already left my husband because he's still in love with his former girlfriend.'

Gina grimaced. 'It sounds sort of cut and dried when you put it like that, but it's not that simple, Carey, is it?'

'It's perfectly simple to me,' she said tautly.

'Look, don't you think you should at least talk things through with Ben first?' asked Gina.

'You were the one who took my phone and told him to sod off,' said Carey.

'I know.' Gina looked uncomfortable. 'You looked so upset that I couldn't help it. But surely you don't want to let it go without a fight.'

'Oh, come on!' Carey took off her tiny glasses and rubbed at the lenses furiously. 'I got these vibes from the sister all the time – Ben was practically living with this Leah person before he met me. They all thought he was going to marry her.'

'But he didn't,' Gina reminded her. 'He married *you*.'

'Only because it was easy,' said Carey. 'And it was a mistake.'

'I liked him,' said Gina sadly.

'I thought I loved him,' Carey whispered. 'But I was wrong.'

202

Chapter 16

French Marjoram

This oil is comforting and fortifying, and is a great anxiety reliever

T he thing that Leah liked best about her job was that it gave her time to think. As her fingers gently kneaded the muscles of her clients her mind would often be so far away that she would twitch with surprise if the person lying on the table in front of her moved or sighed and brought her back to reality. Leah thought allowing your mind to wander was an important part of overall wellbeing. Far too many people didn't give themselves time to think.

She was miles away when the girl who had booked the Swedish massage murmured that it would be nice if Leah could really work on her shoulders today. She was totally stressed, she told Leah, since her swine of a boyfriend had broken up with her and was now going out with a girl he'd once told her he hated. 'Traitorous pig,' she muttered, as Leah obliged by digging her thumbs into her muscles. They were all the same, weren't they?

'I guess so.' Leah wasn't sure what the right response should be. In her opinion the bloke had a good reason for leaving the girl. She was irritating and whiny, and Leah could well understand why he might have had enough of her. She worked even harder to make up for thinking such nasty thoughts about someone who was paying her a lot of money to feel better.

'That's so good,' sighed her client.

Leah said nothing. The hushed plainsong that was playing on the CD filled the silence. She felt the girl unwind again, the texture of her skin changing beneath her touch. She loved that moment when

203

she could sense a client move into a different mode, when she could literally feel them loosen under her fingers.

She wondered how relaxed Ben was feeling today. How he was feeling full stop. It was almost two weeks since the party, two weeks since she'd kissed him and only a couple of hours since she'd learned that his wife had left him. Freya had phoned her with the news. Ben's sister had sounded deeply shocked and very angry. She said that she hadn't trusted herself to phone before now.

'You promised,' she told Leah. 'You promised nothing would happen.'

Leah hadn't been able to think of the proper response to that. She was feeling somewhat guilty at how she'd behaved that night. But how the hell was she expected to behave? It was all very well to think she should be calm and accepting about everything, but Ben Russell had bloody humiliated her like no man ever had before. It was all very well too, to tell herself that she could get over him because she'd got over him at least three times already, but the thing was, she didn't want to get over him. As far as she was concerned, Ben was *her* long-term boyfriend. And surely that counted for more than being someone else's short-term husband? Besides, Freya was right – Carey hadn't been anything much to look at, although Leah conceded that there was something striking about the shock of dark curls framing her oval face and lively brown eyes. However, she wasn't beautiful or groomed or elegant in the way Leah knew that she was herself. She simply couldn't understand what Ben saw in her. Besides which, the girl was a bitch. She'd been sharp and sparky in their encounters and not in the least sympathetic to Leah's own plight. At this point Leah stabbed her fingers into her client's shoulders and the girl protested that she wanted to be destressed, not physically hurt. Leah apologised and tipped more oil onto her palms, lightening her touch as she worked along the girl's spine.

So what now? she wondered. Now that the stupid marriage was up in smoke, would Ben come running back to her like he always did? And would she take him back? She smiled slightly. If and when he came running, she'd be the one holding all the cards. And this time she'd play them to her advantage.

Ben hadn't been at an evening football practice since before

Christmas. He pulled the *Herbal Matters* van into the car park near the training grounds and walked out onto the pitch.

'Yo! Ben!' Phil sauntered over and banged his pal on the shoulder. 'I wasn't expecting to see you for another couple of weeks. I didn't think you'd be let out for footie practice so soon.'

'Don't be a fool,' said Ben shortly.

'Sorry for opening my mouth.' Phil looked at his friend in surprise. 'What's the matter with you?'

'Nothing,' said Ben.

'Suit yourself, mate.' Phil picked up a football and began bouncing it on his knee.

'Quit messing.' Ben took the ball mid-bounce. 'I want to stretch my legs.' He dribbled the ball down the pitch, Phil in hot pursuit. Ben approached the open goal and steadied himself just as Phil caught up with him and tapped him on the ankles, causing his shot to drift past the post.

'What a player!' cried Phil. 'A crucial tackle at a crucial moment of the game.'

'Oh, piss off,' said Ben. 'It was a foul.'

'Rubbish.'

'A foul,' Ben repeated. He retrieved the ball and placed it on the penalty spot. Then he kicked it low and hard into the back of the net.

'And he scores!' Phil laughed. 'Deadly from six inches, as my old man used to say.' He grinned at Ben. 'Or does the new Mrs Russell disagree?'

'Who knows,' said Ben.

'What d'you mean?'

Ben hesitated for a moment then glanced back down the pitch to where the other footballers were waiting. 'They're picking the teams.' He tucked the ball under his arm and jogged towards the other players. Phil frowned as he followed him.

Carey sat in the bedroom and looked at the walls. The paper was alive with cartoon characters dancing and jumping and cartwheeling – it made her feel tired just looking at it. But she was in the bedroom that had once belonged to Peter's son, Aaron, and she couldn't expect that a two year old's walls would be papered in gentle pastel

205

shades or that there wouldn't be crayon marks on the window sill and mysterious stains on the bright yellow carpet.

It was quiet in the house. Today was her day off and she was already exhausted. She'd woken far too early that morning, pitching into wakefulness as she had every day since she'd moved in with Peter. She'd heard him getting up, heard the splash of the shower and the buzz of his electric toothbrush. She'd heard him clatter down the stairs and bang the front door behind him and she'd burrowed down beneath the sheets and tried, desperately, to get back to sleep. Only she couldn't. She wondered if she'd ever be able to sleep properly again.

Later she got up and walked around the house in her grey marl pyjamas. She hadn't had the inclination or the opportunity to do it before. She stood in the kitchen and thought how this was the second time in a few short weeks that she'd stood in the kitchen of some bloke's house and looked inside his cupboards for coffee and cups and she felt herself start to tremble. Peter's house – the house that he'd shared with Sandra and Aaron – was very different from Ben's. Even though some of the original pictures or decorations were missing (there were lighter patches on the wallpaper which pointed to things that had been removed) it was clear to Carey that, unlike Ben's, it was a home which had had the input of a woman in its decoration. There were pinks and pastels in some of the rooms, frills in others and an entire ambience of femininity which was completely lacking in Portobello. But, Carey thought moodily as she spooned coffee from a patterned jar into a bright red mug, she'd felt more comfortable in Ben's. The pinks and the frills weren't really her thing.

She spent the day in her pyjamas watching TV, gorging herself on a diet of Oprah, Sally Jesse Raphael, Judge Judy and Australian soaps, and telling herself that no matter how bad her life was, it paled into insignificance beside the insane traumas of Sally Jesse's guests – although she supposed that she could appear in an episode captioned 'My Love Rat Husband Had It Off With His Girlfriend At Our Wedding'. When she heard Peter's car pull into the driveway she disappeared up the stairs and into the room where she now sat, her legs drawn up beneath her chin, her arms wrapped round them.

She didn't want to talk to Peter. She didn't want him to ask her about Ben or what had gone wrong or why she'd left him so suddenly. She didn't want him to look sympathetically at her – Peter was good at the soulful, sympathetic look which, along with his trim and toned body, made him almost irresistible. Really, all she wanted was to disappear off the face of the earth so that she didn't have to talk to anyone ever again.

She blinked away the tears that filled her eyes. She was damned if she was going to cry over Ben or Peter or whoever was making her feel like this. She focused her gaze on her thirty-nine boxes of shoes, trying instead to remember which shoes were in which box, forcing herself to think of things that had nothing to do with the way she felt right now. Her mobile phone rang and she grabbed it.

'Yvette,' she said blankly, glancing at the caller ID as she answered it.

'Hi, Carey.' Yvette was a controller on another team. 'How're things?'

'Fine,' lied Carey.

'I was wondering if there was any chance you could swap shifts with me tomorrow?' asked Yvette. 'I'm on the six a.m. one but I've got a meeting in Roberta's school which I completely forgot about. I'm a bit stuck.'

'No problem.' Carey wasn't due in until the afternoon and she was delighted at the opportunity to get out of the house earlier. She knew that she'd be awake anyway.

'Thanks a million.' Yvette sighed in relief. One of the most difficult things about being a single mother who worked shift hours was trying to remember where she was meant to be at any given moment. It wasn't surprising that sometimes she got things wrong. 'How's married life treating you, Carey?'

'I'll tell you about it another time.'

Yvette frowned but the tone of Carey's voice stopped her from asking any more. 'Thanks again,' she said instead. 'We must get together for a drink sometime soon.'

'Yes, we must.'

When she'd ended the call Carey scrolled through the menu on her phone. She looked at the list of received calls. There weren't that many. Although the word was beginning to spread among some of her friends about her renewed single status, the word was also that she wasn't prepared to talk about it yet. She looked at her list of missed calls. Two from Gina and one from Elena. They'd left messages. She'd already called them back. She dialled her message minder service.

'You have no messages,' the automated voice told her cheerfully.

Carey closed her eyes. She hadn't expected to have messages. She hadn't expected to suddenly see a missed call which she knew she hadn't missed. But she really and truly couldn't believe that, despite what she'd said to Ben and despite Gina yelling at him down the phone, he hadn't once tried to call her again.

She knew that her brother, Tony, would tell her that she was being a typically irrational woman. She knew that when she'd written the note, she hadn't wanted Ben to call. And she knew that she'd still been furious when he did call. When Gina had taken the phone away from her, she'd been half-relieved. But now she was torn about what she really wanted. Falling in love with Ben had been so sudden she was quite prepared to believe that falling out of love could be equally quick. People changed all the time. Not that she'd expected him to change so quickly, but why not? It just meant that she didn't know who she'd married: the Ben of New York and Las Vegas, warm, wonderful and caring, or Irish Ben – womaniser, sullen, kisser of old girl-friends.

Tears welled up in her eyes. Even if she didn't want him back she wished that he'd wanted her. It was hard to accept that none of it had been real. Not his declarations of undying love, not his assurances that Leah meant nothing, not the feeling of completeness she'd felt with him. It had all been in her head; she'd been a bloody fool all over again and when, she asked herself savagely, *when* would she ever learn?

This time she couldn't keep back the tears. They slid down her cheeks and dropped onto the bright yellow quilt. It was difficult to know which was worse, she thought miserably, being a fool or being rejected. The knock at the door startled her and it came again before she answered.

'Yes?' She grabbed a couple of tissues from the box on the bedside locker and scrubbed her eyes.

'You OK?' asked Peter.

'Sure.'

'Can I come in?'

'If you like.'

The door opened and Peter walked in carrying a tray. On it was a big blue teapot, a blue cup, a jug of milk and a plate of warm, buttered toast.

'What's this?' she asked.

'I have the feeling that you're going through a sad and lonely phase,' said Peter. 'I thought this might help.'

She swallowed hard and looked at him tearfully. 'Thanks, but I'm not really hungry.'

'I know,' said Peter. 'When Sandra and I finally split up I went through the not hungry stage, too. I'm sure girls must find it very useful if they're dieting. I lost at least five pounds.'

'I could do with losing at least five pounds.' Carey sniffed.

'No, you couldn't,' said Peter sternly. 'You're not fat, Carey. You're bony.'

'Not thin and bony,' she protested.

'Well, no,' he conceded. 'But you don't need to lose five pounds. You do need to eat properly.'

'You're being very caring,' she told him.

'Not really,' said Peter. He poured tea into the cup and handed it to her. 'I blame myself.'

'Pardon?'

'For you. For what's happened.'

'What on earth are you talking about?'

'Because of me you rushed into getting married to some moron. Because of me you're unhappy again. I'm sorry.'

'It wasn't because of you,' said Carey.

'I feel as if it was.'

She shook her head. 'It was because of me,' she said. 'Because I'm a stupid cow who can't think straight.'

'You're not stupid,' said Peter tenderly. 'You're the cleverest, prettiest, nicest girl I've ever met.'

Carey blinked away the ever-present tears again. 'Don't say things you don't really mean.'

'I'm not. I told you, Carey, it was me who was stupid before. I'm not being stupid now.'

209

She gulped a mouthful of tea. 'You're not trying to get off with me again, are you?'

He grinned. 'It's a bit transparent, I'll admit. But all the best men's magazines encourage us to be nice to women when they're at their most vulnerable. And I do care about you very much.'

'I care about you too, Peter,' she said. 'But I don't want you getting the wrong idea of why I'm here.'

'How could I get the wrong idea?' he asked wryly. 'You've spent all your time holed up in this room.'

'I'm not ready for anything else yet,' she told him. 'I don't want to talk to anyone else either.'

He looked at her appraisingly. 'I love you,' he said.

'Don't.'

'I can't help it.'

'Don't tell me.' She put the cup back on the tray. 'I can't hear it right now, Peter. I really can't. And if you really do feel like that then I can't stay here either.'

'Stay,' he said. 'I shouldn't have said that. I won't in future.'

She swallowed. 'All the same, maybe this isn't such a good idea.'

'It's a fine idea,' said Peter. 'Really, Carey. Stay. It's not for long anyway. And if you want to spend the entire time locked in this room that's OK by me.'

'Thanks.' She smiled bleakly at him.

He opened the bedroom door. 'But feel free to come downstairs any time you want either.'

Her smile was stronger this time. 'Sure.'

She poured herself another cup of tea after he'd gone. As she was about to take the first sip, her phone rang again. She reached out hastily for it and knocked the cup over, the tea spilling across the bright yellow carpet.

'Oh bugger!' she said under her breath as she grabbed some tissues to soak it up while at the same time looking at her phone. 'Double bugger,' she muttered as she realised that it was Sylvia who was calling.

Chapter 17

Eucalyptus

A fresh, stimulating and penetrating oil which is also antiseptic

A week later Sylvia Lynch got out of her green Mondeo and walked up the pathway to her mother's house. She hesitated for a moment before sliding her key into the front door and pushing it open. Then she called out that she was there.

'I'm in the conservatory,' rasped Maude.

Sylvia walked through the house and stood at the conservatory door. Maude was sitting in a wicker chair, a tartan blanket wrapped round her.

'How are you feeling?' asked Sylvia.

'I'm fine,' replied Maude testily. 'I have laryngitis, that's all. I don't even have a cold. Your father insisted on trussing me up before he went out.'

'He worries about you.' Sylvia tucked the blanket more tightly around her mother.

'Will you stop!' ordered Maude. 'I'm perfectly all right and I was only keeping this on me until you arrived so that you could report back to him that I was still wrapped up when you got here.'

Sylvia grinned at her mother. 'You seem to be your usual self.'

'I am,' said Maude. 'Just a huskier version of it.'

'Would you like a cup of tea?' asked Sylvia.

'That'd be nice,' said Maude. She sat back in her chair and listened to the sounds of Sylvia in the kitchen. She really hadn't wanted her elder daughter to call round today; she felt perfectly well even though her voice was a whisper, but Arthur had rung Sylvia because

211

he was due at his weekly chess game and he hadn't wanted to leave Maude on her own. Silly old fool, Maude had thought, as he brought the blanket from upstairs. Fusses far too much though I'd hate it if he stopped.

'What are these for?' Sylvia appeared at the door holding a brightly coloured box.

'Drinking, of course,' said Maude. She made a face. 'Herbal teas. I bought them last month, after meeting that Freya girl. She told me they were excellent.'

'Actually I knew what they were, I just didn't think you were a herbal tea person.'

'I'm not.' Maude suddenly looked angry. 'You can bloody well throw those out, Sylvia. I'm sure *he* drinks herbal teas. Make me a pot of Lyons.'

'Have you been talking to Carey lately?' asked Sylvia when she returned with two mugs of strong tea and sat down beside her mother.

'No,' croaked Maude. 'She came to see us last week but she was so distant . . . I don't really know what to do. You know how she is, Sylvia. She won't talk about it.'

'She was so stupid to get involved with him in the first place!' cried Sylvia. 'We all knew it would end in disaster.'

'Not quite so quickly perhaps,' said Maude.

'No.' Sylvia sighed. 'I can't believe it really. He seemed so nice.'

'True.' Maude looked disappointed. 'I enjoyed talking to him while he was here. And the party was such fun. I haven't had as good a time in years!'

'What about our anniversary night out?' asked Sylvia abruptly. 'You said you enjoyed that.'

'And I did, of course,' Maude rasped hastily. 'It was just that this was so different from anything I'd been at in ages. I really enjoyed myself. I liked talking to him. And his sister seemed really nice.'

'Southsiders,' said Sylvia in her most scathing tone.

Maude laughed painfully and then coughed while Sylvia looked at her anxiously.

'I'm all right,' Maude assured her. 'So have you seen her?'

Sylvia shook her head. 'I'm meeting her for a sandwich at lunchtime, but it took me ages to persuade her.'

212

'Has she said anything about a divorce?'

'Not to me,' said Sylvia, 'but I bet she can get one easily enough. Sure they're hardly even married, are they?'

'I don't know,' said Maude worriedly. 'I just wish that for once she'd think before she did anything.'

'So do I,' said Sylvia. She hesitated and then went on, 'you know where she's living now?'

'She told me she was sharing a house with a friend.' Maude looked anxiously at Sylvia. 'Why? Is there a problem?'

'The friend she's sharing a house with is the bloke she was going out with before she got married.'

'Sylvia!' Maude's voice was somewhere between a squeak and a croak. 'Not the married man!'

'I don't know anything about a married man,' said Sylvia in surprise. 'I know so little about her life that she could be keeping a harem of blokes and I wouldn't have a clue. But if there *was* a married man then she's currently sharing his house.'

'And the wife?'

Sylvia shrugged expressively. 'Who knows.'

'Oh, God.' Maude pressed her fingers against her forehead. 'Where did I go wrong with that girl? I brought her up the same way as I brought you up. I thought I was doing all the right things. How come it's all gone haywire?'

'I don't know,' said Sylvia. 'I do know that she was always hopeless with boyfriends and that she clearly hasn't got any better.' She smiled at Maude. 'But I'll try and find out how things are progressing at lunch.'

'Tell her to call me,' asked Maude. 'If I ring she just says she's busy and puts the phone down.'

'I'll tell her.'

'And be nice to her. Tell her we love her.'

'I'll tell her that too.'

'And tell her not to do anything really silly.'

Sylvia looked helplessly at her mother. 'I think it's a bit late for that,' she said. 'Don't you?'

Carey stood in the huge furniture store at the Airside Shopping Centre and gazed longingly at the dark leather sofa. It was the coolest-looking sofa in the entire shop and she thought that it would look absolutely wonderful in her new apartment. There were still a few weeks to go before the sale of the apartment would finally be complete and she'd be able to move in, but she wanted to get some things now.

Of course, as she told herself, the apartment was already furnished with a perfectly good two-seater sofa and a matching armchair. She didn't need the leather sofa. She couldn't actually afford the leather sofa. But she really, really wanted it. However, she was going to be sensible. She was going to walk away from the sofa and she was going to walk out of this shop and she was going to meet Sylvia for lunch without having done something stupid like buy a totally unnecessary piece of furniture.

'It's lovely, isn't it?' The woman beside her gazed at the sofa too.

Carey nodded.

'Only quite impractical for me,' the woman said. 'My kids would have it destroyed in five seconds. And I know that some salesperson will tell me that leather cleans up great but not after an eight year old with a Pritt Stick and Rice Krispies.'

Carey didn't really care about the woman and her cleaning problems but she nodded again.

'I'd really love to buy it though.' The woman sighed. 'Oh well, can't have everything, I suppose.' She looked around her and yelled at a tousle-haired boy in faded jeans, 'Come on, Ivan. Time to go.'

Carey supposed she could always sell the other furniture. That way she could make back some of the price of the leather piece. She looked around for a sales assistant.

'There's up to eight weeks delivery period on this,' he told her. 'Though we'll get it to you as quickly as we can. It's hugely popular. You could have it in black or white or dark green if you prefer.'

'No, I like this maroon colour,' said Carey as she took out her credit card.

'I bought one myself,' the sales assistant confided. 'I love it.'

'I'm sure I will too.' Carey signed her slip for the deposit price and folded her receipt.

'Our warehouse will be in touch to organise delivery,' said the sales assistant.

'Great.' Carey beamed at him. 'Thanks for all your help.' She left the shop and got into her car. She was late for lunch with Sylvia but she didn't care. She swung into the car park at the Pavilions Centre and hurried inside.

'What kept you?' grumbled Sylvia as they sat down in the café and ordered coffee and sandwiches. 'I was waiting ages.'

'I'm only ten minutes late,' said Carey. 'Sorry. I was buying furniture.'

'Furniture?'

'I've bought an apartment,' said Carey. 'I needed furniture.' She decided not to tell Sylvia that the apartment came ready furnished.

'You've bought an apartment? Where? Have you moved in yet? Honestly, Carey . . .'

'I mentioned that I was getting my own place,' said Carey, 'when I told you I was living with Peter.'

'You told me it was temporary because you were looking at somewhere,' Sylvia said accusingly. 'You didn't say you were buying a place of your own.'

'Time to settle down,' said Carey blithely.

'Oh, for God's sake!' Sylvia looked at her younger sister in frustration. 'Settle down – you? The girl who got married and divorced in a fortnight?'

'I haven't actually got divorced yet,' said Carey.

'Are you sure you even got married?'

'Sod off,' snapped Carey. 'I didn't come here to listen to you lecture me.'

'I'm sorry, I'm sorry.' Sylvia made a face. 'I didn't mean to lecture. I wanted to be caring and understanding.'

'Yeah, right.'

'I did. I do,' said Sylvia. 'Come on, Carey. I worry about you.'

Carey sighed. 'There's no need to worry. I have everything sorted. At least, I will have as soon as the divorce happens and I move into my own place.'

'So you're not in it yet. Where is it?'

'Not far from here,' she said. 'That new development off the main road.'

215

'Oh well, at least that's handy,' agreed Sylvia. 'But in the meantime you're living with a married man with whom you've had an affair.'

'You've been talking to Mum, haven't you?'

'Of course I've bloody well been talking to her. She's worried about you too. She wants you to call her. You're practically the only topic of conversation these days.'

'I suppose.'

'What went wrong, Carey?' asked Sylvia.

Carey was tired of telling people what had gone wrong and she'd already had this conversation with Sylvia when her sister had phoned, breathless and unbelieving, to ask if it was true that she'd walked out on Ben. She shrugged. 'Boy meets girl, boy marries girl, boy gets off with previous girlfriend again, girl realises the error of her ways . . . that's it in a nutshell, Syl, and talking about it over and over won't change it.'

'But couldn't you sort it out?' asked Sylvia. 'I mean, I realise that kissing Leah was a horrible thing to do and all, but maybe, you know, drink taken, all that sort of thing?'

'Maybe we could've if he'd tried,' said Carey, 'but he didn't want to. Besides, I heard things . . . well, it doesn't really matter now. Afterwards I had a nightmare day and I nearly had a loss of separation – can you imagine? Me of all people. It was all his fault and if I stayed with him it would happen again.'

'Carey, you can't blame him because you were distracted at work.'

'Of course I can,' said Carey. 'If I hadn't been so upset I would've been concentrating properly.'

'It wasn't a safety issue, was it?'

'No,' said Carey. 'Even as it was happening I realised my mistake. But I don't make mistakes, Syl. I don't.'

Sylvia raised her eyebrows.

'Not those sort of mistakes,' snapped Carey.

'It's just that you seemed to click,' said Sylvia. 'When you brought him to Mum's for lunch I was ready to hate him. Yet I didn't. And I know I warned you about the whole thing, but I thought that it'd work out, Carey. You were so happy with him.'

'So? I'm always happy when I get a new boyfriend,' Carey shrugged.

216

'This was different,' Sylvia told her. 'It was as if you and he had been together for years. You were comfortable with each other. You—'

'Oh, shut up,' said Carey. 'Look, Syl, I admit I thought that Ben and me were different, I really did. But when it came down to it, we weren't. And all the closeness and sharing and feeling that I had actually known him for years came down to nothing because I didn't ever really know him at all. I didn't want to break up with him, but staying with him would've been even worse.' She exhaled slowly and looked down at the table.

'So what's the story with the married man?' asked Sylvia after a moment's silence.

'I was going out with him and discovered he was married and split up with him.'

'And now you're back with him? In his house? And his wife is . . . where, exactly?'

'Moved out ages ago.' Carey picked at the tandoori chicken sandwich which the waitress had just put in front of her. 'If I'd kept in touch with him, maybe I wouldn't have gone to the States and met Ben.'

'Oh, Carey.' Sylvia looked at her despairingly. 'What on earth are we going to do with you?'

'Nothing,' said Carey angrily. 'I'm fine. I was a bit wobbly for a few days but everything's OK now.'

'I don't think you're OK,' said Sylvia.

'It's difficult to be on top form when you've messed up your life, but I'm getting over it.'

'Fine, fine.' Sylvia shook her head. 'All I'm saying is that you have a habit of doing things on the spur of the moment and if it's a mistake you're too stubborn to admit it.'

'I've admitted my mistake about Ben,' said Carey.

'Not just that.'

'What?'

'Loads of things,' said Sylvia dismissively.

'Rubbish,' said Carey.

They sat in silence while they ate their sandwiches. Carey couldn't decide whether or not she was pissed at Sylvia for calling her stubborn. And for saying that she did things on the spur of the

217

moment. Well, of course she did. Everyone did. There was nothing wrong with acting on instinct.

'I want to tell you something.' Sylvia put the remains of her sandwich on the plate and pushed it to one side.

'Fire ahead.'

'You'll admit that I have lots of experience in the marriage stakes?'

'Without a doubt,' said Carey.

'John and I once went through a bad patch,' Sylvia said.

'I guess if you've been married for half your life to the one person you're bound to hit a bad patch sooner or later,' said Carey lightly.

'A really bad patch,' Sylvia told her, unsmiling.

'Oh?'

'When Jeanne was about ten.' Sylvia stared into the distance. 'It was a difficult time. The kids were really tiring. I was knackered all the time – you know.'

'Well, I don't know,' said Carey, 'but I can imagine. I've read the magazines and listened to the radio programmes.'

Sylvia looked at her wearily. 'Believe me, they only scratch the surface of what it's like. For me, it was awful. I could only think of the kids. My whole day was taken up with them. Bringing them to school. Picking them up. Driving them to ballet or soccer or swimming or whatever bloody thing was on that night.'

'And you and John grew apart because of it?'

'I guess so,' said Sylvia. 'It sounds so predictable, doesn't it? Wife at home with kids; husband has affair.'

'John had an affair!' Carey stared at Sylvia. 'John? You're joking.'

'Don't be facetious,' said Sylvia. 'Of course I'm not joking.'

'Yes, but – John!' Carey couldn't keep the incredulity out of her voice. 'I mean, predictable old John.'

'My husband isn't predictable,' said Sylvia angrily.

'I didn't mean it like that.' Carey was contrite. 'I just meant – oh well, you know what I meant, Syl. You and John are like two twigs on the same branch.'

'We work at it,' said Sylvia. 'We worked at it especially hard after his affair.'

218

'Who with?'

Sylvia shrugged. 'A woman in work,' she told Carey. 'Isn't it always?'

'How did you feel?' asked Carey.

'How d'you think?' Sylvia ran her fingers through her fine hair. 'Devastated. He moved into the spare room. I didn't know what to do. But after a while I knew that I loved him and I wanted to save what we had together.'

'Does Mum know about this?'

'I told her a few years later,' said Sylvia. 'She guessed. She has a horrible habit of guessing correctly about our private lives.'

'I wouldn't have known,' said Carey. 'I really wouldn't.'

'Thing is . . .' Sylvia stirred her coffee idly. 'We could've just as easily split up. We had to make a decision to stay together. We had to want to make it work.'

'Yes, but . . .' Carey stirred her coffee too, 'you *did* want to make it work. You had time together behind you. You were a couple. Me and Ben – we're practically strangers.'

'You didn't seem like strangers at lunch,' Sylvia said gently. 'Or at the party.'

'If his bloody sister hadn't interfered and organised that damned party, then none of this would've happened!'

'Tell me about the girlfriend.'

'Leah?' Carey sighed. 'I hardly know anything about her. Other than they were practically joined at the hip. And, as you probably noticed, she's sensational to look at. To be honest, I don't know why he left her in the first place.'

'Maybe she set him up that night.'

'It was more than that.' Carey gulped back her coffee. 'I'm an idiot, Sylvia. I'm utterly useless when it comes to men. I can't get it right. I'm the kind of emotional half-wit that they write about in the *Living* sections of the newspapers, the thirty-something woman who's a whizz at work but hopeless at relationships. I keep ending up with totally unsuitable men because I wouldn't recognise true love if it hit me over the head with a hammer!'

'It's not that bad.'

'Actually, it is,' said Carey. 'I'm clearly not capable of forming a decent relationship and I'm usually bad at being on my own.' She

219

traced a pattern in a mound of sugar granules that she'd spilled on the table earlier. 'I rush into things with men because I like male company. You'd think, working with so many of them, I'd be a better judge of their characters, wouldn't you? But I seem to pick the wrong man every time.'

'So what's the story with the married bloke?'

'I told you. He's letting me rent out his spare room. That's all it is.'

'And is he divorced?'

'Not yet, obviously,' said Carey. 'But since his wife has moved in with someone else it's only a matter of time.'

'At the risk of you hitting me – are you absolutely sure it's irretrievable?'

'Peter seems to think so.'

'Not *him*! You and Ben.'

'Oh God, yes. If he'd wanted to do something about it he would've got in touch by now so he clearly doesn't. He obviously can't be bothered. He's probably shagging that black-haired nymphomaniac as we speak.'

Chapter 18

Patchouli

This is an earthy and sensual oil

B en was sitting at the kitchen table, his laptop open in front of him. He was supposed to be looking at sample brochures which their advertising company had e-mailed to them but instead he was surfing the web. He'd been in touch with his solicitor about getting a divorce and, to his horror, Gerry Buckley had told him that under Irish law he'd have to wait four years before he was eligible. He'd argued with Gerry about it, saying that surely the fact that he'd married in a sleazy US ceremony counted for something and the solicitor had sighed and said that yes, it had counted as a valid marriage. He'd told Ben to check it out with the relevant government departments if he liked, which was why Ben was fruitlessly surfing the web. Somehow, though, he seemed to keep getting wedding sites instead of divorce ones. He'd even managed to access the site of the Church of Everlasting Love and had stared at a photograph of a newly-married couple standing outside its arched doorway just as he and Carey had done a few weeks earlier. He'd stabbed at the keyboard to get rid of the picture but had only succeeded in crashing the computer instead. He'd just logged on again and typed the words 'quickie+divorce' into his search engine when the doorbell rang. He logged off before going to answer it.

'Hi, Ben.'

Leah looked lovelier than ever. Her dark hair was pinned loosely at the back of her head in a style he'd always liked. Her eyes looked dark and soulful, lashes long and black.

'Leah.'

'Can I come in?'

He opened the door a little wider and she walked through to the kitchen.

'Working?' She nodded at the open laptop.

'Yes.'

'Sorry to interrupt you.'

He shrugged.

'I called the shop and Freya told me you were out. I tried here on the off-chance.'

'What do you want?'

'To see how you're doing.'

'I'm fine,' he said.

'Are you?'

'Of course I am.'

She smoothed her perfectly shaped eyebrows. 'I also wanted to say that I'm really sorry. I shouldn't have gone to the party, I shouldn't have said the things I said to . . .' she hesitated, 'to Carey, and I certainly shouldn't have let you kiss me.'

'Doesn't matter,' he said. 'She had her own agenda that night.'

'Oh?'

He shook his head dismissively. 'Nothing.'

'Freya is mad at me,' Leah said. 'She thinks I deliberately tried to sabotage your marriage.'

'The thought had occurred to me too,' said Ben dryly. 'Though I don't think anything you did really made any difference. It was probably doomed from the start.'

'I didn't mean to make things worse,' Leah told him. 'I know I might have been a bit over the top, but . . .'

'You said you wanted to make me suffer,' said Ben.

'Oh, come on!' She looked angrily at him. 'That was in the heat of the moment. That was when you'd slept with me a week earlier. Of course I wanted to make you suffer.'

'You have,' said Ben.

'Although from what you're saying, it's not all my fault.'

'No.' Ben's voice was dispirited. 'It was a mistake, Leah. I thought there was something but there wasn't. No such thing as love at first sight.'

'I brought some essential oils with me,' said Leah. 'I know you like patchouli and it's very relaxing. Freya said you were totally stressed by everything.'

'You've got to be joking if you think I could possibly let you give me a massage!'

'Ben, don't be stupid. You're stressed. I'm a therapist. That's all.'

'*No.*' He saw the hurt expression in her eyes. 'No,' he repeated more gently.

'Would you mind if I had a cup of tea?' she asked.

He shook his head. 'Help yourself.'

Leah opened the cupboard and took out the mugs while Ben wandered back into the living area and sat in one of the armchairs. He couldn't believe that Leah was here. She shouldn't have come even though he had to admit that she was being utterly straightforward. No lies and half-truths with Leah. She'd admitted her anger and apologised to him and – even though he felt uncomfortable in her presence right now – he was grateful to her too. He imagined that Freya had exchanged some pretty sharp words with her. Freya had been like a cat on a hot tin roof the past few days, and if she was feeling mad at Leah then it was always going to be Leah who'd come out the worst.

Though it was strange how Freya's allegiance had shifted. She'd been totally against the marriage from the start and yet now she was hinting that he should call Carey and apologise and try to sort things out. But then Freya didn't know that Carey had a lot to apologise for too.

Ben wasn't good at saying sorry and much of the time he wasn't sure why people wanted apologies anyway. He didn't know whether it was a trait he'd inherited from his father or whether he'd developed the habit in his previous job where admitting you were wrong about anything was corporate suicide. Anyway, it wasn't up to him to apologise. There was no difference between his kissing Leah and Carey kissing that bloke. Except in location. He was fed up with feeling that he was to blame for everything! And, of course, Carey was being supported by her awful friends. He'd almost phoned her once more, had even picked up the receiver and started to punch in her number, but what was the point when they were clearly sitting round in a man-hating coven together thinking dreadful thoughts about him. In the end he wasn't sure whether or not he'd ever loved her enough to get over something like this. Or whether she'd loved him enough either. And even if they had loved each other, no matter how little or how briefly, they hadn't known each other at all. Carey obviously still had feelings for her old boyfriend, maybe she'd started to regret her impulsiveness. It hadn't seemed that way at the start, he admitted to himself, but everything had changed. It was unfortunate that he'd allowed himself to be carried away by his damned testosterone in the States because that's what it came down to in the end. He'd seen her, he'd wanted her, he'd married her. Fool that he was.

'Here.' Leah came over to him with a mug of steaming tea. 'Drink it.'

'I'm not ill,' he said irritably. 'You don't have to fuss over me.'

'I'm not.' Her tone was mild. 'I'm just giving you a drink.' She sat down in the armchair opposite him. 'Look, I know you probably hate me right now. I know that you're probably feeling messed up. But I'm your friend, Ben. I care about you.'

'Thanks.'

'I do,' said Leah firmly. 'And I know that it's partly my fault all this has happened. Personally, I think you're right and it would've happened anyway. She was a nice girl, Ben, but not for you. Still, I might be biased.' She smiled, a cute lopsided smile that she knew melted Ben's heart. 'I was really mad at you because you behaved like a complete shit. Even if you'd come home with her, told me about her, married her later . . .' A lock of her dark hair escaped from her clip as she spoke and fell softly across her face. She pushed it back behind her ear in a languid move. 'Still, it doesn't matter now. I'm over it. And I came round to say that I never really wanted to make you suffer. I'm sorry if you're suffering now.'

'Leah, you're right about one thing. I'm totally messed up right now,' said Ben. 'I thought I'd found something and I hadn't and I'm feeling . . .' he shrugged. 'Oh well, who cares how I'm feeling. But I'm in a wanting to be alone with my thoughts mood. I do appreciate you coming round and everything, but I just don't know what I want to do.'

'Call me,' said Leah. 'Over the last few years we've been through

224

so much together, you and me. Remember when I split up with William? You were there for me. And when you split up with Annabel? We helped each other get through it. We can do it again.'

'You think?'

'I'm certain,' said Leah.

They finished their tea in silence, then she took the cups into the kitchen, washed and dried them and put them away. She looked around her. There were no signs of Carey's presence, nothing to prove that she'd ever lived here. Leah folded the tea-towel into a neat square and told Ben that she had to go.

Freya sat in Dr O'Donnell's waiting room and read the notices on the walls. They were mainly about ensuring that elderly patients got their flu jabs or that young children were inoculated against the myriad diseases that could threaten them. Part of Freya wanted to rip them up and put up other notices instead, telling people to eat healthily and extolling the virtues of herbal remedies, but she knew she wasn't as radical as all that. Besides, she thought, she was here now in an ordinary doctor's surgery awaiting the results of a blood test because herbal remedies hadn't had any impact on her sudden bouts of trembling which always ended up with her breaking into a sweat and feeling panicked.

She was 99 per cent sure that it was stress. And 100 per cent sure that the stress was being caused by Ben. Over the last few weeks she hadn't been able to have a normal conversation with him even though she wanted to tell him that she and Brian had decided to get married. But she was afraid that talking about her own engagement would send him into a complete depression and she'd told Brian that they should keep it quiet for a few weeks, until the whole Ben and Carey thing had blown over. Brian had been great about it, as always, and had told her that waiting a little longer wouldn't make any difference when he'd been waiting for her his whole life. At which point he'd kissed her and they'd made love on her coloured sofa – since he'd proposed to her, their sex-life had improved enormously!

But whenever Brian wasn't around she couldn't help worrying about Ben. He never joined her for drinks after work any more and he was spending hours in the office drawing up over-elaborate plans for marketing campaigns that they couldn't possibly afford to run. His disastrous personal life was having a bad effect on his work, and it was stressing her out, too.

She'd told all this to Dr O'Donnell when she'd first visited him and he'd nodded at her, checked her blood pressure, listened to her heart and her lungs, talked to her in a general way about the state of her health and then suggested the blood test. She'd had a phone call from the surgery the previous day to say that the results of the test were in; there was nothing to unduly worry herself about but Dr O'Donnell would like to talk to her. Freya was comforted by the 'nothing to worry about' part of it and almost didn't bother to come in for what she imagined would be a lecture about her lifestyle. She knew that, despite the vitamin supplements, she didn't always eat properly or get enough sleep or take enough time off to do silly things. But it wasn't in her nature to be like that.

'Freya Russell, please.' Her name was announced over the intercom and Freya got up and went into the consulting room.

'Hi, Freya.' Dr O'Donnell smiled at her from behind his small, pine-coloured desk. He was a friendly man in his early fifties and his father had been the Russells' original family doctor. 'Take a seat.'

She sat down and crossed her legs.

'I needed to talk to you about the results of the blood test,' he said.

'I was told there was nothing to worry about.'

'And there isn't, as such,' he assured her. 'You're thirty-nine years old, aren't you?'

'Forty next month.' She smiled at him. 'I'm not worried about my age, Doctor.'

'You're unmarried?'

'Yes.'

'And you don't have any children?'

She raised her eyebrows. 'Fortunately not.'

'The thing is . . .' he glanced down at the piece of paper in front of him and up at her again. 'According to these results, you seem to have entered the menopause.'

Freya stared at him in stunned silence.

226

'It does happen,' he told her. 'A very small percentage of women have early menopause, sometimes much earlier than you.'

She continued to stare at him in silence.

'There are, of course, a number of things we can do about it.'

'Are you telling me that whenever I break out in a sweat it's a hot flush?' she said abruptly. 'Is that it?'

'Hot flushes are particularly symptomatic of menopause,' said Dr O'Donnell calmly.

'You're telling me that my body is shutting down?'

'Not your body,' he said. 'Just your reproductive system.' He looked at her sympathetically. 'This is probably a shock to you, Freya.'

'Yes.' She felt as though the breath had been knocked out of her. 'Yes, it is. Are you sure?'

'Your levels of oestrogen are almost non-existent,' he said.

Freya felt the familiar rush of heat through her body and the prickle of sweat on her head. 'It's happening now,' she said. 'The hot flush.'

'Possibly,' agreed the doctor. 'Or it could simply be reaction to the news. It's not easy to take in.'

She wiped the perspiration from above her eyes. 'So – so what about children?' she asked.

'It's highly unlikely that you'll have children.' His voice was gentle. 'Not completely impossible, because nothing is impossible, but it's not something I think will happen without significant medical intervention.'

'You mean my stock of eggs has dried up.' She looked at him accusingly. 'That's what happens, isn't it? Women have a finite number of eggs and mine are finished. So I'm having the menopause.'

'I have a lot of literature here,' he said. 'Not specifically about premature menopause, of course, but about the change generally.'

'But none of that literature will say that it's possible for me to have a child.'

'Not naturally,' said Dr O'Donnell. 'And, of course, you're somewhat at the upper age for some of the other techniques too.'

Freya swallowed. 'You mean that as an almost forty-year-old woman I'm totally washed up?'

227

'Not at all.' His voice was still gentle. 'Of course you're not washed up, Freya. Reproductively time has rushed on for you, but you're a young woman still.'

'Oh really.' Freya was horrified to realise that she might cry. She blinked hard a couple of times before looking at the doctor again.

'The thing is,' he told her, 'you have to make a decision about this. One of the problems that menopausal and post-menopausal women face is the effect that the lack of hormones has – such as osteoporosis. Particularly osteoporosis, in fact. I'm sure you know that brittle bones can be quite serious in older women. We need to address that issue.'

'For God's sake!' She looked angrily at him. 'You've just told me that I'm young. Now you're telling me that I need a damn Zimmer frame.'

'No, I'm not,' said Dr O'Donnell. 'I am telling you that you need to think carefully about this. In cases like yours I really do recommend hormone replacement therapy. But I know your background, Freya. I know you don't like conventional medicine.'

'Just because I own a herbal-remedy shop it doesn't mean I'm an idiot,' snapped Freya. 'But clearly I'll research the alternatives.'

'I understand.'

'Do you?' She stared at him. '*Do* you understand what it's like for someone to look you in the eye and tell you that you're nothing but a reproductive husk?'

'Freya, you don't have to see it like that.'

'How else?' she demanded.

'Why haven't you had children before now?' he asked.

'Oh, it's my fault for waiting, is it?' She gritted her teeth. 'How perfectly male of you to think like that.'

'I don't think like anything,' he said. 'I just asked you, was there a reason? Did you never want children, perhaps?'

'What difference would it make whether I wanted them or not?' she asked. 'At this point it's pretty damn irrelevant, isn't it?'

'Are you in a relationship?'

'Oh, give it a rest, Doc!' She sighed. 'I suppose there's probably some counselling thing that you do for people like me. But I don't need your counselling. I don't need your sympathy.'

'I'm not trying to counsel you,' he said. 'There are people

228

much better than me at that. But I want to make sure that you're OK.'

'I'll have to be, won't I?' She stood up. 'It's not as if I can change things, is it?'

'Make an appointment with my receptionist to see me again,' said the doctor. 'When you've had time to think through what you want to do.'

'Maybe,' said Freya.

'I'm sorry,' Dr O'Donnell told her.

'Don't be.' Her smile was weak but it was a smile nonetheless. 'I don't have a life-threatening disease. I don't have some serious illness. I'll live, won't I?'

'Yes,' said Dr O'Donnell.

'So I'll be fine.'

'Make an appointment,' he repeated.

She nodded and walked out of the consulting room as quickly as she could. She paused by the receptionist's desk but then hurried on her way, pushing open the surgery door and stepping outside.

The wind rushed along the Rathmines Road, swirling occasional leaves and discarded paper around her legs. She turned right along the canal towards Ranelagh, hugging her wool coat close to her, noticing every woman who walked past and telling herself that they were normal, fertile women while she was someone whose clock had stopped ticking before it had even started.

It was all very well for Dr O'Donnell to ask her if she'd put off having children because of her career or her lifestyle but, despite anything she might say, it was as much because she'd never before met the man that she wanted to have children with. She hadn't realised that Brian was that man. Or maybe she hadn't wanted to realise that Brian could be that man because she'd always been convinced that one day he'd leave her. When, instead, he'd asked her to marry him she'd been surprised at how content and how happy it had made her feel. He'd also said that he wanted them to be a family. Family meant kids, didn't it? Well, no chance of that, she thought bitterly as she strode briskly alongside the weed-choked water, I'm a dead duck as far as Brian's son and heir is concerned.

She shivered as she waited for the traffic-lights at Ranelagh Bridge to change. Then she crossed the road and continued on towards

Baggot Street. She had no idea where she was going but she knew that she had to walk. She wasn't able to keep still. Of course, she told herself, I probably have to do more exercise than normal people now. To keep my muscles from wasting away. But I'll have to be careful that my damned brittle bones don't snap while I'm doing them. She bit her lip. She didn't want to feel like this. She didn't want to be a young person trapped in an older woman's body. And then she told herself that no matter how young she considered herself to be, thirty-nine wasn't that young at all. They tried to tell you that it was, but how many thirty-nine-year-old blokes went round looking for thirty-nine-year-old girlfriends? They wanted younger models, prettier models, models who didn't have reproductive organs the same age as their mothers.

But Brian, her forty-plus-year-old boyfriend, wanted to marry her. He'd asked her and she'd said yes. And he must have known that he was risking the child thing by suggesting it. He must have taken into account that maybe they wouldn't have any, even though he wanted a family.

She sighed and thrust her hands deep into her pockets. Brian probably hadn't thought about it at all. It wasn't the kind of thing that men did think about. They just assumed that everything was in good working order. And she had no idea how he'd react when he found out otherwise.

Chapter 19

Peppermint

An oil that's invigorating and refreshing and good for tired muscles

The sound of the sirens in the distance caught Ben's attention although, as he told everyone afterwards, the sirens had nothing to do with what happened. However, their banshee wail made him look up from the display of Bach flower remedies and out of the shop window. Not that there was much to see initially, other than the rain pelting furiously against the glass. Ben hated rainy days which meant that people didn't bother shopping and the takings were down. The ideal weather for him was slightly overcast, not too warm but mild enough for everyone to want to be outside.

He put the bottle he was holding back on the shelf and looked out of the window again. At first he couldn't quite believe what he was seeing, but his body reacted more quickly than his brain and he yelled out a warning to Susie, the shop assistant, while at the same time vaulting over the nearby counter as a metallic red Mitsubishi jeep ploughed through the plate glass and past the spot where he'd just been standing. Shattered glass cascaded over the shop in a glittering tidal wave as bottles, jars and containers flew into the air before the 4x4 finally came to a halt against the back wall.

'Ben!' Susie's voice was an agonised shriek. 'Ben, are you all right?'

'I'm OK.' Ben got up from the floor behind the counter hardly able to believe his eyes. The entire front of the premises had disappeared and was now open to the pelting rain and gusting winds. Shelves had fallen from the walls, their contents strewn across the floor in a rainbow of colours. He looked at the battered jeep and its occupants. 'But I don't think they are. Call an ambulance, Susie.'

He crunched over broken glass to the jeep, conscious that his ankle hurt and that while his heart was racing his legs trembled. He could see a small group of people begin to cluster round the gaping hole of the shop and he pushed the thought of looters to the back of his mind, annoyed that in a crisis he should be thinking of his livelihood. He opened the door of the jeep and looked at the driver. He was a young man, in his early twenties Ben guessed. 'ABC,' he muttered to himself as he pulled himself onto the door-sill. Airways, breathing, circulation. The driver was knocked out but was breathing raggedly. Ben looked at the passenger and inhaled sharply. It was clear that the passenger, another young man, was in worse shape than the driver. Ben wasn't so sure that he was breathing at all. He jumped down from the driver's side and ran around to the other side.

He was right. He felt himself panic at the thought that there was a dying man beside him and that he should be able to do something about it but he wasn't sure what. Part of him was afraid to move him, but Ben knew from the First Aid classes he'd done before they opened the shop that getting the victim breathing was the most important thing of all.

He opened the young man's mouth and realised why he wasn't breathing. Somehow he'd managed to swallow his tongue. This wasn't as bad as Ben had feared: years ago he'd seen a referee at a football match help a player who'd swallowed his tongue. Ben knew that he could do this. He reached into the man's mouth and hooked his finger behind the tongue. The problem, he thought worriedly, would be if he didn't start to breathe straight away. It was all very well to know what you were supposed to do, but doing it was another thing altogether.

'Ben!' He could hear Freya's voice in the distance. 'Ben, are you OK?'

'A bit busy right now,' he muttered as he finally freed the tongue and looked anxiously at his patient. The man still wasn't breathing. Ben knew that he'd have to start mouth-to-mouth. He pinched the man's nose and breathed into his mouth, the lessons coming back to him. 'Don't make things worse,' the First Aid instructor had told him. 'All you want to do is keep the patient alive until somebody competent gets to him.' Ben prayed that somebody competent would get to him very quickly because he didn't feel very competent himself.

'Excuse me, sir.'

Ben sighed with relief at the quiet authority in the voice beside him.

'He swallowed his tongue,' Ben told the paramedic. 'He wasn't breathing. I don't know how he is now.'

'Leave him to us,' said the paramedic. 'You've done all you can. Maybe you want to sit down.'

Ben realised that there was a crowd of onlookers clustered around the jeep. He shivered and a woman handed him a fleece.

'Put it on,' she said. 'You've had a shock.'

'Ben! Ben!' Freya pushed her way to the front of the crowd. 'Oh God, Ben, I got such a fright. And I thought you – I knew you were down here and I didn't see you.'

'Susie knew I was OK.' Ben's teeth were chattering.

'Susie fainted,' said Freya.

Ben smiled wanly. 'I have that effect on women.'

Freya's return smile was shaky. 'You really are OK then?'

'I think so.' He shook his head and slivers of glass fell out of his hair.

'Are you cut?' demanded Freya.

'I don't know.' Ben looked over to the jeep. The paramedics had now strapped both driver and passenger onto trolleys and were wheeling them to the ambulance outside.

'They got here really quickly,' said Freya.

'Just as well.' Ben's voice was sober. 'I don't know whether or not I was keeping that bloke alive. Without them he had no chance.'

'Here.' A man in the crowd thrust a takeaway cup of steaming coffee into Ben's hand. 'That's from the café across the road. They saw what happened.'

'Thanks.' Ben accepted the cup gratefully.

'You did really well,' said a woman. 'You saved his life.'

'I don't know,' said Ben. 'I don't know at all.'

'Given that they nearly killed you, I wouldn't worry about it.' Another man in the crowd expressed his opinion. 'Maniacs, that's what they are.'

'Your lovely shop.' Ben recognised the elderly lady who spoke. She came in every week for vitamin supplements and herbal teas. 'It's destroyed.'

'Not destroyed.' But as he looked around him Ben knew that his words were hollow. The front of the shop was a wreck. What hadn't been flattened by the jeep was now being pulverised by the rain. And he had a feeling that he'd be picking glass out of everything for weeks.

'Thugs,' said another man. 'Thugs the lot of them.'

'Maybe not.' Ben didn't know why he was taking the side of the jeep's occupants.

'You're in shock,' said the elderly lady. 'Once you come out of it you'll realise that they probably were thugs.'

'I suppose.' He shrugged and drank some more of the scalding coffee. He was freezing now, and wet from the rain. He wished everyone would go home and leave him alone. The crowd suddenly parted and he thought he was getting his wish. Then he realised that the police had arrived and wanted to talk to him.

He tried to be coherent but he knew that he wasn't. All he could do was repeat over and over again that the jeep had quite suddenly swerved towards the shop and there was nothing anyone could have done to stop it. The police, no doubt covering all bases, wanted to know if he'd had any threats made towards him or the shop, and he stared at them in utter disbelief before saying that he ran a bloody healthfood store, not some drug-dealing den, and that there was no need to threaten him because he had nothing to give anyone. The younger of the two gardai shrugged and said that you never knew these days, and that sometimes gangs tried extorting money from keyholders and had anything like that ever happened?

Ben shook his head wearily. The guard got up and shook his hand and said that he'd had a narrow escape and Ben, looking at the damage to the counter he'd jumped over, agreed. Then they talked to a revived Susie who couldn't tell them anything more and whose teeth were chattering so much that anything she did say was totally incomprehensible. Ben suggested that she should be taken home and, since she lived close to the police station in Rathmines, the gardai offered to drive her. She kissed Ben tearfully on the cheek and told him she'd be in tomorrow. At which he told her not to

234

bother. There was no chance of them being open for business; she should take the day off and he'd phone her later.

'We'll have to get on to the insurance company,' said Freya after Susie had gone, 'and see what we can do about getting plastic put over that hole.'

Ben nodded then shivered again.

'Are you really OK?' asked Freya. 'Maybe you should've gone to hospital too.'

'I just can't believe what happened,' said Ben. 'One minute everything was fine. Next – bang!'

'Was it deliberate?' asked Freya. 'I mean, I know it sounds fantastic, but have we ever been threatened by gangs demanding protection money or anything?'

'No.' Ben made a face at her. 'Honestly, no. Nobody is out to get me . . .' His voice trailed off.

'What?' Freya looked at him anxiously. 'Who have you thought of?'

Ben grinned. 'Both my wife and my girlfriend might want to have a go.'

'Ben!' Freya gasped. 'You surely don't think . . .'

'Get a grip, Freya,' he said. 'I was only joking.'

'Right now I'm not able to take a joke.'

'I'm sorry.' Ben put his arm round her shoulder. 'I felt like being silly for a moment.'

'If only it was just a moment!'

'Don't worry about me,' he said. 'And don't worry about the shop either. We'll get through it.'

'I hope so,' she said as she picked a glittering shard of glass from his collar.

Carey had decided that it was not having a definite place to live that was making her feel so unsettled. She'd had three different homes since the end of January and she missed the security of knowing that the place she was coming back to after work was the place where she was staying for good. Of course, she'd always known that she wouldn't stay with Gina for ever but it had been a base for three years. Living with Peter was uncomfortable. She'd got over her inclination to lock herself away in the bedroom and now sat in the living room with him on the evenings she wasn't working, but she never felt relaxed.

There were two reasons for her unease. The first was that this was the home that he'd shared with Sandra at the same time as he was having an affair with her and she felt, very strongly, that she really didn't belong here. The second was that platonically sharing a house with a man with whom she'd once slept was a difficult thing to do.

It wasn't as though Peter was jumping on her at every available opportunity – quite the opposite, in fact. He was being nice and sympathetic and utterly caring. But there was an undercurrent between them that was impossible to ignore. So they were ultra-polite to each other and carefully avoided talking about anything other than the most superficial of things, but it seemed to Carey that if she wasn't careful she could suddenly find herself involved with Peter Furness again and she really didn't want that to happen.

Now they sat at opposite ends of the sofa while Peter watched the nine o'clock news and Carey flicked through the newspaper and hoped that the purchase of her apartment would come through quickly.

'Two men were seriously injured and another had a lucky escape when a jeep went out of control and ploughed into a shop in Rathmines earlier today.'

Carey glanced at the TV as the news announcer's words penetrated her consciousness. 'The owner of the shop, Mr Ben Russell, saved himself by jumping out of the path of the vehicle. He subsequently administered first aid to one of the jeep's occupants.'

She stared at the screen, her mouth open. The news crew had arrived on the scene before the jeep had been removed and the cameras lingered on its battered bonnet as well as the destruction it had wrought on the shop.

'Can you describe what happened?' The reporter was talking to one of the bystanders, a young woman with a toddler dragging out of her arm.

'All I saw was the jeep suddenly turn towards the shop,' she said. 'It didn't slow down or anything. And there was a terrible noise.'

The cameras panned out from the shop again.

'Ben Russell is the owner of *Herbal Matters*,' said the reporter. 'He saved the life of the passenger in the jeep after miraculously escaping being killed himself. How are you feeling now, Mr Russell?'

'I'm fine,' said Ben. 'I wasn't injured. I got out of the way in time.'

'You saved the life of the passenger,' repeated the reporter. 'It was an act of bravery following your own narrow escape.'

'Not bravery,' said Ben. 'The man was unconscious. And I didn't save his life, the ambulance people did.'

'Have you any idea what caused the accident?'

Ben shook his head. 'None whatsoever.'

The cameras panned away from him and back to the reporter.

'That's him?' Peter turned to Carey. 'That's your Ben?'

She nodded slowly.

'A hero,' said Peter.

Carey glanced at him. 'Lucky to be alive.'

'So it seems.'

'I wonder what it was all about.'

'Maybe the driver lost control,' said Peter. 'Maybe he was high on something.' He shrugged. 'If your Ben hadn't been agile enough to get out of the way, you'd be a widow right now.'

'Don't!' She reached for her mobile phone which was on the coffee-table beside her. 'I should talk to him.'

'Why?' asked Peter.

'I just—' She was about to hit the speed dial when the reporter began talking again, giving some more information about Ben and the shop. The cameras moved to Freya, who was now standing beside Ben, then quickly to the other side of him where they stopped and focused on Leah Ryder. Carey held her breath as the reporter spoke to Leah.

'You're a close friend of Mr Russell,' he said. 'How did you feel when you heard about today's events?'

'I rushed over straight away.' Leah looked directly into the camera, her eyes wide. 'I heard the reports on the radio and I was so worried I had to come immediately. Fortunately Ben was unhurt. But I think he did a great job in looking after the man who was.' She turned and smiled at Ben.

'Is that her?' asked Peter.

237

'Shut up,' said Carey. 'I want to listen.' But the reporter was now wrapping up the piece and had nothing new to add.

'Are you OK?' asked Peter.

'Of course,' said Carey. 'I wasn't there, was I? I didn't nearly get run over by a jeep.'

'Nor did he,' said Peter.

'If he didn't, he probably got the most awful fright. And the shop is ruined.' Carey felt tears prick at the back of her eyes. 'His lovely shop.'

'Insurance will pay for it,' said Peter practically.

'I know, but . . .'

'Was that the girlfriend?' Peter asked the question again.

'Leah,' said Carey. 'That's her.'

'Very pretty.'

'I know.'

'Back by his side.'

'Never fucking left it,' said Carey.

Freya turned down the volume on the TV in her apartment and grinned at Ben.

'My hero,' she said with a hint of amusement in her voice. 'Hopefully people will see you and think that herbal remedies are responsible for your rugged charm and amazing agility.'

'Sod off,' he said amiably. 'At least they managed to show the shop name quite a bit. Even if we can't get any sales in Rathmines, with a bit of luck the Tallaght and Drumcondra branches will draw in a few customers looking for the healthy option.'

'Oh Ben, surely you're not really thinking of customers at a time like this?' Leah turned her brown eyes on him. 'I'm more concerned with your health than anyone else's.'

'I'm perfectly OK,' Ben assured her. 'I know that I got a fright when it happened and I'm sure I was in shock afterwards, but everything's all right now.'

'Although the shop is a disaster area.' Freya sighed. 'And those bloody insurance people will probably wait for ages before paying out.'

'I'll have a word with Mick Delahunty,' said Brian. 'Make sure there's no delay.'

238

'Thanks, Brian,' said Ben. 'It's good to have a financial brain in the family.'

Ben didn't see the dark flicker in Freya's eyes as Brian replied that it was due to his recommendation that they'd taken the insurance out with Mick's company and he'd do his best to get things sorted out as quickly as possible.

'How long will it be before you can open the shop again?' asked Leah.

'I don't know,' said Ben. 'We'll have to assess it when the insurance guy comes round. If we get it sorted quickly then obviously we'll re-open as soon as we can.'

'You know I almost died of fright myself when I heard it on the radio news,' she said.

'I almost died of fright when I heard the sound of the jeep coming through the window,' Freya told her. 'I thought it was an earthquake. Or a bomb. I was on the phone to Gerry Donovan and I just dropped it onto my desk without telling him what was going on.'

Ben yawned and then looked at his watch. 'I'd better get home. I'm really tired now and I could do with falling into bed.'

'I should get going myself.' Leah stood up and reached for her red velvet jacket which was draped over the back of a chair.

'Thanks for calling round,' said Freya.

'I'm just glad you're both OK,' Leah told her.

'Needs more than a four-by-four to take out a Russell.' Ben grinned. 'Come on, Leah. Do you want to share a cab as far as Portobello?'

'Fine.' Her smile was brief.

'See you tomorrow, Freya,' said Ben and kissed his sister on the cheek. 'Look after her, Brian. Make sure she doesn't suddenly start to panic about how secure the premises are tonight and all that sort of thing. You know she's a worrier.'

'I am not!' Freya looked affronted and then relented. 'Oh, all right, I am.'

'Good luck,' said Brian. 'See you soon, Ben. And I'd milk the hero thing if I were you. That guy probably would've choked to death if you hadn't done something.'

'Maybe,' said Ben. 'Though looking round the place afterwards I have to say that I could've cheerfully choked him myself.'

When her brother and Leah had left, Freya leaned her head back and closed her eyes.

'You OK?' asked Brian.

'Sure,' she said.

'So what's all that about?'

'What?'

'Ben and Leah. Together.'

'God knows.' Freya opened one eye. 'I'm past caring. If he wants to start going out with her again, that's fine by me.'

'Actually I thought you might be pleased.'

Freya opened the other eye. 'So did I. But I don't know how I feel about him and his women any more.'

Brian laughed. 'Him and his women? You make it sound like there's a queue.'

'He's a philanderer,' said Freya. 'You know that. Maybe he just wants someone new every so often.'

'He's a good-looking bloke,' said Brian.

'Looks aren't everything,' snapped Freya. 'Not that it matters. It's his life.'

Brian looked at her curiously. 'Are you totally stressed out about today?' he asked. 'Don't be. Insurance will cover a lot of it and you'll get back on track.'

'It's not that.' Freya swallowed. 'I was shattered when it happened, of course, but you're right. It's only money or property. It's not important.'

'Goodness, Freya, that sounds odd coming from you.'

'Why?' she asked. 'I gave up my exciting job in banking to pursue alternative remedies. Why should my lack of concern bother you?'

'Because you might have gone another route but you're still a businesswoman at heart,' said Brian. 'And there's something wrong, isn't there?'

'Like what?'

'Freya, don't play games with me.'

'I'm not,' she said.

'Well, what's up with you?'

'Our – engagement,' she said slowly.

'What about it?' He looked at her. 'I've said nothing because that's what you wanted. I understood that, given the circumstances.

Anyway, at our age it doesn't much matter, does it? We can do the deed whenever you want.'

'I know. It's not that.'

'What then?'

'Afterwards. When we get married.'

'Yes?'

She lifted her blue eyes to meet his puzzled stare. 'You said you hoped to have a child.'

'Yes.'

'Have you thought about it much?'

'Not a lot.' Brian looked at her uncomfortably.

'And is it important to you?'

'If it's important to you.'

Freya picked at the sequins on one of her brightly coloured cushions. 'So you don't feel the need to have a child?' she asked.

'I – I don't know.' Brian looked even more uncomfortable. 'I'm not in a rush, I suppose.'

'But you should be,' said Freya. 'You're not getting any younger. And neither am I.'

Brian raised his eyebrows. 'But I'm sure I'm as potent as ever!'

'You may be,' Freya told him almost inaudibly. 'But I'm not.'

'What d'you mean?'

She pulled at a thread and purple beads slid onto the sofa.

'Freya?'

She had to tell him. It was only fair. 'I can't have children,' she said blankly.

He stared at her in silence.

'Sorry,' she added.

'If you can't have children, then why the hell have I been investing in condoms for the past three years?' he demanded.

'I thought I could. I could have, a few years ago. But I can't now.'

'Why?'

'I'm – I'm going through the menopause,' she said.

'What?!'

'You heard me.'

'Freya, you're only thirty-nine years old. You can't be.'

'I am,' she said. 'I saw Dr O'Donnell and he sent me for a

241

blood test. I might be only thirty-nine outside but inside I'm a dried-out crone.'

'Oh, sweetheart.'

'You see?' She shrugged. 'The kid thing won't happen with me. So I kind of think that we might be wasting our time.'

'But what about all those women who have kids in their fifties?' asked Brian.

'I don't know,' she replied. 'Maybe they're not menopausal yet. Though I'm sure, like me, they're not exactly rolling in eggs.'

'Freya!'

'Sorry.' She made a face at him. 'The whole thing is sort of awful.'

'Is this absolutely certain?'

'Dr O'Donnell seems to think so.'

'Surely there are ways, though?' Brian looked at her questioningly. 'I mean, I realise that it might be difficult but what about test-tube babies?'

'I don't know for sure,' she said.

'Because it wouldn't bother me if we had to lend nature a helping hand,' said Brian.

'I'll check it out,' said Freya.

Brian put his arm round her. 'Don't worry,' he said, but she could hear the edginess in his voice. 'I bet you anything that we'll have a kid. We probably just need to work fast. Don't they recommend that women still take contraceptives even when they're going through the menopause?'

She nodded.

'There you go.' This time his tone was calming. 'This is probably just a warning, telling us that we can't be complacent – but we knew that anyway.'

'I suppose so,' she said.

'I know so.'

She gathered the purple beads from the cushion where they'd fallen. 'But what if it isn't?'

'Huh?'

'If it isn't just a warning. Brian, I think it's more than that. What if I simply can't have kids, full stop?'

'Don't start thinking like that,' said Brian. 'You're a positive person, Freya. Think positively. Anyway, surely there's a flower that you can distil or something that will pep up the egg production?'

'I have absolutely no idea,' said Freya. 'I never thought about it because it never mattered to me before. I'll find out. But I thought you should know.'

'I'm glad you told me,' said Brian. He rubbed his face with his hands. 'It's difficult . . .'

'I know it's difficult.' Freya interrupted him. 'And that's why we needed to talk. But you're right, Brian. Maybe I'm over-reacting. I'll go back to the doctor. Talk to him again.'

'When?'

'As soon as I can.'

'Fine.' Brian looked at her for a moment, opened his mouth then closed it again. 'Whatever you think,' he added after a moment's silence. 'Whatever you want to do.'

'How's your ankle?' asked Leah as she and Ben waited at the side of the road for a cab to appear.

'Not bad.' Spurred on by adrenaline at the time, Ben hadn't realised that he'd twisted his ankle quite badly in his gazelle-like leap over the counter. But during the following hours it had swollen so that now walking on it hurt. 'I'll rub some arnica on it later.'

'Why don't you come back to my place?' suggested Leah. 'I've lots of oils that I could rub in for you.'

Ben shook his head. 'I'm tired,' he said. 'But thanks anyway.'

'No problem.' Leah gritted her teeth. She wished Ben wasn't being quite so distant with her, but she was putting it down to delayed reaction. She'd hoped, though, that he'd let her look after him after what was clearly a major ordeal. She had been truly shocked when she'd heard the first news bulletin about the accident and quite convinced that it was Ben who had been seriously injured, which was why she'd cancelled the rest of her appointments and rushed over to Rathmines. She arrived at the same time as the TV crew and she'd enjoyed the attention of the cameras and the reporters. But she'd also enjoyed being there for Ben, supporting him when he suddenly realised that he couldn't walk, fetching more coffee from the place across the road and generally being part of the family again.

No sign of the wife, she'd thought with grim satisfaction. No

243

chance of Carey turning up like a ministering angel. The girl was a complete cow who really couldn't have cared less. Ben was well rid of her.

'Taxi!' Ben flapped his arm in front of the approaching cab and slid thankfully into the back seat. 'Portobello, then Ballsbridge,' he told the driver.

'You're sure you don't want to come back with me?' The journey from Rathgar to Portobello was very short and they were approaching Portobello Bridge when Leah spoke.

'No, really. You've been great, Leah. Thanks.'

'It's OK,' she said. 'I'll give you a call tomorrow.'

'Sure.'

The cab pulled up outside Ben's house. He got out and waved briefly at Leah before opening his front door. The message indicator on his phone was blinking. He hit play immediately.

'Ben, you old dog!' Phil's voice filled the room. 'Hero, life-saver, all round Wonderman. We're ready to buy you a drink on Saturday after the match – if you come down to earth on time. Listen, pal, glad you're OK, it looked a bit of a nightmare on the telly. See you soon.'

Ben erased the message then hobbled into the kitchen. There was no chance of him playing in any football match next Saturday with a crocked ankle. He took a bottle of beer from the fridge and flopped onto the sofa. He was getting tired of people telling him how great he was, when all he'd done was jump higher than he'd ever managed in his life before. Admittedly, and from the reports that they'd got back from the hospital, he possibly had saved the passenger's life – but it was all instinct as far as he was concerned. He hadn't thought about it, he'd just done it. He felt a bit of a fraud accepting people's praise for something he'd done without thinking.

He wondered whether Carey had seen the news. Whether she thought he was a hero. Or whether, as far as she was concerned, he was still the shit who'd kissed his ex-girlfriend at their wedding party. Not that it mattered, of course. But he'd like to think that she'd looked at the TV and realised he wasn't as bad as she'd thought. Wasn't as bad as her, in fact. And now there was Leah again. He'd been surprised when she'd shown up but also touched by her concern. Leah put him first, Carey had never really done that.

From the moment they'd left New York she'd been thinking of her job, she'd made suggestions about moving to the northside of the city, she hadn't looked up to him in the way that Leah did. All she cared about was her work, her friends and her ridiculous collection of shoes. And she'd managed to cut him out of her life completely.

Whereas Leah had come back, just as she always did. Perhaps she was right, perhaps they were meant to be together. How did you know, though? How did all the people who got married to the right person realise that they were marrying the right person? How come they didn't mess it all up?

He rubbed his forehead. He really wasn't much good at the self-analysis stuff. All he knew was that he had a pain in his ankle and a pain in his head and he didn't want to think about anything else right now. He drained the beer, left the bottle on the floor beside the armchair and went up to bed.

Chapter 20

Grapefruit

A highly revitalising and uplifting oil with a sharp, zesty fragrance

For the first time in weeks Carey woke up without a nagging headache and an over-riding sense of gloom. The fact that the sun was shining and the screaming winds of the past month had faded into warm breezes certainly helped, she thought as she opened the door of her Audi, but the most likely reason was that today she was completing the purchase of her apartment and by twelve o'clock she would be a real live homeowner and in charge of her life at last.

As she turned the key in the ignition, she told herself that this was the start of a new chapter in being Carey Browne. The grown-up and sensible chapter. The one where her friends and family stopped thinking of her as slightly mad and irresponsible Carey and began to treat her as a true adult capable of making mature and informed decisions. Well, maybe not her family, she sighed as she turned onto the main road and headed towards the solicitor's office. Whatever about Tony, safely distant in Perth, Arthur, Maude and Sylvia would never think of her as being capable of making mature and informed decisions. She'd always be the scatty baby of the Browne family as far as they were concerned. But other people might be impressed.

The traffic into the city centre wasn't as bad as usual and she was lucky, too, in finding a parking meter just a short walk away from the solicitor's office. She locked the car and walked along Pembroke Row until she arrived at the door of Savage & Savage. Not the most comforting name for a solicitor's, she thought, as she pressed the buzzer on the intercom.

The door opened and she walked into the small tiled reception area in the hallway of the old Georgian building. A studious-looking receptionist looked at her enquiringly.

'Carey Browne,' she told her. 'Here to close a sale.'

The receptionist looked at the list in front of her. 'Your solicitor isn't here yet,' she said dismissively. 'You'll be meeting Mrs Harris.'

'Fine.' Carey was intimidated by the chilliness of the receptionist and the clinical atmosphere of the reception area. She perched on the edge of one of the navy tub chairs either side of a smoked-glass coffee-table and flicked through the day's edition of the *Irish Times*. Then she put it down and took up a two-week-old copy of *Hello!* instead. She'd wanted to look at *Hello!* from the start, but had felt that might make her look like an air-head in front of the snooty receptionist. But then she'd decided that if they left *Hello!* lying around they expected people to read it, so what the heck. Besides, she was too excited to concentrate on anything more demanding than the details of the dress that Nicole Kidman had worn to the latest Hollywood awards ceremony. Nicole looked great, Carey thought as she peered at the dress, and everyone agreed that her career had really taken off as soon as she'd been granted her divorce from Tom Cruise. Which just went to prove that sometimes a girl was better off doing things on her own. And that so-called matches made in heaven were usually anything but. She turned the page and sighed wistfully at the sight of ex-Spice Girl Mel B walking along a beach somewhere in the Caribbean. She wondered how it was that Mel, whose hair was even more corkscrewed and surely more difficult to manage than her own, appeared so groomed and elegant while she perpetually looked as though someone had given her an electric shock.

'Good morning, Carey.' Eddie Kelly, her solicitor, walked into the office and she dropped *Hello!* back onto the table.

'Hi,' she said.

'Ready to rock and roll?' Eddie looked like a solicitor, Carey thought, with his snappy suit and the gold cuff-links in his Thomas Pink shirt, but he didn't talk like one. She'd found the firm of Kelly, Smith & Clarkson in the *Golden Pages* and had chosen them precisely because the telephonist had been cheerful, friendly and very unlegal and, when she was put through to Eddie, he'd sounded cheerful and friendly too.

'I can't wait,' she confessed.

'It won't take long,' he promised, just as Savage & Savage's Mrs Harris walked into reception. She was tall and beaky and Carey wondered whether or not she'd been a Savage before turning into a Harris.

Eddie was right about the timing and, despite Mrs Harris's somewhat pedantic approach to dotting the Is and crossing the Ts, it was a mere twenty minutes later when Carey stood outside the office with the key to the apartment in her hand. It had all been a bit of a blur but now she was a person with her own place and, no matter what happened, it would always be hers. She thanked Eddie for his help, shook his hand then waved goodbye as he went in the opposite direction to his car. She tuned into 98FM as she drove back to Swords, singing along to Robbie Williams and feeling a frisson of excitement every time she thought about her new home ready and waiting for her. She'd discovered that a few other employees at the airport had bought apartments in the development, too: the last day she'd gone to look at it she'd seen a girl whom she knew worked for Aer Rianta, and they'd had a brief chat about how convenient it was. It was nice to know that there would be a few familiar faces around the place and it made her feel that her choice of home was all the more fortunate.

In the end, Peter Furness hadn't bought one of the apartments. He'd put a deposit on a place nearer Blanchardstown. He was a real home-bird at heart, he'd told Carey; he liked the area where he lived and he didn't want to move. 'Which is maybe why me and Sandra never really worked,' he'd added ruefully. 'She was always looking for something more than I was able to give her.'

Carey was relieved that she'd finally be moving out of his house. It had been very convenient to be able to stay there, but it had never been comfortable. And she felt guilty every time she opened one of the kitchen cupboards which had undoubtedly been chosen by Sandra when she and Peter were in the first flush of happiness together.

Does it always wear off, she wondered as she turned onto the M1. Are there any married couples out there who truly love each other as much as they did on the first day they met? Her parents, maybe, but she remembered fierce arguments (which they'd tried and failed to hide from their children) between Arthur and Maude in the past. They seemed perfectly content now, but how could anyone be certain? And she still hadn't quite recovered from Sylvia's revelation about John's affair. If Sylvia and John's marriage had almost foundered, then anyone's could.

So maybe I'm not a total failure after all, she thought. I gave it a go and it went wrong. It's not my fault. And better to have found it out now than in a few years' time. At least this way I've motivated myself to do something I've talked about for ages. At least this way I've managed to prioritise my life.

She turned into the development and parked in the space marked *Apt 2A*. 'My apartment,' she murmured as she stood outside and looked up at the first floor. 'My apartment. My life.'

She unlocked the main door and walked up the stairs. It was quiet inside the block and she wondered if many of the other apartments were occupied yet. She slid the key into her door and pushed it open.

She supposed, as she stood in the middle of her living room, that she should have asked Sylvia or Maude or anyone at all really to come with her to share the moment. But it hadn't occurred to her to ask and now she regretted not having someone here to wish her luck and to hug her and tell her that she'd made the right decision.

'You're being silly,' she said out loud. 'You don't need anyone.' She strode across the room and opened the balcony doors to let fresh air into the room. 'You've done it all by yourself.' She walked into her kitchen and opened and closed her own cupboards. Then she went into the bedroom and did the same with the wardrobes. She sat on the sofa and draped her legs over the arms. She got up again, pushed it against a different wall and looked at it with a critical eye. And then she remembered that it didn't make much difference where she put the sofa because her new leather couch would be ready soon. She winced at the thought of how much that had set her back, and then shrugged because it was only money and what was the point in worrying? She earned a good salary and she had a great credit-card limit so she might as well use it.

She looked at her watch. It was lunch-time, she was starving and she had lots to do today. She wanted to pick up all her stuff from Peter's as well as call into the shopping centre and buy essentials like bedlinen, kitchen equipment and, of course, some instant meals for the freezer. Her mobile chirped and she took it out of her bag.

'So?' asked Peter.

'So what?'

'So, is it done?'

'Yes.' Her voice bubbled with the excitement she'd wanted to share. 'And it's great. I love it.'

'I'm glad,' said Peter.

'I've loads to do,' she said. 'I've to buy mountains of stuff.'

'Why don't we celebrate first?'

'Celebrate?'

'I'm in Swords,' he said. 'Let's push the boat out and go to lunch.'

'I don't know if—'

'I've already booked it,' said Peter. 'The Old Schoolhouse. One o'clock.'

'That was cutting it a bit fine!' she exclaimed. 'I might've still been in town at one o'clock.'

'Ah, but I knew you wouldn't.'

'That's one of the things that always irritated me about you,' she told him sternly. 'Your always being right.'

'Not always,' Peter said. 'But about this I am. Come on, Carey, you want to celebrate, surely?'

'Well, yes, I do,' she admitted. 'I was standing here wishing I had someone with me earlier.'

'You have me now,' said Peter. 'Or at least you will at one o'clock. The reservation's in my name.'

'You're amazing.'

'See you there,' he said and rang off.

The Old Schoolhouse was exactly that. Set off on a side road from the village it had been a small school at the early part of the twentieth century and, though it had clearly been renovated and altered to become a restaurant, it still retained the high ceilings and a background atmosphere of sloping desks, inkwells and scab-kneed children.

Carey walked inside and looked around for Peter without expecting to see him. But, once again, he was there before her, reading the menu in front of him.

'Hi,' she said as she sat down at the table beside him.

'Hello there.' He beamed at her. 'Well, what's it like?'

'A bit strange actually,' she said. 'I was moving furniture around before I came out and I suddenly realised that I could put it anywhere I liked because I didn't have to please anyone else.'

Peter laughed. 'I don't want to burst your bubble but those apartments don't exactly lend themselves to a wide range of furniture configurations. They're not what you might call huge.'

'They're fine,' she said sternly. 'And you're not to start pointing out defects when I've only just moved in.'

'I'm sorry,' said Peter. 'I was just teasing.' He looked up as a waiter stood beside the table and ordered two glasses of champagne.

'Peter!' cried Carey.

'Why not?' he asked. 'It's your first place. And I told you we should celebrate.'

'This is really good of you,' she said after the waiter had returned with their champagne and taken their lunch order. 'And it is nice to mark the occasion.'

'When Sandra and I first bought our house we celebrated by going to Burger King,' Peter told her wryly. 'I'd left my credit cards at home and we only had enough for a couple of quarter-pounders instead of the slap-up meal I'd planned.'

'Idiot,' said Carey.

'No wonder she left me.' Peter sighed.

'I'd leave you if you were celebrating our first home together with a couple of quarter-pounders,' said Carey.

'You're leaving me anyway,' he told her.

She made a face at him.

'I'll miss you,' he said. 'I'll miss knowing you're there.'

'You won't,' she said. 'You'll be glad to get your spare room back.'

'You know I'll miss you,' he said. 'Even though you've practically hung a sign round your neck saying Do Not Touch and even though I'm afraid of saying the wrong thing to you half the time, it's still been great having you there.'

'Don't say things like that.' She fiddled with the linen napkin.

'I'm just telling you how I feel,' said Peter.

'And you already know how I feel,' she said sharply. 'So just stop.'

'OK, OK.' He picked up his glass of champagne and held it towards her. 'Right. To you, my sweet, and your new apartment, and may God Bless All Who Sleep In It.'

'Fool.' But she giggled and clinked glasses with him.

'So are you going to live on your own?' asked Peter. 'Or will you have someone share?'

'I'm going to be on my own for a while,' she replied. 'It's about time I tried it.'

'It's not half as much fun as it's cracked up to be,' remarked Peter.

Carey didn't respond but picked up her fork and prodded the tagliatelle carbonara which the waiter had just placed in front of her.

'Two more glasses of champagne,' said Peter.

'Oh no,' she protested.

'One more won't hurt,' he told her. 'You'll be fine.'

'OK,' she said, 'but that's it. I told you I've loads of things to do today.'

'The first thing you have to do is to chill out and enjoy yourself,' said Peter.

'I will so long as you don't keep getting at me,' she told him.

'Not another word,' he promised.

'You're terribly bossy,' she complained, but smiled at him all the same.

He kept his promise; the lunch was perfect and somehow she didn't find herself objecting when he ordered yet more champagne. She felt herself relax with him in a way that she hadn't been able to when she was living in his house, and she remembered why it was that she'd fallen for him in the first place. He was totally charming. He said the right thing at the right time and he made her feel special. He'd been good at that when they'd been seeing each other, she remembered, sending her flowers at home, or surprising her with tickets to a concert she'd wanted to see when she thought they were simply meeting for a drink, or unexpectedly turning up at the gates to the ATC Centre on one of the only hot days of the summer with a picnic hamper and whisking her off to the coast for the afternoon when her shift had ended. Rushing into an impetuous marriage with Ben Russell might have seemed romantic, she thought suddenly, but Peter Furness actually *was* romantic.

'You OK?' asked Peter.

'Sure, fine.' She clattered back to the present. 'Daydreaming.'

'Pleasant thoughts?'

She flushed. 'Partly.'

'You should only be having beautiful thoughts today,' he told her as he waved at the waiter and ordered still more champagne. 'So drink up, girl, and keep on celebrating.'

'Anything you say,' she agreed. 'Anything you say.'

'Now I'm drunk.' Carey hiccoughed as she pushed another empty glass away. 'You said we were only having one drink but we've had lots and now I'm drunk.'

'I'm a bit under the weather myself,' admitted Peter. 'But it was fun.'

'You're really nice,' she said. 'And I'm sorry that I was nasty to you when I found out you were married.'

'You were entitled to be nasty to me.'

'Maybe.' She closed her eyes. 'I don't know if anyone is ever entitled to be nasty to anyone else though. People should be kind to each other, shouldn't they?'

'I guess so.' Peter watched her as she sat there with her closed eyes and then signalled for the bill. 'And could you order us a taxi?' he asked.

The waiter nodded and ten minutes later told them that the cab had arrived.

'This is totally inconvenient,' murmured Carey as Peter led her outside. 'I'm abandoning my car here and I really need it to get to work and do shopping.'

'You're not on until tomorrow afternoon, are you?' asked Peter. 'You'll have plenty of time to collect it.'

'But I wanted to be organised,' she wailed. 'I wanted to get all my stuff together and spend the night in my new apartment.'

'You can do all that in the morning,' said Peter.

'I can't spend the night in my apartment in the morning.'

Carey frowned in confusion at her own sentence and closed her eyes again.

They made the journey in silence and Peter asked the taxi-driver to stop at the pub in Blanchardstown village.

'What are we doing now?' Carey opened her eyes again and looked round.

'Hair of the dog,' said Peter.

'It's a bit soon for hair of the dog,' she objected.

'Well, how about sheep as a lamb?' he suggested.

'Sorry?'

'Both of us have skived off today. We might as well have a few more drinks and make it worthwhile.'

She laughed. 'I am not going to get pissed in the middle of the afternoon and have a hangover by nine o'clock,' she told him.

'Just the one,' said Peter.

'Oh, all right.'

They had two. And then Carey said that she was knackered and that she really did need to get back and pack some stuff. 'Because I honestly do want to be ready to move,' she told him. 'Tomorrow, seeing as I've made such a mess of today.'

'You'll have plenty of nights to spend in your new apartment,' Peter said. 'Spend one more night with me instead.'

She looked at him, recognising that the tone of his voice had changed. He met her gaze, and smiled.

'You mean sleep with you, don't you?' she said.

'Look, we're both free agents,' said Peter. 'There's nothing wrong with us sleeping together.'

'We're both married to other people,' said Carey.

Peter laughed. 'And you think those other people will care?'

'Well, no,' she acknowledged. 'I was being facetious.'

'I know.'

'I don't know if I want to sleep with you,' said Carey.

'Why not?'

'I loved you and then I stopped loving you. I only slept with you when I loved you.'

'And how do you feel about me now?' he asked.

'I like you,' she said. 'I'm grateful to you.'

He made a face. 'But you don't love me any more?'

'I'm drunk,' she told him. 'I'm not really at my best, judgement-wise, when I'm drunk.'

'I love you, Carey,' said Peter. 'From the moment I met you.'

'Ben said that.' She took off her glasses and polished them on the corner of her shirt. 'But it didn't last.'

'With me it would,' said Peter. 'I promise you.'

She sighed. 'I'm getting out of one relationship,' she said. 'I'm not sure I'm ready to get right back into another one again. Especially one I've been in before.'

'Doesn't seem to be bothering Ben,' said Peter.

'I know.'

'Stay with me tonight anyway,' he said. 'I'm not going to do anything awful like force myself on you if you don't want me to.'

She smiled. 'I guess if you were going to do that you could've done it before now.'

'Exactly,' said Peter. 'But don't think the thought hasn't crossed my mind.'

It had crossed Carey's mind, certainly. Some nights as she'd lain in the narrow single bed she'd thought about getting up and sliding into bed beside Peter instead. She'd imagined the feel of his arms around her and the taste of his lips on hers and it had been very hard to pull the duvet round her shoulders and make herself go to sleep on her own.

'I'll stay the night,' she said. 'But I don't think I'm ready to sleep with you yet, Peter.'

'As long as you're not ruling out the possibility in the future, that's OK with me,' he said and kissed her on the lips.

Chapter 21

Mandarin

An oil with a cheering fragrance that's also calm and gentle

Freya stood in the middle of the Rathmines branch of *Herbal Matters* and surveyed the work so far. The huge plate-glass window had been replaced and new carpets had been put down, but they were still working on the shelving and it would be another week before the store was finally ready to re-open. Ben and Freya had taken the opportunity to redesign the layout so that there was more space for customers to browse and (said Freya hopefully) more space for goods that might entice them to buy. Freya was going through a despairing phase about the loyalty of their clients and the effect that the accident was having on their cashflow. And it *had* been an accident. The police had called round to tell them that the two men in the jeep were brothers. The younger brother, in the passenger seat, was an epileptic who'd forgotten to take his medication and had had a fit which had distracted the driver so much that he'd lost control of the jeep; that was why it had ploughed so dramatically into the shop. The doctors thought it was the impact of the accident that had caused the younger man to swallow his tongue rather than the fit, since that was a relatively rare occurrence, but they still praised Ben for his handling of the situation.

Freya looked up and smiled at him as he walked into the shop.

'Things are improving round here,' he said. 'We should be on schedule to re-open soon.'

'Maybe.' Freya had to raise her voice to be heard over the sound of an electric drill.

256

'Definitely,' said Ben. 'I know it's still a mess but it's the kind of mess that you can deal with.'

'I don't feel like dealing with any messes right now.' Freya sighed. 'I'm exhausted by everything.'

'I know it's tiring,' he said, 'but at least we're managing to do the re-fit and that insurance friend of Brian's came through with the goods.'

'Which is something,' agreed Freya.

'He's an efficient bloke, Brian, when he puts his mind to it.' Ben stepped over a supply of cardboard boxes. 'I can see why he's so successful.'

'More efficient than me?' asked Freya.

'God no.' Ben grinned at her. 'Nobody could be more efficient than you.'

She returned his smile but her eyes were troubled.

'What's the matter?' asked Ben. 'You've been really down this last while. I thought it was the shop, but . . .'

'Oh, just some things on my plate,' said Freya. 'Nothing you need to worry about.'

'I don't worry about things I can't change,' said Ben. 'But of course I worry about you. Just like you worry about me.'

'I never worry about you,' retorted Freya.

Ben laughed then put his arm round his sister's shoulders. 'Is there something wrong?' he asked.

'Not really.'

Ben looked at her curiously. Her tone was flat and lacking in the optimism he always associated with her. 'Let's go for a coffee,' he suggested. 'We haven't sat down and talked about non-shop things in ages.'

'I know,' said Freya.

'Come on.' Ben watched as one of the carpenters fixed an architrave around the doorframe. 'We'll leave the professionals to it. They'll probably be glad to have us out of their hair.'

The owner of the café across the road smiled at them as they entered. Ben wondered if she remembered that he was the embarrassed customer who'd been yelled at by a demented Leah in what seemed like another lifetime – she certainly gave no sign of any memories now.

'Hello, Ben. Hello, Freya,' she said. 'What can I get you?'

'Double espresso for me,' said Ben. He turned to Freya.

'Latte,' she said.

They sat at a window table where they could still see the shop.

'So what's wrong?' asked Ben when the coffees were placed in front of them.

'Brian's asked me to marry him,' said Freya.

Ben looked at her in delight. He'd wondered, after his conversation with Brian, whether or not they'd ever get married and had been concerned by Brian's comments about Freya's reluctance to even talk about it. He was worried that because she'd looked after him so wonderfully after their parents died, she now continued (unwittingly) to see herself in the role of surrogate mother which somehow held her back from taking the plunge herself.

'I think that's great,' he told her.

'Do you?'

'Well, of course I do,' he said. 'I've always thought that you and Brian should get hitched. You spend more time together than most married couples and he's the only bloke I know who's laid back enough to put up with you.'

'You think I'm difficult to get on with?' she demanded.

'Sometimes,' he told her. 'You like doing things your way, Freya. You always have.'

'I know. Brian's forever telling me that I'm difficult.'

Ben laughed. 'So there you go! Difficult and he still wants to marry you.' His voice softened. 'I think it's great. I really do.'

'You recommend it then?' she said dryly. 'Even though your own didn't last long enough for the ink to dry on the page?'

'OK, I'll admit that you were right and I was wrong about me and Carey.'

Freya raised an eyebrow. 'Actually, what was wrong was that you hadn't finished with Leah properly. And that's why you messed it up.'

'Can we not talk about me?' asked Ben. 'We're here to discuss you, aren't we?'

'Not discuss me,' said Freya. 'Just to chill out and chat.'

'Right,' said Ben. 'So he's asked you to marry him but it has

258

you wandering mournfully round the place . . . don't you want to marry him?'

'I'm not sure.'

'Why?' Ben looked puzzled. 'You've been with him for ages. Don't you think it's time to move on to another level with him?'

'Maybe.' Freya stared into her coffee. 'There's one question I really want to ask you.'

'What?'

'When, eventually, you get married to someone properly, will you want a family?'

'Huh?'

'Kids, Ben. Will you want them?'

He considered the question for a moment. 'I suppose so. They weren't on my agenda with Carey straight away. We didn't really discuss it much but I guess there was an understanding that some day . . .'

'And if you discovered that she didn't want any?'

'Things would hardly have been any worse, would they?' He smiled wryly. 'I mean, we've split up, Freya. Regardless of the kid thing.'

'I suppose.'

'Is it an issue with you and Brian?' he asked.

Although she desperately wanted to talk to someone about it, Freya knew that it wasn't a subject she could discuss with Ben.

'Not exactly,' she compromised. 'I just wondered how you felt about it, that's all.'

'I guess I want kids some day,' said Ben. 'And I bet Brian would love 'em. He'd probably be really good father material.'

'You think so?' Freya frowned. 'Surely he's as picky as me about stuff. Don't you think he'd freak out if he found toys lying round the house or if he was asked to change a dirty nappy?'

'Just because he mightn't like the trappings – and don't tell me that you wouldn't freak out at a dirty nappy, Freya Russell – it doesn't mean he wouldn't want the children,' said Ben. 'Maybe most men are better at family stuff when they get older. You know, when we finally mature at age fifty or something!'

'D'you think so?'

259

'I'm probably the worst person in the world to ask,' said Ben. 'But yes.'

Freya dumped another sachet of sugar into her coffee.

'Is there a problem with Brian over it?' Ben rephrased his earlier question.

'Who knows?' she responded. 'Seriously – what would you have said if Carey didn't want children and you did?'

'I've no idea,' said Ben. 'Look, Freya, we didn't get that far in our relationship, OK?' He shrugged. 'We talked and talked about loads of things but never that.'

'Did you ever talk to Leah abut it?'

'God, no.'

'Will you?' asked Freya.

Ben looked uncomfortable. 'I don't know yet.'

'Don't string her along again.' Freya pushed her cup to one side. 'She deserves better than that.'

'I know.' He nodded. 'I just don't want to make another mistake. But Leah and I keep coming back to each other and that has to count for something.'

'She rang me,' Freya told him.

'Oh?'

'I called her and told her about you and Carey and I was really quite short with her. And she got upset, understandably, I suppose. Then she phoned back the next day to say that she absolutely didn't mean for anything to happen, and that the fact that it did might have proved something to her but she wasn't going to do anything about it.'

'Not quite true,' said Ben. 'She called round to see me.'

'And?'

'And nothing,' he said. 'She was just Leah. And it was nice to have her fussing round me instead of that mad whirlwind spinning around the place.'

Freya laughed. 'Maybe we're neither of us good with whirlwinds,' she said. 'You could never accuse Brian of being one.'

'No.' Ben laughed too. 'So are you actually going to announce your engagement, Freya, or are you just going to get married?'

'We haven't decided yet,' she said. 'But there hardly seems any point in getting engaged.' She wrinkled her forehead. 'I'd like the ring, though.'

'You women are all the same!' cried Ben. 'It's jewellery all the way!'

'Once you remember that, you won't go too far wrong,' said Freya as she got up from the table.

'Now she gives me the important advice,' groaned Ben.

When Carey walked into the control centre the following afternoon Chris Brady asked her if she'd mind taking her shift in the tower. She smiled at him and told him that she'd be happy to. She rarely got to work in the tower these days but she always enjoyed it. While air traffic control centres didn't have to be anywhere near an airport (and many of them were, in fact, being located further and further away), the tower was the place where the whole jigsaw of arrivals and departures came together. From their vantage point in the glass room the controllers could see the spread of the airport and its runways and watch every plane that landed and took off.

Carey took the lift to the top of the tower and then the short flight of stairs into the control room with its panoramic views of the surrounding countryside as well as the airport itself.

'Hello, there!' She hadn't seen Jennifer O'Carroll in ages. 'Still seducing them with your husky Mariella tones, Jen?'

'You know me,' said Jennifer. 'The honey-pot of the airwaves.'

Ciaran Geoghegan, the ground controller working with her, spoke into his mike. 'Shamrock 156, ground, start-up approved. ATIS J is current. Expect Runway One Zero for departure.'

Carey knew that she'd take over from Jennifer after the Aer Lingus plane had taken off. Gerry Ferguson, who was taking over with her, had also arrived. They stood and watched as Ciaran instructed the Aer Lingus plane to taxi to the holding point.

An incoming British Airways plane touched down and Jennifer pulled her baseball cap tighter on her head as it thundered along the runway. 'He's going to miss his turnoff if he doesn't hold it up a bit quicker,' she said. 'What the fuck does he think he's doing?' She clicked her mike. 'Tower, Speedbird 349, turn right at end of runway if able. If not, please proceed to M1 motorway and take airport exit from roundabout.'

Carey shook with laughter as the clipped tones of the British Airways pilot informed them that he hoped to be able to make the

261

correct turn off the runway. 'And no need to be sarcastic, Mariella,' he added to Jennifer.

'Oh, it's things like this that make the job so exciting.' Jennifer unplugged her headset and got up. 'Have a nice day, Browne. By the way, are you entering the bowling league?'

'I don't know,' said Carey. 'I'm hopeless at it and I'm up to my neck at the moment. I moved into my new apartment this morning.'

'I heard you'd bought a place,' said Jennifer. 'I hope you're going to have a really good housewarming.'

'Maybe.' Carey grinned at her. 'But maybe I don't want my lovely new home trashed by irresponsible ATCs.'

'Irresponsible my arse,' said Jennifer. 'Haven't I just got that hulking great 747 off the runway with flair and precision, and without leaving you to deal with the headache of a blocked runway and irate pilots?'

'You're so sweet! And I'll let you know about the party,' said Carey as she slid into the seat. Of course before she had a party she'd have to kit out the apartment, something she'd intended to make a start on the previous day but which, thanks to Peter's intervention, she hadn't got round to yet. It had taken ages to get to Swords that morning and retrieve her car from the car park beside The Old Schoolhouse, then to go back to Blanchardstown to collect her stuff. By the time she'd brought it all to the apartment she'd only just managed to rush into Dunnes Stores and buy a few bits and pieces (including bedlinen) before heading off to the airport for her shift. Part of her was annoyed that she'd allowed herself to spend the whole day with Peter. Getting to know him again. Getting to like him again. Feeling herself drawn by his charm and made careless by the effects of the alcohol.

So careless that she had allowed him to take her in his arms when they got into his house the previous evening. And to hold her face between his hands and kiss her, very gently, on the lips. And then she'd let herself kiss him back, familiarising herself again with how accomplished a kisser he was, and she'd put her arms around him, hugging him to her. She'd allowed his fingers to slide from her cheeks to her breasts and she'd allowed him to unbutton the cotton shirt she'd been wearing. She'd responded to the touch of his hand and

262

the taste of his kisses but she'd finally pulled away from him and told him that she wasn't ready. He'd looked at her with frustration in his eyes and had asked her what the hell the matter was. They were both adults, he said. They were both free agents. So it wasn't as though either of them was betraying anyone now, was it?

'It's not that.' She stood uneasily in front of him twisting closed the buttons of her shirt.

'What then?' he asked.

'I just – can't!'

'You don't think that your ex-husband isn't doing exactly this with that girl?' asked Peter harshly. 'You don't think he isn't getting what he wants, do you?'

'I've no idea what Ben is doing,' said Carey shakily. 'And he's not my ex-husband yet. Sandra isn't your ex-wife either.'

'Stop splitting hairs,' said Peter.

Carey winced.

'I thought you wanted it,' said Peter. 'I wouldn't have done anything if I hadn't thought that.'

'I'm not ready,' Carey told him unhappily. 'I'm sorry, I really am. If I was . . . if there was anyone . . . well, I care about you a lot. But I—'

Then he'd leaned towards her and placed his index finger over her lips. 'It doesn't matter,' he said. 'Forget about it.'

He went into his bedroom and closed the door firmly behind him.

'Delta 207, cleared for takeoff, contact departure on 124.65.' She glanced out of the tinted windows at the Delta plane shimmering in the sunlight. She watched it gather speed as it rolled along the runway and lifted into the air.

'Tower, Delta 207, switching to Departure. By the way, after we lifted off we saw some kind of dead animal on the far end of the runway.'

Carey made a face and turned to her next plane. 'Shamrock 165, cleared for takeoff, contact departure on 118.6. Did you copy that report from Delta?'

'Shamrock 165, cleared for takeoff, roger. Yes, we copied Delta and we've informed our caterers that they left something behind.'

Carey laughed. 'Thank you, Shamrock.'

Gerry Ferguson, who was sitting beside her, looked at her in disgust. 'Those guys are fucking revolting.'

'Oh, come on, Gerry.' She grinned. 'Dead badger is probably a delicacy somewhere.'

Although Carey enjoyed her shift in the tower, she was also glad when it finished. She got into her car (still packed with her morning's shopping) and drove to her apartment. She hurried inside the building and opened her door. Everything was exactly as she'd left it the previous day. Going back out to the car, she unloaded her stuff. She hung her clothes in her built-in wardrobes and stacked her set of black and white crockery in the kitchen cupboards. Finally she filled the kettle and switched it on.

While she was waiting for it to boil she went out and stood on the balcony. The night air held the merest hint of warmth.

'My place,' she said as she heard the kettle click off. 'My place. No one else's.'

She turned back into the apartment and made herself a cup of coffee. As she walked from room to room, she acknowledged that she hadn't felt this sense of security and ownership in Ben's house. In the second bedroom she stopped and looked at her pile of shoe-boxes. At least there was room for them here and she didn't have to feel guilty about them cluttering up the place. Her mobile phone buzzed to alert her to a text message. She picked it up and read it.

'Sleep well, miss u. Luv Peter.'

She smiled and simply replied 'Tks.'

264

Chapter 22

Bergamot

This is a light oil with a calming effect and a fruity scent

Although one of the benefits of her shift rota was that she could go into town at off-peak times and so miss the weekend crowds, Carey got up early the next morning and drove into the city anyway. Her Saturday shift didn't start until nine that evening and she wanted to potter round places like Habitat where, according to Gina, there was a fantastic sale on, and Stock Design, who were advertising a new range of pots and pans, to look at things for the apartment. She felt that she was possibly going a bit overboard, but Gina had told her not to be stupid – one of the joys of having a place of your own was spending far too much money on it.

She parked in the Dawson Street car park and cut through the Royal Hibernian Way (resolutely ignoring its designer boutiques) to Grafton Street where she was instantly seduced by a pair of knock 'em dead burgundy stilettos in Carl Scarpa. She tried them on, they fitted perfectly and, as she handed over her credit card, she reminded herself forcefully that she must *not* visit Nine West or Bally or any of the other shoe shops on her way to the top of the street.

It was, she thought as she stepped out of the shop, very strange to walk along Grafton Street and ignore the footwear displays. Not surprisingly there seemed to be hundreds of gorgeous pairs of shoes begging her to buy them today. 'I will be strong,' she said out loud. 'I will think only household thoughts.' Though the idea of her, Carey Browne, thinking longingly of tea-towels and wastepaper bins made her giggle.

She managed to get to Habitat without inflicting further shoe-related damage to her credit card and walked inside. It wasn't a shop she'd ever bothered with before but now she spent ages browsing round their displays and she began to worry that she might find herself as equally enticed by sofas and coffee-tables as she was by shoes. She had to make herself walk by a really lovely black recliner which she knew would look stupid in the apartment even though it looked great in the shop. And she reminded herself that she actually possessed two sofas even though the new leather one she'd bought hadn't been delivered yet. She worried at her lower lip as she thought about her multi-sofa state and wondered how she'd get rid of the one that was already in the apartment. It was actually quite comfortable. She wasn't sure whether or not the leather one would even be as comfortable. Although it was clearly way more stylish.

She wandered down the stairs to the lighting department and was instantly charmed by a round orange table-light which gave off a warm glow. Perfect for the living area, she decided, and 10 per cent off! She was also fascinated by a very utilitarian but totally modern stainless steel lamp. She stepped backwards to look at the lamp from a greater distance and bumped into the man behind her.

The sense of shock she felt when she realised that she'd stood on Ben Russell's foot was overwhelming. She could hardly believe that, after the events of the last few weeks, she would bump into him here in the middle of a furniture store, looking at a lighting display. In her most secret of dreams she'd imagined their next meeting to be at some as-yet undecided function where she'd be guest of honour receiving an award for – she didn't know but something dramatic anyway – smiling coolly at him, acknowledging him but in a vague, half-remembering kind of way, and saying something witty yet slightly cutting so that he'd wonder why on earth he hadn't loved her and cherished her the way she deserved to be loved and cherished. She simply couldn't believe she'd met him in Habitat. It was far too mundane.

'Oh,' she said.

'Carey.'

'Hi.'

'Hi.'

266

'What are you doing here?' she asked.

He raised an eyebrow. 'Looking at lights.'

'Me too,' she said.

'Obviously.'

'Yes, well, yes, obviously.'

They stared at each other in silence. She searched his face for signs of sleepless nights and worry but she couldn't see any. He looked as handsome as ever, his eyes bright and carefree, his fair hair spiked with gel.

'I heard about the incident at the shop,' she said eventually. 'It sounded very dramatic.'

'At the time it was,' he said.

'Why did they do it?' she asked. 'Was it a burglary attempt?'

He explained about the two brothers. 'I called into the hospital to see the younger one,' he told her. 'Nice guy. Very apologetic.'

'Well, hopefully the insurance will cover you.'

'Yes,' said Ben.

'I saw the report on the news,' she added.

'Did you?'

'I would've rung . . .'

'It doesn't matter,' he interrupted her. 'How's work?'

'Oh, fine,' she said.

'Easier now that you're on the northside of the city again?'

'Well, yes. More convenient.'

'Where are you living?'

'I bought an apartment,' she told him. 'That's why I'm here looking at lights.'

'Oh.' His eyes darkened. 'Where?'

'Near Swords.'

'I hope you'll be very happy,' he said.

'I hope so too.' I can't believe we're having this conversation, thought Carey. I made love to this man three times in one night. I stood naked with him in a Vegas swimming pool. I once told him that I loved him and meant it. And now we're having a conversation about apartment locations. How did this happen?

'I'm sorry it didn't work out.' His casual words broke in on her thoughts.

Carey felt a lump in her throat. 'Yes, well, nobody's fault.'

'Both our faults actually,' said Ben. 'Too much unfinished business in our pasts.'

'Maybe.' Suddenly she wanted him to go. If he stayed she might cry, and she didn't want to cry in front of him. If he thought that she was still in love with Peter Furness that was a good thing. She didn't want to be his cast-off. One of his many cast-offs.

'We should have dealt with it better.'

'I tried,' she said tightly.

'By throwing shoes at me when I was in bed.'

'You shouldn't have gone to bed.'

'I was tired. I thought you were tired. And overwrought.'

'You wouldn't talk.'

'I didn't think it was worth talking about.'

'Well, maybe not.' She tightened her grip on the Carl Scarpa bag. 'After all, you were continuing your life exactly as it was before. I guess you thought I should too.'

'I never—'

'We're starting again,' she interrupted him. 'And we don't need to argue, do we? It's over. There's no reason to fight.'

'I just want to be painted in my true light.'

'Don't worry, I know what your true light is.'

'You're so convinced you're in the right all the time.'

'So are you.'

'That's because . . .' he broke off. 'Oh hell, Carey, it doesn't matter any more, does it? You're back living near the airport where you always wanted to be and I'm up to my neck re-fitting the shop. I suppose we'll look back on it as a mad month in both our lives. Maybe someday we won't even regret it.'

'I don't regret our time together,' she said slowly, 'but I'm sorry that we were so stupid as to think it could be long-term. And I suppose I should really ask you – have you done anything about a divorce yet?' She was astonished at how together she was managing to remain.

'I got some information sorted,' said Ben, 'but I haven't followed it through. I was side-tracked by the whole shop disaster.'

'Do you want me to deal with it instead?' asked Carey.

'I thought you had a solicitor on the case already,' said Ben.

'I haven't quite got round to the solicitor part,' she told him.

'To be honest, I just wanted it all to go away and pretend it never happened. But I'll get on with it soon.'

'You know it takes four years,' he said.

'What!' She looked at him in shock. 'Four years! We weren't even together four weeks!'

'I know. I know. But you can do a package in the Dominican Republic – a one-night stay and home you go again. I checked it out on the net. Apparently Sylvester Stallone, Michael Jackson and Jane Fonda have all done it. So we'd be in good celebrity company.'

'Is it legal?'

'Probably as legal as our marriage.'

She laughed suddenly. 'We built things up out of all proportion. Just because it was great sex . . .'

He laughed too. 'Yes, I know. Hormones got in the way of judgement.'

'So.' She exhaled slowly. 'I'd better get going.'

'Are you going to buy it?'

'What?'

'The lamp. You were looking at it for ages.'

'You were watching me!'

'I couldn't help noticing you,' said Ben. 'You're a noticeable woman.'

She made a face at him. 'I don't think so. And I don't know about the lamp. What d'you think?'

'I like it,' he said. 'What's your apartment like?'

'Nothing special,' she told him. 'I bought a show apartment which meant that it was already decorated and you know how that is. Modern but fairly neutral.'

'Convenient,' he said.

'Yes.' She grinned suddenly. 'Except that having bought a place with a perfectly good three-piece suite I then went out and bought a leather sofa too.'

'Ouch.' Ben winced. 'So what are you doing with the suite?'

'Dunno,' she said. 'I suppose I could put an ad in *Buy & Sell* or something.'

'How much?' he asked.

'What?'

'Are you asking for it?'

She shook her head. 'I haven't a clue.'

'I'll buy it,' said Ben.

'What?'

'You know what my furniture situation is like. You were always complaining about the uncomfortable armchairs. I'll buy it.'

'But you haven't even seen it.'

'I'm sure it's fine. I just want something I can sit in and not feel as though my back is going to break.'

'Well . . .'

'Name your price.'

'Ben, you can have it,' said Carey.

'Oh, no.'

'Please.' She pulled at one of her curls. 'Take it. You'd be doing me a favour anyway.'

'I really think . . .'

'Please,' she said again, more forcefully. 'Think of it as my divorce present to you.'

'OK,' said Ben after a pause. 'D'you think it'll fit in the *Herbal Matters* van?'

Carey scrunched up her face. 'Yeah, I think so.'

'OK,' he repeated. 'Give me a call when you want me to pick it up.'

'Sure.' The unreality of the situation was making her head buzz. Of all the things she'd imagined she'd talk to Ben about if they ever met again, collecting sofas wasn't one of them. 'I kind of dreaded ever having to talk to you again, but it wasn't too bad, was it?'

'No,' said Ben.

'So maybe we're not complete fools after all.'

'Maybe not.'

'Give my – well, give my regards to Freya.'

'I will,' said Ben.

'Though she never liked me, did she?'

Ben shrugged. 'She never got to know you. That's different.'

'You didn't get to know me but you liked me,' said Carey. 'Or, more accurately, you liked me at the start.'

'I still like you,' said Ben. 'If things had been different . . .'

'They were different enough as it was,' she said quickly.

'You still like buying shoes?' He nodded at the Carl Scarpa carrier bag to break the sudden, uncomfortable silence between them.

'A bit of a weakness,' she admitted.

'I was surprised you left some behind,' said Ben.

'Out of fashion ones only,' she told him.

'Ah.'

'Give my regards to Brian too,' said Carey. 'If you meet him soon.'

'They're getting married,' said Ben. 'Freya and Brian.'

Carey smiled. 'I'm glad,' she said, 'but surprised. I didn't think your sister was the marrying type.'

'I don't think she did either,' said Ben. 'Maybe we changed her mind.'

'God only knows why,' said Carey. 'I'd've thought that seeing us would've put even the most dedicated wedding-goer off.'

'Maybe they're looking at it as a triumph of hope over experience.'

'Maybe. At least we've got over the hating each other part.'

'I never hated you,' said Ben.

Carey felt a lump in her throat again. 'No. I never hated you either.'

'We should've been honest with each other from the start.'

'Don't go down that road again,' she said. 'It's over. Forget it.'

'Yes. Sure.' He glanced at his watch. 'I'd better go.'

'Meeting people?'

'Leah,' he said uncomfortably. 'For brunch.'

'Have a good one.'

'You too,' said Ben.

For a moment she thought he was going to kiss her but he simply smiled shortly and walked away. She stood there for a moment, then brought the orange light and the stainless steel lamp to the cash desk, paid for them and left the store.

Leah was already sitting at the window table of South Anne Street's Gotham Café when Ben arrived.

'Sorry,' he said as he sat down beside her. 'Got delayed.'

'Punctuality was never your strongest point,' she said. 'I always allow you an extra ten minutes.'

271

'Do you?' He looked surprised.

'Of course.'

'I'm not always late.'

'Ninety per cent of the time,' she said.

'Have you ordered?'

She nodded. 'Pizza. Pepperoni for you, vegetarian for me. Deep pan,' she added as she saw him about to speak again.

'You know me too well,' he said.

'Years of experience.'

A waitress put two large glasses of Coke in front of them.

'Far too well,' he amended.

He leaned back in his chair. He was still shocked at having bumped into Carey in Habitat and surprised at how civil they'd been to each other. Not just civil, friendly, he thought. He'd imagined that if he ever met her again there'd be more heated words and snarled accusations but she seemed to have got over it. His first instinct when he'd seen her gazing at the stainless steel lamp had been to leave the store at once, but he hadn't been able to do that. Instead he'd watched her critically, wondering what it had been about her that had made him act so out of character and wondering why she'd married him in the first place.

'Ben, you're not listening to me!'

He blinked out of his daydream and looked at Leah who was frowning at him. 'Sorry, what did you say?'

'I was wondering if you'd like to stay in town, do some shopping and go to a movie later?' she asked.

He shook his head. 'I told Freya I'd get back to Rathmines and check things out with her. There's still a heap of work to be done if we want to open on schedule.'

'I thought you were going in tomorrow?'

'Yes, but I need to make sure that everything the shopfitters are doing is OK. They won't be around on Sunday,' he explained.

'You love that shop, don't you?'

'Of course,' he said. 'It's something that Freya and I did for ourselves. It means a lot.'

'I have an opportunity to do something that means a lot to me too,' said Leah.

'Oh?'

272

'Karen and Juliette have asked me to go into partnership with them.'

'Really?' Ben looked at her with interest. 'Where?'

'A new salon,' she said. 'In the Rathmines town centre. A unit has come up for lease there and it's ideal.'

'And do you want to go ahead?' asked Ben.

'I think so.' She tore off a piece of the pizza which the waitress had just put in front of her. 'I like working at Eden but I'm only an employee there. A partner would be much better.'

'More stressful,' remarked Ben.

'I'm good with stress,' she reminded him.

'Clearly.' He grinned. 'That was stupid of me.'

'Anyway, we have to come up with three months' rent in advance, plus there's all the outfitting costs.'

'You should set up a company,' said Ben.

'I think that's what we'll do all right,' agreed Leah. 'Juliette is the brains behind it, she knows the business stuff. Thing is, we all have to put in some money of our own. About ten grand each.'

'Wow.' He made a face. 'Aren't you borrowing?'

'Some. But let's face it, as Juliette says, we probably won't get as much as we want.'

'True.'

'And if it's our own money we'll have to work hard.'

'Equally true.'

'So it's just a matter of getting it.'

'You don't have a spare ten grand lying around then?'

She made a face at him. 'Give me a break! If I had ten grand lying around I probably wouldn't be sitting here right now. I'd be off on a Pacific Coast cruise or something.'

'Probably.'

'I went in to see my bank manager but the most he'll lend me is five thousand,' said Leah.

'Ah.'

'I wondered whether you and Freya would like to make an investment of five thousand?' She popped another piece of pizza into her mouth and looked at him earnestly.

Ben ate a slice of pizza himself while he mulled over her proposal. It wasn't a huge amount of money but, given what had happened

273

at Rathmines and the current cash-flow situation in the chain, it was probably the wrong time for her to ask.

She didn't look at him while he thought but busied herself with picking the courgette slices from her pizza and laying them down on the side of her plate.

'Let me have a word with Freya,' said Ben. 'See what she thinks.'

'I was hoping you wouldn't have to ask Freya,' said Leah, turning her chocolate-brown eyes on him. 'I don't think she likes me very much at the moment.'

'What? Of course she does. I thought you two were friends. In fact, I'm surprised that you asked me about the investment, not her.'

'Freya's still mad at me about the party,' said Leah. 'I haven't spoken to her in ages.'

'Call her,' said Ben. 'She's over it.'

'That's just it,' Leah said. 'She doesn't even return my calls.'

'Doesn't she?' Ben looked surprised.

Leah shook her head. 'Well, last time she did but I was out. She left a really terse message saying she was busy.'

'Then that's exactly what she was,' said Ben. 'You're reading the situation all wrong. Anyway, if she was mad at anyone it was me, not you.'

'Poor Ben.' Leah smiled sympathetically. 'All these women being mad at you.'

'Oh, I've got used to it.'

'Anyway, let me tell you about our plans.'

He listened as Leah spoke but he didn't really hear what she was saying. He didn't really see her in front of him either; the image that filled his head was Carey. Carey as he'd seen her today in Habitat. Standing with her weight slightly on one leg. Long knitted coat almost to her ankles. Hair billowing out around her face, black-rimmed glasses perched on her nose. No matter how he felt about her as a person, he still thought she was one of the sexiest women he'd ever met. Not beautiful, like Leah. Just sexy.

'You're not listening,' Leah accused him again.

'I am,' he said. 'Really. And I think you'll make a great success of it.'

'Huh.' She looked unconvinced.

274

'Actually, I was thinking that I can help you with the money.'

'I thought you were going to ask Freya first.'

'I'll lend it to you myself,' he said. 'Nothing to do with Freya or *Herbal Matters*. Not an investment, just a loan. From me. Personally.' He took his chequebook out of his pocket and wrote the cheque straight away. 'Repay it when you can,' he said as he handed it to her.

'Really? Can you afford to do this?'

'Yes,' he told her.

'Oh, Ben!' She leaned across the table and kissed him.

It felt good, he thought as he basked in the glow of her approval, to make someone happy.

Chapter 23

Virginian Cedarwood

A very soothing tree oil with a dry, woody aroma

C arey stood on the third storey of the Dawson Street car park and looked at the spot where her car was supposed to be. The space was occupied by a lime-green Volkswagen Beetle with a bright orange flower in the little chrome vase on its dashbord. She turned round and scanned the row of cars behind her but she knew that the Audi wouldn't be among them. She'd parked here, opposite the stairs, she remembered it clearly.

She put her carrier bags and the stainless steel lamp on the ground. Her arms were aching from the weight of her purchases – she'd engaged in some post-traumatic stress shopping after meeting Ben which included another two pairs of shoes, a soft red cashmere cardigan and a pair of rhinestone-studded jeans. It wasn't really fair to think of the shopping as a post-traumatic stress event, she told herself as she stared blankly at the rows of cars. Meeting Ben hadn't been stressful at all. Not in the sense that she might have expected. Talking to him had been easy and spontaneous, and suddenly she'd remembered why she'd fallen for him in the first place. And so, when he'd told her that he was meeting Leah for brunch, she'd experienced a feeling of regret and a totally unexpected burst of jealousy which upset her more than she would've imagined. It was to get rid of those feelings that she'd gone shopping. The frenzy of trying on clothes and shoes had pushed all thoughts of Ben and Leah from her mind. But as soon as she'd signed her last credit-card slip she began to think about them again.

She'd still been thinking about them as she got out of the lift in the car park. She rubbed her arm muscles and forced herself to focus on her parking problem instead. There was no question in her mind but that this was the spot where she'd left her Audi. Someone had clearly stolen her car. She felt a wave of panic rise inside her. She needed her car, it was essential to her. Already her mind was juggling with the hassle of reporting it stolen and waiting around in case it reappeared and of ordering taxis to get to and from work. And then, probably, the police finding it burnt out somewhere. She hated to think of her little Audi burnt out at the side of the road.

She thought evil thoughts about the kind of people who preyed on cars in city centre car parks. Then she frowned. If someone had stolen her car, then how had they got it out of the car park? She had the ticket. Surely getting it out would be almost impossible without the ticket?

She looked round her again. She was definitely in the right place, but maybe she was on the wrong level. She'd got out at level three because everyone else in the lift had got out at level three. Now she wasn't quite sure where she'd left the Audi. Parking the car now seemed to be something that had happened in a different reality. She picked up her bags again and walked up the pedestrian ramp to the next parking area. A navy BMW was parked in the space. Down a level, she thought. Perhaps I'm too high. But on the second storey she found a silver-grey Porsche which, while very desirable, still wasn't her Audi.

'This is fucking stupid,' she muttered angrily to herself. 'It's not like I'm in the Stephen's Green car park where you could mislay a bloody bus because the place is so huge. Or an equally awful place like the Ilac Centre. This is an ordinary, straightforward place and surely I should be able to find my damned car!' She ground her teeth with rage and tears of frustration pricked at her eyes. 'I parked it here, I know I did. It can't have been stolen. I'm just totally thick.' She couldn't remember how many levels there were in the car park but the idea of trudging along them all, lugging her bags with her, was almost too much to bear. Plus – the thought suddenly struck her – it would probably take so long to find it that her ticket would elapse and the barrier wouldn't lift and there'd be some sort of scene . . .

Then, just as she felt that the tears would spill down her face, she thought of her central locking system. She sniffed, rubbed her hand over the end of her nose and pressed the button on her key. She heard the beep of the Audi's alarm system disarming. A beep that definitely came from higher than level two. 'Right,' she said aloud, 'it's here somewhere.' She pressed the button on her key again and heard the alarm system reset. Not on level three. Not on level four. Not on level five. But closer, she thought. Her car was here somewhere.

It was on level six. She saw the amber glow of the indicator lights and heard the beeps as she pressed the alarm key again. The car was parked in the bay she'd expected. She sighed with relief as she opened the boot and let down the back seat so that the stainless steel lamp would fit before piling all her bags inside.

She got into the driver's seat and took a tissue from the box in the door pocket. She wiped her eyes, blew her nose and then took out a fresh tissue to clean her glasses. 'Stupid, pathetic woman,' she said to her reflection in the rearview mirror. 'Stupid, pathetic, loser woman.' She started the engine and took extra care in reversing out of the space. She didn't trust herself not to smash into one of the concrete pillars and completely ruin her day.

She was utterly amazed to see Sylvia's car outside her apartment building when she got home.

'You've forgotten, haven't you?' said Sylvia as she got out, followed by Jeanne.

'Forgotten?' Carey stalled for time.

'You told Jeanne and me that we could come over today,' Sylvia reminded her. 'You said that it would be a good day to look round.'

'Yes, I did.' Carey smiled at her niece. 'And I hadn't exactly forgotten. Just slightly.'

'Slightly?' asked Jeanne.

'Now that I see you I remember,' said Carey. 'I hope you haven't been waiting too long.'

'Ten minutes,' said Sylvia. 'I rang but your phone is switched off.'

'It's in the bottom of my bag,' said Carey. 'I probably didn't hear it. Sorry.'

'You've been shopping!' Jeanne was peering into the back of Carey's car. 'D'you want me to bring some stuff in for you?'

'That'd be great,' said Carey. She took her keys out of her bag. 'Syl, could you grab the lamp and then we needn't come back for anything.'

Sylvia sighed but picked the lamp out of the car and followed Carey along the flagstone pavement to the building's entrance.

'I don't know how you can afford to buy clothes and stuff,' she observed. 'Buying a place of your own is ruinously expensive.'

'Credit card,' said Carey succinctly as she opened the apartment door and ushered them inside.

'Oh, wow, Carey it's way cool,' breathed Jeanne as she looked around her. 'I really, really like it.'

'Very nice,' said Sylvia.

'Thanks.' Carey felt bathed in a proprietorial glow. She beamed at them as they wandered from room to room, exclaiming in delight over the kitchen appliances and the built-in wardrobes. 'To think,' she murmured to herself, 'that I even care about the fact that I have cherrywood wardrobes!'

'Oh, sorry, Carey, this is for you.' Jeanne handed her a box wrapped in bright yellow paper and topped with a rosette. 'From all of us.'

'Thanks,' said Carey again. She pulled the paper from the box and opened it to reveal a delicately cut John Rocha vase.

'I really wasn't sure that vases would be your thing,' said Sylvia. 'But it's a modern design so I hope you like it.'

'It's fantastic,' said Carey. 'Now all I have to do is get flowers!'

'And remember to change the water,' added Sylvia. She walked over to the patio doors and peered over the balcony. 'That garden will be lovely when it matures a bit.'

'I know,' said Carey. 'It's very peaceful, isn't it?'

'Gorgeous,' agreed Jeanne, who'd joined them. 'I'd love a place of my own, I really would.'

'No chance,' said her mother. 'By the time you can afford a property you'll probably be middle-aged.'

'God, Sylvia, that's cheerful!' Carey made a face at her sister. 'Jeanne might get a brilliant job, earn a fortune and buy some fabulous penthouse overlooking the Bay.'

'I want to be a controller, like you,' said Jeanne.

'Really?'

Jeanne nodded. 'Absolutely.'

Sylvia sighed. 'She's been talking about it for ages.'

'It's hard work,' Carey told her. 'Just because I'm a bit of a messer from time to time doesn't mean it's all like that.'

'I know,' said Jeanne. 'And you're not a messer, Carey. You just live life to the full.'

'I'm not so sure about that.' Carey stepped back into the apartment. 'I do my best but I've had a few spectacular failures.'

'At least you tried,' said Jeanne passionately. 'That's what counts, isn't it? What's the point of never doing anything because you're afraid you'll get it wrong? Better off giving it a go.'

'But looking before you leap isn't exactly the worst thing you could do either,' said Sylvia.

'I know.' Jeanne glanced at her mother. 'You should weigh up the possibilities. All I'm saying is that you don't always have to go for the safe option.'

'Actually, if you're directing a plane, you do.' Carey grinned at her.

'Well, yes, for that,' admitted Jeanne.

'I'm glad we're in agreement on the safety issue,' said Carey.

'I think that's why you do some mad things in your personal life,' Jeanne added. 'You're safe and sensible at work so you're not when you're at home.'

'Jeanne!' cried Sylvia. 'You can't say things like that to Carey.'

'Why not?' Carey shrugged. 'Maybe she's right, Syl. Maybe I do like to take chances at home.'

'That's why she took the chance on getting married,' said Jeanne.

'And we all know where that led,' said Sylvia tartly.

'It was worth it. Anyway, I'm not discussing it any more,' Carey told them. 'It's past. This is the present – me and my apartment. A single woman doing it for herself.'

'Will you get lonely, d'you think?' asked Jeanne.

'Nope.' Carey grinned. 'When I shared the house with Gina I used to dream of being on my own. She was so untidy it drove me mad.'

'Are you a tidiness freak?' Jeanne sounded surprised. 'I didn't think so.'

'Not like Sylvia,' Carey told her. 'Your mother used to go round folding her knickers into neat little different coloured bundles when we lived at home and tying each bundle with a different colour ribbon.'

'Carey!' Sylvia blushed.

'She still does,' said Jeanne. 'Well, I don't know about her knickers, of course, but she colour codes everything else. Folds everything into neat little parcels, too.'

Carey snorted with laughter.

'There's nothing wrong with that,' said Sylvia defensively. 'At least that way I know where things are. There are three women and three men in our house. I need to know. Anyway,' she added, 'it makes sense.'

Carey laughed again.

'It's no different to your boxes of shoes,' said Sylvia.

'My shoes are works of art,' Carey told her. 'Investments even.'

'Well, so are my knickers,' said Sylvia.

This time both Jeanne and Carey laughed.

'The price I paid for the La Perla ones, they damn well are an investment!'

'I hope they are,' said Carey. 'I hope they do the trick for you.'

'Stop it!' But Sylvia was smiling too now.

'Maybe I'd have better luck with men if I spent the money on knickers instead of shoes,' mused Carey. 'Though Peter likes my shoe collection.'

'You're not going out with him, though.' Sylvia stared at her sister. 'Are you? You told me you were just renting a room from him.'

'Oh, he took me to lunch to celebrate the apartment,' said Carey. 'Nothing special.'

'Don't, Carey,' said Sylvia. 'Don't do something really stupid.'

'I won't,' said Carey. 'Don't fuss.'

'Is this the married bloke?' asked Jeanne interestedly.

Carey glared at Sylvia.

'Mum told me about him,' Jeanne explained. 'She said he damaged you emotionally.'

'Sylvia!'

'I explained to Jeanne why it is that having a relationship with someone who's married isn't a good idea,' said Sylvia.

'I wish you wouldn't use me as an example of all that's wrong in relationships,' Carey told her. 'I didn't know he was married at the time. Why doesn't anyone believe me?'

'I believe you,' said Jeanne robustly.

'Jeanne, I'm a hopeless role model for you, obviously,' Carey said. 'Certainly when it comes to men.'

Jeanne laughed. 'I dunno. At least while she's fretting about you and your men, Mum leaves me alone.'

Sylvia turned to her. 'I certainly don't intend to leave you alone.'

'What you don't know won't hurt you,' said Jeanne, her voice bubbling with laughter.

'Anyone want some tea or coffee?' asked Carey hastily.

'Do you have Diet Coke?' asked Jeanne.

'In the fridge.'

'Let me make the tea,' said Sylvia.

'OK,' said Carey. 'I'll unwrap my lights and you guys can help me decide where to put them.'

The orange blob looked well on the low sideboard but it took her and Jeanne a while to decide on the best place for the stainless steel lamp. Eventually they put it in the far corner of the room where it threw a small pool of light onto the polished floor.

'It'll be fabulous in the evening,' Jeanne assured her.

'I think so too,' agreed Carey.

Sylvia handed her a coffee in one of the new black and white cups. They stood side by side in the middle of the living area.

'These places are so cute,' she said. 'It makes me wish for one myself.'

'All you have to do is divorce John,' said Carey. 'Then you can find a place of your own.'

'Mum would never divorce Dad,' Jeanne said. 'They're too much of a pair.'

'You think so?' Sylvia looked at her daughter curiously.

'Oh, absolutely,' said Jeanne. 'You finish each other's sentences, you know what the other one is thinking . . . you're very definitely married.'

'I guess that's good to know,' said Sylvia.

'How about you, Jeanne?' asked Carey. 'Any romance on the horizon?'

Jeanne blushed which made Carey smile. Her niece had been so self-assured until now that it was nice to see that she could still be embarrassed.

'Gary,' said Sylvia dryly.

'Gary?'

'She met him at your party,' Sylvia told her.

'Oh!' Carey nodded. 'The football guy.'

'Yes.' Jeanne's cheeks were still bright pink. 'He phoned me.'

'And you've been going out with him?'

'Only a couple of times,' said Jeanne. 'And, of course, Mum is like the secret police every time we do, wanting to know where we're going and how long we'll be and all that sort of thing.'

'Oh, Sylvia.' Carey grinned. 'Cut the girl some slack.'

'I'm her mother,' said Sylvia grimly. 'It's not in my nature to cut her any slack.'

Both Carey and Jeanne laughed.

'It's a pity you and Ben didn't stay together,' sighed Jeanne. 'You could've had a kid and I could've babysat and invited Gary over for heavy snogging sessions and it would've been very convenient.'

Sylvia glared at her daughter and Carey laughed again. 'By the time I got round to having a baby you'd have moved on to someone else,' she assured Jeanne. 'But I promise you that if I ever do have a kid, my apartment is available for you.'

'Carey!' Sylvia sounded angry. 'Not even in a joke.'

'Sorry,' said Carey. 'I sometimes forget I'm supposed to be an example.'

'A bad example,' Jeanne reminded her.

'Oh bloody hell!' Carey drained her coffee. 'I don't really want to be an example at all.'

Sylvia and Jeanne stayed for another hour. Carey enjoyed their company although she was glad when they finally left and she had some time to herself. She went into the spare bedroom and stacked her new shoes along the wall with the rest of her collection. Then she tried on the rhinestone jeans and the cashmere cardigan together and gazed at her reflection in the full-length mirror. Not bad, she thought. She looked strong. The red cashmere brought out the colour in her cheeks and the mahogany tints in her hair. The jeans were figure-hugging. Carey had to admit that even though hers was the sort of figure that wasn't flattered by floating dresses and short skirts, she always looked well in jeans.

It doesn't matter how I look, she told herself as she took off the jeans and hung them up. Not from the potential boyfriend point of view anyway. I'm taking some time out for myself. Today was a watershed because I met Ben and I talked to him and we were adult about everything even though I never expected us to be. And I know that I'm over it. She grinned at her reflection in the mirror. I even have the apartment to prove it.

She pulled on her tracksuit and went into the kitchen. She opened the fridge door and took out a Tesco lasagne for one. It was a pity, she thought as she popped it into the microwave, that the apartment had such a gorgeous oven and hob and she hadn't got round to using them yet. At some point she'd try cooking. But it seemed so much effort for a person on her own.

Chapter 24

Myrrh

A soothing resin oil with a musky and smoky scent

B rian and Freya sat at a corner table in Oleg's, a half-finished bottle of Beaune between them. Colman, the owner, came over and refilled their glasses at the same time asking them if they'd enjoyed the meal.

'As always,' said Brian. 'It's a great place, Colman.'

'Thanks.' Colman smiled at him. 'We want to become an institution. Any time anyone thinks of eating Russian food in Dublin we want them to think of here.'

'I'm sure they do already,' said Freya. 'And I don't want to appear picky, but there probably aren't that many places in Dublin serving Russian food.'

'Not just Russian food, obviously,' added Colman. 'Good food. That's our aim. And good service.'

Brian laughed. 'You have the loan, Colman, you don't have to pitch the business plan every time we meet.'

'I guess not,' Colman acknowledged. 'But I feel that I have to assure you that we're doing well.'

'That's pretty obvious,' remarked Freya. 'The place is almost full.'

'Yes,' said Colman. He looked in satisfaction at the occupied tables around them. 'And we have had a lot of functions as well. Since I did the party for your brother, Freya, we've had three other weddings.'

'Really?'

He nodded. 'How is your brother?' he asked. 'And his lovely, lovely wife?'

'Actually—'

'They're great,' Brian interrupted Freya. 'It was a fantastic night, Colman, and we appreciated it very much.'

'I'm glad.' He smiled at them and moved off to another table.

Brian looked at Freya. 'I just didn't see the point in telling him that it had all blown up in their faces,' he told her. 'Colman and Dimitri put so much effort into making everything just right . . .'

'It wasn't their fault,' said Freya.

'I know,' said Brian. 'But why make him feel bad?'

'I didn't realise you were so thoughtful,' she said.

'No?'

'Maybe I did.' She took a sip of her wine and then looked at him. 'Were you thinking of us having our wedding reception here too?'

'What?' Brian looked startled.

'It's something we should start thinking about,' said Freya. 'Always provided that you still want to go through with it.'

'What makes you think I don't?' he asked warily.

'The fact that you've just asked that question.'

Brian cracked his fingers and Freya winced. It was a nervous gesture of his, one that he used to buy time, and she recognised it as such. She said nothing.

'I suppose I haven't given it a lot of thought,' said Brian.

'The wedding? Or the reception?'

'Any of it,' he admitted.

'Haven't you?'

'It didn't seem urgent.' He looked uncomfortably at her.

'No. But you were the one who asked me to marry you and I said yes so I suppose we should get a move on,' she told him. 'Unless you just want us to get engaged and stay like that for ever?'

'Don't be silly,' he said.

'I'm not.' She drank some more wine. 'I'm bringing things into the open, Brian, because I can see that I have to.'

'What d'you mean?'

'Oh, for heaven's sake!' Her impatience was evident. 'You asked me to marry you and I told you that I couldn't have kids and we haven't talked about it ever since.'

'You said you were going to check out the whole children thing,' he said uneasily.

'I know. I have, and it's not very promising. I didn't expect it to be. Yes, it's possible – just like winning the lottery is possible. But it's not very probable. So, Brian, you have to make a decision. Given that I'm unlikely to produce any kids for you, and given that you've said already that you want them . . .' Suddenly Freya's voice trailed off and she reached for her wine glass again.

'You don't have to make it sound so stark,' he complained.

'I do,' said Freya. 'Because it is stark. Oh sure, I can try all sorts of treatments if I want to. And we could do insane things like using someone else's egg.' She shivered. 'I don't even want to think about that, to be honest. But the bottom line is that you and I as a unit would probably be childless. We're too old to adopt.' She snorted. 'I never realised before just how on the scrapheap a thirty-nine-year-old woman is in our society. I always thought that with our age-defying make-up and our aerobics classes we were as young as anyone. But we're not.'

'Freya—'

'So you have to decide, Brian. An old husk like me or someone young and fertile?'

'Freya—'

'If you opt for the young and fertile, I'll understand.' She reached out and touched his hand. 'I will, honestly. Just because you've never had to think about the kid issue before doesn't mean you're not entitled to better options now.'

'I don't know any young fertile women,' he said.

'But you could find one,' said Freya.

'I'm not looking,' said Brian.

'But you might.'

He picked up his starched white napkin and folded it neatly. 'How do we know that you won't get pregnant?' he asked. 'I've done a bit of research too since you told me. Other women going through the menopause still get pregnant. They warn about it, in fact.'

'Very few,' said Freya. 'And I doubt that any of them are women whose bodies have given it all up before forty.'

'I always thought we'd be together,' said Brian. 'There didn't seem to be any need to rush things.'

'You know, people don't think about getting old any more,' said Freya. 'All we do is think about how we can stay looking young and doing the things we've always done. But our bodies have different ideas.'

'You look young,' said Brian. 'You look lovely, Freya. You always do.'

She smiled at him. 'Thank you. But in my case, it literally is only skin-deep.'

He sighed and rubbed the back of his head.

'You've got to think of it like this,' she said. 'If you and I get married, we won't have children. If that's what you want, then I'm happy to start thinking about when and how we tie the knot. But if children are an important issue then there's no point in marrying me.'

'I don't see it that way.'

'You've got to,' she told him. 'Because I don't want you marrying me thinking that there's more to the package than you're getting. I don't want to be the second Russell to get divorced before making it to the first wedding anniversary.'

'Let me think about it,' said Brian.

'No.' Freya finished her glass of wine. 'You *have* been thinking about it. You said you'd done some research. And you must have a bottom line yourself because that's the way you are.' She stood up. 'I'm going to the Ladies. If you're still here when I come back then it's wedding bells all the way. If you're not . . . well, I'll understand why, Brian. And I won't hate you for it because if it was me I might do the same.'

She walked up the stairs and pushed open the door of the ornate Ladies room. She sat down on the same gilt and brocade chair that Carey had sat on during the night of her wedding party and looked at herself in the enormous mirror. She didn't look like a woman who was over the hill. The shadows under her eyes, which she knew were caused by sleepless nights lately, were hidden by her expensive, light-refracting concealer. Her skin, though not flawless, still appeared dewy and smooth and it wasn't all down to the latest L'Oreal foundation. She'd always had clear skin, rarely had to worry about spots, even as a teenager. Her golden-blonde hair gleamed under the mirror's white light. Sure she had it coloured once a

288

month, but so did everyone. She didn't look like some ancient crone, she certainly didn't feel like one and yet her body was telling her that she was.

She opened her handbag and took out her pale pink lipstick. She wished she knew how Brian really felt about her situation. She'd hoped, although not really expected, that he'd bring up the subject first. But really she'd known all along that it would be up to her because Brian was the kind of person who believed that if he said nothing and did nothing, any unpleasantness would go away. Deep down she knew she was that sort of person too. Sometimes she wondered if she'd secretly known what was the matter with her but had pushed it to the recesses of her mind so that she wouldn't have to deal with it. And yet she'd been genuinely shocked when Dr O'Donnell had told her.

It wasn't because of the fact that she'd never now have children. In some ways she'd almost accepted that beforehand. But her acceptance had been based on the fact that it was her choice. Now the choice had been taken away from her. There was no use in thinking that she might have a baby in some distant future – despite the fact that time was running out – because the distant future had become the past. And the loss of time was almost mind-numbingly painful to her.

She couldn't understand why it was she felt like this. All she knew was that she was flawed. And that this flaw could cost her the one relationship in her life that really meant something to her.

She dropped the lipstick back into her handbag. Then she took out her mascara and swept it over her lashes, thickening and lengthening them so that they framed her Scandinavian blue eyes. Not even a wrinkle around them. Naturally smooth even without the aid of Botox. She looked at her watch. Ten minutes had elapsed since she'd left Brian downstairs. Ten minutes was surely enough for him to leave the restaurant if that was what he wanted. And ten minutes was too long to leave him on his own if he'd stayed.

She readjusted her royal-blue jacket and took a deep breath.

She was still holding her breath as she turned into the dining area and looked at the corner table.

He was gone.

*   *   *

289

Maude and Arthur walked into Oleg's five minutes after Freya, holding her head high, had walked out of the door. Maude looked at the gilt mirrors and the ornate décor and reflected that it was nice to be somewhere where the walls weren't painted white, the tables weren't sandblasted glass and the cutlery wasn't some kind of design statement. Oleg's brought her back to a time when eating out was a deeply comforting and elegant experience rather than a trendy thing to do.

She hadn't expected Colman to remember them but his brow furrowed in semi-recognition as he showed Maude and Arthur to a table beside the one so recently vacated by Brian and Freya. He handed them two leather-bound menus and left them to look over the contents while he tried to remember where he'd seen them before. It was when he brought the complimentary vodka shots to the table that it came to him. He wondered if they knew that they'd only just missed the other couple but decided against saying anything. Brian had paid the bill and left before Freya, telling Colman that his girlfriend would follow shortly. Colman had sensed that something was the matter but, despite his natural curiosity, he reminded himself that the personal lives of his clients was none of his concern.

'It does seem kind of disrespectful to Carey to come here,' said Maude as she looked at the menu. 'But I really did want to try it out as a restaurant.'

'It's nice, isn't it?' Arthur too liked the warmth of his surroundings. 'Though a long way to come for a night out.'

'Oh, why not?' asked Maude. 'It's not as if we had anything more exciting to do, is it?'

'No.' Arthur shook his head. 'But I have to tell you, woman, that you're exhausting me with these weekly nights out.'

Maude laughed. 'I think it's fun.'

'So do I,' he admitted. 'You were right, you know, we were getting terribly staid.'

'I suppose you fall into it.' Maude sipped her vodka cautiously. 'It becomes too much of an effort to shift out of the house.'

'We've been out more in the past couple of months than in the last two years,' declared Arthur.

'And it's been worth it.'

Maude felt that it had definitely been worth it. Friday nights had become their designated eating-out nights and they'd swapped their traditional fish supper from the local chipper for a table for two in a variety of restaurants around the city. Mostly they'd picked ones closer to home but Maude had wanted to try Oleg's again because she'd liked it so much on the night of the party. Even though she knew that it had some bad associations for her.

She hadn't known, of course, that her new son-in-law had been cavorting here with his ex-girlfriend while Carey was completely oblivious to the fact. She was very angry with Ben and disappointed too because, like everyone, she'd thought he was a nice guy. She'd also been extremely shocked at Carey's immediate departure from Ben's home. While she didn't expect her daughter to stay in an unhappy marriage she rather wished that she'd given it more time. But it was hypocritical, she thought, to have wanted Carey to give it more time when she hadn't truly approved of the marriage in the first place.

'Are you sure this was a good idea?' asked Arthur.

'Why?'

'Because you're thinking about them, aren't you?'

Maude smiled at him. 'Of course – I expected to. And I'm just sorry that it all ended up being such a mess. Only not very surprised.'

'D'you blame him?'

'Yes,' said Maude. 'But I wish Carey had more sense too. It was such a rebound thing for her after Peter . . .'

'Peter?'

'Her previous boyfriend,' said Maude dismissively. Arthur didn't know much about Peter and Maude certainly wasn't going to enlighten him.

'What is it with girls now?' demanded Arthur. 'It was different in our day.'

'Of course it was,' said Maude. 'You had to marry us to have your evil way with us.'

Arthur laughed. 'Not always.'

'Indeed,' said Maude primly. 'But generally.'

They gave their order to Colman, who praised their choices of borsch and minsky salad to start with and who, at their request,

291

recommended a bottle of red wine which he thought would go well with their main courses of buglama, a dish of lamb stewed in spices, for Maude and fish galki for Arthur.

'Anyway, this takes me back a bit,' said Arthur. 'Remember that restaurant we went to in London when we were on our honeymoon?'

'Yes.' Maude nodded. 'It's quite similar, isn't it?'

'Except that the London one is probably long gone by now,' said Arthur.

'Probably,' agreed Maude. 'But at least we're still standing.'

'And still together,' said Arthur.

'It's because I pander to you,' Maude told him.

'Rubbish.'

Maude smiled at Arthur and buttered a bread roll. He might think it was amusing (and so did she) but the reality was that they'd stayed together because she'd adapted. When she'd married Arthur in the 1950s, that was what women did. If she'd discovered he was being unfaithful to her she wouldn't have been able to walk out on him as Carey had done with Ben. She would have had to put up and shut up because there was nothing else for her to do. There had been times, particularly in the first few years of their marriage, that Maude would have left him if she'd had the opportunity. Not because of other women, simply because he'd treated her as many men had treated their wives then, as a housekeeper with whom he could sleep whenever he liked. She'd hated being taken for granted by him, hated being referred to as 'the little woman' or 'her indoors'. And it had taken a lot of self-will to stick with it, to make it work and make him see that she was more than that. It had been worth it in the end, she thought. And she was glad now to have him. But she hadn't always felt like this.

'I admire you,' said Arthur suddenly. 'I admire the way you brought up our family and I admire the way you did things that you didn't really want to do because you thought it was for the best, and I'm really glad that you never walked out on me.'

Maude looked up from the bread roll.

'I know you wanted to,' said Arthur. 'Especially when you had to give up your job in that little office and stay at home.'

292

'It was what people did,' said Maude. 'And it wasn't a "little office" it was a big company.'

'Sorry,' said Arthur. 'I know it was a good job. That's why I came on a bit heavy sometimes. I was afraid you'd get bored with me and leave.'

'Really?'

He nodded. 'I'm so glad you didn't.'

'So am I now,' she said. 'But I wasn't always.'

'I should make it up to you more,' he told her. 'Bringing you out on Friday nights is all very well, but . . .'

'Arthur, shut up,' said Maude. 'Every now and then I get a bit sentimental and do some reminiscing about my days as a glamour girl but not very often, I assure you. And I'm happy that things ended up between us the way they did. I'm also very happy that in the last couple of months we seem to have grown closer.'

'So am I,' said Arthur.

'And even though it all went horribly wrong for Ben and Carey I'm glad that their marriage opened my eyes to the fact that you still need to work at it, even after more than forty years.'

'I'm not sure how good a silver lining that is,' said Arthur, 'but I know what you mean.'

They'd finished their starters and were waiting for their main courses to arrive at the table when Freya Russell walked into the restaurant. Maude recognised the tall, elegant woman instantly. Colman acknowledged her and went to the bar area while Freya stood in the restaurant with her arms folded tightly across her chest. Maude wondered whether or not she should say hello. And then Freya's gaze fell on Arthur and Maude and her eyes widened in surprise.

'Hello,' said Maude.

'Hello.' Freya looked at her uncomfortably. 'I dropped my purse when I was here a little earlier,' she said. 'I'm just collecting it.'

'We must have barely missed each other,' said Maude. 'You remember my husband, Arthur?'

Arthur stood up and extended his hand. Freya shook it.

'We decided to try it out as a restaurant,' said Maude.

'It's very nice,' added Arthur.

'Yes.'

'So how are you?' asked Maude with interest. She could see that Freya, while as cool as she remembered, was clearly upset.

'Oh, you know.' Freya's smile was clipped. 'Fine and all that.'

'How's your brother?' asked Arthur.

Maude shot him a look but Arthur ignored her.

'He's OK too,' said Freya. 'We had some trouble recently when a jeep smashed into our shop but he wasn't hurt.'

'Pity,' said Arthur.

Freya stared at him. 'I don't think you really mean that, do you?'

Arthur shrugged.

'Not exactly,' Maude said. 'But he's still obviously very upset on Carey's behalf.'

'Carey left Ben,' said Freya shakily.

'Yes, but – ow!'

Maude kicked Arthur under the table. Freya looked frantically towards the bar in the hope that Colman would soon return with her purse.

'Would you like to sit down?' asked Maude. 'While you're waiting?'

'Oh no, thanks.' Freya shook her head.

'Please do,' said Maude more firmly. 'Unless you've someone waiting for you?'

'No,' said Freya and immediately wished she'd said yes.

'Then join us for a moment.' Arthur waved her at the banquette. 'We'd like to talk.'

'I don't really think there's anything to talk about,' said Freya desperately as she perched on the edge of the seat.

'Maybe not.' Maude's voice was gentle. 'We're not going to be nasty to you, Freya. We just wanted to ask you some questions, since you've arrived here so opportunely.'

Freya sat down and looked at both of them. 'I'm really sorry about your daughter and my brother,' she said. 'But it's nothing to do with me.'

'Of course not,' said Maude. 'We understand that.'

'We're just curious,' said Arthur, 'about why he would've married her when he was still holding a candle for this other girl.'

Freya smiled faintly. 'That's an expression I haven't heard in a long time.'

294

'While he still had the hots for the other girl,' said Maude prosaically and Freya winced.

'I don't know,' she said. 'I only know what you know. They met, they married, they split up. I know that there's all sorts of gossip about him and Leah, but Ben says there were other issues. I don't know why they got married in the first place, I really don't. I thought he was mad.'

'We thought *she* was mad,' Arthur said grimly.

'The whole thing was insane,' said Freya.

'But he was the one who had another girlfriend.' Arthur got back to the point. 'I mean, if he had this girl already, why did he hitch up with Carey? What was the point?'

Freya shook her head. 'I honestly, really and truly don't know.' She wasn't able to look this rather nice elderly couple in the eye and tell them, as Ben had told her, that Carey was the sexiest woman he'd ever met and he hadn't been able to keep his hands off her. And she couldn't say that she supposed that this was the reason he'd married her, stupid and all though it was.

She sighed with relief as Colman arrived at the table with her purse.

'I knew,' he said to Maude and Arthur. 'I knew you were here the night of the wedding party. I recognised you but I wasn't certain.'

'We thought we'd try it out,' said Maude.

'I'm delighted you did,' Colman said, 'and I'd love it if you'd have a drink on the house. You too, Freya.'

'Oh, not for me,' she said hastily. 'I have to go.'

'Stay a little longer.' Maude's voice was authoritative. She turned to Colman. 'We won't have a drink, thank you, because we're having wine with our meal and we don't want to end up blotto, but please bring one for Freya.'

'Sure.' Colman beamed and disappeared while Freya gritted her teeth.

'So how's your boyfriend?' asked Maude.

'Oh, fine.' Freya wondered if it was possible for her voice to be any more brittle.

'I liked him,' said Arthur. 'He told me a filthy joke.'

'Arthur!' But Maude smiled.

'He said some nice things about you to me,' Maude told her.

Freya swallowed the lump that had suddenly appeared in her throat. 'Really?'

'Yes.' Maude nodded.

'Well, he obviously didn't mean them.' As soon as the words were out of her mouth, Freya gasped in horror at what she'd said. Maude and Arthur stared at her.

'Why?' asked Maude.

'I – look, sorry, I shouldn't have said anything.' Freya pinched the bridge of her nose and swallowed hard again.

Colman returned to the table, slid a vodka shot in front of Freya and placed the buglama and galki before Maude and Arthur.

'Are you all right?' asked Maude when he'd gone.

'Yes. Fine.'

'Sure?'

'Oh, please!' Freya looked up at her, her blue eyes swimming with tears. 'I'm as fine as I can be. I'm just not fine enough for him.'

Arthur scooped an enormous portion of food onto his fork and swallowed it. This was not how he'd intended the evening to turn out. He hated seeing a woman upset and Freya was clearly very upset. He hoped that she wouldn't cry because he truly couldn't cope with them when they cried, but he wasn't certain that she'd be able to keep the tears at bay. And as he watched her, a single tear tumbled from her eye and rolled down her cheek.

'Do you want to talk about it?' asked Maude.

'I can't.' Freya gasped. 'I really can't.'

'If it's a problem maybe I can help.' Maude gestured. 'Not that I was ever much help with my own daughters but you never know.'

Freya said nothing.

'Your parents died, didn't they?' Maude continued. 'I'm sure you did really well on your own but it's nice to have someone to share things with from time to time.'

'I really don't need to share this,' said Freya. She glanced at Arthur who was eating as though someone would take the plate away from him at any time.

'You remind me of Carey,' said Maude. 'Determined to do your

296

own thing even if it means making a mistake. Determined not to admit that you might need help.'

'She's like that?' Freya wiped her hand over her cheek.

'Absolutely,' said Maude. 'Thinks she can work it all out by herself, but of course she can't. She's being really offhand about the break-up of her marriage to your brother but I know she was devastated.'

'Was she?' Freya was genuinely surprised. 'I got the impression that she was annoyed at first but that she'd almost expected it to go wrong. And, well, I kind of heard that she might have someone else, too.'

'You got that impression from *him*, I suppose,' said Arthur, unable to stay silent at what he thought could be a slur on Carey.

'Sort of,' said Freya. 'Ben wouldn't talk about it much. He said that they were both complete fools and that it was doomed from the start. And that there was someone else in her life anyway.' She looked apologetically at the two older people.

'D'you blame her for telling him that?' asked Arthur hotly.

'I suppose not.' Freya sighed. 'I love my brother, but I'm not sure that he's that good with women.'

Maude smiled at her. 'Carey's not that good with men either. Perhaps they were both to blame.'

'Perhaps.'

'But neither of them have anything to do with why you're so unhappy.'

'It's really nice of you to take an interest, Mrs Browne . . .'

'Maude,' she interrupted.

'Yes. Well. Maude. It's nice of you to ask, but it's a private matter.'

'Of course,' said Maude, 'I understand. But if you'd like to talk to me, you can phone me any time.'

Freya looked at her in puzzlement. 'Why? I'm nothing to you,' she said.

'At the moment you're still connected to me by marriage.' Maude grinned and Freya suddenly realised that she'd probably been a very beautiful woman when she was younger. There was a sparkle in her dark eyes that held the promise of mischief and more. 'I keep telling Carey that she needs to sort things out legally, but – like I said – she

297

pretends to herself that they'll sort themselves out without her ever having to do anything. I haven't pushed her yet because I think she needs a bit of time. I will eventually, and she'll hate me for it. But not yet.'

'I doubt that anyone could hate you,' said Freya.

'You'd be surprised.' Maude grinned again. 'I remember when my elder daughter, Sylvia, was about sixteen and going out with the most unsuitable boy. I wouldn't let her go away for a weekend with him and a group of friends. She yelled at me that she hated me then. And I'm sure she did.'

'I talked to Sylvia on the night of the party,' said Freya. 'I liked her.'

'Sylvia's very likeable,' said Maude. 'We all are. Even Carey.'

'I'm sure.'

'Anyway,' she told Freya, 'if you do feel like getting something off your chest at any time, ring me. It's not as if I have so much else to do that I don't have the time. And Arthur insists that I'm an old busybody anyway.'

'I never said that,' said Arthur.

'You think it sometimes.' Maude looked fondly at him.

Freya drank the vodka shot and stood up. 'Perhaps I will phone some time,' she said. 'You never know.'

'It'd be lovely to hear from you,' said Maude.

'It was nice meeting you again,' Freya told her, 'though I wouldn't have dreamed that it would be.'

'Take care of yourself,' said Maude.

'Thanks.' Freya smiled faintly at her and at Arthur and walked out of the restaurant.

Maude dug her fork into her buglama and said nothing. Arthur had almost finished his food. 'You're an interfering old woman,' he said eventually.

'She's very unhappy,' Maude told him.

'It's none of your business. And if Carey knew . . .'

'This has nothing to do with Carey,' said Maude.

'You're not trying to win the boy back through the sister?'

'No!' Maude looked shocked. 'No,' she repeated. 'I liked Freya the night we first met her. She does remind me a little of Carey, but she reminds me more of me.'

'She's nothing like you.' Arthur looked at his wife in bewilderment.

'It's a woman thing,' said Maude. 'Trust me.'

'Oh God.' Arthur groaned. 'I hate it when you say that. I really do.'

Chapter 25

Ylang-Ylang

A well-known soothing oil with an exotic fragrance

Some of the reporters who'd covered the story of the jeep ploughing into *Herbal Matters* were there to cover the re-opening. Ben, Freya and the shopfitters had worked really hard to get everything done and the paint was still a little tacky when they opened the doors at noon on Monday, but they were finally back in business. The shop looked wonderful with its new displays, better lighting and additional stock. Mike and Des, the two men in the jeep, had turned up too despite the fact that Des's right arm was still in plaster. The reporters joked that maybe Ben could treat him with some kind of herbal remedy and Ben, beaming broadly at the marketing opportunity, presented the brothers with two baskets which he'd already made up containing a variety of different potions. Including arnica for bruises, he told them, and Hypercal cream for the cuts. Photographers snapped away happily as the men shook hands and a small knot of customers applauded. Then the reporters drifted off to file their stories while Susie, the sales assistant, had one of her busiest days in ages.

Later in the afternoon Ben and Freya opened the pile of cards that had come from well-wishers, from other local stores, from their friends and even from people they'd never met before. Ben was astonished to realise that there was still a community spirit in existence, that others were genuinely sympathetic to the accident and full of praise for his promptness in administering first aid to Mike.

300

'It's your fifteen minutes of fame,' Freya told him as she opened yet another card. 'Better lap it up while you can.'

'I don't want the fame for me,' said Ben, 'but I sure as hell want the publicity for the shop. D'you know both Tallaght and Drumcondra have seen increased sales since the accident?'

'Yes.' Freya laughed at him. 'If you recall, it was me who printed out the report.'

'I know, I know. Sorry.' He opened another card and grinned. 'From Phil and the blokes on the footie team.'

'That probably means more to you than any of the others.'

'Probably.'

Freya slid her finger under the flap of the last envelope and drew out the card. She opened her eyes wide when she read it.

'Who's it from?' asked Ben.

'Um – Carey,' said Freya baldly.

'Give it to me.' Ben held out his hand and Freya handed him the card. *Best wishes on your re-opening,* it said. *Carey.*

'That was nice of her,' he said carefully.

'Why did she bother?' asked Freya. 'Is she looking for something?'

'Why should she be looking for anything?'

'Maybe she's decided that she's going to sue you for maintenance or something.'

'Hardly,' said Ben. 'She wouldn't get very far. Besides, she's not like that.'

'She's not your best friend either,' remarked Freya as she threw the envelope into their recycling bin.

'No. But I'd like to think that she might be a friend.'

'I beg your pardon?' Freya stared at him. 'Are you joking?'

'Well, maybe not exactly a friend,' admitted Ben. 'But not an enemy either.'

'I thought the last time you spoke to her, one of her manic housemates grabbed the phone and told you to fuck off,' said Freya. 'I wouldn't call that the hand of friendship.'

'I've seen her since then,' he said defensively, 'and we've patched things up.'

'You've seen her? And patched things up!' Freya's voice rose an octave. 'What d'you mean "patched things up"?'

301

'Not that kind of patching,' said Ben hastily. 'We've just agreed that, you know, it was all very silly and we were fools and life goes on.'

'So when was this friendly meeting?' demanded Freya.

'I met her in Habitat.'

'Habitat?'

'Yes,' he said. 'I was meeting . . . I was meeting Leah for brunch and I had some time and I was thinking of buying some new furniture for the house so I went into Habitat and there she was.'

'You never said anything to me about it.'

'What did you want me to say?' he asked. 'We spoke, we were polite, that was it.'

'What was she doing in Habitat?'

'What d'you think?' Ben looked at his sister impatiently. 'She was buying furniture and stuff too.'

'Why?'

'Because she's bought a new apartment.' He laughed. 'Though she bought it furnished and then went out and bought a second sofa.'

'Ben, that girl is a complete nutter,' said Freya.

'No, she's not. Just a bit impulsive. So I'm taking the extra sofa from her.'

Freya stared at him. 'Why?'

'Because that's what I was looking for myself. I wanted to buy it but she's giving it to me as a divorce present.'

'I'm bewildered,' said Freya. 'I thought I understood you but I just don't.'

'And I thought you'd be pleased,' said Ben, 'that I've managed to get through a difficult situation and come out on top.'

'You think taking her unwanted furniture is coming out on top?' asked Freya.

'From where things were a few weeks ago, probably.' Ben grinned at her and Freya couldn't help laughing. 'Anyway, where's Brian?' Ben had had enough of talking about his meeting with Carey. 'I thought he was coming along today.'

'No,' said Freya.

'Busy?'

'No,' said Freya again.

'What then?'

'OK, don't freak out on me,' she said, 'but me and Brian have split up.'

It was Ben's turn to open his eyes wide in surprise. 'You've what?'

'I don't want to talk about it.'

'But you were engaged!'

'No,' she corrected him. 'We were going to get married. We changed our minds.'

'When?'

'Recently.'

'Freya, I don't believe this. I thought—'

'Listen,' she said. 'I thought the wrong things about you and Leah and, apparently, about you and Carey too. So don't tell me what you thought, Ben Russell, because I just don't want to hear it.'

'OK, OK,' he said quickly. He looked at her with concern in his eyes. 'Are you all right?'

'Perfectly,' she assured him. 'There were reasons and good reasons, but they're personal.'

'God Almighty,' said Ben. 'You didn't discover that he had a criminal past or anything, did you?'

'You have a totally over-active imagination, you know that?' said Freya. 'Of course not. Now can we please drop the subject?'

'One more question.'

'What?'

'Did you dump him for another man?'

'I haven't quite managed to rack up your conquests of the opposite sex,' said Freya tartly. 'No other man, nothing like that. Just personal. Now forget it.'

'Sure, sure,' said Ben. 'I've forgotten it. For now.'

They were closing the shop for the night when Leah arrived wearing a new wool coat with a red fake-fur collar, a black beret sitting jauntily on her head.

'It's starting to rain,' she informed them as she pushed the door open. 'Oh, my goodness, this looks wonderful.'

'Glad you like it,' said Ben.

303

'I wish I'd been here for the actual re-opening. Did the news-papers come?'

He nodded. 'Though we'll probably be bumped out of the pages by a cocaine-snorting celebrity who's had her boobs reduced or something.'

'I hope not,' said Leah. She kissed Ben on the cheek. 'I met Karen and Juliette just before I came here. We're signing the lease at the end of the week.'

'Great,' he said.

'Lease?' Freya looked at her enquiringly.

'I'll tell you later,' said Leah. 'Meanwhile I'm taking this man out to dinner.'

'You are?' asked Ben.

'Absolutely,' Leah told him. 'I've booked a table in that new place in Ranelagh.'

'I hadn't—'

'You've been working like a maniac,' she told him. 'It's your night off.'

'Go on, Ben,' said Freya. 'I'll lock up.'

'Are you sure?' he asked.

'Certain.'

'You wouldn't like to come too, would you? I don't like to think—'

'Ben, just go,' said Freya impatiently. 'I'm fine. I've stuff to do at home. I don't want to go out tonight, honestly.'

'OK.' He couldn't quite keep the reluctance out of his voice.

'Come on,' said Leah. 'We're doubly celebrating, Ben. You and your place. Me and mine.'

'True.' He smiled while Freya shot him a puzzled look. 'See you later,' he told her.

Freya liked being in the Rathmines shop on her own. Although she enjoyed visiting both the Tallaght and Drumcondra stores too, this was their start-up shop and the one with which she identified the most. And while she'd been totally horrified at the idea of having to completely refurbish the place, she had to admit that it had worked out well in the end. The displays were less cluttered, the lights were brighter, the stock more inviting. Regardless of anything else that goes on in my life, she thought, as she ran a cloth over the glass-topped counter, this is something that I achieved for myself. And even though Ben was with me, I could've done it without him. Maybe I wouldn't have expanded to the same extent, but this would have been a success anyway. I would've made it a success. I wouldn't have been a failure.

She sprayed more glass cleaner on the counter. Just because there's one little thing that I can't do it doesn't mean to say that I'm useless, she told herself as she rubbed at a nonexistent stain. She folded the yellow cloth and closed her eyes. She couldn't pretend that being a woman and unable to have a baby wasn't useless. It was like being a computer with no software, a perfume with no scent. Brian had been right to walk out of Oleg's and out of her life. If they'd married, the day would have come when he'd resent her uselessness in the baby department and he'd think of all the other women he could have married instead. Women who weren't reproductive failures. And perhaps he would eventually have left her and found someone else. Someone who hadn't been stupid enough to leave having a kid until it was far too late. Someone who'd already realised what her primary purpose on earth was. Not spending years in the boring trade department of a boring bank. Not building up a chain of damned herbal shops. Just having babies. Like women were supposed to do.

It wasn't fair, she thought miserably. She'd had it all mapped out, all planned and everything had turned upside down. She wished that she could turn back the clock. If she'd known a few months ago that the baby issue would suddenly become so important, if she'd known then what she knew now, maybe she could have talked to Brian about it. Maybe they could have tried for a baby then. Only maybe he wouldn't have wanted one a few months ago. She rubbed the back of her neck. Why was life so bloody complicated? Why didn't people love each other at the same time, want babies together at the same time, want the same things at the same time? And why did you never realise the value of what you had until one day you found out that it was gone?

Leah opened the door to her apartment and stepped inside followed by Ben. She slid out of the dark wool coat and removed her beret, shaking her river of black hair so that it shimmered across her shoulders.

'Coffee?' she asked. 'Or a drink?'

'Coffee,' said Ben, although he'd made a promise to himself to cut back on it. He hadn't been sleeping well lately and he knew that his increased intake of caffeine over the past few weeks was probably to blame.

'Java or Colombian?'

'I don't care.'

'I thought you were fussy about coffee.'

'Only when I'm making it,' he said.

Leah went into the kitchen and Ben flopped onto her squashy sofa. The last time he'd been in this apartment had been the day before he'd gone to New York. It made him dizzy to think that his life had taken a different road since then and yet he'd ended up here all over again. And he wondered, uneasily, whether or not he'd spend tonight with Leah lying on her exquisite cream silk sheets with her equally exquisite body wrapped around him. Was being together their destiny, like she sometimes said? He'd thought so too once. Maybe he'd been a fool ever to leave her. Women were better at these things than men.

She walked into the living room carrying two bone-china mugs of coffee, put them down on the black lacquer table and then began to light the candles dotted around the room. Ben exhaled slowly.

'Don't,' said Leah.

'Don't what?'

'Breathe disapproval like that,' she said.

'I'm not.'

'Yes, you are. It's the candles, isn't it?'

'I don't like the smell of jasmine,' he told her.

She turned to him, the match still flickering between her fingers. 'I do,' she told him and lit another one.

'I know.'

'When we're in your house I don't ask you to turn down the lights,' she said. 'This is my place. I want to light candles.'

'Fine. No problem.'

'They're restful. Therapeutic. You'd think you'd understand that,' she added.

'I'm not disputing it. I just don't like the smell, that's all. It's no big deal.'

'But you're making it a big deal.'

'How?' he asked.

'Breathing like that.' She blew out the match and looked at the cluster of half-a-dozen cream-coloured candles which flickered gently in the draught from the doorway. 'Six,' she said. 'That's not too many.'

'I said it's OK.'

'I'll put them out,' she told him. 'On one condition.'

'Which is?'

'That you promise me it's over between you and the curly crazy woman.'

'What?' He stared at her.

'I need to know,' she said.

They stared at each other in silence for a moment.

'Why do you need to know?' he asked. 'I thought we were just friends.'

'Oh, come on, Ben,' she snapped. 'I really think that you have to make up your mind about things.'

'I don't have to make up my mind about anything yet,' he said.

'You do,' said Leah. 'You can't go on living your life like this.'

'Like what?' he asked.

'Drifting,' she said.

'I'm not drifting,' said Ben. 'I drifted with you for a few years, I admit – and I'm sorry if that wasn't really what you wanted. But I didn't drift into getting married and I didn't drift into splitting up. Those things happened pretty damn quick.'

'It's just . . .' She sighed. 'I need to know if I'm wasting my time with you, Ben. I need to know whether you think there's something between us.'

'Of course there's something between us,' he said. 'Leah, I care about you. I always have. But . . .'

'But only as someone to sleep with, not to marry,' she finished.

'You're being unfair,' he told her.

'I need to know,' she repeated.

'I can't tell you right now,' said Ben. 'I wish I could, but I can't.'

307

'You can't tell me because you want to keep your options open.'

Ben stood up. 'I have to leave,' he said shakily. 'I can't keep making the same mistake over and over. Not with Carey. And not with you.'

'Don't go.' Suddenly the anger had left her face and her eyes were melted chocolate again. 'I'm sorry. I'll put out the candles.'

'It's not the candles,' he said. 'It's everything.'

'Ben . . .'

'I need to be on my own for a while,' he said. 'I'm sorry for all the fucking-up I've done, Leah, I really am. You deserve better than me.'

'Ben . . .'

He put on his jacket.

'Call me,' she said. 'When you've got yourself sorted out. Call me then.'

'Sure,' he said. 'Thanks for this evening, Leah.'

'Yeah, right.' She didn't try to kiss him before he left. And when he closed the door behind him she blew out all of the candles.

He was tired but he didn't want to go home and he didn't want to go to bed. He walked along the canal, hands thrust deep into the pockets of his jacket, shoulders hunched against the cold wind. He was utterly useless, he decided. Because of Carey he'd hurt Leah. Because of Leah, he'd hurt Carey. His mouth twisted into a bitter smile. Somewhere surely it was a sign of his masculine success that he had two women fighting over him. Well, maybe not exactly fighting over him but he was the apex of a kind of love triangle. Except that in his triangle nobody loved anybody any more. Which somehow defeated the purpose of the whole thing.

Now Leah was moving things on. Since the accident in the shop she'd slotted back into his life without saying what she wanted from him. But tonight was different. Tonight she'd made it clear to him that she wanted more than they'd had before. The thing was, he had no idea what he wanted himself. And did what he want really matter any more? He'd wanted Carey but he'd made such a complete mess of that, that he didn't trust himself to know his own mind about anything to do with women. Not that any bloke really did. He comforted himself with the thought. But he hated lumping himself in with the pool of men that women defined as emotional fuckwits. He'd kind of hoped he was a cut above that. Clearly, though, he wasn't.

He groaned and shoved his hands deeper into his pockets.

'I don't understand Leah,' he muttered aloud. 'I don't understand Carey, and even though I thought I understood Freya I clearly don't because I have absolutely no idea why she and Brian would split up so soon after they decided they were going to get married.' He'd been utterly shocked by Freya's announcement and he knew that he'd have to get to the bottom of it. He hoped it wasn't because Brian Hayes had behaved like a fuckwit too. He'd always liked Brian. Got on with him. Imagined that one day he probably would marry Freya even though she always seemed to be perfectly content to stay single.

He stopped and looked into the murky water of the canal. Maybe it was Freya and him. Maybe there was something about them which stopped them forming proper relationships with people and making that final leap into total commitment. Not that anyone could exactly blame them, he thought. After all, Charles and Gail weren't exactly fun role models of what marriage was all about. They'd been so close, so wrapped up in each other that they hadn't had time for anyone else, not even their children. Maybe both he and Freya were afraid of turning out like Charles and Gail.

Ben Russell, pop-psychiatrist, he said to himself as he began walking again. He put his head down and strode onwards, not thinking any more. He reached Crumlin before the real tiredness started to kick in, then leaned against the bridge and wished that he hadn't come so far. His calf muscles were aching now and his feet hurt. He saw an unoccupied taxi and hailed it, falling gratefully into the back seat. Surreptitiously he eased off his leather shoes and began to rub the soles of his feet. At least they were comfortable shoes, otherwise he'd never have managed the distance between Ballsbridge and Crumlin without blisters.

Looking at his shoes made him think of Carey again. Shoes and Carey were inextricably linked in his head. He wondered if she'd phone him about the sofa, or whether she regretted her offer. Not that it mattered really. He'd lived with the uncomfortable armchairs for a long time now. A bit longer wouldn't make any difference.

Chapter 26

Atlas Cedarwood

A sensual oil with a woody aroma which helps to raise the spirit

'I am so hopeless at this,' wailed Carey as her fourth ball of the night veered into the left-hand gully of the bowling lane. 'I can't seem to co-ordinate at all.'

'You've got to follow through,' Elena told her. 'You're just dropping the ball and hoping for the best.'

'Story of my life!' Carey grinned at her friend. 'This must surely be the last round.'

'One more each,' said Elena. 'Then you can finish in the knowledge that even though you were utterly crap, our team still won tonight.'

Carey shook her head. 'Not right,' she said. 'I don't like being a passenger on the team. I want to compete, not just take part.'

'That's my girl, all right.' Chris Brady put his arm around her shoulders and hugged her. 'But you're a truly awful bowler, aren't you?'

'I knew I would be,' Carey told him. 'I swore I wouldn't get involved, but Jennifer persuaded me against my much better judgement.'

'Are you coming into town with us afterwards?' asked Chris. 'We're going to a club.'

'I haven't been clubbing in months,' said Carey. 'Of course I'm coming.'

'Excellent.' Elena picked up a fourteen-pound ball and eyed up the pins. 'As soon as I get a strike with this little lot I've put our victory beyond doubt.'

Carey watched as Elena strode up to the lane and delivered the ball, curling in from the right across the bowling lane so that it reached the pins at exactly the right place to knock them all down.

'I don't know how she does that.' She sighed deeply. 'I wish I could get to grips with this, I really do.'

'You can't be good at everything,' Chris told her.

'The odd thing might be nice.'

'You're good at your job.'

'I'm supposed to be,' said Carey. 'That doesn't count.' She looked at him warily. 'At least, I hope I'm still good at my job.'

'You are,' he said. 'Though I thought you might be interested in the refresher course they're running at Shannon next month.'

'I didn't hear about it.' She frowned.

'There's a notice on the board,' said Chris. 'You might enjoy it.'

'Enjoy?' she grinned. 'I don't know. But it'd be nice to get away for a week.'

'Put your name down,' he told her. 'It'd be good for you.'

She looked at him anxiously. 'You're saying this because you think it would be a break for me and because I have to do a course at some point this year – *not* because you think I'm utterly useless?'

'Carey, why do you look for hidden agendas when there aren't any?' asked Chris. 'I went on the last course, I thought you might benefit from this one.'

'If you're sure that's the only reason?'

'Positive,' he said. 'Now come on, it's your last ball. See if you can't get a strike.'

Two hours later the bowlers were in the latest hot spot night-club, chugging bottles of beer or designer alcohol and dancing enthusiastically. Carey had completely lost herself in the beat of the music and she felt freer than she'd done in months. Every so often guys that she didn't know would come and dance opposite her and she'd smile at them and allow them to dance, but she didn't bother to try to communicate with them. It was good to be back on the circuit again, she thought. Good to be with her friends, good to be clubbing, good not to care. It was a pity Gina couldn't come but Gina had gone to Scotland for a couple of days to meet with Steve's grandparents. She hadn't been looking forward to it that much but, as she said to Carey, it was one of those things you had to do to keep the prospective in-laws happy. Something Carey didn't have to worry about any more. She smiled to herself and jumped up and down to the beat of the bass, her hair flying out around her head, her arms waving in the air.

It was nearly four o'clock by the time she got home but her shift the next day wasn't until nine in the evening so the time didn't matter. She opened the fridge and poured herself a tall glass of cranberry juice. She was thirsty from dancing but not from alcohol because she'd restricted herself to just two bottles of Smirnoff Ice. Anyway, she hadn't needed alcohol for a buzz tonight. She drank the juice, then a glass of water and then she filled the kettle for a cup of tea. It was, she felt, very uncool to want to drink a cup of tea before going to bed but she always did, it was part of her sleep ritual.

She leaned her head against the balcony doors while she waited for the kettle to boil. In the distance she could see the sodium fizz of the motorway lights and the white glow from the airport. She liked knowing that it was so near. She'd felt cut off in the brief time she'd lived in Portobello. Maybe I'm just a sad work-obsessed fool, she thought. But at least it's better than being obsessed about anything else.

She heard the click of the kettle as it boiled and she made herself her cup of tea. She turned on the TV and flicked through the channels. Sky One was showing an episode of *Stargate*. Carey liked *Stargate* though she was sceptical of wormholes as a means of transport across the galaxy. She reckoned that there was a place for a decent controller helping them to arrive in the right place at the right time on the show. Good control would stop them ending up in so much trouble every week.

Sylvia Lynch was awake too. She was trying not to look at the alarm clock beside her bed because the last time she'd looked it was ten to four and she'd made a pact with God and with herself that if she didn't look again, Jeanne would be home before the hour. But she knew that more than ten minutes had passed and Jeanne still wasn't home. Jeanne was a sensible girl – as sensible as a just seventeen year old could be, at any rate. She shouldn't worry about her, she shouldn't want to phone her to check where she was but it was hard to lie here and not conjure up images of Jeanne and that boy Gary. Or Jeanne and Gary's friends. Or Jeanne and goodness knew who else. She didn't want to think that Jeanne might be sleeping with Gary but it was a possibility. She always told Jeanne that there was nothing she couldn't tell her, but so far there was nothing that Jeanne ever wanted to tell her. She wondered whether other parents had this problem with their children. As far as she could see, these days mothers and daughters were supposed to get on tremendously well all the time but that didn't happen with her and Jeanne. They liked different things, they laughed at different jokes and they differed wildly about the acceptable time to come home on a Friday night. She should be grateful that Jeanne was at least just going out with one boyfriend – unlike Carey who, Sylvia remembered, had been surrounded by them at seventeen. She'd never been able to get Carey to babysit for her on Fridays because her younger sister had always been off having fun. 'Plenty of time for babysitting when I've actually got the babies,' Carey would laugh, and then tell Sylvia that there were much better babysitters than her around the place anyway.

Sylvia opened her eye and looked at the clock. A quarter past four. They were going to Tamango's, Jeanne had told her. A gang of them. And then they might go back to one of the girls' houses nearby. Sylvia had wanted to know what was wrong with coming directly home after Tamango's but Jeanne had just looked pityingly at her and said that she wouldn't be too late. But a quarter past four was too late. It really was.

She stiffened as she heard footsteps on the gravel driveway outside and then, thankfully, the sound of a key in the front door. She felt every muscle in her body relax as Jeanne tiptoed up the stairs. She was going to call out to her daughter but then decided not to. She didn't want Jeanne to know that she hadn't gone to sleep. She didn't want Jeanne to know how much she worried.

Freya burrowed into her green armchair and readjusted the yellow cushion behind her head. She opened the book she'd bought that day entitled *Change Can Be Good – A Woman's Guide to the Menopause*.

313

She had decided to be positive about this, just as the book suggested. She wasn't going to look at it as a bad thing in her life, but just something that had happened to her. And it wasn't as though it was the worst thing in the world that could have happened – she might, for example, have been standing in the middle of the shop the day the jeep had driven through the window and been seriously injured. But she hadn't. Dr O'Donnell could just as easily have told her she had some serious illness. But – excluding the menopause – she was in perfect health. And if that wasn't good enough for Brian bloody Hayes, well, *he'd* never been good enough for her in the first place.

Then she felt the rush of prickling heat begin to envelop her so that suddenly she was covered in a lather of perspiration, until not just her forehead but her back, her shoulders, her neck and even the top of her head were soaking wet. Her light cotton top was drenched. She snapped the book closed, got up and changed into another top. She was going to have to buy more clothes, she decided as she sat down again. She couldn't be sure whether that was a positive or a negative.

Leah awoke with a jump, her eyes snapping open. It was the sudden squall of rain beating against the bedroom window that had disturbed her. She slid out of bed and peeked through the curtains, wondering whether or not the weather would ever settle into a more spring-like pattern. It had been dry and almost warm earlier but now she shivered as she watched a stream of water cascade down the glass. She pulled on her jade-green robe and went into the kitchen. She filled a mug with milk and put it in the microwave while she took a jar of hot chocolate from the cupboard. When the milk had heated enough she spooned the chocolate in and stirred it vigorously. Then she brought the drink back to bed and got between the covers again.

She wished she hadn't annoyed Ben by lighting the candles tonight. She hadn't intended to have a serious make-or-break type conversation because she thought it was too early to start issuing ultimatums, but she'd somehow managed to do it anyway and now she didn't know where she stood with him. She was worried because since he'd lent her the money for her salon she didn't want to irritate, annoy or pressurise him so much that he asked for it back. Fuck, she thought as she sipped her hot chocolate. I hope I haven't blown it.

314

Chapter 27

Black Pepper

A spicy, warm oil which is both stimulating and useful for helping muscle fatigue

C arey was pleased when she got home from her 6 a.m. to 2 p.m. shift to find a message on her answering machine saying that her furniture was ready to be delivered. As she dialled the warehouse number she told herself that she'd certainly come a long way when she was as thrilled about a leather couch as she normally would be about a pair of Manolos. She waited impatiently for the phone to be answered, planning where she'd put the couch and wondering whether or not she could do with another blue and red Joan Miró print on the far wall for extra colour.

The delivery was arranged for the following Wednesday morning. It irritated her that she'd have to wait for a few days but she acknowledged that not every business was as immediate as hers. When she had to deal with an incoming aircraft she had to do it straight away. She couldn't tell the pilot that she only accepted travellers from Italy on Wednesday mornings, or that he should pop back in a few hours when she wasn't as busy. But she never quite got used to the fact that other people expected customers to wait.

Thinking about her furniture reminded her of her Visa bill which had arrived the day before and which she'd flung away from her as though it was radioactive. Visa would certainly have to wait for payment. She'd barely paid off the minimum amount the previous month and she'd racked up even more purchases in the last four weeks. She'd never before let her finances spiral so completely out of control and she knew that she would have to begin cutting back if she didn't want to dig herself the kind of money-pit that, even with her generous salary, she'd never manage to get out of. Of course, a lot of her spending was on once-off items. All the same she winced as she looked at the balance and swore that she wouldn't go into a shop for anything except groceries for the next two weeks.

She looked again at her current furniture arrangement. If she'd been really sensible she would have charged Ben for the sofa she was giving him, as it would at least have dented the Visa bill. But it was too late now. She picked up the phone, hesitant about ringing to tell him that he could collect it. It hadn't been too bad talking to him in Habitat, but perhaps that was because it had been unexpected. This time he'd have plenty of opportunity to think up awkward questions and accusations to throw at her, and she wasn't in the mood to defend herself.

She looked at her watch and yawned. Her next shift began at ten this evening. She couldn't talk to Ben before she'd had some sleep. And she was nervous about contacting him anyway. She knew it was silly but she couldn't help it.

In the end she simply sent him a text message. Then she turned off her phone, got into bed and fell asleep straight away.

Ben was on the line to his New York supplier when his mobile alerted him to Carey's message. He slid it across the small desk and accessed it while still talking to Denton Huyler about a new range of pre-blended oils. He frowned as he tried to figure out a message that said 'furn avl fr coll whn u r fone me 18r' but he eventually worked out what she meant. It would have been useful, he thought, if she'd given him an actual time to phone. Telling him to call later must mean that right now she was either in work or asleep. He'd never really got to grips with her shift schedule. He knew that it was four days on and two days off but, without knowing what week was the start of the cycle, he had no idea what shift she was on now. It didn't matter really. He'd do what she said, call later and if he woke her up that was her bad luck.

'You guys heard anything from Palmarosa?' Denton's question broke in on his thoughts.

Ben raised his eyebrows at the name of one of the biggest herbal stores in the States. 'Funnily enough, Diane Geddes called me last week wanting to know when I'd next be in the US,' he said. 'I told her I was going over later this month. Why?'

'They're on the acquisition trail,' said Denton. 'Looking to expand into Europe.'

'I doubt they'd be interested in us,' Ben told him. 'We're too small and too isolated to matter to them.'

'Maybe,' agreed Denton, 'but you know how it is when these guys want to get a foothold in the market. They'll do anything.'

'It'd make more sense for them to buy up a German chain or a French chain though,' Ben said lightly.

'Who knows what goes through the minds of the big corps.' Denton laughed. 'But, buddy, I'd hate to lose you.'

Ben laughed too. 'I know that we're probably more trouble than we're worth to you,' he said. 'Still, I always enjoy doing business with you too.'

'I don't know about small,' said Denton cheerfully. 'This order'll keep us going for a while.'

'Thanks,' said Ben. 'Talk soon.' He hung up and dialled Carey's mobile but got her message-minder. He left a message to say that he'd pick up the sofa whenever it suited her and then turned his attention back to his new brochures on revitalising and comforting oils.

In the end the arrangement to pick up the furniture was made entirely by text message since when Ben phoned Carey later that day, as she requested, he got her message-minder again. Message-minders and answering machines drove him nuts so he sent her a text almost as cryptic as her own.

He arrived at her apartment late on Tuesday afternoon having decided to tie in his stint as a furniture-removal man with a friendly football match in Raheny Park that evening. He hadn't played football in ages and Phil had been delighted when he said he'd turn up for the match. Ben and Phil hadn't talked much about Ben's disastrous foray into marriage other than to shrug shoulders together and tell each other that everyone made mistakes now and again and that there were plenty more fish in the sea. But Phil had been concerned that Ben was using his still-injured ankle as an excuse not to come either to footie practice or to play in any of their competitive games but simply sit at home instead, so he was glad to see that his friend had started to get back into the real world again.

'It's me,' he said as Carey answered the bell. 'Russell's Removals.'

She buzzed him in and was waiting at the apartment door when he got up the stairs.

'Nice place,' he said when she ushered him inside. 'Certainly knocks spots off mine.'

'Oh no,' she protested. 'Your house is lovely.'

He said nothing but allowed her to show him round. 'At least you've got room for your shoes,' he remarked as they stood in the spare bedroom where she kept her collection.

'I know.' She looked at him shamefacedly. 'It was one of the reasons I bought a two-bedroomed place.'

He chuckled. 'I should've known that it'd all go horribly wrong the night you brought over fifty-odd shoe boxes. I mean, look!' He opened the nearest box and took out a pair of emerald-green sandals with chrome stiletto heels. 'Where on earth would you actually get to wear these?'

'To Sylvia's wedding anniversary dinner,' said Carey promptly. 'I wore a skin-tight printed dress in almost the same colour and I looked gorgeous.'

'I bet,' said Ben.

'I did. Well,' she amended, 'maybe not gorgeous. But striking.'

'You always look striking,' he said mildly. 'So what other occasions have been graced by them?'

She shrugged. 'Nothing specific.'

'So you bought a pair of shoes and wore them once.'

'But they were the perfect pair,' she protested. 'And when you find perfection you have to have it. Even if it's only a brief outing.'

'Rather like us,' remarked Ben as he put the shoes back in the box.

Carey flushed and walked into the living room.

'Sorry,' he said as he followed her. 'I didn't mean that the way it sounded.'

'It's OK.' She stood beside the sofa. 'How exactly did you plan to carry this?'

318

'I didn't.' He looked at it appraisingly. 'I thought I'd formulate a plan when I got here.'

'D'you still want it?' she asked. 'You didn't see it before so you don't have to take it if you hate it.'

'It's fine,' he told her. 'And I don't know why you're changing it anyway.'

'The new piece is perfection,' she said blandly.

'Right.' Ben stood and contemplated the oatmeal-coloured sofa. 'First things first, let's take all the seat cushions off.'

They piled the cushions into the corner of the room.

'Were you intending to help me carry this down the stairs?' he asked.

She shrugged. 'I hadn't really thought about it one way or the other.'

'Because I can't manage it on my own.'

'I thought you could do anything on your own,' she said.

'Are you being bitchy?'

She made a face. 'Possibly.'

'It could wait,' he told her. 'I'm playing football with Phil and the rest of them in Raheny later. I could get him to come and help me.'

'Don't be totally stupid.' She stood at one end of the sofa. 'I'll help you.'

They got as far as the door and stopped. Ben eyed the opening and the sofa and scratched his head. 'I wonder did they bring this in before they put the door on?'

'I hope not,' said Carey. 'Because that'd mean my new one wouldn't fit in either.'

'True.' He frowned. 'If we turn it on one side we might be able to slide it out.'

'Nope,' she said. 'You need it at an angle. Otherwise it'll get stuck against the landing wall.'

'But the arms are too fat,' objected Ben. 'If we do that they'll get jammed in the doorway.'

'I don't think so.'

'Let's try it my way first,' he suggested.

'Whatever you say.'

They got the sofa halfway out and then Ben stopped her. 'There

319

isn't enough room on the landing,' he said. 'We can't push it all the way out.'

Carey said nothing.

'Is that what you meant?' he asked.

'Kind of.' She made a face at him. 'I'm good at thinking three-dimensionally.'

'OK,' he said. 'Let's move it back in.'

'Wait! Wait!' she cried as he started to push it. 'I need to tilt – ow!'

'You all right?' He peered over the huge arm of the sofa.

'Yes.' She blinked away the tears in her eyes. 'Just a near self-amputation of my thumb in the doorway. Nothing too serious.' She stuck her thumb in her mouth.

'Sorry,' he said. 'Didn't mean it.'

'I hope not.'

'I didn't.' He looked at her over the arm again. 'Do you want to stop?'

'Stop?' She took her thumb out of her mouth and giggled. 'And leave a sofa half-in and half-out of my apartment?'

'OK, we won't stop.' Ben grinned at her.

'Thank you. Are you ready to start again? Following my instructions this time?'

'Whatever you say. You want to lift and turn it, don't you?'

She nodded.

'Sure it's not too heavy?'

She gave him a withering look.

'Come on then.'

It was heavier than she'd expected but she gritted her teeth even though she felt that her fingers were going to break and her thumb was still throbbing.

'Nearly there,' panted Ben as he stood at the top of the stairs. 'Just turn it a little, will you?'

'I'm doing my best.' She edged the sofa a little bit more and then suddenly it popped through the doorway so that it was outside the apartment.

'Well done,' said Ben as he wiped the sweat from his forehead. 'Now all we have to do is get it down the stairs.'

'Wait till I put the latch on the door,' said Carey. 'I don't want to get locked out after all that.'

It had taken them nearly half an hour to manoeuvre the sofa through the door. It would have taken less, she thought, as she inched her way down the stairs with him, if he'd believed her about the best way to get it out in the first place. But men never gave women credit for being able to work anything like that out and she hadn't really expected him to be any different. She sighed with relief and rubbed her fingers vigorously as soon as they put the sofa down on the pavement. Ben opened the van and made sure that the old carpet he'd put in the back to protect the furniture was in place. Then he went back upstairs and retrieved the cushions.

'Easy part now,' he said.

'Speak for yourself.' She puffed as she raised the sofa to the height of the van and helped him to push it inside.

'Great,' he said when they'd finally finished. 'Thanks a million, Carey.'

'You're welcome.' She was still puffing.

'Your thumb OK?'

'Sure.' She took off her glasses and wiped them. 'Just my arms feel like they're going to fall out of their sockets.'

'I'm sorry,' he said. 'I should've brought someone to help me.'

She looked at him wickedly. 'You'd have brought another bloke and you'd still be pushing it back and forward through the door.'

'Possibly.' Ben laughed. 'I remember you once telling me that you were always right. I suppose you were this time too.'

'Last time was the delay on the flight fom New York,' she reminded him. 'And I had to be right about that. It *is* my area of expertise, after all!'

'Well, when you give up controlling you can become a furniture-removal girl,' he said. He looked at his watch. 'I've to be in Raheny soon. Not that I'm expecting to be much good at this match – it's a while since I last played. Still carrying some war wounds from the jeep incident, you know.'

'I'm sure you'll be as good at it as you are at everything,' she said. 'Even saving people's lives.'

'And I'm sure there's sarcasm in there somewhere,' said Ben. 'Look, are you certain you want to just give me this sofa? I'll pay for it, you know.'

She shook her head. 'Remember – it's my divorce gift to you.'

'Oh.' He looked enquiringly at her. 'Have you found a quicker way?'

'Unfortunately not,' she replied. 'Though I looked up those sites you mentioned. I think I might do the Dominican Republic thing anyway.'

'The advice I got from my solicitor was that it wouldn't be much use.'

'I know.' She shrugged. 'But it's something. A bit of paper saying that we're not together any more. I'd like to have it even if it's not worth much. You probably think that's stupid.'

'Not really,' said Ben. 'I understand.'

'Good.' She smiled with relief.

'Easier to rush in than rush out again, isn't it?'

'Yes.' Carey sighed. 'At least in my mind, though, I consider myself a soon-to-be-divorced woman.'

'Well, would you like to have a soon-to-be-divorced drink with me?' he asked. 'I need something to eat before I play and I'm dying of thirst too.'

'Thanks for the invitation,' she said, 'but I'm going out later on this evening and I have to wash my hair.'

'Ouch,' he said.

'Ouch?'

'Come on, Carey.' He looked scathing. 'Hair-washing is a very outdated way of giving someone the brush-off.'

She smiled. 'I don't think you can give a nearly ex-husband the brush-off but I really do have to wash my hair.' She ran her fingers through it. 'It's a mess.'

'I like your hair,' he said.

'You wouldn't if you had to wash it,' she informed him. 'Curls are a bloody nightmare.'

'Freya often says that she'd love to have curls,' said Ben.

'She wouldn't,' said Carey definitely. 'People with straight hair often think that, but I promise you curls are more trouble than they're worth.'

'I like yours,' said Ben. 'Always did.'

Carey smiled lopsidedly at him. 'Thanks.'

'Well, look, I'd better get going,' said Ben, breaking the awkward silence that had suddenly developed between them.

'Yes, of course, you don't want to be late.'

'I won't be late. Are you certain you wouldn't like that drink before the hair-washing?' he asked as he opened the door to the van.

'It's a nice thought, but no thanks,' said Carey.

'Well.' He slid slowly into the driver's seat. 'Better be off then. Thanks again for the sofa.'

'You're welcome.'

'And for the help.'

'You're welcome there too.'

'And – well, it was nice to see you again.'

Carey bit her lip. 'You too.'

Ben started the engine. 'I hope everything works out for you.'

'I think it will,' said Carey. 'I've kind of got things together. Admittedly I managed to completely screw up my finances by buying my way back into the human race, but money can be sorted out. Getting your head together is the important thing.' She smiled. 'It was nice to see you again too. It helped a lot.'

'Good,' said Ben. He closed the van door and opened the window. 'Don't forget to take the lycopodium.'

'I don't have an ulcer,' she said. 'I told you that before.'

'It's for the stress,' he said. 'Knowing me was stressful for you.'

'Oh, don't worry,' she said. 'Shoe buying is a much better stress-reliever.'

'More expensive than the lycopodium.'

'But far, far nicer,' she told him as he put the van into gear and began to drive away.

The living room was very bare without the sofa. Carey sat in the armchair and tried to visualise the leather couch in its place. It was going to look fantastic. She thought that she was beginning to develop an eye for interior design; she was good at deciding what should go where. Maybe when I'm all washed up as a controller, she mused, I can go round decorating people's homes instead, get my own TV makeover programme and become a megastar. And then – the thought amused her – Ben and Leah can sit side by side and watch me as I stun the world with the brilliance of my décor. She laughed. Stupid thought, really, and she had no intention of becoming washed up as a controller. Although lately she had considered her future a bit more and had wondered whether or not, at some time, she might not work towards getting an Expert Grade which would qualify her to train in new controllers or commit to other special projects such as reconfiguring the airspace around Dublin. She wasn't quite ready for that yet, though. Above all she still loved bringing the planes into land. As far as she was concerned it was still the best job in the world. Thinking about it reminded her of the refresher course on which she had enrolled and which would soon be held in Shannon. She was looking forward to that. It'd be nice to have a week away. Nice to do something different.

She was rinsing the suds from her curls when the buzzer sounded. She swore under her breath as she wrapped a towel round her soaking tresses and went to the intercom trailing drips of water behind her.

'Delivery for a Miss Carey,' said a voice.

Carey frowned. She wasn't expecting anything. 'Hold on,' she said. 'I'll be down in a moment.'

She rubbed her hair briskly, left the towel on the floor of the hallway and went downstairs. The man outside the entrance door was holding the biggest bouquet of red roses that she'd ever seen. She opened the door.

'Miss Carey?' he said again.

'I'm Carey Browne,' she told him. 'I guess it's for me.'

'Someone likes you.' He grinned at her.

'Apparently.' She took the bouquet from him and walked back upstairs. Ben, she thought. He'd obviously ordered them to thank her for the sofa since she'd been so adamant about not taking any money from him. Which was really terribly sweet because she knew that he didn't like fresh flowers himself. They made him sneeze.

She plopped them in the sink and tore open the envelope. *Hi honey, sorry about tonight. Hope these make up for it. Love, Peter.*

She stared at the note and then her phone rang. 'Hi, Peter.' She picked up the handset.

'Hi, darling,' he said. 'Did you get my message?'

'The flowers?' she said. 'They've just arrived. But what about tonight? I didn't get a message about tonight.'

'I sent you a text earlier,' he told her. 'I'm really sorry but Aaron's running a bit of a temperature today and Sandra and the tekkie are going out tonight. She called me and asked if I'd look after him instead of the babysitter. He's not very unwell but he doesn't want her to go out without him. If I'm there she can go. I sent you the text ages ago.'

'I didn't notice,' she told him. 'I was busy today. I didn't have my phone with me all the time.'

'Are you OK with this?' he asked. 'He's my son, Carey. Soon he'll be living in Scotland. I want to see as much of him as I can first.'

'Of course I'm OK with it,' she said, annoyed with herself for feeling peeved at him. 'And the flowers are beautiful.'

'I'm glad you like them. And I love you,' said Peter. 'I'll call you tomorrow.'

'Sure,' she said. 'Talk to you then.'

She ended the call and rubbed her hair vigorously with her new yellow towel before plugging in her hairdryer and waving it over her curls. What kind of bloody idiot am I, she wondered, to have thought Ben might have sent those flowers. And to feel somehow disappointed that he didn't. Why would I even want him to send me flowers? Blokes don't send flowers to girls they've split up from. Very acrimoniously.

And yet tonight she hadn't felt acrimonious with Ben. She'd felt relaxed with him. And she'd enjoyed being in his company. He'd been friendly. Friendly and normal and the kind of guy that she could still find attractive. Deep down and being really honest with herself, she knew she did still find him attractive. 'But not,' she said out loud, 'husband material.' He was one-night-stand material and that was what she needed to remember. And it was important to be able to differentiate between someone who was good for some breathtaking but ultimately meaningless sex and the person with whom you wanted to spend the rest of your life. It was a distinction that had been blurred for her, but not any more. And surely the person she wanted to spend the rest of her life with would be the kind of bloke who didn't mind sending a girl flowers to tell her he loved her.

There was a cluster of people at the football pitch in St Anne's Park. Carey parked her car in the car park and strolled towards the pitch. She didn't recognise any of the players but it would be difficult given that they were all coated in mud. She frowned as she caught sight of one of the spectators.

'Jeanne!' she cried as her niece approached her. 'What are you doing here?'

'More like what are you doing?' demanded Jeanne. 'I'm supporting the team.'

'Which one?'

'Canal Wanderers. It's Ben's team – and Gary's.'

'Oh yes, Gary.' Carey had forgotten about Jeanne's relationship with Ben's team-mate. 'I didn't realise you and Gary were so close that you were attending his football matches.'

'I didn't realise you and Ben were so close that you were doing the same thing,' retorted Jeanne.

'There is a reason,' said Carey, and she explained about the sofa.

'So why are you here?' asked her niece.

'I was supposed to be going out,' said Carey, 'but it was called off and it was such a nice evening – so much brighter than it's been lately – that I thought I'd go for a walk instead. So I came here.'

'Because of Ben?'

'No.' Carey shook her head. 'I came to the park and then heard the cries so I thought it might be interesting to take a look at them.'

'He doesn't know you're here?'

'Of course not.'

'But if he sees you he'll think . . .'

'He'll think I came here out of curiosity. And he'd be right.'

'You gave him a free sofa and now you're watching him play football?' Jeanne looked at her aunt incredulously. 'And you're still saying that you don't love him any more?'

'I had one sofa too many,' said Carey. 'He had none. And I told you, I'm just passing by. When you're older you'll realise that making a brief appearance at a football match isn't a declaration of undying love.'

'Don't patronise me, Carey,' said Jeanne. 'I'm not a child.'

'No, you're not. I'm sorry.'

'However, I do actually enjoy coming to the matches myself,' she confided. 'I can scream and shout and behave in a way that Mum hates.'

'Screaming and shouting?'

'You know Mum,' said Jeanne. 'So prissy.'

Carey grinned. 'That's our Syl.'

'She freaked out a while back when I was out with Gary and didn't get home until really late.'

'I don't blame her for that,' said Carey. 'She worries.'

'Tsch.' Jeanne made a face. 'What's to worry about? She should trust me.'

'I think she probably finds it hard to trust you when she keeps thinking of how I turned out,' said Carey. 'Oh, bloody hell, they've conceded a penalty!'

'Come on, Canal!' roared Jeanne as the Canal Wanderers' goalie picked the ball despondently from the back of the net. 'Get a move on!' She turned to Carey. 'This is the third match I've been at. They lost one and drew one so it'd be nice if they won.'

'Which of them is Gary?' asked Carey as the players raced along the pitch.

'The good-looking one.' Jeanne laughed. 'Number seven.'

'Come on, Gary!' yelled Carey. 'Give it some wellie!!'

Ben heard the call and looked towards the touchline. His eyes widened in surprise as he saw Carey there. Then he recognised Jeanne standing beside her and remembered that Jeanne and Gary had a bit of a thing going. He didn't realise that it was serious enough for Jeanne to come to their matches – he'd missed the previous two she'd attended.

Tony Powell passed the ball to him but Ben, totally distracted by the sight of Carey, missed it completely. Fuck, he thought, as he chased after the opposing player. Now he looked like a useless fool. He tackled the midfielder and, surprising himself, won back the ball, dribbling it towards the goal. It would be nice, he thought, to score spectacularly to prove to Carey that he was good at this. Instead he pitched forward as the midfielder tackled him in return.

'Foul, ref!' shouted Carey. 'Send him off!'

The ref agreed that Ben had been fouled and awarded a free kick. Tony curled the ball towards the goal and Ben, jumping higher than he ever had before, got on the end of it and – as spectacularly as he could have wished for – headed it past the goalie for the equaliser.

'What a score!' Jeanne jumped up and down in delight. 'What a player!'

'Show-off,' muttered Carey. She looked at her watch and turned to Jeanne. 'I'm heading home now,' she said.

'Huh?' Jeanne stared at her. 'It's a good game. Why don't you wait till it's over?'

'I don't want to hang around,' she told her. 'I've things to do anyway.'

'But Ben's playing a blinder,' protested Jeanne.

'I don't care,' said Carey. 'I've had my exercise.'

'OK, if you're sure.' Jeanne looked at her doubtfully.

'Sure I'm sure,' said Carey.

'I still like him,' said Jeanne.

'Surprisingly enough, so do I,' Carey said. 'But I don't love him. And that's what counts.'

Chapter 28

Camomile Roman

A gentle oil with a sweet fragrance

Freya was sitting in her apartment staring at the spring-green leaves on the tree outside her window when she started to cry. She didn't know where the tears had come from, how it was that one minute she was perfectly all right and the next she was sobbing almost uncontrollably. Her entire body heaved with the ferocity of her pain and she hugged her arms around her shoulders as though by doing so she would prevent herself from breaking apart. She wasn't thinking as she cried. Her mind was in a grey fog, unable to formulate thoughts or ideas or even images. All she knew was that she was alone in her apartment and alone with a grief she had never expected to feel. She wiped at her cheeks with her fingertips, the tears sliding down the palms of her hands and dripping onto the multi-colours of her cushions. She wished that there was someone with her to put an arm around her and tell her that everything would be OK, just as her mother had done when she'd been a little girl, upset by something that her father had said or done. Gail had always told her that Charles didn't mean to shout or snap, it was his short temper that did it, that he loved Freya dearly. And while she was telling her those things Gail would hug Freya close to her and stroke her long blonde hair and make her feel totally secure.

But there was no one now to make Freya feel totally secure. And there was nothing in her life that made her believe people ever could be totally secure. She'd felt secure with Brian but it hadn't been enough and she understood that. But she ached for him now and ached for the fact that he hadn't waited in the restaurant to make her feel, even for another hour or so, that he did love her and that everything could be all right. He'd called her once since then but had deliberately phoned the apartment during working hours so that all he had to do was to leave a message. He'd sounded upset and unhappy, telling her that he'd needed a little time, that there were other issues – he'd stopped then and hung up mid-sentence, which was totally unlike him. She appreciated his honesty but a little part of her would have preferred him to pretend. At least for a while.

A few months ago she might have called Leah and shared her unhappiness with her, but these days she felt uncomfortable in the younger woman's company. She didn't know why, because seeing Ben and Leah together again should have made her feel as though everything was working out the way it was supposed to, but it didn't. She was sure that Leah felt equally uncomfortable with her just now too, and so neither of them had exchanged more than a few half-hearted pleasantries over the last few weeks. Freya doubted that – even if Ben and Leah eventually married – they'd ever get back to their easy friendship.

She rested her head on her knees and cried some more. She'd never been much of a talker, never been one for sharing her emotions with people. But she desperately wanted to talk now. She needed someone to listen to her, to understand how she felt. Anyone. It didn't really matter who.

Maude saw the taxi drive past the house, then turn a little further up the road before coming back to stop outside the gate. She didn't wait until the car door opened but threw her own front door open wide and began to march down the path. This way the girl wouldn't be able to lose her nerve and ignore her. She'd reached the gate when Freya got out of the taxi and looked uncertainly at her.

'Hello, Freya.' Maude smiled at her. 'Come on in.'

Freya said nothing but followed the older woman into the house. Maude led her to the sun-drenched living room at the back and motioned for her to sit down. Freya did so, her blue eyes taking in the serenity of the room; the huge bowl of blaze-red tulips on the deep windowsill gave life and colour to it and the pot of coffee on the table filled it with a warm comforting aroma.

'Like some?' asked Maude. 'There's tea if you prefer.'

'Coffee's fine.' Freya watched as she poured it into two large wide cups.

'Milk?'

'Yes, please.'

Maude handed the cup to Freya who realised suddenly that her hands were trembling. But Maude didn't seem to notice the fact that Freya had to grasp the cup firmly between both hands to stop the coffee splashing over the sides.

'I'm sorry,' said Freya after taking a sip of the Java blend. 'I don't know why I rang.'

'It doesn't matter,' said Maude. 'It's nice to see you again.'

'You said to call you that night at the restaurant,' Freya continued as though Maude hadn't spoken. 'And of course I didn't intend to. There was nothing for us to say.'

Maude was silent.

'Only I needed someone.' Freya looked up from her mug and met Maude's eyes. 'I've never really needed someone, not like this. I can look after myself, you see. But today – today I couldn't deal with it myself because . . .' her voice drifted away and she squeezed her eyes shut. Maude waited until Freya opened them again.

'You see, I found out something,' said Freya. 'Not about Ben or Carey. That's the thing, Maude, that's why I shouldn't really have come. It's nothing to do with them. It's about me. I'm selfish – I'm sorry.'

'I don't think you're selfish,' said Maude gently. 'I do think you're upset. And it doesn't matter to me whether you're here about Ben and Carey or something else altogether. Arthur thinks I have a terrible habit of getting involved in other people's lives but, sure, why not? Especially when they're sort of family.'

Freya's smile was a shadow. 'I didn't think of you as sort of family. I didn't really think at all when I picked up the phone.'

'I'm glad you did,' said Maude. 'And even when Carey and Ben aren't connected any more we'll always be sort of family.' She fixed her grey eyes on Freya. 'So what's the matter, Freya?'

Now that she was here, with someone, Freya's natural reticence wanted to take over. But there was something about Maude's presence that invited confidences. It wasn't as though she was Freya's childhood image of a confidante – the rosy-cheeked, grey-haired grandmother of the books she'd read on her own in bed late at night – but there was an aura of calmness about Maude which made her feel the way she wanted to feel. Secure.

Slowly, she told the older woman about her visit to Dr O'Donnell and his diagnosis of early menopause and of Brian's reaction. And when she'd finished she began to cry again. Only this time the arms around her shoulders were real and the warmth of Maude's embrace was immensely comforting.

'You poor, poor, thing,' whispered Maude. 'No wonder you're crying. You're crying for what you might have had and what you'll never have. You're entitled to cry for those things, Freya. And you're entitled to cry about Brian too.'

'It's selfish, though,' sobbed Freya. 'I've had a good life, Maude. I've done the things I wanted to do. I thought I had all the time in the world for anything else. And maybe this is a kind of punishment for not deciding that I should settle down with someone before now.'

'You may have done all the things you wanted to do but not always on your own terms,' said Maude firmly. 'And you weren't one bit selfish when you went out to work to provide for Ben. You're a good person, Freya. To talk of punishment – that's plain silly and we both know you're not silly.' She held Freya close to her again. 'I'm so sorry for you.'

Freya sniffed. 'Actually, the child thing – well, I always felt that I kind of did it already because of Ben. You see, I knew all about the sleepless nights and the nappies and the mess it makes of your life. And even lately, knowing that I was getting older – it didn't really bother me. So I shouldn't care, should I? But now that I can't – *now* I care.'

'Oh, Freya.' Maude looked at her sympathetically. 'You did what everyone does, you made choices. If you haven't had children you've had your reasons and they're perfectly good ones. But the problem is that sometimes we think we can have it all, whenever we want it – and we can't. We have to make those choices. Unfortunately, some of them get made for us.'

'I wanted Brian to choose me,' said Freya. 'I wanted to think that he loved me for myself but he didn't.' She bit her lip. 'All the times we were together I congratulated myself on having a man like him

332

and then suddenly he was gone. And I've no one, Maude. I've liked being on my own because I'm not a good person with other people, but now I realise that I'll always be on my own.'

'No, you won't,' said Maude. 'You're a good-looking woman and there's no need for you to be on your own at all. Unless that's what you choose.'

'It's not as simple as that,' said Freya. 'It's not as though someone special, something exactly right is just waiting for me.'

'No,' agreed Maude. 'There's compromise all down the way. Particularly as we get older and pickier.'

Freya's smile was a little stronger this time. 'I'm horribly picky,' she said. 'That's why Brian was so good to be with. I want my men to be there when I need them and to leave me alone when I don't. I want them to be loving when I'm in the mood and to back off when I'm not. I don't know how the poor bloke put up with me.'

'Possibly because it suited him,' said Maude calmly. 'Tell me about your mum and dad.'

'They were difficult to have as parents,' admitted Freya. 'Dad was very domineering and Mum always wanted to please him. She did everything for him, gave up her job and her friends . . . she didn't seem to mind though.' She paused. 'I know Dad wasn't very pleased when me and Ben came along. He was fussy, he didn't like kids much and he was absolutely devoted to Mum. I don't mean that he didn't love us too but in a distant kind of way. On his terms. But they were the most important part of each other's lives. We were incidental. Then when he died she had nothing. No job, no friends and somehow neither me nor Ben were able to keep her happy. Everyone says she died of a broken heart.' Freya twisted a lock of hair between her fingers then looked directly at Maude. 'I felt guilty when she died. I thought that if we'd only been better kids then it wouldn't have mattered that Dad had died; she'd still have had us.'

'Oh, Freya.' Maude's voice was gentle. 'Don't feel like that. Maybe she did love your dad so much that nothing and nobody else could fill the gap. But it certainly wasn't your fault.'

'You see, I already know that,' said Freya. 'In my head I know that. But in my heart . . .'

'I think she'd be very proud of you,' Maude announced. 'I know I would be.'

333

'You have your own daughters to be proud of,' said Freya.

'Yes.' Maude sat back and grimaced. 'I *am* proud of them. Even though they have me heart-scalded from time to time.'

Freya smiled shakily. 'How's Carey?' she asked.

Maude shrugged. 'Getting on with things.'

'I heard she bought an apartment,' said Freya.

Maude nodded. 'Which I'm glad about. It's a new focus for her.'

'It's a pity it didn't work out,' said Freya, 'with Ben. I'd have liked us all to get to know each other a bit better.'

'You know me now anyway.' Maude smiled at her. 'And whether I'm family or friend it doesn't matter, Freya. You're welcome to call and see me any time.'

'You're really nice,' said Freya warmly. 'And you give such good advice.'

This time Maude laughed. 'But you're the only one who's ever even considered taking it!' she told her.

They were having a second cup of coffee when the door opened and Sylvia arrived. She stood in amazement at the sight of Maude and Freya sitting side-by-side on the sofa.

'Freya's visiting,' said Maude simply.

'I didn't realise you kept in touch,' said Sylvia.

'We met,' explained Freya, 'and your mother invited me out.'

Sylvia took in Freya's red eyes and blotchy cheeks. 'And is everything OK?' she asked.

'Fine,' said Maude.

'Sure?'

'Yes,' said Freya. She smiled at Sylvia. 'Nice to see you again.'

'Well, you too,' said Sylvia uncertainly. 'Mum, would you like me to go? I was just dropping off some shopping for you, but . . .'

'Stay,' said Maude. 'We're having a right old chat. Freya was telling me about her childhood. Makes me realise how good I was to you all.'

'Huh.' But Sylvia grinned and poured herself some coffee. 'What's she been telling you, Freya? That she was even-handed and generous, that she loved all her children equally?'

'Actually, yes,' said Freya.

'I did. I do.' Maude looked at her daughter with injured innocence.

'Oh, really?' Sylvia smiled. 'So when you gave Tony the money for his first motorbike, that wasn't favouritism?'

Freya looked anxiously between mother and daughter but Maude simply grinned at Sylvia.

'And didn't I pay for you to go on that trip to Rome even though we were skint at the time?' she replied.

Freya realised that the banter between the two women was well-worn and familiar. And that they weren't going to argue or fight over things that had happened years ago. That they were, in fact, simply revisiting past times. Her brow furrowed. She rarely revisited past times with Ben. She never wanted to.

'Did you hear that Carey's bought an apartment and is seeing her old boyfriend?' Sylvia turned to her quite suddenly and jolted Freya out of her thoughts.

'I – yes. He told me about the apartment. Not about the boyfriend. I didn't know about that.'

'*Is* she seeing him again?' Maude looked anxiously at Sylvia who shrugged.

'He took her out for lunch after she closed on the apartment,' said Sylvia, 'and I just got the impression there was something going on.'

'Oh.' Maude pursed her lips.

'And did Ben tell you she gave him a sofa as a breaking-up present?' Sylvia returned to Freya.

'Yes,' said Freya. 'He told me.'

'That was a bit odd, don't you think?'

'Oh Sylvia, everything about them is odd.' Freya sighed. 'When he told me he'd met her he also said they'd patched things up and at first I thought he meant they were getting back together. I nearly fainted. But I guess it just means they've stopped screaming at each other.'

'That'll be the day,' remarked Maude. 'At least,' she added, 'that Carey stops screaming and shouting. You know her, Sylvia, mouth runs away with her all the time.'

'Ben's a bit of a shouter too,' said Freya. 'Gets it from our dad, I'm afraid.' She bit her bottom lip. 'He wasn't an awfully nice man really. I loved him, of course, but he was – difficult.'

'So's Arthur,' said Maude cheerfully.

'I don't think he's difficult in the same way,' Freya said.

335

'All men are difficult,' Sylvia stated. 'It's a penance women have to put up with.' She picked up the coffee pot and refilled Freya's cup. 'Have some more and tell us all about your family. I love hearing about other people's families. It makes me think that maybe my own isn't completely dysfunctional after all.'

Chapter 29

Ginger

A warm and spicy oil which is great for a tired body

B en couldn't remember when he'd ever been so angry. Not on any of the occasions when he'd fought with Leah, not when he'd had the blazing row with Carey, not ever before. But now, as he sat in the *Herbal Matters* van on his way to Brian Hayes's house, he could feel the fury surging through his body so that it was all he could do not to put his foot to the floor and speed recklessly through the suburban streets.

Freya had told him. The day after her afternoon with Maude and Sylvia (an afternoon which hadn't ended until much later in the evening and which she'd enjoyed more than she could ever have imagined), she'd gone to lunch with Ben and explained about the early menopause – how she'd given Brian the choice and the decision he'd made. Ben hadn't said anything but had looked at his confident, capable older sister on whom he'd depended so much in the past and had suddenly seen another, more vulnerable side to her. And he'd wanted, there and then, to flatten Brian Hayes for making Freya cry.

'I'm not crying because of him,' she'd sniffed. 'I'm crying for me.'

But Ben found that hard to believe. He'd liked Brian, got on with him even though he found the other man a little staid and boring, but right now he wanted to wring his neck.

The lights changed to green and Ben turned up Orwell Road. He supposed Brian thought that it was fine to go out with Freya and sleep

337

with her and generally treat her as though she was part of his life until the moment when there was something he wanted that she couldn't give him. Things would have been different if they'd married before, but now, because Freya had been so scared of getting married in the first place, Brian was able to discard her without a second thought. Ben tightened his grip on the gear lever as he shoved the van into fourth. Well, that bastard had made a mistake if he thought he could mess around with Ben Russell's sister. A big, big mistake.

Ben pulled into the kerb outside Brian's house. At nine o'clock in the evening the porch-light was on, illuminating the attractive cobble-locked driveway in which two cars were neatly parked. Ben hesitated when he saw the pale green Micra alongside Brian's shiny black BMW. It might not be a good time to confront him if he had visitors. Although it would never be a good time to confront him. And after all, his friends deserved to know what kind of shit he was. So, what the hell, he said to himself as he got out and slammed the doors of the van. He pressed the bell and held his finger on it so that he could hear the insistent buzz inside the house. The hall light came on and he could see Brian's shadow behind the stained-glass panel of the front door.

'Ben.' Brian, casually dressed in a rugby-shirt and jeans but somehow still with the aura of a banker, looked at him in surprise.

'Brian.'

'Can I help you?'

'Can I come in?'

'It's not hugely convenient just now.'

'It won't take long,' said Ben and pushed past Brian so that he was standing in the tasteful, yet somehow soulless, hallway.

'Come into my study,' said Brian. He opened a door to the left and switched on the light. The study was small, barely accommodating the old-fashioned mahogany desk with green leather inlay, the matching leather chair and a half-size filing cabinet. The desk was laden with papers and files.

'Busy?' asked Ben.

'Very,' said Brian. 'We're advising on a take-over.'

'Good for you,' said Ben.

Brian rested against the desk and looked at Ben. 'So what do you want?' he asked.

'You know,' said Ben.

'No, I don't.'

'Freya told me.'

'Ah.'

'You miserable shit.' Ben's voice rose. 'How could you do this to her?'

'Do what, exactly?'

'You dumped her!' cried Ben. 'Dumped her – because of her age.'

'I didn't dump her,' said Brian evenly. 'I told her I needed time.'

'Oh come on!'

'That's exactly what I did. I didn't dump her. Not in the way you mean.'

'You left her on her own in a fucking restaurant, you bastard!' This time Ben shouted. 'You left her on her own when she was already upset and unhappy, and you phoned her to say that you needed some time because you had issues – for fuck's sake, Brian, "issues"! D'you think you're living some kind of pop-psychology life? Now Freya is devastated.'

'Is she?' Brian looked guiltily at Ben. 'I thought maybe she wouldn't care in the end.'

'How could you think that?' said Ben furiously. 'When you know how much she loves you? Just because she doesn't swoon in your arms all the time. Just because she has a career of her own. Just because—'

'OK, OK,' said Brian. 'I get the message.'

'And you just left her there.' Ben's voice rose again. 'I can't believe you did that. I really can't. You utter, utter pr—'

He broke off as the door to the study opened and a stunningly beautiful girl walked in. Ben reckoned that she couldn't have been more than nineteen. Her strawberry-blonde hair fell around a flawless, ivory-skinned face, and her green eyes glittered behind enormous dark lashes. She wore a short black skirt, emerald-green figure-hugging T-shirt and knee-high black suede boots.

'Is everything all right?' she asked.

'You total fuck!!!' Unable to stop himself, Ben clenched his right hand into a fist, raised his arm and caught Brian a blow to the side of the face. Almost at the same time, Brian grabbed Ben by the collar of his well-worn navy fleece and began shaking him so hard that his teeth clattered off each other. Ben heard the beautiful girl scream as he lashed out again at Brian, this time missing him completely and losing his balance in the process. Brian took the opportunity to try to land a blow of his own, grazing Ben's temple but not inflicting any real damage.

'For God's sake, stop it!' The girl's shrill cry burst through the air. 'Dad, stop! You'll kill each other.'

As the words penetrated Ben's head he stopped struggling and turned towards the girl, allowing Brian to finally land a retaliatory punch which caught him on the nose.

'Fuck.' Ben heard the crunch of tissue and felt the blood begin to flow.

'Shit.' Brian turned to his desk and grabbed a bundle of tissues from the box.

'You maniacs!' The girl stared at both of them. 'What the hell d'you think you're doing?'

Ben took the proffered tissues from Brian and held them to his nose, at the same time realising that, in their struggle, some of the files had been knocked from Brian's desk and now lay scattered across the floor while the ones that hadn't fallen were covered with a decorative spray pattern of blood.

'Will I call the police?' The girl looked at Brian, her eyes wide and her face flushed.

'No, Linnet, it's OK. We don't need the police.' Brian turned to Ben. 'You all right?' he asked.

'Yes.' Ben's voice was muffled. 'Though I think you broke my nose.'

'You didn't do my jaw much good either.' Brian massaged it gently.

'It's swollen,' Linnet said, her voice accusing.

'Sorry.' Ben's eyes darted from one to the other.

'Ben, this is my daughter, Linnet,' said Brian, still rubbing his jaw. 'Linnet, this is a friend of mine. Ben Russell.'

'A friend!' Linnet looked at her father in astonishment. 'A friend barges into your house and tries to beat you up?'

'I had my reasons.' Ben took the tissues from his nose. It had stopped bleeding but was now red and sore.

'And those reasons were?' Linnet looked angrily at him.

'I understand his reasons,' said Brian. 'Lin, be a good girl and leave us alone for a bit, will you?'

'Don't talk to me as though I was five years old,' she snapped. 'And I certainly won't leave you alone. The two of you might start beating each other up again.'

'I doubt it.' Brian opened and closed his mouth gingerly.

'Don't bet on it,' said Ben.

'You see!' Linnet looked worried. 'Maybe I *should* call the police.'

'Don't be silly,' said Brian. He turned to Ben. 'Come into the living room,' he said. 'I'll deal with in here later.'

Ben's head was throbbing as he walked behind Brian and Linnet. He was trying to get his mind around the fact that Brian had introduced this absolutely stunning creature as his daughter. Ben had never heard Brian say anything about a daughter before and certainly nothing about someone as beautiful as this. Freya had never said anything about a daughter either.

'Would you like a drink?'

Ben nodded and set off a chain reaction of pain bouncing round his skull. Brian opened a rosewood cabinet and took out two crystal glasses and a bottle of Bushmills. He poured a generous measure into a glass and handed it to Ben.

'We won't start beating each other up again,' Brian told Linnet who was standing anxiously at the door. 'I promise.'

'You're too old for this!' his daughter reproved him. 'I really can't believe I saw it.'

'Don't tell your mother, eh?'

Suddenly Linnet smiled and Ben saw the resemblance between herself and Brian in the way her eyes crinkled. 'Bloody maniac,' she said, although her tone was milder.

'Leave us for a bit,' said Brian. 'I'll yell if he throws another punch.'

'I don't think I can,' said Ben. 'I nearly broke my fingers on your jaw. Must be made of cement or something.'

'Feels like crumbling cement at the moment.' Brian rubbed it gently.

'OK,' said Linnet after a moment. 'I'll go. But the slightest noise and I'm on the phone to the cops. And I don't care if you spend the night in the slammer!' She walked out of the room and closed the door firmly behind her.

Ben said nothing. Brian refilled both their glasses before sitting down in a maroon armchair. He waved Ben to the opposite one.

'Some explanations?' Brian looked at Ben. 'My daughter, as I said. From a brief but intense liaison with a rather gorgeous-looking woman twenty years ago.'

'Clearly she didn't get the looks from you,' Ben said rudely.

'I know,' said Brian. 'Every time I see her I can't quite believe she's mine. But she is.'

'Where's her mother?' asked Ben.

'Marijka went back to the Netherlands ten years ago,' said Brian. 'Took Linnet with her. I didn't want her to go but you know how it is with women. She got homesick.'

'Does Freya know?' asked Ben.

Brian shook his head slowly. 'No.' He stared into his glass of whiskey for a moment then looked up at Ben. 'It wasn't that I held it back deliberately. At first – well, at first when we were going out it was fun and everything, but I wasn't particularly expecting it to last. And I didn't see the need to tell her. Let's face it, Ben, what woman wants to hear that the guy she's dating has a teenage kid?'

'But later?' asked Ben. 'Why didn't you say something later?'

'I should have,' admitted Brian. 'But it got harder and harder. Freya wasn't into family stuff – she hardly ever talked about your parents, Ben. And she didn't seem to care much for kids anyway. So I was afraid that the whole idea of me having a child would turn her off. It wasn't as though Linnet was on the doorstep and was going to pop up at any moment.' He exhaled slowly. 'Later, when things were getting more serious between us, I knew I'd have to tell her but the right moment never seemed to come. And then it was too late. We were going out for a long time and I hadn't said anything and then it would be like confessing to a secret.'

'It *would've* been confessing to a secret,' Ben pointed out. 'And Freya wouldn't have minded that you had a child. Especially a child who was being brought up by someone else.'

'Maybe not. But I wasn't sure.'

'So – do you want to have another child? Is that why you dumped Freya?'

342

'I wanted to marry Freya,' said Brian. 'And I was happy to think that children would be part of our marriage. I know it sounds callous but the night I asked her – the night of your party, Ben – I didn't want to ruin it by telling her about Linnet. But I would've told her. OK, it could've been a problem but we'd have got over it, I know we would. Then when she told me that she couldn't have any children herself . . . I thought that if I talked about Linnet right then she'd feel even worse. And she'd wonder why I hadn't told her before. And the whole kid thing would be an even bigger issue. Even though Freya matters to me more than anything else.' He rubbed his jaw again. 'After that I simply didn't know what to do.'

'She said that if her not being able to have children wasn't a problem that you should stay in the restaurant, but that if it was you should leave. You left, Brian. So the kid thing matters more.'

'No.' Brian shook his head. 'To be honest with you, Ben, I didn't know what to do at that point. I panicked. I know that sounds really, really stupid but that's what happened. I wasn't sure that even if I stayed she'd believe I didn't want kids. In any event I'd have had to tell her about Linnet regardless, and that was the difficulty. How do you tell someone who's just told you that she can't have kids that it doesn't matter because you have one already?'

'And doesn't it matter really?' asked Ben.

Brian sighed. 'I can't say that it doesn't completely. I thought that we might have a child together. I got excited by the idea of bringing up my own son or daughter. Watching them grow up rather than receiving progress reports on them. I missed out so much with Linnet and I regret it more than anything. Marijka was good about access but it was difficult given that they were in Amsterdam. I adore my daughter but sometimes it does feel as though she's simply a distant relative. This is only the second time she's actually stayed with me. I wanted the closeness of bringing up my own child. To see it through properly. So when Freya said . . . when she told me . . . well, I was disappointed.'

'I always thought you were a bit boring,' said Ben. 'I didn't realise you had a secret past.'

'All of us have secret pasts,' said Brian. 'You can't get to forty-six without having a secret past.' He swallowed the rest of his drink. 'Just think, when you have kids of your own they'll find out that

343

you and a woman they've never heard of got married in Las Vegas and split up a couple of weeks later.'

'Thanks,' said Ben.

'I'm simply making the point. It's not as though I tried to keep it a secret, it's just that it already was. And it's hard to talk about these things.'

'Freya doesn't have a secret past,' said Ben.

'She probably does. You just don't know about it.' Brian tried to grin but winced instead.

'I must ask her,' said Ben.

'Don't,' said Brian. 'If she wants to tell you, she will.'

'You mean there is something?' Ben looked at him incredulously. 'Something she's told you but not me?'

'I don't know,' said Brian. 'All I'm saying is that she doesn't have to have told you everything about her life. And you don't necessarily have to know.'

'I suppose you're right.' Ben rubbed his hand over his face. 'So what now?'

'Why did you come here in the first place?' asked Brian.

'She's unhappy,' said Ben. 'She feels betrayed by you. I came to . . . to get revenge for Freya.'

Brian touched his jaw gingerly. 'Revenge hurts,' he said. He sighed. 'I was afraid, Ben. Of what to say to Freya and how to say it. It was easier to let her assume I was upset because she couldn't have kids. Though I know that's wrong too.'

'You're doing her an injustice,' said Ben. 'Maybe she wouldn't be able to cope. But that's her decision.'

'You're sounding very wise all of a sudden,' said Brian wryly.

'I've had lots of experience the last few weeks,' said Ben.

'So how are your own relationships going?'

'I don't have any relationships,' said Ben glumly. 'I just lurch from a series of crises with different women.'

Brian laughed. 'One day it'll all come right.'

'Maybe.' Ben finished his drink too. 'So – are you going to contact her?'

'Yes,' said Brian. 'Maybe not tonight or tomorrow night, but I will be in touch. It's unfinished business no matter how it turns out.'

'Good.' Ben held out his hand and Brian grasped it firmly. 'I won't tell her I was here.'

'Thanks,' said Brian. 'And, Ben, just one more thing . . .'

'What?'

'In your lurching from woman to woman, please do me a favour and keep my daughter out of the equation.'

Chapter 30

Lime

A refreshing oil with a zesty aroma which is uplifting for tired minds

Carey enjoyed the training course at Shannon. The drive from Dublin had been a good deal less fraught than she'd feared and it had given her time on her own which she'd enjoyed. She'd opened the sun-roof and basked in the unexpectedly warm fresh air as she sang along (tunelessly) to her *Heart of a Woman* CD. She'd arrived at Shannon in a good mood and eager to start the course.

If the training centre had been located in the airport itself she would have flown down, but the Irish Aviation Authority's modern glass building was located in an industrial park a few miles from the airport, surrounded by well-tended lawns and ponds. The advantage of this was that during the breaks, the people attending the course could sit outside and recharge their batteries in the warmth of the spring sunshine. Once inside again, the replicated control centre could have been any control centre in the world. Carey and the others had battled with a range of different scenarios that the course instructors had thrown at them, dealing with them as though they were real-life situations even though they all knew that the captain of the 747 which had just executed an emergency landing in appalling weather conditions was really a twenty-five-year-old Aviation Authority employee in the next room.

The course finished on Thursday night but most of the participants stayed in the airport hotel until Friday morning where they had a last breakfast together. Carey was just sitting down at the table when her mobile phone rang.

'Hi, Syl,' she said. 'What's up?'

'It's Jeanne.' Sylvia's anxious voice was choked with tears and Carey felt a chill wrap itself around her.

'What's the matter?' she asked.

'She didn't come home last night.'

'What?'

'She went out . . .' Sylvia gulped '. . . she went out with her friends and she hasn't come back.'

'Hasn't she ever done that before?' asked Carey. 'Stayed over with people?'

'Well, naturally she has, but she always tells me first,' said Sylvia. 'She's seventeen, Carey. I expect her to stay with friends sometimes, but not without telling me.'

'Did she leave a note or anything?' asked Carey.

'Of course she bloody didn't!' snapped Sylvia. 'I'm not stupid.'

'No, you're not, I'm sorry,' said Carey quickly. 'But maybe that's what she's done, Syl. Maybe they went back to someone's house and she stayed over and she hasn't even woken up yet. Have you tried ringing her?'

'Yes, yes,' said Sylvia. 'But I got her message-minder. And that's worrying in itself. She never has her phone switched off.'

'Have you called the police?'

Sylvia started to cry again. 'Yes, I had to. I mean, oh Carey, it's as if this is happening to someone else. I keep thinking of all those news stories about girls . . . she's my baby, Carey. I know she's supposed to be grown-up but she's not. She's a kid really.'

'I know,' said Carey, 'but don't start imagining the worst.'

'How can I not?' demanded Sylvia. 'She knows how worried I'd be.'

'I'll leave here now,' said Carey, 'and I'll be with you in a few hours. Look, Syl, did you and Jeanne have a row?'

'The police asked that too,' said Sylvia. 'No, we didn't have a row, not really. She wanted to go away for the weekend with some of her friends and I said no but she didn't throw a fit about it or anything. I thought it was all right.'

'So maybe she's gone anyway?' said Carey hopefully.

347

'That's what I thought at first,' said Sylvia, 'but I rang Deirdre Barr's mother and she called Deirdre and they said that Jeanne wasn't with them. So that's not where she is.'

'What about Gary?' asked Carey. 'Could she be with him?'

'I don't know,' said Sylvia. 'We did have a bit of an argument about him but it was last week The usual stuff – I said she was seeing too much of him and she told me not to interfere. The thing is, Carey, I don't even know his surname or where he lives or anything. I wanted to find out but she wouldn't tell me. She didn't want to tell me anything about him.'

'Don't you think it's more likely she's with him than anyone else though?' suggested Carey.

'Maybe. But she wouldn't just go off with him and not say something.' Sylvia's voice rose into a wail. 'I mean, she might be with him but she wouldn't stay out all night. Carey, she knows I'd be worried stiff. She really does.'

'She'll be OK,' said Carey as convincingly as she could. 'She's a sensible girl really.'

'It doesn't matter how sensible she is if some maniac has her,' cried Sylvia.

'No maniac has her,' said Carey. 'She's with Gary or one of her other friends and for whatever reason she's behaving really badly, but I promise you, Sylvia – she's OK.'

'I want to believe you.'

'Believe me,' said Carey.

'I'll try.'

'And I'll be there soon.'

'OK,' said Sylvia.

Carey ended the call and told the course supervisor that she had to get back to Dublin for a family emergency. When she explained the situation the supervisor pursed his lips and told her that he thought there was an Aer Lingus commuter flight leaving Shannon for Dublin very soon and did she want him to see if he could get her on it. Carey nodded and before she knew it she was boarding the flight and being shown to her seat over the wing.

She liked flying in commuter planes; because of their lower altitude passengers got a much better view of the lush green countryside even though they were more likely to be buffeted by the winds. But today was gloriously clear and still and if she hadn't been so worried about Jeanne she would have enjoyed the flight. She was almost certain that her niece was with her boyfriend, but Carey simply couldn't understand why Jeanne would do something so thoughtless as to stay out all night and worry Sylvia so much.

She wondered where Gary lived. She also wondered what he was like – whether he'd treat Jeanne properly or whether he was a totally unsuitable boyfriend for her in the first place. And she felt terribly guilty that Jeanne had met Gary at her wedding party and so, indirectly, if Gary was to blame for whatever Jeanne was up to, it was her fault too. And then Carey sat bolt upright in the plane because of course she could find out where Gary lived or at least get his phone number. All she had to do was to ring Ben.

They were making their final approach to Dublin Airport. Carey waited impatiently until the female captain had touched the plane down in a featherlight landing on Runway One Zero and taxied to the stand before pulling out her phone and pressing Ben's speed-dial number.

'Hello?'

She could hear the sound of people in the shop and knew that he was behind the counter at *Herbal Matters*.

'Hi,' she said. 'It's me.'

'I know. What do you want?'

'It's an emergency,' she said. 'I need Gary's number.'

'Gary?'

'Gary,' she repeated impatiently. 'The bloke on your football team. Going out with my niece.'

'Oh, that Gary,' he said. 'Why?'

'For Christ's sake, Ben, just give me the number, will you?' she cried. 'He's probably with Jeanne. She didn't come home last night and Sylvia's sick with worry.'

'Bloody hell.' Ben sounded shocked. 'It's on this phone but I don't know how to read a number without cutting you off. Can I ring you back?'

'Sure.' Carey had disembarked first and was now striding through the baggage hall. She planned to get a taxi to Sylvia's but, she thought, if she got Gary's number and Jeanne was with him then she'd go to wherever he was and forcibly drag her niece home with her. Her phone beeped.

'Hi,' she said.

Ben called out Gary's number to her. 'Let me know if you contact him,' he said.

'Thanks.' Carey punched in the numbers and then almost cried with frustration as she heard Gary's message-minder. She stood in the centre of the arrivals area and cursed under her breath. Then she swore out loud when she got outside and saw the length of the queue for the taxis. Her phone rang again.

'Any luck?' asked Ben.

'No.' Her voice was tight.

'Where are you?' asked Ben. 'With Sylvia or at home?'

Carey explained about the controllers' course and her early morning flight up to Dublin.

'So you weren't in the apartment last week?' asked Ben.

'No,' said Carey.

'Or last night obviously.'

'Obviously.'

'I know this might sound a bit off the wall, but – Jeanne wouldn't have the key to it by any chance, would she?'

'Oh my God.' Carey gripped the phone so tightly that she heard the press-on cover creak. 'She might have. We joked about her using it once. And she knows I was away.'

'I'm in Drumcondra today,' said Ben. 'I'll meet you there if you like.'

'Would you?'

'Sure.'

'Thanks,' said Carey. 'I'm waiting for a bloody taxi. I'd probably be quicker running to the apartment.'

'I'd pick you up but even if there's a queue you'll get a taxi quicker,' said Ben.

'I know. It's OK,' said Carey.

'Don't worry,' said Ben. 'Gary's not a bad bloke.'

'I'm not worrying about *him*,' said Carey. 'But if she's not with him . . . oh Ben, if she's not with him then I don't know where she might be. Maybe she's run off or something, but I can't see her doing that. I really can't.'

350

'Let's try your apartment first.' Ben had left the shop while he was talking to her and was already in the van. 'If she's not there then we'll worry a bit more.'

'Thanks,' she said again.

She debated about whether or not to ring Sylvia but decided to wait until she got to the apartment. If Jeanne *was* there then she'd be able to ring Sylvia and explain that all was well. If she wasn't – well, Carey didn't want to get her sister's hopes up unnecessarily. And going to the apartment would only add an extra few minutes on the journey to Sylvia's anyway. She tumbled into the next taxi that arrived and gave him her address. She was astonished to see the white *Herbal Matters* van arriving at her apartment block at the same time as the taxi. And her eyes widened as she noticed the angry bruise beneath Ben's left eye as well as his swollen nose. But she didn't have time to ask him about it.

'You must have raced out here,' she remarked instead.

'Exceeded the speed limit slightly,' he admitted as he waited for her to pay the taxi driver. 'Have you spoken to Sylvia yet?'

Carey shook her head. 'This'll only take a minute.' She took out her keys and let herself into the block. Then she ran up the stairs and unlocked her apartment door.

The sickly sweet smell of cannabis floated out to meet her and she could hear the low drone of the TV. Her heart leapt as she exchanged looks with Ben and the two of them went inside. Carey knew that she was giggling with relief but she didn't want to laugh at all as she looked at her semi-naked niece and the guy stretched out beside her on the off-white rug in the living room. Both of them had clearly passed out but were perfectly well.

'Wake up, you moron!' Ben kicked Gary Hannigan in the back and the young man stirred languidly.

Carey took out her phone and called Sylvia.

Ben and Carey sat on the new leather couch while Jeanne perched anxiously on the edge of the armchair. Ben had ordered a taxi and Gary had gone home but not before being sick in Carey's bathroom. Ben and Carey had rushed him out of the apartment so that he wouldn't be there when Sylvia arrived.

'She's going to kill me,' muttered Jeanne. 'She really is, Carey. She's going to kill me.'

'I don't blame her,' said Ben.

'It wasn't – we didn't mean – it was just . . .' Jeanne couldn't finish her sentences.

'I thought you had more sense, Jeanne,' said Carey. 'I mean, drink and drugs!' Jeanne moistened her lips nervously as the buzzer of the apartment sounded and pulled at a curl in her hair. Then she straightened up and looked defiantly in front of her.

'Hi, Sylvia.' Carey opened the door and Sylvia strode into the room. When she saw her mother, Jeanne's defiant expression immediately disappeared and she started to cry. Sylvia stood beside her for a moment then knelt down to hug her daughter. Ben and Carey exchanged relieved glances.

After a couple of minutes Sylvia released her hold on Jeanne and stood up. 'Well, young lady,' she said, her voice grim but still a little shaky, 'what have you got to say for yourself?'

Jeanne said nothing but twisted a sodden tissue in her hand.

'I gather,' Carey told Sylvia, 'that after the night-club they came here. Jeanne took the spare set of keys that I gave you.'

'I didn't plan it.' Jeanne spoke through her tears. 'I just saw them on the rack when I went to get my coat and I took them. I didn't think. He didn't know.'

'But he got a few joints in advance,' pointed out Ben.

'I only smoked one,' wailed Jeanne.

'You were drinking as well!' cried Sylvia.

'Not that much,' protested Jeanne. 'Not really. We got some miniatures in the off-licence earlier.'

Sylvia looked at her wordlessly.

'It was only vodka,' said Jeanne. 'And it's not as though I'm a child.'

'You've certainly behaved like one,' said Sylvia angrily. 'And you're too young to buy drink in off-licences in the first place. I suppose he bought them, did he?'

Jeanne nodded miserably.

'How many?' asked Carey.

'What?' asked Jeanne.

'Vodkas.'

Jeanne shrugged. 'Not that many.'

'And when did you intend to come home?' demanded Sylvia. 'Or when did you intend to let me know where you were?'

'I thought I'd be home at my usual time,' said Jeanne. 'We only came here for some – some privacy.'

'Privacy!' Sylvia snorted. 'Privacy! For what?'

Jeanne blushed, her cheeks two red spots on her chalk-white face.

'I've tried to be good with you,' said Sylvia despairingly. 'I tried to give you a certain amount of freedom. I do know that you're supposed to be old enough to look after yourself. And this is how you repay me. Not to mention the nerve, the absolute cheek of you, to use Carey's apartment for furtive fumblings.'

'It wasn't furtive fumblings,' muttered Jeanne. 'And I didn't think—'

'You certainly did not!' Sylvia interrupted her. 'What I want to know now, before you get home and face your father – who I can tell you will be a lot less lenient with you than me – is whether or not you are in any danger whatsoever of being pregnant.'

'Oh, Mum.' Tears cascaded down Jeanne's cheeks. The tissue disintegrated in her hand.

Sylvia pinched the bridge of her nose. Carey put her arm round her sister.

'Do you want us to leave the two of you here for a while?' she asked. 'So that you can have a more private conversation?'

'No.' Sylvia shook her head. 'I'll get her home. John's sick with worry too and I know he won't rest until he sees her. He wanted to come and pick her up but I was afraid that Gary would still be here and John would've absolutely gone for him. Next thing I know, I would've had a husband being arrested for assault on top of everything else. You know how bloody stupid men can be. Solve everything with a punch-up.'

Carey glanced at Ben as Sylvia spoke and frowned. He looked at her uncomfortably, especially when Sylvia suddenly looked at him and frowned too. But nobody mentioned the fact that his face bore all of the trademarks of a punch-up. If they say a word, Ben thought, I'm out of here.

But Carey looked away from Ben and at her sister. 'Would you like some tea before you go?' she asked Sylvia. 'Or coffee, or anything?'

'No, thanks,' said Sylvia. 'We've taken up enough of your time already, Carey. And you've been great. You and Ben.' She smiled waterily at him.

'No problem,' said Ben.

'Come on.' Sylvia pulled Jeanne out of the chair. 'Let's go.'

'I'm really sorry,' wailed Jeanne again. 'I didn't mean to come here and mess it up for you, Carey. We just wanted to be on our own. And it was such a good opportunity.'

'Sometimes opportunities aren't all they seem,' said Carey. 'Take care, Jeanne. I'll talk to you again soon.'

'You'll still talk to me?' Jeanne sniffed.

'We'll see,' said Sylvia. 'No more hanging round. We're off home.' She turned to Carey. 'Thanks again.'

'It's OK,' said Carey. 'Call me later tonight.'

'Will do,' said Sylvia and left.

As soon as the door had closed behind them Carey flopped down onto the couch and closed her eyes.

'Are you OK?' asked Ben.

'Sure. Just exhausted,' replied Carey. 'I was so worried about her. Then I was mad with her. Then sorry for her. Then worried for her again – Sylvia can get pretty angry.'

'I think she was too relieved to be angry,' said Ben.

'I guess so.' Carey opened her eyes again. 'Thanks for everything, Ben.'

'Glad I could help,' he said.

Suddenly neither of them could think of anything else to say. Eventually Carey got up. 'I know Sylvia didn't want anything, but would you like a tea or coffee?' she asked. 'Or something stronger?'

'Tea would be lovely,' said Ben.

'Sit down,' she said. 'It'll only take a minute.'

Ben sat in the recently vacated armchair and listened to the sound of Carey bustling about in the kitchen. He looked round her living room. It was very different from the living room in his own house in Portobello. That was darker and less spacious because of the design,

354

despite the architect's best efforts to filter light through it. But the wide patio doors allowed Carey's south-west-facing room to be flooded with light even before midday. He liked her leather couch too. It was very stylish, much more appropriate than the sofa she'd given him. And the lamps that she'd bought, the ones he'd seen her looking at in Habitat, were perfect. He could see why she'd be happy here.

'Here you are.' She handed him a big yellow mug filled to the brim. 'Sorry I don't have any biscuits or cakes or anything to offer you. I was going to do some shopping this evening.'

'That's OK.' He sipped the tea gingerly. It was far too hot. He liked lots of milk but since Carey drank hers black he knew that she didn't have a clue as to how much she should put in.

'Eejit,' said Carey as she sat down on the couch.

'Pardon?'

'Eejit,' she repeated. 'Jeanne. Getting drunk and spaced out on bloody joints! After all the trouble I go to telling Sylvia to treat her as an adult she has to go and behave like a child.'

'Hardly like a child.' Ben grinned.

'You know what I mean,' said Carey. She frowned suddenly and stared at Ben. 'I noticed it earlier and didn't want to say anything, but what on earth's wrong with your nose?'

'Oh nothing,' said Ben uncomfortably.

'It's not from the car smash, is it?' she asked. 'I thought you looked all right after that.'

'Nothing to do with the car smash,' Ben assured her. 'Different kind of smash altogether.'

'Oh?'

'I don't want to talk about it,' he said.

'Right,' said Carey hastily. 'I wasn't trying to probe or anything.'

Suddenly he laughed. 'I know, I'm sorry. I'm kind of sensitive about it.' He felt his nose carefully. 'It's still quite sore.' He looked at her appraisingly for a moment then shrugged. 'I got it in a fight.'

'Ben!' Carey jerked in surprise and slopped some tea onto the rug. She put the cup onto the coffee-table and got some kitchen towel to wipe up the mess. 'Not that it really matters,' she commented looking at the burn marks from where Jeanne and Gary had allowed a joint to singe it. 'I think I'll be getting another one.

I'll never be able to look at this one without visualising the two of them on it.'

Ben laughed again.

'So tell me about this fight,' she said.

'It was about Freya.' Ben looked at Carey hesitantly. 'It's sort of personal.'

'Don't tell me Freya did that to you!' she exclaimed. 'I know she's tough, but . . .'

'Don't be stupid, Carey, of course she didn't.'

'So who did?' she asked.

Ben hesitated.

'It doesn't matter,' said Carey immediately. 'Forget I asked.'

'I was so angry for her,' said Ben. 'And so sorry for her too . . .' His voice trailed off. 'She didn't deserve it,' he said shakily. 'She's a good person.'

'Didn't deserve *what*?' Carey couldn't stop herself asking.

Ben breathed deeply. 'You'll understand, I know you will.' The words spilled out and he told her about Freya's sorrow and his rage-filled visit to Brian's house while Carey listened, wide-eyed.

'Poor, poor Freya,' she said when he'd finished. 'How is she now?'

'You know my sister,' Ben said. 'Hard outside but maybe not so hard underneath.'

'I'm beginning to see that,' said Carey.

'You won't say anything?' Ben looked at her anxiously. 'I mean, I'm sure she doesn't want anyone to know and if she thought I'd told you . . .'

'Of course I won't say anything,' said Carey. 'Anyway, there's no one I'm likely to tell, is there?'

'I suppose not.'

'Still, it's horrible for her.' Carey sighed. 'And for Brian too, I guess.'

'You think?'

'But of course,' she told him. 'How can it be easy to tell your infertile girlfriend you have a kid already? He had no idea how she'd react. Has he told her yet?'

'I don't know,' said Ben. 'I haven't seen Freya because I've been in Drumcondra and she hasn't phoned me. But I'm sure she'll let

356

me know, even if it's still all off between them. I'm hoping not. I'm hoping to prove that you can solve problems by a punch-up after all.'

Carey laughed. 'Very gallant of you all the same,' she told him.

'Gallant?'

'Rushing to his house and clocking him on the jaw.'

'It wasn't really,' he said. 'It was just blind fury.'

'I'm glad I wasn't there, but it's certainly shown me a whole new side to your character.'

'The gallant side or the violent side?'

She laughed again. 'Both, probably. Anyway it was really good of you to come here today. And I'm glad you didn't clock poor Gary.'

Ben grinned at her. 'He was in bad enough shape as it was. And I was glad to be able to help.'

'Still, we appreciate it.'

'I'm relieved that it turned out all right,' said Ben.

'Yes.' Carey sighed. 'I suppose she's entitled to do something stupid,' she said. 'She's still a kid, after all.'

'And most of us go on doing stupid things right through our lives,' agreed Ben. 'Only we don't have to face the fury of our parents.'

'You're right.' Carey smiled and her brown eyes met his. 'Anyway,' she said quickly after a moment's silence, 'at least Jeanne was OK, which is the main thing.'

'Yes,' said Ben.

'So all's well that ends well.'

'Yes.' He winced suddenly.

'What's wrong?' she asked.

'My nose,' he told her. 'Every so often the pain just seems to rush through it. And my head aches a bit.'

She chuckled. 'Serves you right. D'you want some paracetamol?' He nodded. She went into the kitchen and returned with a glass of water and some Nurofen. 'Don't have paracetamol but will these do?'

He nodded again and took the glass from her. She stiffened as his fingers grazed hers.

'Sorry,' he said.

'It's OK.'

He swallowed the tablets.

'You'll be drummed out of the alternative medicine society,' she told him.

'I don't care,' he said.

'Actually, you're awfully pale.' Carey looked at him anxiously. 'Are you all right?'

'I'm fine,' he said. 'I don't know what's the matter. Just a bit dizzy all of a sudden.'

'You'd better sit down again,' she told him. 'I really can't face the thought of you passing out on me or anything.'

'Just for a minute,' he said. 'I'm sorry about this.'

'Don't worry,' she said. 'You're the one who came to help me out.'

He sat on the leather sofa. The room, which had begun to spin, seemed to have settled down again. Carey stood by the patio doors, looking out into the courtyard. The sun shafted across the room, picking up copper strands in her hair. Ben wondered why he'd never noticed copper in her hair before. He closed his eyes, conscious of a stirring of desire for her again. He thought, briefly, how wonderful the male body was that in the midst of the sudden blinding pain that his injured nose had caused he could still get a hard-on for a woman he didn't love any more. He shifted on the couch and hoped that she hadn't noticed.

He heard her footsteps move into the kitchen and then the bedroom. The memory of her in his bedroom on the night of the party fiasco came back to him and he could see her once again, naked except for her high-heeled shoes, hair cascading down her back, brown eyes full of mischief. How could he have let her get away, he wondered. Why *did* he let her get away? And then he reminded himself that it was because of sex, not love, he'd married her and that she was, in fact, now seeing someone else. Someone she'd been in love with before.

He sighed deeply and breathed slowly. Thinking of her was making his headache worse. Better to think of nothing at all. Better, in fact, to leave. But he lay there for a little longer, fragments of thought spinning incoherently round in his head, merging together so that they were suddenly incomprehensible.

Suddenly she was leaning over him wearing her slit-to-the-waist wedding dress, her loose hair tumbling down her cheeks in wild abandon. He stared at her in amazement, his eyes drawn to the hollow between her breasts. Why was she doing this? Had she actually noticed that he'd had an erection simply by looking at her? Had it awoken a sudden desire in her too? Did she miss the joy of the wanton sex they'd once had? Did she still love him after all? He reached out for her.

His mobile phone rang. His eyes snapped open. The phone was on the coffee-table. He reached for it and answered it. 'Sorry,' he said as he rubbed his eyes cautiously. 'I got caught up in something. I'll be back as soon as I can.' He heard Carey's footsteps and looked at her accusingly. 'You let me sleep!'

'You must have been tired,' she said. 'You were out for the count.'

'I can't believe I fell asleep here,' he said. 'I really can't. I'm busy – I've things to do.' He stood up abruptly.

'Your head's better then,' she said.

'I have a meeting,' he told her. 'Freya's there already.'

'Better not tell her you were here so,' said Carey. 'That'd freak her out altogether.'

'I'm sorry. I have to go,' said Ben.

'I know.'

They looked at each other silently for a moment.

'What were you doing?' he asked.

'What?'

'While I was asleep?'

'Washing my underwear,' she said calmly. 'Why?'

Ben didn't tell her that he'd been dreaming of her. That in his dream she'd been sliding her wedding dress slowly from her shoulders as she'd done on their wedding night. He shrugged. 'I'm disoriented,' he said. 'I didn't think I'd fall asleep.'

'You looked wretched,' she told him. 'And I thought it might do you good.'

'Well, thanks.' He pulled on his jacket and put the phone in his inside pocket.

'I haven't done anything about that Dominican Republic divorce yet,' she said abruptly. 'But I intend to.'

Ben stared at her. 'You do?'

359

'It's important, I think,' she said. 'To put things behind us.'

'Yes,' said Ben.

'I'll let you know when I've got it sorted.'

'OK.'

They looked at each other.

'Headache definitely gone?' she asked. 'You're OK to drive, are you?'

'Yes, absolutely.'

'So – well, thanks again.' She held out her hand.

He looked at her.

'Friends?' she said.

'Sure.' He grasped her hand. It was warm and dry. He felt a tingle of electricity, the same frisson as when she'd handed him the glass. But she didn't seem to have felt anything. She was smiling at him in a normal, friendly fashion. He squeezed her hand and then kissed her hastily on the cheek.

'Best be off then,' he said brightly as he released her.

'Sure.'

'Thanks for the drugs.' He smiled faintly.

'Thanks for everything else.' Her smile was equally faint.

'Anytime.'

'I'll – I'll be in touch about the divorce.'

'Yes. Fine.' He turned and hurried out of the apartment.

She closed the door slowly and leaned her back against it. Then she walked out to the balcony and leaned over the rail. She could just see him getting into the van and driving off. He didn't look back.

Chapter 31

Melissa

Derived from leaves and flowers, this is both soothing and uplifting with a sweet, fruity fragrance

L ater that evening, Freya was very glad to lock up the store and finally pull down the shutters at the Rathmines branch of *Herbal Matters*. It had been truly hectic all day and there was no doubt in her mind that the publicity from the jeep crashing through the windows, added to the subsequent refurbishing of the shop, had increased sales dramatically. Which just went to prove, she thought as she checked the main padlock, that the cloud and silver lining cliché actually had some merit.

She unfurled her brightly coloured pink and blue umbrella as she began walking along the Rathmines Road. She wondered if there was some kind of cliché to deal with the fact that the hours when she was cooped up inside the shop were more likely to be mild and sunny while as soon as she stepped outside it began to rain.

'Mind if I join you?'

She looked around, startled, as she recognised Brian's voice. She felt a lump in her throat and was quite unable to answer him.

'Let me,' he said, and took the umbrella from her, holding it so that it sheltered both of them from the persistent drizzle.

She said nothing but allowed him to walk beside her, matching her step to his, wishing that her heart wasn't thumping so much within her chest.

'Have you been talking to Ben lately?' he asked.

She glanced at him. 'No. He's been in Drumcondra the last couple of days.'

'No news of him and Carey or him and Leah?'

'If you want to know about Ben's love-life, why don't you ask *him*,' said Freya spiritedly.

'It's my love-life I'm more concerned about really,' said Brian. 'You know how much you mean to me, don't you?'

Freya stopped walking and turned to look at him. 'You've told me before,' she said. 'But sometimes it isn't enough, is it?'

'I'm bloody hopeless at this,' said Brian. 'I'm not good at saying how I feel. Not deep down. I'm not good at emotional stuff. I hate talking about things, I really do. That's why I love you, Freya. Because you don't go for Valentine cards and huge boxes of chocolates and bouquets of flowers either.'

'The odd bunch of flowers is nice,' she remarked. 'The odd box of chocs too.'

'I'm sorry,' he said. 'I'm trying to joke my way out of this and I can't, can I?'

'There's no way you can joke your way out of leaving me in a restaurant on my own,' she said. 'I know I told you to, but it still wasn't the best moment of my life when I realised that you'd taken me at my word. All the same I understand why, Brian. I really do. It was just that when it happened I found it more difficult to deal with than I expected. Still, I'm fine now. So don't feel that you have to apologise to me for it or anything.'

'I shouldn't have left you,' said Brian. 'It was cruel. And unnecessary.'

She shrugged and began walking again.

'Freya!'

She stopped. 'Brian, if you want me to forgive you, I absolutely do. I know that this menopause thing isn't easy for you to deal with. And maybe if I were you I'd have reacted the same way. It doesn't matter. Really it doesn't. I'm over it and you can do whatever you want. I did love you. I still care about you. But I'm not about to go into a decline over you.' She smiled suddenly and her ice-blue eyes warmed. 'I'm not some silly teenager who believes that her heart is broken, never to be mended. At least that's one advantage of getting older. You know that no matter what happens you get over it.'

'I don't doubt for a second that you'd get over anything,' he said feelingly. 'You're a remarkable woman, Freya. But before you put me into your getting-over box there's stuff that I have to tell you that I didn't before now.'

She heard the seriousness of his voice and looked enquiringly at him.

'We need to go somewhere private,' said Brian. 'Your place or mine?'

Nadia Lynch pushed the bedroom door open. Jeanne was lying on her bed, her eyes closed. 'Mum says do you want to come downstairs and watch the movie?'

Jeanne shook her head.

'We're all going to watch it,' said Nadia. 'Nobody's going out tonight. Not even Donny and his girlfriend rang to ask him.'

Jeanne kept her eyes shut.

'It's a good movie,' said Nadia. 'And Dad's doing popcorn in the microwave.'

'Go away,' said Jeanne.

'OK,' said Nadia. 'But you'll be sorry you missed it.'

Jeanne listened to the sound of the door closing and opened her eyes again. They were red and sore from the entire day's crying that she'd done as well as (she supposed) the reaction to the amount of vodka she'd drunk the night before. She didn't know whether smoking a joint could give you red eyes too but she was prepared to accept that it might.

How could she have been so stupid! When she'd seen the keys to Carey's apartment she'd picked them up because knowing that Carey was away she'd thought that it would be a really cool thing to be able to say to Gary that they'd got a place for the night if he wanted. He'd been totally impressed when she told him and totally impressed, too, by Carey's place. They'd wanted somewhere to be on their own. It wasn't just, as Sylvia had suggested, so that they could fumble furtively, it had been the whole feeling of being somewhere with each other, without other people, somewhere that nobody else was going to barge into and disturb them.

She wished they hadn't smoked the joints. She'd felt great afterwards but then sleepy so that curling up beside Gary had been a perfect thing to do. She flushed as she remembered Carey's expression at the sight of them together.

To be fair to Carey she'd been really good, thought Jeanne. She hadn't lectured her or given out to her or anything. She'd simply told her that Sylvia was worried out of her mind and she'd rung her mother and told her to come and collect her. Ben had been pretty good too. He'd called a cab for Gary straight away, told them that he didn't think it would be a good idea if Gary was there when Sylvia came, and had then been sympathetic when the younger guy had thrown up in the bathroom. Jeanne frowned suddenly. In all of the fuss and bother she hadn't wondered before why Ben and Carey had arrived at the apartment together . . .

There was another knock at the bedroom door and she sighed deeply. She wished they'd leave her alone. The door opened. She bit the inside of her lip as John walked in. Her father had been furious with her when she arrived home. Truly furious. She'd seen the veins on his temple actually pulsate as he spoke. He'd made it clear to her that he thought her only barely better than a prostitute.

'Nadia told you we were going to watch a movie?' he said.

She nodded wordlessly.

'We'd like you to come down and watch it with us.'

'I'm OK,' she said.

'I know,' said John. 'But we'd still like you downstairs.'

'I don't want to be downstairs.'

He sat on the end of her bed. 'I might have been a bit harsh with you earlier,' he said, 'but you frightened us beyond belief, Jeanne. You've no idea what it was like.'

She bit her lip harder, wanting to keep the tears in but knowing that they were going to fall again.

'When we called the police – well, all I could think of was those newscasts where parents appeal for news of their missing children. And how so many times those children never come home.'

'I'm not a child,' she said.

'You're not a grown-up either,' said John.

'I'm sorry.' The tears spilled down her face again.

John put his arms round her and hugged her to him. 'You won't go through life without making mistakes,' he said. 'But you see, you're my daughter and I don't want you to make mistakes. I don't want

364

you ever to feel hurt or unhappy. I don't want to think that some bloke looks at you and thinks he's on to a sure thing . . .'

'Gary didn't think like that,' said Jeanne rapidly. 'It was me who took the keys and me who told him about Carey's apartment.'

'So your mum told me.'

'So don't blame Gary just because I wanted to do something.'

'I won't,' said John.

'And I know it was wrong but I did it anyway,' said Jeanne.

John held her closer. 'Life would be pretty boring if we did the right thing all the time,' he murmured.

Jeanne sniffed loudly.

'Blow your nose,' said her father. 'And come downstairs.'

She sniffed again and took a tissue from the almost empty box beside her bed.

'OK,' she said.

Carey and Peter went into town for something to eat that night. They sat in one of Temple Bar's myriad ethnic restaurants and ate Mexican food to the soundtrack of a Mariachi band. Carey told him about Jeanne and Gary and her race up from Shannon to find them in her apartment. She was going to have to go back to Shannon in the morning, she told him, to retrieve her car which was still parked in the hotel car park, but really it was a small inconvenience against the fact that Jeanne was OK and that everything had turned out all right. Although, she added, she hadn't envied Jeanne the undoubted trauma that John and Sylvia would put her through.

'I'm surprised you didn't think of the apartment yourself,' said Peter as he loaded a tortilla chip with hot salsa. 'It wasn't a difficult leap to make.'

'I wasn't thinking at all,' she said. 'D'you know, it's funny, you can watch a detective drama on telly and you don't understand why some of the characters don't ask the obvious question, but when it's happening to you – well, you just don't!'

'So it was lucky that Ben asked it for you,' said Peter.

Carey looked at him. 'Are you jealous?' she asked.

'Jealous!' He laughed.

'You sounded a bit bitchy just then.' She dipped her tortilla chip into the bowl of guacamole.

365

'Not bitchy, just sarcastic,' admitted Peter. 'Come on, Carey, you've got to admit that he comes out of the whole thing looking like some knight in shining armour. Just like he did out of that damned jeep episode too.'

'Not really,' she said. 'He reacted to the circumstances, that's all.'

They were silent for a moment then Peter said suddenly: 'Actually, you're right. I *was* jealous.'

'Oh?'

'You're married to him, Carey, not me. And he was there when you needed him, not me.'

'I'm out to dinner with you, not him,' she reminded him. 'We've been out together half-a-dozen times since I bought the apartment. I haven't been out with him at all.'

'But you haven't slept with me,' said Peter.

Carey stared at him. 'I haven't slept with Ben either.' And she felt her face flush because she couldn't admit to Peter that when Ben had been sleeping on the sofa of her apartment she had, for an instant, stood beside him and wondered what would happen if she slid her hands beneath the black T-shirt he'd been wearing and pulled him to her as she unexpectedly wanted to do.

'I'm sorry.' Peter hadn't noticed her blush. 'I can't help feeling jealous of someone who actually married you.'

'I don't think my marriage is anything to get jealous about,' she told him. 'Anyway, I've decided to do the Dominican Republic divorce.'

'Why?' asked Peter. 'From what you said before, it's not likely to mean much in Ireland and surely it's just hassle to go there.'

'I have to do it,' she said. 'Closure.' She stabbed another tortilla chip into the guacamole. 'I know closure is an over-used term these days, but I definitely need closure about this.'

'And when you have closure, what then?'

She shrugged.

'Will you want to get married again?'

She smiled. 'Getting married is less important than getting the right guy.'

'And am I the right guy?' asked Peter.

'You could be,' said Carey.

366

'That's good to know.'

'You could be, but I'm still kind of bruised about everything,' she said. 'All the same, I'm really glad you were there when I needed someone.'

'No problem,' said Peter. 'I was glad to be there. And glad to help with easing the bruising too.'

Carey almost said that part of the bruising was his fault in the first place, that she'd been carrying the scars when she met Ben. That maybe because of Peter, Ben had been her big rebound thing. But she knew that wouldn't be fair. She couldn't blame anyone else for her own silliness.

'Why don't you combine the divorce with your apartment-warming,' suggested Peter. 'Have a big closure and opening party at the same time.'

'Not a bad idea,' she conceded as she scooped up the last of the guacamole.

'It'd be fun.'

She nodded. 'I'll think about it. It's time I did something just for fun.'

Freya sat on her sofa and looked at the photograph of Linnet van Roost. She saw, as Ben had seen, a stunningly beautiful girl with Brian's eyes and Brian's way of half looking out from beneath a fringe of hair.

'She's amazing,' said Freya.

'I know,' said Brian. 'I find it hard to believe that she's mine.'

Freya nodded. 'I can imagine. Especially if you only see her occasionally.'

'It worked out best that way. Marijka is a wonderful mother.'

'Did you ever want to marry her?' asked Freya.

'No.' Brian shook his head. 'It wasn't that kind of relationship, Freya. I was infatuated with her. It was great while it lasted. But it was never serious.'

'When did you find out?'

'About Linnet?'

She nodded.

'When she was six months old,' said Brian. 'I went to Amsterdam to see her.'

367

'What was that like?' asked Freya.

'Very strange,' he admitted. 'When you see your own child – well, there's nothing like it.' He looked at her. 'I'm sorry.'

'Don't be.' She handed the photograph back to him. 'I'm glad for you, Brian. I really am.'

'I should've told you before now.'

'Of course you should.'

'I know I had my reasons but now those reasons seem really daft.'

She shook her head. 'Not to me they don't. I understand.'

'Do you?'

'Yes,' she said.

'I definitely shouldn't have left you in the restaurant,' said Brian.

'You definitely shouldn't have done that,' she agreed.

'I couldn't deal with it.' He looked surprised at himself. 'Think of all the things I can deal with, Freya – mergers and acquisitions and loans and all sorts of bullshit like that, but I couldn't deal with telling the woman I love that I have a daughter.'

'The last few months have been laced with shocks,' observed Freya. 'What with Ben and Carey and then the accident and then finding out about the menopause and Linnet – it's no wonder I'm going grey.'

Brian looked at her golden hair. 'Not from where I'm sitting.'

'I hate to tell you this, but I get my highlights done once a month,' she told him. 'Otherwise things might look very different from where you're sitting.'

'They never will,' said Brian. 'Freya, I love you. I always have.'

'Always?' She looked enquiringly at him.

'Always,' he said firmly.

'I thought we were just good friends for a long time.'

'So what?' said Brian. 'I still fancied you like crazy.'

Freya laughed.

'And I fancy you like crazy now,' he said. 'Only it's more than that, Freya.'

She smiled at him. 'Thanks.'

'I'm sorry that I hurt you. I'm sorry that I kept stuff from you. I'm sorry that I wasn't confident enough to be able to talk about it.'

'A lot of apologies,' said Freya.

'I feel that there's a lot to apologise for,' Brian said.

'Not really.' Freya shrugged.

'I don't want to keep things from you any more,' said Brian.

'I don't want you to keep things from me either.'

'Oh, Freya.' He put his arms round her and pulled her close to him. And neither of them felt like talking then.

Chapter 32

Rosewood

Ideal for relaxation, this has a subtle woody aroma

Maude was ready and waiting when Sylvia arrived in the cab. She opened the hall door and waved to let her daughter know that she'd seen her arrive, then went into the living room where Arthur was watching a garden make-over programme, his feet propped on the coffee-table in front of him. He looked guiltily at Maude who told him that she didn't care where he put his feet but that if he scratched that table she'd have his guts for garters.

'I won't,' he promised, nevertheless rearranging his viewing position so that he wasn't using the table as a footrest any more.

'I'll see you later.' Maude grinned.

'Have a good time,' said Arthur. 'Mind yourself.'

'I'm sure I'll have a great time,' said Maude. 'And I won't be too late.'

'Be as late as you like.' Arthur smiled up at her and she kissed him on the lips before going out to the waiting cab.

'Everything OK?' asked Sylvia as Maude settled in beside her.

'Great,' said Maude. 'I'm really looking forward to this.'

'Me too,' said Sylvia. 'I do like Freya, don't you?'

'Very much,' said Maude. She looked at her watch. 'We're in plenty of time, aren't we?'

Sylvia nodded. 'She said half-seven. It's a quarter to now. We'll be early.'

They arrived at the Clarence Hotel with five minutes to spare but Freya was already in the small bar waiting for them. She beamed at them in delight and kissed Maude on the cheek.

'Thanks for coming,' she said. 'I booked the table for eight so we can have a celebratory drink first.'

'Celebratory?' Maude twinkled at her.

Freya said nothing but ordered champagne from the bar.

'Goodness,' said Maude as she looked at her glass. 'You really did mean celebratory!'

'A toast,' said Freya. 'To you and Sylvia, Maude, for being so bloody nice to me. And to me and Brian.'

Sylvia looked at her enquiringly.

'We're getting married,' said Freya.

'That's great!' Sylvia hugged the other girl. 'I'm really happy for you.'

'Thanks,' said Freya. She looked at them and smiled. 'I wanted you guys to come out with me because you've been fantastic. Maude, when I was so upset and uncertain about the menopause, you helped me put it in perspective. You did too, Sylvia. And maybe because of that, I knew that even without Brian I'd be all right. In the end, though, it didn't matter because he . . . well,' she smiled, 'he came back to me. And it's not that I couldn't have coped without him, but – I love him. I hadn't realised how much I loved him until he'd gone.'

'So his explanation for leaving you was satisfactory?' asked Maude.

'He had some issues of his own,' Freya told her.

'Issues?' Sylvia paused with her glass halfway to her mouth.

Freya nodded and told them about Linnet.

'And how do you feel about that?' Maude wanted to know. 'After all, he has a child of his own and you know that you and he won't have one. Can you cope with that?'

She nodded again. 'It isn't exactly easy,' she admitted, 'and I still get this aching feeling in the pit of my stomach sometimes. But I do know that I love Brian and I know he loves me too and so . . .' She shrugged. 'We can get through it together.'

'I'm glad,' said Sylvia warmly.

'It's a great feeling,' said Freya, 'to know that you love someone and they love you – and you love each other despite everything that's happened!'

'Or maybe because of it,' Sylvia said knowingly.

371

'Why didn't he say something about his daughter before now?' asked Maude.

'He had his reasons and I accept them,' said Freya. 'But he eventually told me everything because of Ben.'

'Ben?' Maude and Sylvia spoke together.

'He called to Brian's house and punched him on the jaw.'

'Freya!' Sylvia stared at her. 'You're saving the juiciest bit till last!'

'I know.' Freya looked at them contritely. 'I wasn't sure whether or not I should mention Ben.'

'Actually he's not quite persona non grata among the Brownes at the moment,' said Sylvia. 'Which I'll tell you about in a minute. But come on, Freya, why did he punch Brian on the jaw?'

Freya explained while Maude and Sylvia listened wordlessly.

'Wow,' said Sylvia at the end. 'I didn't realise he was so – so determined.'

'I didn't realise he was such a bad fighter,' said Freya. 'You should've seen him the next day!'

'That explains it,' said Sylvia thoughtfully. 'I knew he looked odd.'

'Looked odd?' said Freya. 'You met him?'

'Quite recently,' said Sylvia and related the tale of Jeanne's all-night drinking session.

'And they were both at Carey's?' Freya shook her head. 'You must have been out of your mind with worry, Sylvia.'

'Demented,' said Sylvia. 'But I have to say that Ben was great. So was Carey.'

'He never said anything about it to me,' said Freya.

'Maybe he was embarrassed,' suggested Maude.

'Maybe he was being discreet about my wayward daughter,' Sylvia said.

The three of them drained their glasses and looked at each other.

'Is there any chance,' Freya said doubtfully, 'that they might get back together?'

'They looked very at ease with each other when I saw them,' said Sylvia.

'But Carey's going out with that other man again,' objected Maude.

'Don't even think about it.' Sylvia shuddered. 'It was bad enough the first time, I couldn't take it all over again.'

'Neither could I,' said Freya. 'Although . . .'

'Although what?' asked Maude.

'I don't think I was as fair as I could've been to Carey,' Freya said. 'I'd wanted to meet her and she was never around and I felt sorry for Leah—'

'The girl he kissed?' Maude interrupted.

Freya nodded. 'I'd known her a long time. And so maybe I wasn't as welcoming . . .'

'Hey, it wasn't *your* fault,' said Sylvia.

'I know, but . . .' Freya sighed.

'Look, let Carey and Ben worry about their own lives,' said Maude briskly. 'The good thing that's come out of everything is that we've met you, Freya. And it's nice to be out celebrating with you tonight. So let's concentrate on that and forget about everything else.'

'Absolutely,' agreed Sylvia and they trooped into the dining room to help Freya celebrate some more.

Jennifer O'Carroll was going ballistic in the tower. The captain of an outbound flight to Paris had inexplicably taken the wrong taxiway to Runway One Zero despite her clear instructions, and was now in the way of a recently landed holiday flight from Majorca. The fact that the holiday flight couldn't immediately turn off the runway, plus the fact that the Paris flight was now going to have to make a round trip back to the ramp before setting off again, meant that all other flights were being delayed. The pilot of the Majorcan plane was already bitching at Jennifer who was trying to work out the quickest way to unravel the mess.

'Don't fucking move,' she yelled at the hapless French captain, who requested further instructions. 'Don't fucking move until I tell you! And at that point, move *exactly where* I tell you, *when* I tell you.'

The other controllers knew that later they'd laugh at Jennifer's outburst but right now they were busy assessing what to do with their incoming flights. Carey busily reissued instructions to the stack of planes she'd intended to bring in on Runway One Zero. Two Eight was the alternative but the weather suited One Zero better, which was why it was in use that night. Still, as she muttered to herself, this was why the pilots were paid the big bucks. They were supposed to be able to land anywhere. And conditions weren't really bad. Low cloud, persistent drizzle and moderate winds, but nothing too awful.

'Speedbird 2522, Dublin. Descend two thousand feet. Turn left heading 310. Establish on localiser. Report established.' Carey watched the blip of the plane on her screen while the captain of the flight repeated her instructions before turning her attention to the traffic behind. 'Shamrock 165, Dublin. Descend three thousand feet. Turn left heading 340. Your position now is fifteen miles east of Dublin.'

'Dublin, Lufthansa 1634, now established on the localiser.'

The first plane in her stack was ready to be passed to the tower. She hoped that Jennifer would treat him kindly.

'Lufthansa 1634, Dublin. Roger. Nine miles from touchdown. Cleared approach Runway Two Eight. Contact tower 118.3.'

'Shamrock 165, Dublin. Descend two thousand feet. Turn further left heading 310, intercept localiser Runway Two Eight. Report established.'

Suddenly the alarm in the control centre went off. All of the controllers looked at their screens to see whether the problem was in their area. The siren always sounded when two planes were on a collision course. That happened more often than people thought, but usually because a controller had issued a set of instructions to one pilot and was in the process of issuing instructions to the other. The computerised alarm went off anyway. So the sound of the siren didn't necessarily mean an actual crisis.

But of course it could also signify a genuine emergency, perhaps one declared by the captain on board a flight. By looking at the call-sign on the radar the controllers could identify the type of emergency in question. Once a controller knew that the emergency was out of their area they ignored it. They had enough to worry about with their own planes without taking on concern for someone else's.

Finola Hartigan saw that it was a real problem and the plane concerned was under her control. It was a recently departed flight to Glasgow which had developed engine trouble and now the captain was requesting a return to Dublin. Finola gave him a new heading

374

and watched her radar screen as the plane turned and descended. The instructions between Finola and the captain of the troubled flight were calm and businesslike. He knew what he had to do while she opened an exclusive approach vector for it.

Forty miles out from Dublin, Finola transferred the plane to Carey on approach control. Trevor, the team's co-ordinator, contacted the tower who were responsible for ensuring the emergency services were informed. He also kept Chris Brady, the station manager, up to date with what was happening while Carey spoke to the captain. There was a lot of information she needed – the number of passengers and crew, fuel remaining, which engine had been shut down – but she also wanted to keep her transmissions to a minimum so that the pilot could get on with what he had to do.

Her other aircraft had been taken over by Chris Brady while she dealt with the emergency flight.

'Is One Zero open yet?' she asked Trevor Hughes. 'I'll keep his options open but I'd really like to bring him in that way if I can.'

It was typical, she thought, that the night there was an emergency was also the night when an Airbus and a Boeing were nose to nose on the damn runway. She hoped that Jennifer and Gerry, who was working the tower with her, would rise to the occasion.

'You've got One Zero,' said Trevor after speaking to Gerry.

'Excellent.'

Although she was totally focused on the incoming craft, Carey could feel the heightened tension in the control room. At this point the entire responsibility for the aircraft was hers. There was nothing anyone else could do. Carey knew she was in a zone and nothing could distract her. She did her job and expected anyone else involved to do theirs. Gerry Ferguson, in the tower, instructed the rescue vehicles to position themselves at the correct points nearby so that some of them could follow the plane once it had landed while others would be ready at the other end. Carey watched the green blip descend along the approach vector until the plane was no longer under her control but low enough to be passed to the tower.

'Good luck,' she said to the pilot.

'Thanks,' he replied briefly.

When the control room heard that the plane had landed safely and that the passengers had been evacuated without any problems, she exchanged high fives with Chris, stretched her arms over her head and went for her overdue break where she knocked back a strong black coffee and devoured a Crunchie while Finola propped her feet up on the table in front of her.

'Oh, there was never anything to worry about.' Now Finola unwrapped a Mars bar and took a bite. 'Not with the top team in control.'

'Your faith in our abilities – and the abilities of our beloved pilots – is touching.'

'It is, isn't it,' said Finola. 'I have a bit of news for you, by the way.'

'Oh?'

'Dennis and I are getting married.'

'Finola!' Carey looked at her friend in delight. 'When?'

'The end of the year,' said Finola.

'I'm thrilled for you,' said Carey. 'Good to know that you can live with someone for two years and still want to marry them.'

Finola laughed. 'We have an ulterior motive,' she said.

'Which is?'

'I'm pregnant.'

'Finola!' This time Carey's voice held a mixture of congratulation and query. 'Planned?'

'Not exactly,' admitted Finola, 'but it's been on our agenda. Dennis and I have been talking about getting married for a while and then this news just crystallised it for us.'

'I'm really pleased for you,' said Carey. 'I bet you'll be a great mother.'

'Are you mad?' Finola laughed. 'I'll be a terrible mother. I'll keep informing the poor child to establish itself in the pram and contact its father for further instructions.'

Carey laughed too. 'And he'll refer the little mite back to you.'

'I know. Still, I suppose we'll manage.' She paused. 'It's a challenge.'

'I'm sure you're ready for it.'

'I'm not so sure, to be honest,' admitted Finola. 'But Dennis and I wanted a family at some point, so I guess it's no harm to start now.'

'What about work?' asked Carey.

'I haven't decided yet,' said Finola. 'Maybe I'll move out of control and into some other area. The shifts will be difficult. I know Yvette manages, but that girl is a superwoman.'

'I know.' Carey nodded. 'Well, I wish you the best of luck with the whole thing, Finola.'

'Thanks,' said her friend. She finished the Mars bar and licked her fingers. 'You may have noticed I've given up the fags. Unfortunately I've replaced them by eating chocolate which I'm sure is terribly unhealthy. But I can't help myself.'

'I wouldn't worry,' advised Carey. 'My sister Sylvia gorged herself on popcorn during her last pregnancy.'

'Did she?' Finola looked interested. 'I wonder if there's a reason for that? Was she deficient in some vitamin or other?'

Carey shrugged. 'No idea.'

'Of course, your soon-to-be-ex is a vitamin expert, isn't he?' asked Finola.

'Yes,' replied Carey. 'And feel free to ransack his shop for folic acid or whatever it is you mothers need. Unfortunately, though, the soon-to-be-ex part is going to take longer than I thought.' She told Finola about the four-year divorce wait and the overseas options. 'It might be possible to get it annulled in Vegas but I'm not certain about that either,' she sighed.

'I like the sound of going to the Dominican Republic myself,' said Finola. 'Lap up a bit of Caribbean sun and come home divorced. So what if it's not entirely watertight. At least you've had the holiday and you've got a bit of paper.'

'It's really just a question of drawing a line in the sand, you know?'

'Sure,' said Finola. She looked at Carey sympathetically. 'I understand. And I know that we all laugh and joke about it, honey, but we do care about you.'

Carey felt tears prick at the back of her eyes. 'I know you do. And thanks. We'll sort it out eventually, you know.'

'In the meantime, how's the apartment coming along?' Finola decided to change the subject.

'Great,' said Carey. 'Really great. I love it.'

'Housewarming?' asked her friend.

Carey grimaced. 'Everyone keeps asking me and I do intend to.

It's just I haven't got round to it yet. Peter wants me to combine it with a divorce party.'

'That might take ages,' complained Finola. 'I haven't been to a decent party in months!'

'OK, OK.' Carey grinned then stood up. 'Last lap,' she said as she looked at her watch. 'Come on, Finola. Let's do it all over again.'

When she'd finished her shift, Carey decided to call and see Maude. She felt guilty that she hadn't dropped in to see her mother in ages but she hadn't wanted to get involved in deep discussions about her personal life – which she knew was bound to happen if she called at the house. However, popping in after this shift would mean that she didn't have to stay too long, and she hoped that she might be able to keep away from the subject of the men in her life for half an hour or so.

She was surprised to find Arthur at home on his own.

'Your mum's gone into town,' he informed her.

'Town!' Carey looked at him in astonishment. 'At night – on her own?'

'She's a grown woman,' said Arthur mildly.

'Yes, but . . .' Carey blinked a couple of times. 'She doesn't go into town on her own often, does she?'

'She's celebrating tonight,' said Arthur.

'Celebrating what?' demanded Carey.

'With Sylvia.'

'Sylvia's celebrating something with Mum?'

'And Freya.' Arthur zapped the remote control and changed stations.

'Dad!' Carey looked at him in exasperation. 'Where have they gone? Why? And why with Freya? How does Mum even know Freya?'

'She's met her a couple of times,' said Arthur. 'They get on together.'

'But Freya is Ben's sister!' cried Carey.

'Maude doesn't hold that against her,' said Arthur.

'You're so impossible!' Carey glared at him.

'Look,' said Arthur, 'all I know is that they've gone into town for

378

a meal and a bit of a celebration because Freya got engaged. And she asked your mum and Sylvia to go out with her.'

'Engaged!' Carey frowned. 'But I thought – never mind. Why has she asked *them* to go out with her? Doesn't she have other friends?'

'Maybe she prefers Maude and Sylvia to any of her other friends,' said Arthur.

'That's ridiculous,' snapped Carey.

'Why?'

'Because – because they can't be friends with Ben's sister.'

'Why not?'

'It's weird,' said Carey.

Arthur hit mute on the remote control and looked at his daughter. 'You're calling them weird?' he said mildly. 'You? You're the one who rushed off and . . .'

'OK, OK!' she cried. 'It's weird that after Ben and me split up, they've become friends.'

'Perhaps,' said Arthur. 'But I'm sure your mother knows what she's doing.'

'I'm not,' said Carey darkly and went to make some tea.

It was nearly midnight when Maude arrived home, her cheeks flushed and her eyes sparkling. She looked at Carey with surprised delight.

'Well, hello,' she said. 'What do you want?'

'Nothing,' said Carey. 'I just called in to say hi. But you weren't here.'

Maude shrugged off her light coat. 'No,' she said, 'I was out to dinner.' She hung up the coat and raised her eyebrows at Carey. 'We haven't seen you for ages.'

'I've been busy,' said Carey. 'I'm sorry.'

'Did you have a good time?' asked Arthur.

'Wonderful,' said Maude. 'I haven't been in the Clarence since that pop-star guy took it over.'

'Bono,' said Carey. 'I think he regards himself as a rock star really. And it wasn't just him who took it over.'

'Who cares?' asked Maude. 'The important thing was that we had a lovely meal and a lovely time.'

'With Freya,' said Carey.

379

'Yes.'

'Mum!'

'What?'

'Freya? Ben's sister?'

'That doesn't make her a bad person,' said Maude. 'In fact, she's a very nice person.'

'She's the person who invited his ex-bloody-girlfriend to our party and broke up our marriage,' exploded Carey.

'So it's all her fault?'

'Yes,' said Carey.

'Nothing to do with you and Ben?'

'You're missing the point,' said Carey. 'She never wanted me to marry him in the first place and she did everything she could to make sure it didn't work – and I just don't see how you can be friends with her!'

'She's had a tough time,' said Maude.

'Oh, I know. I've heard all about the early menopause. So what?'

'Carey!' Maude looked at her daughter angrily.

Carey flushed. 'I'm sorry,' she said. 'I know that was probably horrible for her. And then her boyfriend dumped her.'

'How do you know all this?' asked Maude.

'Ben told me – when we went to the apartment in search of Jeanne and Gary.'

'It wasn't very discreet of him.'

'I haven't told anyone,' said Carey. 'I wouldn't. You obviously knew already.'

'But why did he tell you?' asked Maude.

'He had to explain why his nose was squashed,' Carey told her. 'He got into a fight with Brian.'

'Yes, Freya told me.'

Carey grinned. 'Apparently they really went for each other.'

'Well, it worked,' said Maude. 'Because Freya and Brian are now engaged.'

'Dad said.' Carey smiled faintly. 'That's nice for her, I guess.'

'Have you seen him since?' asked Maude.

'Brian?' Carey shook her head. 'How would I . . .'

'You know perfectly well I don't mean Brian,' said Maude. 'I meant Ben.'

380

'No, I haven't seen him,' said Carey. 'I don't expect to see him. My plan is to go to the Dominican Republic and get a divorce and never see him again.'

'Carey—'

'And I don't want to talk about it any more.' Carey picked up her jacket from the chair. 'Anyway, I'd better get home. It's late.'

'OK,' said Maude. 'It was nice of you to drop round.'

'I won't leave it so long next time,' said Carey. 'I promise.'

Chapter 33

Juniper

A berry oil, it is clear and refreshing

B en looked up from his computer as Freya walked into his office.
He hadn't seen his sister in almost a week – since she'd informed
him that she was taking a few days off and was going to the Sheen
Falls Hotel in Killarney to recharge her batteries. 'With Brian,' she'd
added, and kissed Ben fondly on the forehead.

She looked great today, he thought, as she smiled at him. Bright
and cheerful and quite unlike the pale and tired woman she'd
been such a short time earlier. She sat on the edge of his desk
and extended her hand to show him the glittering sapphire and
diamond engagement ring she now wore.

'He bought it for me before we went,' she told him. 'And he gave
it to me on our first night there.'

'It's lovely,' said Ben. 'Really lovely.'

'And it's thanks to you,' said Freya. 'Who would've believed
that my kid brother would be the one to sort out my relationship
problems!'

'In the time-honoured way of beating up the man who upset you.'
Ben grinned. 'I'm really happy it worked out, Freya. At the time, all
I was thinking of was killing him.'

'I know,' she said. 'And even though I would've been very upset
if I'd known what you were up to, I'm glad that you did it.'

'So am I,' said Ben. 'But I acted totally without thinking. I was
so mad at him, you know. Because you're a brilliant sister and you
did everything for me and – well . . .' his voice trailed off. 'I just

knew that the two of you were supposed to be together.'

'Did you?'

'Yes,' said Ben. 'I know I teased you about it and called him Boring Brian sometimes – I think that once I even told you that your relationship with him was a bit sad – but actually, it wasn't. It was exactly what it should be. You're made for each other.'

'OK, OK, stop with the soppiness,' commanded Freya.

'Besides, I like him,' said Ben, 'despite having tried to beat him to a pulp and getting a squashed nose for my troubles. He's easy to get on with, and how could I be sure you wouldn't bring home some kind of ridiculous toy-boy next?'

'Ben Russell!' Freya hit him on the shoulder.

'I know, I know, you're not that sort of girl.' Ben smiled at her. 'So when's the big day?'

'July, I think,' said Freya. 'I've always wanted a summer wedding.'

'Really?' asked Ben. 'I never even knew you thought about it.'

'Not often,' Freya told him. 'But sometimes.'

Ben glanced at his computer screen then looked at Freya again. 'So – two Russell weddings in the one year,' he said tonelessly.

'Don't get upset by me saying this, but I rather hope mine lasts a bit longer,' said Freya.

Ben grimaced. 'Shouldn't be too difficult.'

'All the same, I hear you've been lending a helping hand to the Brownes recently.'

'What?' He looked at her, startled.

'Finding Sylvia's missing daughter. Dealing with the drug-crazed boyfriend. That sort of thing.'

'Who on earth told you about that?' demanded Ben.

'I have my sources.'

'Freya!' His voice rose. 'Who told you?'

'Keep your hair on,' she said. 'Sylvia told me. And Maude.'

'Sylvia?' He stared at her. 'Carey's sister? And her mother? Why did they tell you? How did they meet you?'

'It may surprise you to know that I've kept in touch with them,' said Freya nonchalantly. 'We went for dinner to celebrate my engagement.'

'Freya!' This time his tone was incredulous.

'We get on with each other,' she told him simply.

'How the hell did you manage to stay in touch with them?' asked Ben. 'I didn't think you even knew where they lived.'

'The how is irrelevant,' said Freya. 'Accidentally, to tell you the truth. And the why is that I like Maude and I like Sylvia too.'

'How often do you meet them?'

'Not that often. But we chat on the phone sometimes. They give me good advice.'

'You're not serious.'

'I am.'

'So – you're getting advice from my ex-in-laws?'

Freya grinned. 'Sometimes.'

'But . . .' He looked helplessly at her. 'You're getting involved with them while I'm trying to get uninvolved with Carey.'

'It's you that's got involved,' Freya pointed out. 'You're the one helping out, not me.'

'That was completely accidental, too,' said Ben. 'And I haven't seen or talked to Carey since. What you're doing is different. You're becoming involved on a regular basis and that's not going to make it easy on me or her.'

'It's not going to make any difference,' said Freya. 'You're not the one meeting Maude and Sylvia.'

He rubbed his temples. 'This is bizarre, Freya,' he said. 'Really bizarre.'

'It is a bit,' she agreed. 'But there's something about them that I like.'

'If only you'd felt like that about Carey at the start,' he said bitterly.

'That wouldn't have changed anything,' said Freya. 'I had nothing to do with your – your difficulties.'

'No, but you might not have invited Leah to the party,' said Ben. 'And a lot of things might have been different then.'

Freya looked at him speculatively. 'Do you really think so?'

Ben sighed deeply. 'Well, maybe not.'

'So it wasn't my fault, but the silver lining is that I've made some new friends in Maude and Sylvia and that's a good thing.'

'I suppose so. It's still bizarre though.'

'Have you seen Leah at all lately?' asked Freya.

'That's a bit bizarre too,' said Ben. 'We had a row – well, not a flaming row, just she wanted to know where we stood, that sort of thing. I left and I didn't know whether or not I'd even talk to her again. Then a few days later she rings me up and asks me for some PR contacts for her salon opening. Next thing I know I'm having coffee with her and she's a totally different person because she's focused on her business and she doesn't even mention the fact that she wanted some kind of long-term commitment from me.'

'So where does that leave you?' asked Freya.

'I don't know.' He scratched the back of his head. 'The thing is, I know she'd like to get married and settle down and have children, but I don't know whether or not she should do any of those things with me. And . . .' he looked doubtfully at Freya '. . . she's not getting any younger. I mean, it's not like she's old, or anything, but . . .'

'You're eyeing her up and wondering if she'll end up like me?'

'Kind of,' he admitted. 'And although I'd be shocked if at some point in my life I didn't have kids, I know that it would be much worse for her.'

'You can't hang around for ever, Ben,' said Freya. 'You've got to make your choices.'

'See, the problem is that when I do, they always turn out to be rotten choices.'

Freya looked at him sympathetically.

'I'm hopeless,' said Ben. He shook his head resignedly. 'You'd imagine that human beings would have got over this whole love thing by now, wouldn't you? That we'd have evolved past it. It causes so much bloody trouble.'

'But when it works it's great,' said Freya.

Ben smiled suddenly. 'And it's worked out for you, hasn't it?'

'Yes,' she said. 'It really has.'

Carey was on her own in the apartment. She had a headache, not a bad one but a nagging ache at the back of her neck, so she lay stretched along the leather couch with her eyes closed. She was trying to get rid of the pain without taking any pills. In the first week she'd met him Ben had told her that the body had a wonderful system of self-healing which most people resisted rather than assisted. He'd tried to teach her how to relax although he'd given up in despair when she'd told him that she was at her most relaxed when she was doing things, and then had reached out for him and pulled him towards her and they'd made love. For the third time that day, she remembered.

She moved her head and stopped thinking about making love to Ben. Instead she concentrated on the sounds of waves gently lapping upon the shore which were coming from her recently bought *Restful Moments* CD. There were lots of natural sounds on it, including hissing rain and summer breezes rippling through the trees but it was the easy sound of the sea that Carey found the most soothing. While she listened she could almost see the waves gathering momentum as they travelled towards the beach before tumbling casually in a splash of multi-coloured drops onto the golden sand.

In her imaginings the waves were always white-tipped azure blue and the sands were always golden, lit by a hot sun spilling from a cloudless sky. She shifted on the couch, almost feeling the warmth of the sun on her face. It had been another sunless day in Dublin, the skies hidden by a film of grey cloud. It would be nice, she thought as she shifted again, to get away to somewhere warm. To get away to the beach of her dreams and the real sound of the waves. Peter was talking about going to the South of France for the summer holidays. She hadn't given it much thought herself, hadn't really considered going anywhere, but the last night they'd been out together he'd told her about the little town of Cap d'Agde where he'd gone the year before he'd married Sandra and which, he said, was beautiful and unspoiled and utterly gorgeous. Not touristy, he'd said, and had made a face at her when she asked him why all tourists considered themselves to be above the tourist hordes. And she'd told him that she'd think about it but that maybe her ideal holiday this year would be an all-inclusive break somewhere totally touristy where she wouldn't be expected to immerse herself in culture but could behave outrageously instead.

'I like the thought of behaving outrageously with you,' Peter said.

'Do you?'

'Even behaving normally with you would be nice.'

'Sorry?'

'Come on, Carey. We're going out together again, but you still won't sleep with me. And I'm beginning to feel—'

'I'm not ready to sleep with you,' she interrupted him. 'I told you.'

'It's not like you haven't slept with me already,' he pointed out.

'That was different,' she said. 'It's just that I'm – it's still being married to Ben. It just feels wrong, Peter. It's not that I don't find you hugely attractive because you know I do. But I can't get this feeling of being attached to someone else out of my head. I'm sorry.'

'Do you still love him?' asked Peter.

'Oh, don't be ridiculous,' she said crossly.

'Do you love me?' he asked.

She turned to him. 'I don't trust myself to know,' she whispered. 'That's the problem. I really have no idea how I feel about anything any more.'

'I love you,' he said. 'You know I do. And I'll give you some more time.'

Then he kissed her gently on the lips and she held him to her and wondered how long he'd wait for her before dumping her for someone who didn't seem to have completely lost her marbles when it came to falling in love.

She opened her eyes. Thinking about Peter had pushed the azure seas and lapping waves completely out of her mind. What was even worse, her headache hadn't improved in the slightest. She sat up and rotated her head slowly from side to side. She wished she didn't feel so unsettled all of a sudden. When she'd first moved into the apartment it had been like a safe haven for her and she'd expected that the uneasiness that seemed to be with her constantly would lift. But it hadn't. She still felt edgy and out of sorts and, even though she knew that she was back to top form as far as work was concerned, her personal life was ragged round the edges. It's the bloody closure thing, she thought savagely as she rubbed at her neck. It's knowing that this marriage is like a damn sentence that I have to serve even if I go ahead with the dinky Dominican divorce.

She stood up and stretched, then picked up the brochures from the table in front of her. They were full of pictures of pale beaches, blue skies and shimmering seas. She looked at the divorce information she'd downloaded from the web and read through it again. What the hell, she thought. The holiday will be nice.

Sitting down at her computer, she logged on. She looked up the divorce sites again and filled out all of the information requested: then she submitted the form. There was no point in drifting any longer. When she heard back from the lawyers she'd book a flight and go. With luck, it wouldn't take too long. And then she'd feel like a single person again, a person who could go to bed with her boyfriend and not feel bothered about it.

It was funny, she thought, that sleeping with someone else even though he was married to Sandra hadn't bothered Peter in the slightest. She had the feeling that sleeping with Leah even though he was married to someone else wouldn't bother Ben either. And they were right not to be bothered! It was just Carey herself who was being silly.

Gathering up the forms which she'd printed off, she clipped them together. Then she put them into her big handbag, picked up her car keys and left the apartment. Her headache was gone.

She hadn't meant to drive to Portobello. She hadn't really given any thought at all to her destination when she'd started the engine and eased out of her parking space. But suddenly she was on the M1 heading towards the city and she knew that she was driving to Ben's house. What she didn't know was why. She tried to analyse it now as she sat stuck in the commuter traffic. Why did she want to see him? To talk about the divorce? To ask him if he thought it was really a good idea before she booked her flight? Or – she shoved the car into first and edged forward about a yard – did she want him to change his mind? To tell her that he was sorry about everything and that he really loved her after all? She made a disgusted face at herself in her rearview mirror. That was plain silly – she knew it was. And yet . . .

She sighed. It was still hard to accept the mistake. It was hard to admit that she'd got it so wrong. If only they'd been able to give it some more time. After all, they'd behaved really well towards each other over the sofa, like real grown-ups, no screaming and shouting. And Ben had been wonderful about Jeanne. Carey bit her lip. Far too wonderful, she thought. Far too nice and understanding and helpful for someone she would have preferred to hate.

Anyway, it was too late now. She knew what she was going to do.

She was going to post all these papers through his letter-box so that he'd know that she was ready to make a fresh start. He'd probably be relieved and happy about that. After all, he'd been perfectly prepared to go to the Dominican Republic himself. He probably would have gone ages ago except she'd been the one to insist on going.

Although, she wondered as the traffic ground its way forward, would it be better to wait until she'd heard back from the lawyers and had something useful to give him rather than shoving the stuff she had through the door? According to the information, he was going to have to sign some papers too. Perhaps it'd make more sense to wait until she had them? She edged towards Ben's street. I won't stop, she thought. I'll go back home and wait until I have the right papers. No point in—

'Shit!!!'

She slammed on the brakes as the girl in the red coat stepped off the pavement in front of her. Silly bitch, thought Carey, her heart thumping with fright. Didn't even look! And then she swallowed hard. Because the girl who was now glaring at the car was Leah Ryder.

Carey pressed the button and her electric window slid down. 'Are you all right?' she asked.

'You stupid cow!' cried Leah. 'What were you—' Then she stopped as she realised who the stupid cow who'd nearly hit her actually was.

'Hi,' said Carey in her most offhand tone.

'Hi?' Leah stared at her. 'You nearly kill me and that's all you can say?'

'You stepped out without looking.'

'You were going too fast.'

'Don't be daft, you can't go fast on these roads.' Carey got out of the car and drew herself up to her full height so that she was head and shoulders taller than Leah.

'What are you doing here?' demanded Leah.

Carey shrugged.

'Come to try and get him back?' Leah looked disdainfully at her.

'No,' said Carey.

'Because you won't,' said Leah. 'You never will. He doesn't love you.'

'I know,' said Carey.

Leah stared at her. 'You know?'

'Of course he doesn't love me,' said Carey. 'He'd hardly be with someone like you if he did.'

'Someone like me?'

'Shallow, selfish, bitchy.'

'Fuck you!' cried Leah. 'He loved me until he met you. You destroyed him.'

'No, I didn't,' Carey smiled sweetly. 'Anyway, what difference does it make now? I'm not living with him any more, we're going to get a divorce and you're clearly on your way to meet him. So what's your problem?'

'My problem is that you're like a damn thorn in my side,' snapped Leah. 'You're the one-night stand who accidentally outstayed her welcome and you keep on doing it.'

'You were the thorn in mine,' said Carey. 'Wonderful, gorgeous, sensitive Leah who's so good in the sack that he can't stay away.'

'You are such a bitch!' hissed Leah.

'I'm not.' Carey sighed. 'Really, I'm not. Look, d'you think I'd have married him if I'd realised the kind of relationship you two had? I'm not a complete fool. He didn't tell me about you. If he had, maybe things would be different.'

'So it's his fault?'

'I don't know,' said Carey. 'I don't care.'

'Why are you here?' asked Leah.

'I don't know that either,' replied Carey.

'Yeah, well, you can just fuck off back wherever you came from. He doesn't need you fussing around causing trouble. Neither do I.'

'I know,' said Carey.

'Good.'

'We're getting a divorce,' Carey told her. 'I'm going to the Dominican Republic.'

'I heard about this stupid divorce,' said Leah. 'It doesn't really mean anything. It's not as though he can get married . . .' She bit her lip.

'I'm sorry.' Carey watched the other girl. 'I really am. I didn't think that this would happen and I'm sorry he can't marry you if that's what you want, and I'm sorry if you think it's my fault.'

Leah was silent for a moment. Then she looked up at the taller girl. 'So why are you here?' she asked edgily.

Carey reached into her bag and took out the divorce information. 'To give him this,' she said. 'To say that as soon as I hear back from them I'll be booking my flight.'

'I suppose it's better than nothing.' Leah glanced at the printouts.

'So you can stop worrying that I'm trying to win him back or anything,' said Carey.

'Oh, I wouldn't worry about that,' Leah told her. 'He's an investor in my company now as well as a dear friend.'

'What company?' asked Carey.

'Beauty salon.' Leah looked her up and down. 'Helping people to make the most of their appearance.'

'I'm sure you'll be really good at that,' said Carey.

'I'm sure I will.' Leah flicked through the papers again. 'Do you want me to give these to him for you?'

Carey hesitated.

'Or perhaps you wanted to see him one last time?' asked Leah dryly.

'No,' said Carey. 'Of course you can give them to him.'

'Excellent,' said Leah. 'That's what I'll do. I'm sure he'll be glad to know that you're making progress. Such as it is.'

'Thanks.' Carey got back into her car.

'Drive carefully,' said Leah.

'Oh, fuck off, you bimbo bitch,' muttered Carey as she put the Audi into gear and drove down the street.

Chapter 34

Geranium

With a delightful floral scent, this oil is cleansing and refreshing

Freya was surprised to receive an invitation to the opening of the new beauty salon in which Leah was a partner. She was even more surprised to see that she and Brian were invited to the post-launch dinner which was being held (astonishing her still more) in Oleg's. She hadn't spoken to Leah in ages and she wondered whether or not the other girl really wanted her to show up or not. But she would go, she decided. She regretted the fact that her friendship with Leah had fractured, especially since Ben and Leah were involved with each other again. There was no point in allowing the awkwardness between herself and Leah to grow. Going to the launch would be an indication of her support for both her brother and his girlfriend.

Ben was already at the salon when she arrived. He was standing uncomfortably at the edge of a clique of women, a glass of Amé in his hand. Leah, looking effortlessly beautiful in royal blue trousers teamed with a dazzling white top and with her raven hair pulled tightly into a knot on the back of her head, was chatting to a woman whom Freya recognised as the wife of a local politician and who was clearly going to do the official opening. Because of the politician's wife (a good publicity catch, thought Freya) there was a small group of photographers at the event too.

A pretty girl at the door handed Freya a glass of the non-alcoholic drink and a small black-and-white striped carrier bag, both of which she accepted before walking over to Ben.

'Hi,' he said. 'I thought you mightn't make it.'

'I accepted the invitation, didn't I?' said Freya. 'I was held up at the shop.' She looked around her. 'Good crowd.'

'Mm.' Ben nodded. 'I think they're happy with the turnout.'

'And the place looks great,' said Freya. 'Really modern but restful.'

The salon, which they'd named *Shiki*, using the Japanese word for the four seasons, was very simply styled with soft white walls and walnut furnishings. Freya could almost feel herself relax on the spot.

'Hello, Freya.' Leah detached herself from the politician's wife and came over to her. 'Glad you could make it.'

'Thanks for asking me,' said Freya. 'I'm very impressed. It looks fantastic.'

'Yes.' Leah nodded. 'We had our plan and we stuck to it. We wanted to give people a feeling of contentment and tranquillity.'

'You've succeeded,' said Freya. 'I'll have to book a treatment as soon as possible.'

'We're already fully booked for next week,' Leah told her. 'Although that's partly because you've got a voucher in your goody-bag and people have been using them like crazy.'

Freya glanced at the black-and-white bag. 'I haven't checked it out yet.'

'Some sample products,' said Leah. 'And the voucher.'

'Thanks.'

'Oh, everybody got one,' said Leah dismissively.

Freya smiled. 'It's a good idea. So is the politician's wife.'

Leah shrugged. 'An election this year – she was only too delighted.'

'I'm glad to see you have your marketing head screwed on,' said Freya.

'Don't be so patronising,' said Leah curtly.

'I'm sorry.' Freya looked surprised. 'I didn't mean to be.'

At that point Juliette, one of Leah's partners, came over to her and told her that they were ready to start the speeches. Leah excused herself and followed Juliette to the top of the room. Freya stayed where she was and listened to the girls extolling the virtues of a healthy lifestyle and taking time out for yourself. They were right, Freya thought as she drained her drink. She felt a million times better since she'd come back from her break at the Sheen Falls. She'd started taking a variety of supplements to help with her menopausal symptoms and so far they seemed to be having some effect. Certainly her energy levels had improved and she wasn't as lethargic and cranky as she'd been before. She was doing further investigation into natural therapies for the menopause and had decided that she should beef up that whole area of *Herbal Matters*, maybe even holding some workshops for women who were concerned with the issue. She was enthusiastic about the prospect.

The politician's wife started to speak, praised the girls for their business skills, wished them every success and then mentioned the tax breaks that were given to start-up ventures courtesy of her husband's political party. The assembled group of people applauded politely when she'd finished and went back to chatting among themselves. Freya wandered around the salon and went into the four different treatment rooms, named *haru*, *natsu*, *aki* and *fuyu* after the seasons. Like the reception area, they were simply but elegantly decorated and Freya knew that this was mainly due to Leah who loved plain lines and hated clutter. She frowned as she looked at Ben and Leah who were standing side by side but talking to other people. Then Ben turned to Leah, said something to her, and walked away.

'Hi,' she said as he joined her. 'Anything the matter?'

'The matter?'

'You and Leah. You looked . . .'

'You know, I didn't realise that she had it in her,' Ben interrupted her.

'What?' asked Freya.

'The desire to do something like this herself. The drive to do it, I guess.'

'You've always underestimated Leah,' Freya told him. 'Always.'

'I know,' he said. 'And even this time when she was telling me about it I probably didn't think they'd succeed. Not like this anyway.'

'They haven't succeeded yet,' said Freya.

'But they will,' Ben said. 'This place is really great. When she told me about it first I suppose I thought of a little suburban salon with pink walls and middle-aged women getting their make-up done.'

'Ben!' Freya laughed. 'That's sexist and misogynistic and just plain ridiculous all in one.'

'I'm stuck in male myth territory as far as beauty salons go,' he admitted. 'Besides, the place she worked, Eden – that was a bit pink and fluffy, wasn't it?'

'I suppose so.' Freya chuckled.

'But this is definitely the sort of place that a bloke could come into and not feel his masculinity being threatened.'

'I'm glad you think so,' said Leah, who had walked over to them. 'Although I'm pretty sure that ninety per cent of our clientèle will be female.'

'But this room,' he nodded toward *fuyu*, 'is quite masculine.'

'If we do get men in we want them to feel comfortable,' said Leah.

'I'd feel comfortable there,' said Ben. 'I really would.'

'I designed it with you in mind.'

Ben looked at her. 'Really?'

'Of course,' she said. 'You were my role model. A man who didn't want to feel overpowered by the scent of candles or oils. Who wanted things clinically clean. Sort of industrialised health.'

Ben laughed. 'Industrialised?'

'Most women like the candles and the oils and the music,' explained Leah. 'But a lot of guys are like you, Ben. They want things sterile and silent.'

'Makes us sound a bit clinical ourselves,' he observed.

'But at least we cater for you.' Leah smiled thinly at him then glanced at her watch and at Freya. 'You and Brian will be joining us for dinner, Freya? It's a private dinner, close friends only, no media or suppliers.'

'We're looking forward to it,' she said.

'Good.'

'Though I'm surprised you didn't stick with the Japanese theme for a restaurant,' added Freya.

'Actually we wanted to,' said Leah, 'but neither of the restaurants we tried could fit us in. So I called Oleg's. They've promised to do tempura for us anyway.'

'And I guess after a few vodkas we won't care what we're eating,' said Ben.

'I won't be lashing back the vodkas tonight,' Leah said coolly. 'Not that I want to dredge up painful memories or anything, but last time I was there I really drank far too much.'

'I'll make sure you stay teetotal,' said Ben.

'Not teetotal,' Leah told him. 'Just not drunk.'

There were twenty-five of them for dinner and Colman had organised a private dining room for them. He'd also (at Ben's request) strung up a banner which said *Congratulations Leah, Juliette &* *Karen* and had ordered in a supply of saki.

'He goes to so much trouble,' Freya murmured to Brian who'd met them at Oleg's.

'He wants to talk to us about opening another restaurant,' Brian told her. 'But we're not sure about that yet.'

'Don't you think it would be equally successful?' asked Freya.

Brian shrugged. 'The trouble with chefs is that they think they can run businesses too. Just because the place is crowded doesn't mean he's making a fortune.'

'Isn't he?' Freya looked worried. 'I was hoping that he was.'

'They're making money,' agreed Brian. 'But I don't want them to bite off more than they can chew.'

'Rather like this piece of fish,' said Freya as she looked at the battered lump on her plate. 'I think it got mixed up with something else!'

Brian laughed and put his arm around her shoulders. He squeezed her gently and hugged her to him and she allowed herself to mould into the contours of his embrace. In the past she would never have allowed him to hug her in public. Now she was happy for him to do so. It was a pity Maude and Sylvia couldn't be here tonight, she thought, as he finally released her and she turned her attention back to her food. Maude would have loved the buzz and she was dying to have a heart-to-heart with Sylvia about the Jeanne and Gary episode. Of course, she reminded herself, neither Maude nor Sylvia could possibly have sat at the same table as Leah. At least not without World War Three breaking out.

She caught the eye of the other girl who was sitting almost directly opposite her.

'Love the ring,' said Leah. 'Meant to say that earlier.'

'Thanks.' Freya glanced proprietorially at it.

'I'm glad for you, Freya,' said Leah.

Freya frowned but Leah's expression was sincere. Freya found it hard to accept that people were happy for her. It was only in the last few weeks – only since her meeting with Maude, in fact – that she was able to believe that other people could be happy for her. She'd always believed that they were lying before, that nobody was actually pleased when good things happened to someone else. She didn't want to blame that feeling on her parents but she knew that it had been fostered by them. Charles had always been so begrudging of the good fortune of others, wanting to know why it was that he hadn't been the recipient of it instead. But you have to make your own luck and good fortune, thought Freya. You have to do it yourself and let other people help you, and you can't expect it to happen from nothing. That was what Charles had expected though. He could never understand why he wasn't promoted at work or why he didn't have the success of less able men, but Freya knew why now. It was because he'd lived in a closed world, shutting people out, jealous of them. Bitter too.

She shivered. She could have been like that. She knew that she often shut people out, and she'd sometimes told herself that her life hadn't been fair. But she hadn't brooded like Charles. She'd come close to it, especially recently, but people had made the difference to her. Maude and Sylvia. And Ben. His ridiculous testosterone-charged fight with Brian. She couldn't help smiling to herself at the thought.

'What?' asked Brian who'd seen the range of emotions run across her face.

'Nothing,' she said.

'What?' he repeated softly.

'I love you,' she told him.

'I love you too,' he replied.

Ben was astonished at the outward change in Freya and Brian's relationship. He'd never seen them so obviously happy with each other before. He'd never known Freya to laugh so much or to make so many jokes. These days when she came into the shop her first words were always cheerful and friendly rather than a comment on their sales figures. The staff had noticed it too. Susie had told him that she wished Freya had got engaged long before now because it would have made her life so much easier.

As for Boring Brian, Ben had never seen him look so relaxed either. He wondered whether it was because Brian had finally told Freya about his stunning daughter or whether he was simply happy to have made his feelings for her public at last. Whatever it was, the guy was a positive ray of sunshine these days.

He pushed his plate of half-eaten food to one side. He wasn't really hungry and he didn't like fish very much anyway. Particularly deep-fried fish so that he didn't know exactly what he was eating.

'What's wrong?' asked Leah.

'Nothing,' he told her.

'Regretting having come?'

'I said I'd come, didn't I?'

'Worried?'

'About what?'

She shrugged.

'I'm not worried,' said Ben. 'I'm glad I came. I want you to be successful.'

'Do you?' she asked.

'Of course.'

'You didn't believe I could do it.'

'Yes, I did.'

'But you didn't trust us to get it right.'

'Of course I did.' He paused for thought. 'I'm just not up to speed with beauty salons. Tell you the truth, Leah, I'm just glad you've done something for yourself.'

'Why?'

He frowned. 'Why not?'

'You always looked down on me, didn't you?'

'No,' he said. 'Why would you think that?'

'Because I wasn't like your sister. Wasn't a go-getting career-woman. Because having a fulfilling relationship was more important to me.'

'That's complete bullshit and you know it,' said Ben. 'Besides,

398

look at my go-getting sister. Totally smoochy with the international banker!'

'But now that I'm a go-getting woman myself, do you find me more interesting?' asked Leah.

'I've always found you interesting,' he said honestly.

'More desirable?'

'I've always found you desirable too.'

'But not desirable enough.'

'Leah . . .'

'Do you trust me?' she asked.

'Trust you?'

'About everything.'

'I guess so.' He looked at her curiously.

'That's good.' She took a sip of her water. 'D'you mind if I make the announcement tonight?'

'You want to make an announcement?' He looked at her aghast. 'A formal announcement?'

'Trust me,' she said.

She stood up. He looked at her. There was no question but that she looked at her absolute loveliest tonight. He was proud and pleased that she'd turned herself into a success. But no, he didn't trust her.

'Ladies and gentlemen,' she said. 'I have an announcement to make this evening. Nothing to do with our wonderful salon either. This time it's personal.' Her hand slid across the table and closed over his. He looked straight ahead as she relaxed her hold and began to speak.

Chapter 35

Orange blossom

A floral oil that has a sweet perfume with warm and rejuvenating results

It was entirely co-incidental that Carey's housewarming party (which she decided after all to have before going to the Dominican Republic) was on the same day as Leah's official opening. She'd finally buckled under the pressure of her team's constant nagging and then panicked because she didn't know what sort of party she should have.

'One with lots of drink,' Gina told her. 'And loads of sausages. That's all you need.'

'I don't know how much drink to get,' Carey wailed. 'And I always burn sausages.'

'Most people will bring their own alcohol,' said Gina. 'But I'll go to the off-licence with you and we can order in a few crates anyway. As for the sausages, girl, don't you ever look at the shelves in the supermarket? You can buy 'em ready-cooked these days.'

Once she got over the initial worry, Carey enjoyed getting things ready. She ordered double the amount of drink that the guy in the off-licence recommended because, she told him, she wasn't dealing with normal people at her party. Everyone she knew had a vast capacity for free booze. Then she went to the supermarket with Gina and loaded her trolley with multiple packets of ready-cooked sausages as well as the vast number of variety party packs that enticed her too.

'I'll see you later tonight,' Gina told her when they'd packed everything into the boot of the Audi. 'And I'm really looking forward to it.'

So was Carey. She'd invited everyone from her team as well as some of her friends from other teams; she'd asked a group of girls from the gym which she sometimes went to and which reminded her, guiltily, that she hadn't been for a workout in ages; and, of course, she'd asked Sylvia and her family too. She'd also asked Maude and Arthur if they wanted to come but Maude had told her not to be stupid – that much and all as though she'd like to think she could hack it with the young free and single set, she really didn't think that the house-warming would be her thing. Arthur's either, she said. Besides which they were going to dinner in Malahide. But she called over in the afternoon with a bottle of champagne and a tray of canapés.

'You didn't go to the trouble of making these for me!' said Carey in surprise as she took the tray.

'Dead right I didn't,' retorted Maude. 'I picked them up from the deli in Swords. What d'you take me for?'

Carey giggled. 'I suppose I had a brief moment of thinking that you were turning into a kids'-book grandmother figure.'

'I've done that,' said Maude spiritedly. 'When Sylvia's were small, I fed them ice cream and jelly and allowed them to run riot in my house while Sylvia tried to keep hers looking nice.'

'I heard you were back to baking scones again,' said Carey. 'That's what made me wonder.'

'One morning,' Maude said. 'Once, that's all, for the fun of it. And who told you anyway?'

'Sylvia, when I rang her up about the party. We were just chatting and she told me that she'd seen you up to your armpits in flour.'

'Not something that's really worthwhile doing now,' said Maude. 'Not with just me and your father. But it was nice to do it again.'

'You hated it, didn't you?'

'Hated it?'

'The domestic stuff.'

'Not really.' Maude shook her head. 'I hated that people expected it of me. Even when I was doing something I enjoyed I resented it. I think I was missing a gene somewhere.'

'Me too,' said Carey. 'I keep thinking that one day the cooking and cleaning thing will come out in me but it hasn't so far.'

Maude laughed. 'Don't be ridiculous,' she said. 'Look at this place. It's like an ad for *House and Home*!'

'Only because I spent yesterday evening tidying up,' Carey informed her. 'You should have seen it before then.'

'It looks great now,' said Maude comfortingly. 'And I'm sure you'll have a lovely time tonight.'

'I hope so,' said Carey. 'I'm looking forward to it.'

'So's Jeanne,' said Maude. 'It'll be the first time she's been out since the episode.'

Carey frowned. 'Has she broken it off with Gary? I haven't been talking to Sylvia about it at all.'

'I think so,' said Maude. 'And the poor little thing is stricken with remorse.'

'Oh, for heaven's sake! It wasn't that bad.' Carey rearranged some glasses on her sideboard. 'There's plenty of kids having an active sex-life at seventeen.'

'Maybe so,' agreed Maude, 'but it depends on the circumstances. And Jeanne – despite the short skirts and the make-up and the rest of it – is still quite innocent.'

Carey didn't want to tell her mother that the sight of Jeanne and Gary stretched out on the rug in her apartment hadn't exactly been innocent but she said nothing.

'I think she feels she can't trust herself right now,' added Maude. 'She blames it all on herself, you know.'

'That's silly.'

'She was the one to take your keys,' Maude reminded her. 'And that implies a degree of planning.'

'Spur-of-the-moment planning,' said Carey.

Maude laughed. 'Poor Jeanne. I know it ended up OK, but Sylvia was frantic.'

'Of course she was,' said Carey. 'To be honest I was pretty frantic myself. Part of me was convinced that Jeanne couldn't possibly have come to any harm but, well, you can never be sure, can you?'

'No.' Maude sighed and picked up the jacket she'd taken off earlier. 'Anyway, I suppose they'll all get over it.'

'I suppose so,' agreed Carey. 'Have a great evening yourself tonight.'

'I will.' Maude kissed her on the cheek. 'You too.'

'Don't worry about me,' said Carey. 'If there's one thing I can do it's party.'

She was a bit worried by nine o'clock though, when the only people to have arrived were Sylvia, John and their family. It was the first time she'd seen her brother-in-law since Sylvia's revelations about his affair. She found it hard to reconcile the man she'd always considered slightly dull with a bloke who'd had an office affair and almost ruined his marriage. He sat beside Sylvia, his arm draped casually across her shoulders, sharing a joke with her. Carey watched her sister laugh with him and lean towards him and she felt a sudden surge of envy that Sylvia had managed to work it all out while she hadn't. She wondered how hard Sylvia had found it. And, fleetingly, how hard it had been for John too. It was the first time she'd seen Jeanne, too, since finding her in the flat with Gary. Her niece looked stunning in a white top and pale pink skin-tight trousers cut low so that they showed off the silver ring in her belly-button but she sat demurely in the corner of the room and sipped Diet 7UP. Donny and Zac immediately laid into the food while Nadia walked around the apartment telling everyone that she really, really loved it and wanted to live somewhere exactly the same when she was older.

'Don't you feel a bit cooped up, though?' asked John. 'I'd miss being able to walk into the garden if I lived in an apartment.'

Carey shook her head and pointed out the window to where the city lights shimmered in the dusk. 'How can I feel cooped up when I can see that?' she demanded. 'Besides, I'm a bloody useless gardener.'

She got up and refreshed their glasses and prayed fervently that some of the others would arrive soon. She didn't want this to be the kind of party where people sat around and had interesting conversations. She wanted everyone to have fun. She sighed with relief as the buzzer went and the CCTV showed that it was Gina, Rachel, Finola and some of the other girls.

'I've died and gone to heaven,' muttered Donny to Zac as they swept into the apartment in a waft of perfume and chatter. 'That one's bloody gorgeous. And I don't care if she is the same age as Carey. Sometimes those older ones can be better, you know.'

Finola, quite unaware of the effect she was having on Carey's nephew, kissed her friend on both cheeks and handed over another bottle of champagne.

'It's fabulous,' she declared as she sashayed across the room to look out the window. 'Absolutely gorgeous, Carey. I hope you're really happy here.'

'I already am.' Carey grinned and introduced the girls to Sylvia and John. Then, much to Donny's disappointment, the male contingent of the team arrived and soon the apartment was full of people who were laughing and joking and wishing Carey well.

'I've just managed to char the ready-cooked sausages,' she muttered to Gina as her friend walked by. 'I'm utterly useless.'

'I wouldn't worry,' Gina told her. 'You know these guys. They'll eat anything.'

And they did. Carey enlisted the help of Donny, Zac and Nadia who circulated round the room with trays of party mix and cocktail sausages and nobody refused anything on the basis that it was too well done.

'Is Peter going to be here?' asked Sylvia as Carey handed her another gin and tonic.

'I invited him,' said Carey, 'so he'd better turn up.'

'Are you seriously dating him?'

Carey made a face. 'We've gone out together, yes.'

'Do you love him?'

'Oh, for heaven's sake, Syl, give me a break. I'm not even divorced yet.'

'But—'

'I'm not going to discuss this with you.' Carey leaned towards the sideboard and grabbed a Smirnoff Ice. 'This is a party not an inquisition. Now go and do party things.'

Sylvia shrugged and moved away from her sister. Carey wandered over to the group of controllers who were arguing about the latest plans to reconfigure the airspace over Dublin. 'Guys, guys!' she admonished. 'Shop talk. When you could be having fun.'

'Sad to say, some of us actually get our kicks talking about this sort of stuff,' said Chris. 'By the way, did you see that they're looking for more people to train as instructors?'

Carey nodded. 'I'm not ready for that yet,' she told him. 'I like what I'm doing too much.'

'Nice to work in Shannon, though,' he mused. 'Get out of the city for a while.'

'I love the city,' Carey said. 'I love the noise and the crowds and the traffic jams . . .'

Chris laughed. 'But the facility in Shannon is great, though.'

'Oh sure.' Carey nodded in agreement. 'But, like I said, not for me. Not yet. Besides . . .' she dug him in the ribs. 'I've just bought this place. I can't start thinking of moving already!'

'Suppose not,' said Chris. 'But you'd make a great instructor, Carey.'

'You think so?' She wrinkled up her brow. 'I doubt that I have the patience.'

'Maybe not a couple of years ago,' agreed Chris. 'But now.'

Carey smiled at him. 'I still doubt it, but thanks for saying so. All the same, it'll be a bit longer before you get rid of me.'

'I'd hate to lose you,' Chris said, 'but I also want you to do well.'

'Thanks.' Carey was touched by his comments.

'Hey, Browne, quit with the deep discussions and come over here,' Finola called. 'We're discussing potential names for my unborn. What d'you think of Roxy?'

It was later in the evening and Carey was feeling pleasantly light-headed when Donny nudged her to say that there was someone at the door and would she let them in. Carey peered at the monitor for a few seconds before realising that it was Peter. She pressed the button to unlock the entrance door.

'Wow!' he said when he stepped inside. 'What a crowd.'

'It's kind of expanded all right,' she agreed. 'At nine o'clock there wasn't a sinner except my sister and her crew, but suddenly there seems to be twice as many people as I expected.'

'Excellent party,' he told her. 'Am I too late for the food?'

'You might have missed the burnt sausages,' she told him, 'but I think there's a few garlic mushrooms still lurking in the kitchen.'

She loaded a selection of food onto his plate and handed him a

405

can of beer. Finola had found her *Beatles No. 1* CD and the entire apartment was heaving to the beat of 'Love Me Do'. Donny and Zac formed a conga line which snaked its way through the kitchen and out again while Carey and Peter squashed themselves against the worktops and promised to join in later. He put his arm round her and led her back into the living room where they stood by the open balcony doors.

'Hope you invited the neighbours,' he observed as 'Yellow Submarine' blared into the darkness.

'Actually yes,' she snuggled against him, suddenly chilled in the cooler night air. 'But very fortunately the apartment below me is still unoccupied.'

'So when the floor collapses under the weight of all these people it won't be a complete disaster,' said Peter.

'You're so comforting.'

She watched the conga line, laughing as Gina fell off her extremely high-heeled shoes and lay panting on the floor. Donny chivalrously gave her a hand up and then blushed furiously as she kissed him on the lips. Just as well Steve isn't here to see that, thought Carey in amusement. He'd think that Gina was getting it on with a sixteen-year-old boy! Especially since Donny had turned into a rather attractive sixteen-year-old boy. Carey hadn't noticed it before because she never considered her nephew as someone who might be attractive to the opposite sex. Jeanne was an extremely pretty girl too. She groaned to herself. It was too, too depressing to think that her nieces and nephews were growing old enough to be attractive while she was still . . . well, still . . .

'You OK?' asked Peter.

She nodded. 'Just thinking stupid things.'

'Like what?'

'Too stupid to mention,' she told him. 'I think I'll get another drink.' She was rummaging in the fridge for a beer when the phone rang. She tucked it under her chin while she popped open the bottle.

'Hi,' said Ben.

'Oh, hello.' She glanced round. Nobody was taking any notice of her. They'd started another conga line.

'I rang to – em – to ask if—'

'Whey-hey-hey-Browne!!!!' Gerry Ferguson waved at her as he conga-ed past.

'What the hell was that?' asked Ben.

'Party,' she said.

'Party?'

'My housewarming,' she told him.

'Oh.'

'I'd have invited you,' she giggled, 'only the last party we were both at ended a bit dismally.'

'This one doesn't sound at all dismal,' said Ben.

'No,' she told him. 'It's good fun actually.'

'Who's there?' he asked.

'Everyone,' she replied.

'Right.'

'Was there a reason you called?' she asked after a moment's silence.

'Oh – yes. Yes. Actually, I rang to say that I got that stuff about the divorce you sent me.' She'd received further papers from the lawyers and had posted them on to him.

'I'm still trying to book a flight,' she told him. 'My travel agent said that if I waited for another week or so they'll have some bargain flights.'

'You're sure you want to go?' he asked.

Her heart lurched. 'What d'you mean?'

'Well, if you don't have the time or anything, I'll still do it.'

'No,' she said. 'That's OK. I'll do it.'

'Right then,' he said. 'That's sorted.'

'Was there anything else?' she asked. 'Anything important?'

'What d'you mean?'

'It's just that you've rung me at,' she glanced at her watch, 'nearly midnight. People don't usually ring other people at nearly midnight to discuss their divorce travel arrangements.'

'I thought it was as good a time as any,' he said. 'Given the kind of hours you work.'

'Oh, right.'

'So, great,' said Ben. 'You're on top of things. Let me know when everything's organised.'

She looked unseeingly into the crowd of people at her party.

They'd all been at her wedding party. They didn't know that they were at her divorce party too.

'Carey?' he said uncertainly. 'Are you still there?'

'Yes.'

'Are you OK?'

'Of course.'

'Well, look, have a fantastic party.'

'Thanks,' she said and ended the call. She walked into the bathroom and locked the door. Her whole body was shaking. She leaned her head against the mirror of her elegant bathroom cabinet.

'Hey, Browne, you in there?'

She turned on the tap and began to splash water onto her face. 'Yes,' she called. 'What's up?'

'Nothing.' It was Finola who was outside. 'I saw you go in there and you looked a bit frazzled.'

'How could you see how I looked?' demanded Carey as she opened the bathroom door. 'You're at a party.'

'Yes, but I'm not drinking.' Finola gazed at her friend. 'Sure everything's all right?'

'Of course it is,' said Carey. 'I just got a bit warm, that's all. I'm ready for action again now.'

Pushing past Finola, she grabbed a bottle of Miller from the sideboard and then joined the dancing throng. After a while Peter joined them too and they were whirling round and round together, breathless and laughing. Then the music slowed and the aching melody of George Harrison's 'Something' meant that people either stopped dancing or joined together as couples. Carey felt Peter's arms tighten around her as he held her close.

When the song ended he held her a little way away from him and looked deep into her eyes. 'I didn't know whether tonight would be a good time,' he said. 'I thought maybe it would be better to wait until we were alone?'

'For what?' she asked.

He released her and quite suddenly everyone was looking at them, aware of a change in the atmosphere between them. Peter put his hand into the pocket of his trousers and pulled out a navy velvet box. Carey's eyes widened as she looked at it.

'But maybe it's a good time to ask,' he said. 'In front of witnesses and everything.'

'Peter . . .'

He opened the box. A large solitaire diamond glittered beneath the dimmed lights.

'I love you, Carey Browne,' said Peter. 'And I want you to be my wife.'

Chapter 36

Palmarosa

A grass oil with a floral fragrance that is very refreshing

In order to get to the Dominican Republic Carey had bought a discounted charter holiday from London which meant that – to get her dinky and probably totally useless divorce – she was going to spend six nights at an all-inclusive resort hotel on the tropical island. Peter hadn't wanted her to go by herself, had begged her to wait until the summer when he could take some time off and go with her, but she'd told him that she wanted to get the divorce now so that she could feel right about wearing his engagement ring on her finger.

She still hadn't got used to the idea of being engaged to Peter. When he'd proposed to her at her housewarming party she'd been shocked. Her first impulse had been to say no, that he was mad, that she was still legally caught up in another relationship and so was he – but his eyes, dark and searing, had looked at her with a mixture of passion and pleading that had totally disarmed her. And so she found herself saying yes and allowing him to slide the ring onto her finger while her friends and family oohed and aahed and finally applauded them warmly.

Later that night when everyone had eventually gone home and while Peter lay in an alcohol-induced sleep on her bed, she asked herself why she'd said yes to him when all night she'd been congratulating herself on being a single woman with her own apartment living her own life. Why had she agreed to change all that simply because he'd taken her completely by surprise in such a public

410

way? She wondered whether she was once again being caught up in the romance of the moment rather than thinking ahead; whether she was being silly and impulsive and walking herself into trouble.

But she couldn't walk herself into any worse trouble than she'd done in New York a few short months ago. And Peter loved her. She knew that he loved her. She knew everything about him. There were no murky girlfriends in his past ready to come out and ruin their lives. Admittedly he still had to finalise his divorce with Sandra, but as far as she could tell it was all perfectly straightforward.

She loved Peter too. When she'd first met him she'd been unable to sleep because she couldn't stop thinking about him. And, though his revelations about his marriage had shocked and hurt her to the core, that didn't mean she'd stopped loving him. She'd told herself that she'd stopped loving him, of course. She'd pushed him out of her mind. But she could let herself love him again. Couldn't she?

And in the end, she thought, what was the point of being a woman out there doing it for yourself if there wasn't someone to share it with?

She sat back in her window seat halfway down the Airbus cabin and looked at her watch. They were still in Irish-controlled airspace. Much of the air traffic over the North Atlantic was handled by Shannon. She wondered who was working high-level traffic today. She didn't know many of them in Shannon – in fact, there was a lot of friendly rivalry between their control centre and Dublin. She closed her eyes. She wasn't going to think about work; she was going to think about her holiday. The divorce part was entirely incidental. A week on her own would be fun. It was probably wrong of her to be looking forward to a week on her own, without any man in tow just after getting engaged, but she was enjoying herself already.

'Juice?' The stewardess leaned across with a tray and Carey took the proffered glass of orange. Then she fixed her earphones in her ears and settled back to watch the romantic comedy movie which was being shown to while away the Atlantic crossing. When it was over she got up from her seat and walked up and down the cabin to stretch her legs. She smiled involuntarily as she remembered her last long-distance flight, the much-delayed return from New York where Ben had complained about deep vein thrombosis before they'd even managed to take off. Was that the last time we really loved each other, she wondered suddenly. Was it the last time that we felt truly close?

She sat back in her seat. At least this time there was no chance of her losing her heart to a fellow-traveller since she was sitting beside two comfortably late-middle-aged women who were travelling together. Staying at the same resort hotel as her too, she discovered. They chatted to her for a while, clucked over the fact that she was travelling on her own, hoped she'd have a really nice holiday. She told them that she hoped she would too. She didn't say anything about her reason for visiting the Dominican Republic. She imagined they'd think she was cracked if she did.

Peter had said that it didn't matter that they had to wait to get married, that he wanted her to wear the ring and that she could move in with him any time she liked. He said that he didn't care whether or not she went to the Dominican Republic. But she knew she had to go. She wanted something, she told him, even if it was a nonsense piece of paper, to tell her that she wasn't married to Ben Russell any longer and that it was OK to be engaged to Peter instead. When she finished speaking he'd shrugged in acquiescence and told her to enjoy herself. And her eyes had filled with unexpected tears so that he'd put his arms round her and hugged her and she'd almost changed her mind about going without him.

But now that she was on her way, Carey confidently expected to enjoy herself. Excluding the day's trip to the court in Santo Domingo to deal with the divorce, she planned to while away the week on the beach doing absolutely nothing. The Palmyra Resort had, according to the brochure, unrivalled access to a wide stretch of white sandy beach ideal for doing absolutely nothing.

She opened her bag and checked, for the tenth time, her folder of the necessary documents which she'd had to bring with her. The marriage certificate, the power-of-attorney, the property settlement and her passport. She'd sent an e-mail to Ben giving him the details of everything she needed from him and telling him that she'd be travelling to the Dominican Republic soon but not giving him the exact date. Ben had then appointed a representative to appear for him in the Dominican Republic court.

Then he'd asked her if it was really worth all the trouble, whether or not they would just be better off waiting for their four years to be up and then getting a proper divorce at home, but she'd explained about her engagement to Peter and her uneasiness at wearing his ring until she was divorced, in some shape or form, from Ben. He'd given her everything she needed. And so, she thought with a sense of relief as she closed her eyes, by next week this chapter in my life will be over.

Freya and Sylvia sat in Bewley's in Grafton Street with two cups of frothy white coffee in front of them.

'She went this morning,' said Sylvia. 'Flight to London first thing and then a flight to the Dominican Republic. I think she's off her rocker.'

'Oh, what's another off-her-rocker-like manoeuvre for either Ben or Carey?' asked Freya. 'Let's face it, everything else they've done has been totally insane.'

'I couldn't believe it when Peter took out the engagement ring at her housewarming,' Sylvia said. 'I was hoping that she'd tell him no, that she needed some time, but she just gasped and put it on her finger straight away and of course everyone thought it was the most romantic thing ever. Including my silly, silly daughter.'

Freya sighed. 'How is Jeanne, by the way?'

'Oh fine,' said Sylvia dismissively. 'Actually quite well now. We've kind of got over the whole thing about asking her where's she's going all the time and that's helped.'

'Not something I'll ever have to worry about,' said Freya.

'No,' agreed Sylvia. 'Are you feeling OK these days?'

'More or less,' Freya told her. 'Coming to terms with it has been difficult, but I'm better in myself and the remedies are certainly helping. I was so cranky and tired all the time and my cycle was all over the place. Now I feel much better.'

'You look wonderful,' said Sylvia. 'How are you about the whole baby issue, though?'

Freya was silent for a moment. 'Still a bit sad,' she said eventually. 'I don't know whether it would ever have been on the agenda for me, Sylvia, but I'm sad that it's not me who decides. At the same time I know I can live with it. And I know Brian can too. That's why learning about Linnet was so important.'

'Will you see her from time to time?'

'Mm.' Freya nodded. 'In her case, though, the very last thing I need to do is get involved with her life or tell her what she should and shouldn't do! Fortunately she's grown up so it doesn't matter.' She sipped her coffee. 'Actually we're going to Amsterdam next month. I'll meet her then. I'm looking forward to it even though part of me is terrified.'

'Terrified?'

'That she won't like me.' She smiled faintly. 'Isn't it silly to be worried about the opinion of someone who'll never really get to know you? But I want her to feel OK about Brian and me.'

'I'm sure she will,' said Sylvia comfortingly. 'And I think you're great.'

Freya laughed. 'Not great,' she said. 'Not great at all. But more comfortable about things lately. Definitely.'

'If only I thought anyone in my family had reached that level of comfort.' Sylvia sighed.

'Perhaps Carey has now,' said Freya.

'Perhaps.' Sylvia dumped extra sugar into her coffee. 'And how about Ben? How does he feel about this half-divorce?'

Freya shrugged. 'He doesn't say anything. He's been caught up in work lately. We had an offer from a US chain to take a stake in Herbal Matters.'

'Really? A good offer?'

'Yes.' Freya nodded. 'He's trying to decide what to do about it.'

'Surely it's as much your decision as his?'

'Of course. But I've said I'll go along with whatever he decides. A while ago it would've mattered to me more. Getting the money from the US crowd would be nice, of course, but it's not really that important to me any longer. Knowing that we have a good business is what counts.'

'And that you're both happy?'

'Absolutely,' said Freya.

Ben looked at the spreadsheet in front of him. There was no question but that the offer from Palmarosa for a stake in the *Herbal Matters* chain was a generous one. He was still astonished that they'd made the offer in the first place but Diane, who'd called him about it, had said that their market research had shown that Ireland would be a good place for their first European foothold. Ben wasn't sure that he wanted to be part of a European assault by Palmarosa but he also knew that they were a good, ethical company and that if he had to sell out to anyone they were one of the best.

The money would be helpful, he thought, but not as critical as it might have been a few years ago. It wasn't as though Freya needed it – Brian was extremely well-off and Freya's own investments had done well. It wasn't as though *he* needed it either. Sure, a lump of cash would mean that he could pay off his mortgage, but it wouldn't change his life. He liked his life the way it was.

He didn't want to go back to his technology-crazed days where you were never 100 per cent sure what you were trying to sell or why. With *Herbal Matters* he knew exactly what he was trying to sell. And he thought it was a worthwhile product, too, unlike some of the so-called new generation stuff he'd done before. The field of natural remedies was as competitive as anything else, but he liked it.

He supposed there were other things he could get involved with if he wanted. The one thing about himself that he was really proud of was that he was flexible. He'd decided that in the last few days. He could roll with the punches, he told himself. He could take whatever it was life threw at him. And he could learn from his mistakes. He sighed as he thought about this. He *hoped*, he said out loud, that he could learn from his mistakes. Which was a slightly different thing.

The monitors above the passengers' heads showed that the journey was nearing its end. The stewardess announced that they were about to begin their final descent and the screens switched to showing their altitude. Carey watched as it decreased, sliding through 3,000 feet, 2,000 feet – from where she visualised the captain establishing them on the localiser – 1,000 feet and then suddenly the runway was beneath them; then came the touch of the tyres on the surface and the roar of the reverse thrust being applied.

Carey followed the rest of the passengers into the small terminal building and drank a bottle of mineral water while they waited for their luggage to arrive. It was nearly half an hour later before she emerged into the soup-warm air to look for the minibus to take her to the resort.

The two older women who'd sat beside her had already found it and waved frantically at her. She clambered on board and sat behind them, wiping the perspiration from her forehead. The rest of their group made it in dribs and drabs and it was another half an hour before they finally set off for the resort. Carey felt her energy begin to flag but she was kept interested by the lushness of the island, the worrying signs of poverty belied by the beaming smiles of the children who waved at the minibus as it drove by.

Nevertheless she was thankful when they finally pulled up outside the hotel, pleasantly surprised to see that it was extremely modern with a large marble foyer, chillingly air conditioned so that everyone shivered as they waited to register. Carey's room was on the first floor and, as she discovered to her delight, had a view over the millpond Caribbean Sea. She leaned over the wooden balcony and looked into the luxuriant green gardens below, crammed with extravagantly coloured flowers and shrubs. It was a pity in some ways, she thought, that she couldn't have waited until Peter could have come with her. She was sure he would have loved it. But if she was having closure, she decided, she was having it now and she wasn't waiting for anyone.

Carey never spent long over her unpacking and she didn't this time either. She pulled clothes out of her case and hung them on the wooden hangers in her wardrobe, stuffed her underwear into one of the drawers and then pulled on her swimsuit, a pair of shorts and a T-shirt and went downstairs.

The foyer opened out on to a wide wooden verandah dotted with tables and chairs which, she decided, was almost directly below her room. From here, a wooden path led to a pool area and then, a couple of yards further, to the sea. Catching her breath in delight, Carey walked on to the finest, whitest sand she'd ever seen. It was as though any holiday brochure she'd ever picked up and sighed over had come to life right here in front of her. A huge palm tree, bent almost sideways, reached across the beach towards the sea, its bark bleached white from the sun. Straw-topped sunshades lined up in neat ranks near the hotel but didn't intrude too far onto the glorious sand. Carey walked over to a sunbed and sat down. Almost immediately a hotel employee arrived with a blue and white striped mattress and a bright yellow towel. This is heaven, thought Carey, as she slid off her sandals and lay beneath the shade. Absolute heaven.

*   *   *

416

It was raining in Dublin. Ben hurried up the driveway of Brian's house and rang the bell. When he stepped inside he shook his head so that the drops of rain spattered on to Brian's dark green wallpaper.

'You're not a bloody dog,' said Brian in amusement. 'I'll get you a towel.'

'It's OK.' Ben slicked back his hair with his hands in a practised gesture. 'Just getting the heavy wet out of it.'

'Right,' said Brian and led him into the living room. 'Want a drink?'

'Yes, please.' Ben closed his eyes. 'I'd really like a whiskey. I'm cold and wet and I had to wait ages for a cab.'

'You need a car,' said Brian.

'Nope.' Ben shook his head in disagreement but this time raindrops didn't spray the room. 'Too much trouble. The van is usually fine but Genny from the Tallaght branch has it tonight because they're doing some work tomorrow . . . you know how it is.'

'I keep telling Freya that as joint Managing Directors of a company being courted by a US multinational, the least you could do is have a Merc between you.'

Ben laughed. 'I did all that,' he said. 'At least, I had the Saab – which was a statement car too. I don't care any more.'

'Does that mean you don't care whether or not you sell?'

'Partly,' he said. 'Thing is, we're both happy doing what we're doing. At least . . .' he looked enquiringly at Brian. 'I think we're happy. Unless Freya's said anything else to you?'

'No,' said Brian. 'Let's face it, Ben, *Herbal Matters* is the biggest thing in her life. I'm not sure she wants to sell either especially since her foray into the menopause stuff. I was looking at the sales figures – they're phenomenal.'

'She's certainly touched a chord,' agreed Ben. 'I was astonished myself. And when we've got something new doing so well it makes it even more difficult to consider selling. It's a lot of money, I realise that. But . . .'

Brian grinned at him. 'Neither of you wants to sell, Ben. You're just going through the motions.'

'I know.' Ben laughed suddenly.

417

'Then stop pretending and have a drink. And let's toast the fact that your business is worth a lot of money anyway.'

Brian poured them drinks and they sat in companionable silence for a while.

'How's the nose, by the way?' asked Brian eventually.

'It took ages before it felt normal,' said Ben ruefully. 'And that was with Freya insisting on me rubbing arnica on it every day! You sure can land a punch.'

'Lucky blow,' said Brian. 'I thought you were going to kill me.'

'I felt like it,' admitted Ben.

'I'm glad you thumped me,' Brian told him. 'You knocked some sense into me. I was devastated about what I'd done to Freya . . . only I didn't know what to do instead.'

'Glad to be of help,' said Ben.

'And how about you?' asked Brian. 'Any sense knocked into you yet?'

'I'm perfectly sensible,' said Ben. 'Despite what you might have heard.'

Brian laughed then looked thoughtfully at Ben. 'Carey went to the Dominican Republic today.'

'Did she?' Ben swirled his whiskey in his glass. 'I knew she was going, of course. I didn't think she'd booked it, though. She said she'd tell me when she did so.'

'I suppose that since she got engaged she wanted to do it all as quickly as possible.'

'Not that it probably makes much difference,' said Ben.

Brian looked at Ben curiously. 'D'you mind?' he asked.

'Mind?'

'Her getting engaged.'

'Of course I don't mind,' said Ben tightly. 'Why should I care what she does?'

'No reason.' Brian shrugged.

'We have to get on with our lives,' said Ben. 'I'm glad for her that she's doing that.'

'Do you ever wonder . . .'

'I've got to go.' Ben stood up abruptly. 'I've things to do.'

'Ben—'

'Thanks for the business meeting.' Ben began punching the

418

number of the taxi company into his phone. 'Even if it was probably the shortest one you've ever had.'

'Not quite,' said Brian.

'Hi,' Ben spoke to the cab firm. 'I'd like to order a taxi.'

'She's gone for a week,' said Brian when Ben had finished speaking.

'Huh?'

'Carey. She's gone for a week's holiday, according to Freya.'

'Freya spends far too much time with Carey's bloody sister,' snapped Ben.

'They like gossiping,' said Brian, 'and Freya normally gossips so little I encourage her!'

'You're as bad,' Ben told him. 'I suppose the bloke went with her?'

'Nope.' Brian shook his head. 'She went on her own, apparently. A whole week without male company. Unless, of course, she finds some guy on the beach.'

'Knowing Carey, that wouldn't entirely surprise me,' said Ben. 'In fact, it wouldn't surprise me at all.'

Chapter 37

Damiana

This oil is spicy and sweet and also has both balancing and uplifting effects

Because she was so used to changing her sleeping patterns Carey had no problem in waking the following morning. She blinked a few times in the filtered sunlight, then got out of her bed and opened the slatted wooden blinds. A very tall, thin man was hosing down the area beside the pool while a number of guests wandered round the flower-filled gardens. Carey watched them for a short time and then listened to the rumbling of her stomach which told her that she was absolutely starving.

Breakfast was served on the verandah downstairs. Mounds of food were laid out so that the guests could help themselves and Carey heaped her plate with mango, papaya and melon as well as more breads than she knew she could eat. But it all looked so enticing she was completely unable to resist. She carried her breakfast to a table at the edge of the verandah which overlooked the glassy sea. A long-legged bird hopped onto the back of the chair opposite her and looked hopefully at her banana bread. She tore off a corner and threw it over the rail. The bird swooped on it, swallowed it in a single gulp and hopped onto the back of the chair again.

'This is my breakfast,' she told him sternly as she tore off another piece of bread. 'I wasn't planning on sharing it.'

But the bird ate most of the bread while she gorged herself on the sweet fruit and then drank hot milky coffee.

'Hello again.' One of the two middle-aged ladies pulled out the

420

chair and the bird flew away. 'Mind if we join you since you're all on your own?'

Carey shrugged. She hated the way people automatically assumed that a person travelling on their own was gasping for the company of others. It never seemed to occur to them that someone might be alone because they preferred it that way. She'd gone on plenty of holidays by herself in the past and it never bothered her.

'I was just saying to Rita that you're far too attractive to be by yourself,' said the woman easily. They'd introduced themselves on the plane – Carey remembered that Rita was the older of the two friends. Rita was widowed. The woman sitting opposite her – Carey struggled to remember her name – was married with four grown-up children. She was in her late fifties, Carey guessed.

'Nice spot, Jess.' Rita plonked her tray on the table. 'And how are you this morning?' She beamed at Carey.

'I'm fine,' said Carey. 'It's a lovely place, isn't it?'

'My son was here last year with his wife,' said Jess. 'He recommended it.'

'I'm not surprised.'

'So what have you got planned for the day?' Rita began to attack the bacon and eggs in front of her.

'Nothing,' said Carey. 'I'm going to lie on the beach.'

'You can't spend the whole holiday lying on the beach,' protested Jess. 'There's tours, you know. We checked them out this morning. Different ones to different parts of the island. You have to do a tour.'

'I don't think so.' Carey shook her head. 'I'll just concentrate on my tan. Maybe do a bit of windsurfing.'

'Tomorrow's tour is to the waterfall. You really should do that.' Jess's voice was firm. 'It's the one from *Jurassic Park*.'

'Really?'

'Yes,' said Rita. 'And you have to access it by jeep. If you don't do any of the others you should do that.'

'Perhaps,' said Carey non-committally.

'You have to sign up before two o'clock,' said Jess.

'I'll go after breakfast.' Carey knew when she was defeated. If she didn't go on the tour she'd be pestered by the women all week. Easier to give in early on and then tell them that she'd had enough. She got up from the table and said she'd see them later. She passed the tour noticeboard on her way back to the room and stuck her name down. What the hell, she thought. One day in a bus mightn't be too bad.

However, being on the beach was absolute bliss. She lay on her blue and white sunbed and opened her book but the psychological thriller set in the grey streets of Edinburgh couldn't compete with the sparkling sea and the multicoloured sails of the windsurfers skimming across its surface. Carey put the book to one side and walked to the edge of the water where a blond-haired guy was helping the windsurfers get started.

'Want a go?' he asked. 'You resident?'

She nodded, trying to place his accent.

'Get a life-jacket,' he told her. 'Over by the hut.'

She walked to the wooden hut and selected an orange life jacket which she slid over her swimsuit.

'Ever done this before?' he asked.

'A few times,' she said. 'But not recently.'

'Off you go.' He selected a board for her and led her into waist-high water. She clambered onto the board and struggled to get control of the sail. Almost immediately she toppled off and splashed into the lukewarm sea. She surfaced, spitting water and laughing. The blond-haired man grinned too.

'Try again?' he suggested.

This time she managed to stay on for ten seconds before falling off again. The next time she wobbled for slightly longer.

'You're nearly there,' he assured her.

And then she got the hang of it, the yellow and pink sail filling with the breeze so that the board shot across the water while she gripped it with her toes and wrestled with the sail to try and keep on an even line.

'Excellent,' he said when she returned. 'Did you enjoy it?'

'Oh yes,' she panted. 'It was great.'

'You going to do any other watersports here?' he asked. 'Scuba, snorkelling?'

'I might snorkel,' said Carey.

'You can get equipment from the hut for that too,' he said. He extended his hand. 'My name's Janni. I run the watersports. I'm from Iceland.'

'Iceland!' She stared at him. 'You're a bit far from home.'

'D'you blame me?' He grinned and his blue eyes sparkled. 'There's a beauty about Iceland for sure, but it's a lot colder than the Dominican Republic. And it's not very good for snorkelling.'

Carey laughed.

'I live here,' he explained. 'At the hotel.'

'All year round?'

He nodded.

'Great life,' said Carey.

'Absolutely,' said Janni.

'Thanks for the windsurfing,' she told him. 'Now I'm going to exercise my sleep muscles.'

'OK,' said Janni. 'See you later.'

She walked back to the sunbed and lay down. She was tired from her exertions but it was a physical tiredness, quite unlike the mental exhaustion she sometimes felt. She closed her eyes and fell asleep.

She woke up to the ice-cold drops of water on her stomach. Her eyes snapped open and she sat up. Janni was standing beside her, a glass of lemon in his hand. It was the condensation from the glass that he had allowed to drip onto her.

'I'm on my break,' he said. 'Thought you might like something to drink.'

'Thanks.' She took the glass. 'But I was perfectly happy asleep.'

'You looked perfectly happy,' he said. 'And I didn't really mean to wake you.'

She laughed. 'You think that ice-cold water wouldn't wake me?'

He laughed too. 'I wasn't sure. You looked totally flaked out.' He sat on the sand beside her and stared out at the sea. 'You should do the snorkelling this afternoon,' he told her. 'You don't have to go far.' He nodded at the wooden jetty. 'Right there you see all sorts of fish. Parrot fish. Lovely colours.'

'Maybe,' said Carey.

'If you want to dive you can go with a group,' he said. 'I work with a local guy. He takes some people, I take others. We're both qualified dive masters.'

'I haven't done scuba before,' said Carey. 'If I do anything I'll stick to the snorkelling.'

'Whatever you like,' said Janni. He smiled at her then glanced back at his patch on the beach. A group of people were gathered around the boards. 'I'd better get back.' He drained the can of Coke he'd been drinking. 'See you later.'

'See you,' she said. She watched him as he walked along the beach. Sexy and attractive, she thought. And trying to hit on her too. She smiled to herself. Haven't lost it. Good to know.

She managed to avoid Rita and Jess at dinner that evening, choosing a table in the corner of the restaurant and propping her book in front of her, but they were waiting for her the next morning when the rather dilapidated tour bus arrived to pick them up.

'It's a three-hour drive,' wailed Jess as they got on. 'I didn't realise it would take so long.'

'Oh well.' Carey was already drinking more water. 'It had better be worth it.'

It almost was, she thought later as she walked along a rope bridge which crossed the canyon near the waterfall, although she was being eaten alive by mosquitoes. She held on to the rope with one hand while the bridge swayed precariously as she slapped at the insects.

'Didn't you spray yourself?' asked Rita as she strode past.

'Yes,' said Carey. 'Even so, mosquitoes always seem to regard me as a kind of mobile buffet. Shit!' She squirmed as she felt another one bite her. 'I'm going to look diseased by tomorrow.'

But the waterfall was beautiful and the icy pool beneath was perfect for cooling down. After spending ten minutes in its freezing depths Carey sat on a boulder in the sun while some of the others jumped from the rocks that surrounded it.

'So why are you here on your own?' Jess plonked herself beside Carey and almost tipped her into the pool again.

'Travelling,' said Carey laconically.

'I saw that windsurfer guy with his eye on you yesterday,' said Jess. 'You want to watch yourself, young lady.'

'I'm engaged,' said Carey. 'He's wasting his time.'

Jess glanced down at Carey's left hand.

'My ring's in the hotel safe,' Carey told her. 'I hate wearing jewellery in the heat. But I'll put it on tonight to prove it to you.'

'And your fiancé doesn't mind you being here?'

'No,' said Carey.

'It was different in my day,' Jess told her.

The guide interrupted them and told them that it was time to leave. Carey pulled on her shorts and desert boots, tied back her curly hair and wiped the perspiration from her prescription sunglasses. She wasn't looking forward to three more hours on the bus – the journey out had been over some of the worst roads she'd ever encountered.

It was nearly ten o'clock in the evening before they got back owing to the bus breaking down halfway through the journey. When they finally made it into the hotel bar they toasted their survival with huge glasses of rum and very little juice. Jess clucked at the bumps that were appearing on Carey's arms and legs from the mosquitoes and insisted on giving her a bottle of calamine lotion which she'd brought with her.

'It might be old fashioned but it does the trick,' she told her.

When Jess had gone, Carey sat on the edge of her bed and dabbed herself with the lotion until she was covered in little white blobs. If Peter could see me now he'd call the whole thing off, she decided as she crawled beneath the cotton sheet. And I wouldn't blame him at all.

Jess and Rita had signed up for another tour the next day but Carey told them firmly that she was going to the beach and she wasn't budging. And that she wasn't fit to be seen in public anyway given that her body was still covered in bites.

She parked herself on the sunbed and watched as Janni helped another batch of windsurfers to skim across the tiny bay. What a job, she thought. What a life. Nothing more demanding to worry about than getting all the boards back at the end of the day. No juggling with delayed flights or cranky captains or erratic hours – just get up when the sun comes up and go to bed when it sets.

She sighed. It was all very well to dream of a lifestyle like it but she wasn't quite sure that she could manage to live it. After all, she told herself sternly, she'd been on the island for two days and she still hadn't seen a shoe shop yet. How could she live in a place without multiple shoe shops?

She told this to Janni when he came and sat beside her later that morning. He laughed, his tanned face crinkling around his blue eyes.

425

'Why would you need shoes?' he asked, his voice full of amusement. 'You'd spend your life on the beach. You can't wear high heels on the beach.'

'Good point,' she told him and helped herself to a tequila sunrise from the tray which one of the waiters was carrying.

In the afternoon she went snorkelling. Although Janni had told her how beautiful the fish were, she hadn't anticipated the vividness of their colours or their activity in the water. She followed a shoal of parrot fish and then a black fish with an electric blue stripe and she almost swallowed half the Caribbean Sea when she was startled by a huge turtle floating serenely past.

'Utterly wonderful,' she told Janni afterwards as they walked along the beach, masks in their hands. 'I never knew there was such a fantastic world down there. I mean, you see it on the TV but it doesn't do it justice at all!'

'Glad you liked it.' He grinned at her.

'I did,' she said.

'So have I persuaded you to stay?' he asked.

She laughed. 'It's not me,' she told him. 'It's great, Janni, really great. But it's not real life.'

'It is for me,' he said simply. 'Real life is whatever you want it to be.'

'Perhaps.' She sighed deeply.

'Why are you here?' he asked.

She bit her lip and took off her sunglasses, perching them on top of her twist of curls. 'You really want to know?'

'Yes.' He nodded. 'We often see girls on their own on the island. But they're backpackers. You're not.'

'I'm not a backpacker,' she admitted. 'I could never be a backpacker.' She grinned. 'I wouldn't be able to fit the shoes into my rucksack, for starters!'

'Tragic,' agreed Janni.

'When I was a kid I went on a camping holiday with my parents.' She shuddered. 'It was awful. I like my comforts.'

'Which is why you've come to a safe resort hotel,' said Janni.

'Partly,' she said. 'Though safe wasn't the word I was thinking of yesterday on that damn bus journey. There were moments when my whole life flashed in front of me.'

426

'So you're really just here for the sun and the sand?' asked Janni.

'And the divorce,' said Carey.

'Divorce?'

She shrugged. 'I married in haste and repented at leisure as the saying goes,' she told him. 'Or actually I married in haste and repented almost as quickly. But now we've both found other people and we want to get a divorce. So I came here.'

'I'm sorry,' he said. 'I didn't realise.'

'It's no big deal,' she said dismissively. 'I'm going to Santo Domingo on Thursday and hopefully it'll be all sorted out by then.'

'And you'll come back and celebrate on your own?'

'Yes,' she said.

'When you say that there's someone else – you mean there really is another person?'

'Yes,' she said again.

'But you might be interested in a little holiday fling?'

'I like you, Janni,' she told him. 'But no holiday fling.'

'A holiday kiss?' he suggested.

'Janni!'

'Oh, OK.' He made a face at her. 'You can't blame a man for asking.'

'I can,' she said sternly. 'You shouldn't try to seduce every single woman you find on the beach.'

'I don't find enough of them,' said Janni sadly.

'We saw you with that young man on the beach again,' said Rita after dinner that night. 'Nice young man he is, too.'

'Maybe,' said Carey. 'But as I told you already, I'm engaged to someone else.'

'But we wouldn't recommend him,' Jess said as though Carey hadn't spoken. 'Not your type.'

Carey giggled. 'I have a type?'

'Oh yes,' said Rita. 'Someone with more ambition than him.'

'But he's happy,' said Carey. 'Which is all that matters.'

'Hmm.' Both Jess and Rita looked doubtful.

By Wednesday evening Carey's skin had turned a light nutmeg

427

brown and her mosquito bites had faded. She walked down to the water's edge and stood gazing out over the sea, watching the sun slide slowly towards the horizon and allowing the tiny waves to break over her feet in a stream of silver-pink bubbles. Tomorrow, she told herself. Tomorrow was the day when it would all be neatly packaged up and be behind her at last. She'd tried very hard not to think about Ben and the marriage that had hardly been a marriage at all. She didn't want to go over it all in her head again because that was giving it time and energy that it didn't deserve. But on the island there was so much time to think. Today, when she'd gone on her morning snorkelling trip, she'd remembered her first meeting with him and the mad whirl of their week together in the States, and she'd wondered if it would have been different if she'd met him here, on holiday in the sun. Had it just been the frantic buzz of New York and Vegas that had propelled them along? If they'd been in a laid-back spot like this, would they have taken their time about it? Would it have been different?

Hardly different. She picked up a flat stone and skimmed it over the smooth surface of the sea. Because Leah would still have been there when they got back. Ben would probably still have been able to forget about her in the sun but he couldn't forget about her at home. Leah wouldn't let him forget. Besides, it wasn't only Leah. It was the other women too. The ones he went to and came back from. The group of which she had become a part.

It wasn't Ben's fault that he'd turned out to be a different person from the one she'd expected. It wasn't his fault that he'd brought enough baggage to their relationship to fill an airline terminal. It wasn't his fault that their promises of for ever had actually meant for a few days instead. But it was sad all the same.

She pushed her fingers through her tangle of hair. Would for ever be for ever with Peter? He must have thought Sandra was for ever but it had gone wrong. She breathed deeply. What if it went wrong with her too? What if she was just leaping out of the frying pan and into the fire by getting this divorce and wearing Peter's ring? It doesn't matter, she told herself fiercely as she tightened her lime-green sarong around her waist. It doesn't matter because the divorce is for you, not for Peter. And you can stay engaged as long as you like.

She rubbed at her eyes. Just now, at that very moment, she wished that she wasn't on her own. She wished that there was someone she could turn to, someone she could talk to, say that she hadn't meant to make a mess of things and that she didn't want to make a further mess of things. And that she really only wanted to do what was right.

She'd never had a confidante, someone with whom she could share everything. The girls in ATC were friends but they were colleagues too, and there was always something competitive between them, enough to stop her pouring her heart out and letting them know how badly she felt about anything. You had to be assured in ATC. You couldn't let things get you down. And you couldn't let other people see that you were down either.

The nearest she'd ever got to sharing confidences, oddly enough, had been with Ben. The first night they'd spent together they'd talked about everything, and she'd felt connected to him in a way that she hadn't ever experienced before. And maybe it was that which had tricked her into thinking that she loved him – the opportunity to talk about herself to someone who knew nothing about her already.

You're being maudlin, she told herself, as half of the sun disappeared below the horizon. And you need to snap out of it. Go back to the room, have a shower and get dressed for dinner. And mix with people tonight. Wear a dress that shows off your tan and have a bit of fun. The trailer-trash dress would have been good, she thought wryly. She could have given it a third outing and justified its existence. Then she scrunched up her nose. No, she couldn't have worn the trailer-trash dress. Didn't have the right shoes for it with her.

The sun had almost completely disappeared. It was time to get back to the hotel before darkness fell and the mosquitoes made their night-time appearance. Rita had told her about sandflies that came out at night too. She turned around and walked back towards her sunbed to collect her book and her beachbag.

She stopped short of the sunbed and peered short-sightedly at it. Her vision wasn't that bad without her glasses but she was sure that someone had messed with her stuff. She'd left her bag on the bed itself, not on the sand beside it. Surely nobody had tried to rob her! Carey gritted her teeth because her passport was in the bag and she needed it for her court appearance in the morning.

429

She moved closer to the bed, her heart beating a little faster. And then she stood rooted to the spot. She looked around again but she was alone on the beach. She breathed out very slowly and very silently. In the middle of the sunbed, on her book, was a pair of shoes. Fragile shoes. High, high heels with Perspex uppers and tiny white ribbons. Shoes that she'd last seen in Ben's house. Shoes that she'd left behind. Shoes that she hadn't expected to see again. They were perched neatly on the book, side by side.

They're not really there, she told herself. It's because you were thinking about them. Thinking about *him*. Remembering everything. They're not really there and seeing them is just a manifestation of the stress of the past few months. It's been a stressful time.

She reached out. They seemed real enough. The heel of the right shoe had a slight scuff-mark on it from the first time she'd worn them. She swallowed hard and looked around her again. It was dark now and the black sky glittered with the light of the stars. I'm not crazy she told herself. I'm absolutely not.

She picked up her bag and her book. They were definitely real. She touched the shoes again. How had they got here, she wondered. It would have been difficult to leave them without being seen. And she hadn't seen anyone. Suddenly scared, she picked them up and ran at full tilt along the wooden pathway, through the marble foyer and up the stairs to her room. Her hand was shaking as she put the key in the lock. She switched on the light before stepping inside, afraid of what might be there.

But the room was empty. Exactly as she'd left it. She dropped the shoes, bag and book on her bed then squeezed her eyes closed. 'They'll be gone when I open my eyes,' she said out loud. She kept them shut for almost a minute. But the shoes were still there when she opened them again.

Every other evening she'd left her balcony doors open but now she closed them firmly, sliding the lock into place. She checked the door to her room too and slid the chain across. Then she got into the shower and turned it on full.

Perhaps, she thought as she lathered shampoo into her hair, perhaps I brought them myself. It might be true. Maybe I didn't leave them in Ben's at all but brought them with me. And I've been in denial about it the whole time. Maybe the shoes are a symbol of everything that was wrong with my life. And maybe I brought them here to lose that symbol. She grimaced as soap got into her eyes. It wasn't very likely but she simply couldn't think of any other explanation.

Unless Ben had sent them. She stood under the huge chrome shower head and thought that she'd hit upon a possible answer. Knowing that she'd come here – even though she hadn't told him exactly when she was coming or where she was staying he must have found out from someone – Ben had sent the shoes as a symbol himself. That made sense. Ben probably expected her to throw the shoes into the sea or bury them beneath the white sand or something equally symbolic. Part of his health-freaky kind of stuff, she supposed.

Turning off the water, she reached for her towel. She just hoped that the shoes would still be on the bed when she got out of the shower, otherwise she'd know that she was having some sort of breakdown. And she really couldn't afford a breakdown so far away from home.

The shoes were still there. She sat in front of her mirror and applied her dusting of make-up. Then she opened the wardrobe (a little nervously in case someone was lurking inside) and took out her deep purple dress. She slipped it on, then threaded her long silver earrings into her ears and slicked some lip gloss over her lips. She shook her head so that her curls, almost black because they were still damp, flicked around her face.

Looking good, she said. Looking – well, not certifiable anyway.

The shoes were on her bed where she'd left them. She picked them up and slid her feet into them. Definitely her shoes. They fitted perfectly.

The bar was crowded with people. Jess and Rita waved to her and clucked with appreciation at her appearance.

'Thought you only had shorts and jeans with you,' said Jess. 'Nice to see there's more to you.'

'Thanks – I think.' Carey looked warily round the room.

'Are you all right?' asked Rita.

'Fine,' said Carey.

'Your young man isn't here,' said Jess.

'My young man?' Carey grabbed a margarita from a passing waiter and gulped half of it.

'Surfer Boy.'

'He's not my young man,' said Carey. 'Really he's not. I keep telling you, I'm engaged.' But she realised that she'd forgotten to take her ring out of the safe.

'I thought you'd dressed up for him,' said Rita.

'I didn't dress up for anybody,' said Carey.

'Well, you look very nice all the same,' said Jess. 'You really do. Are you going to join us for dinner tonight?'

She wanted to say no but she said yes. Quite suddenly she was afraid of being on her own, afraid of the tricks her mind might play. She nodded and smiled throughout the meal and washed her food down with more margaritas.

'I think I'll get some fresh air,' she said after dinner while Rita and Jess were having coffee. 'It's very warm in here tonight.'

She walked out of the restaurant, along the verandah and down towards the pool. The outside bar was still open and half a dozen people were sitting on the high stools beside it. Carey didn't feel too bad once there were people nearby. But she needed time on her own again. The margaritas were making her head buzz.

She stumbled as she reached the far end of the pool, falling off her Perspex shoes and landing in an undignified heap in the springy green grass.

'That's what happens when you wear car-to-bar shoes.'

His voice was so clear it was as though he was standing beside her. Carey wondered how badly insane she'd suddenly become. She'd thought that people lost their minds gradually but that hadn't happened with her. She'd been fine when she got out of bed this morning. Now she was losing her marbles completely.

'D'you want a hand up?'

She looked around. He was standing there. Definitely. Not her imagination. Surely not her imagination. He held out his hand to her. She reached out and touched his fingers. They were warm.

'OK,' she said, pleased to discover that though she was trembling inside her voice was steady. 'I don't know whether you're real or not but if you can get me on my feet again I'll be very happy.'

'Of course I'm real,' said Ben. 'Why wouldn't I be real?'

432

Carey brushed her dress with her hands. 'Because you're not meant to be here,' she said calmly.

'I know,' he said. 'But I came anyway.'

She stared at him. 'I don't want you to take this the wrong way or anything,' she said, 'but I've had a few drinks tonight. Because I got a fright earlier. Shoes that I didn't know still existed suddenly materialised on my sunbed. And it scared the hell out of me.'

'It wasn't meant to scare the hell out of you,' said Ben.

'What was it meant to do then?' she demanded.

'I thought it would be kind of symbolic,' he said.

'You see, I *knew* it was symbolic.' She looked at him in relief. 'I just wasn't certain exactly what kind of symbol they were.'

'Neither was I,' said Ben. 'I wanted you to see them and . . .'

'. . . and think I was losing my mind so causing me to knock back far too much drink at dinner.'

'Are you actually pissed?'

'A bit,' she said.

'I'm sorry about the shoe thing,' he said contritely. 'I wanted you to realise I was here.'

'Of course I didn't realise you were here!' she snapped. 'I thought I'd gone bonkers.'

'Sorry,' said Ben again.

'Yes, well!' Her voice was even firmer now. 'Ben, why on earth did you come? Don't you trust me to do this on my own?'

'Of course I trust you to do it on your own,' he said. 'You've done pretty well on your own, haven't you?'

'What d'you mean?'

'Since leaving me you've bought your apartment and regained a lover – as I said, you've done pretty well.'

'So have you,' said Carey. 'Just before I left, Sylvia told me that some American company had made an offer for a share in Herbal Matters. And that you had the chance of becoming really rich.'

'Sylvia said that?'

Carey nodded then laughed shortly. 'Since she's become bosom buddies with Freya – not that I approve of the friendship, the pair of them have turned into conspiratorial gossipers as far as I can see – she's tried to impress upon me that you're not a complete madman.'

433

'Nice of her. But actually we turned down the offer for Herbal Matters. Becoming really rich isn't the most important thing in my life. So maybe she'll think I'm a complete madman after all.'

'Why are you here?' asked Carey again. 'Do you want to come to court in Santo Domingo with me?'

'No,' said Ben.

'What then?'

'Would you like to walk on the beach?' he asked abruptly.

She looked at him disparagingly. 'No, I bloody wouldn't. I can't walk in these damn shoes and there are biting sandflies on the beach.'

'I thought it would be a nice setting,' said Ben.

'Looks can be deceiving,' said Carey.

'Let's sit here then.' He perched on the edge of one of the sunbeds which were neatly arranged around the pool.

'OK.' She sat beside him.

'Oh hell, Carey, this isn't the way I imagined it!' cried Ben after a moment's silence. 'This isn't the effect I was hoping to achieve.'

'What effect was that?' she asked.

'I don't know,' said Ben irritably. 'Romantic, I suppose.'

'Romantic?'

'Yes!' His tone was defiant.

'Why did you want romantic?'

'Because . . .' He sighed deeply. 'Because I wanted to ask you not to go through with the divorce.'

The silence between them was broken by a belly-laugh from the bar on the opposite side of the pool.

'Someone obviously thinks it's funny,' he muttered grimly.

'Ben . . .' Carey pressed her fingers to her temples. 'Ben, am I hearing you right? You don't want me to do the dinky divorce. Why not? I thought you believed it was a good idea.'

'Because I don't want to divorce you,' he said. 'And I don't want you to divorce me.'

'Why?' she asked again.

'Don't be obtuse,' he said. 'I still love you, of course.'

She slid her fingers from her temples to her cheeks and looked at him. 'It's a bit late to decide that, isn't it?'

'Is it?' He caught her hands in his and drew them away from her face. 'We're still married, aren't we?'

'Our marriage was a three-week disaster,' she said.

'It didn't have to be.'

'You kissed your girlfriend at our wedding party.'

'You kissed your boyfriend.'

'Your mates all think you're a serial womaniser.'

'Do they?' He looked at her in astonishment. 'Who says so?'

'Some blokes called Mick and Dick or something,' she said. 'I heard them. The night of the bloody party. Dissecting your reasons for marrying me.'

'You're joking.'

'I never joke about serial womanisers,' she said. 'It wasn't very flattering. They talked about the women you'd had in the past and the way you treated them.'

'Is that why . . . ?'

'No,' she said. 'The why was that you were still in love with Leah.'

'I wasn't,' he said.

'You were. You probably still are. And even if you're not,' added Carey, 'she's demented enough to still want you.'

'I shouldn't have married you in Las Vegas,' said Ben. 'I should have waited till we came home and sorted out my life and given it a proper chance.'

'Gee, thanks.'

'I wanted to marry you straight away because I couldn't bear the thought of not being with you for ever. But I hadn't thought about how things would be when we got home.'

'Clearly not. But,' she added, 'neither had I.'

'The Leah thing . . .' He sighed. 'I didn't know how to deal with her. I wanted to do the right thing. I loved her once and I . . . I shouldn't be saying this really, should I?'

'Go on,' said Carey grimly.

'Everything was so different when we got back. Leah and Freya were friends. I didn't want to hurt Leah but I realised that I'd already hurt her a lot. She totally freaked out when I told her about us.'

'I don't blame her,' said Carey spiritedly. 'You'd slept with her the night before you went to the States.'

'I know,' said Ben miserably. 'It was the first time in ages. I wish

435

I hadn't. I'm sorry. I didn't realise, of course, that I was going to meet you.'

'And I'm supposed to say that it didn't matter?'

'No,' he said. 'But at the party, when your boyfriend arrived, I thought that maybe you believed that we'd made a mistake. You weren't going to tell me about him.'

'I know,' she said uncomfortably.

'And Leah was there being, well, Leah and making me think that maybe I'd got it all wrong with you in the first place.'

'Crap,' said Carey.

'No,' said Ben.

'It *only* went wrong at the wedding party because you snogged her,' said Carey. 'After all, Peter and me was a completely different situation which I could've explained to you. I wouldn't even have been outside if it wasn't for the way she'd spoken to me earlier, telling me that you and she had slept together, making it seem as though . . .' Her voice faltered but she continued, 'And those friends of yours – they were talking about how you always went back to her. I knew it was all wrong. But I was prepared to give it a shot. I wanted to talk. You wouldn't.'

'I hadn't a clue what to say,' Ben told her. 'I knew I'd behaved really badly with Leah but I was furious with you too. I thought that I should be a bit aloof. Set out parameters.'

'Oh, for God's sake! What the hell kind of books do you read?' demanded Carey. 'Don't you bloody know that when you have a row with your wife or your girlfriend, you don't go round setting parameters, you buy them large bunches of flowers and you kiss and make up? What you *don't* do is be nice to the old girlfriend who caused the row in the first place.'

Ben smiled shakily.

'And so what about the drama queen now?' she asked. 'The entrepreneurial drama queen in whose business you have a stake? Who keeps warning me off?'

'When did she warn you off?' Ben looked surprised.

'It doesn't matter,' said Carey. 'But it's etched on my brain.'

'This is the difficult bit,' said Ben, 'because I really, really don't want you to think that I'm here on account of a row with Leah – but we split up.'

436

'When?' asked Carey waspishly. 'Yesterday?'

'No,' said Ben. 'I suppose we broke up officially the day she opened her salon.'

He frowned as he remembered. She'd stood up to make her announcement and he'd held his breath because he hadn't a clue what she was going to say. She squeezed his hand and looked at the assembled group of people and she told them how grateful she was to Ben Russell for having faith in her and for lending her some of the money she'd needed to invest in the salon. And she hoped that it would be hugely successful so that she could repay him. He'd shrugged at that and had muttered that it didn't matter, that he was happy to invest in such a great venture and he was sure that it would be tremendously successful.

Then Leah had smiled and said that she was sure it would be too and that it was Ben himself who had been the motivation behind it. Ben's treatment of her, she said, had given her the strength to become a different person.

'Finally,' she'd said, 'I'd like you all to know that I have given up on Ben Russell as a prospective husband. Not because he already has a wife, although that's another one of his relationships on the rocks even though he probably still loves her – which he won't bloody admit to himself. Nor, more shockingly, because she's probably mad enough to still want him but because, despite lending me the money, I think that he's a complete shit and I've no idea why on earth I wasted so much of my life on him.'

There was a murmur round the table. Freya made as though to stand up but Brian's hand restrained her.

'We made this decision some time ago,' said Leah, 'though we agreed not to talk about it until after today. I wanted Ben to come along to our opening because he's an investor in our company and I need to thank him for that, no matter how else I feel. But now I want to make our personal split public, so that I can't go back. I'm asking for you all to join me in a toast. To the success of *Shiki* and to my own success. I'm glad that I have something else to be the focus of my attention.'

The chuckle from the women round the table was embarrassed but they raised their glasses anyway while Ben sat in his seat and didn't move a muscle. He could feel Freya's eyes on him but he didn't look round.

437

When Leah sat down again she turned to him and smiled. 'I realise that was petty and childish – but now you know how I felt when you came back from America with a wife. And that's why I did it. For revenge. And for closure.'

Ben breathed out slowly as he remembered the evening. It had been hugely humiliating. Freya had been angry on his behalf, had muttered that Leah Ryder was a demented bitch and that Ben wasn't the shit that she made him out to be. But he'd told her that it didn't matter any more and they'd left almost immediately.

'Closure.' Carey echoed the words as Ben finished speaking. 'Seems like we're all looking for it, doesn't it?'

'What sort of closure are you looking for?'

'Getting you out of my life too,' she told him bluntly.

'Great,' said Ben. 'It's good to know I'm such a bastard that two women want to get rid of me.'

'You're not really that bad,' said Carey. 'I always thought Leah was a demented bitch too.'

'That makes me feel a whole lot better,' he said ruefully.

'So you came here hoping for a reconciliation?' asked Carey. 'Thinking that because she dumped you I'd be here, willing and waiting? You must really think I'm pathetic.'

'Of course I don't!' cried Ben. 'And, like I said, she didn't dump me that evening. We'd talked about it before then. She'd asked if she could call around to the house one evening, picked up the keys from Rathmines, met me there. When I got home and saw her it was as though everything had suddenly come back into focus. I hadn't been able to think straight for ages. I knew that it was really and truly over between us. Surprisingly, so did she. And then she gave me a whole bundle of divorce stuff and told me she didn't know whether or not we'd ever do it. Although she did say that nobody could ever go back.'

'Most intelligent thing she's ever said,' remarked Carey. 'People can't go back. Neither can we.'

'I'm not asking us to go back,' said Ben. 'But we could go forward.'

Carey stood up and walked to the edge of the pool. She dangled her bare feet in the lukewarm water.

'I have gone forward,' she said slowly, without looking round. 'I'm engaged to Peter now.'

'I know. But everyone thinks it's on the rebound.'

'Everyone?'

'Your mum, Freya, Sylvia . . .'

'God Almighty.' Carey shook her head. 'They're talking about me?'

'Naturally.' Ben stood beside her. 'They care about you.'

'But Freya's involved too.'

'Well, they're all very friendly. And she feels that our problems are partly her fault because of the party and everything.'

'That's silly,' said Carey.

'I know. But she's changed over the last few months. She's so caught up in her own happiness she wants everyone else to be happy too.'

'And she thinks you and me getting back together would be a good thing?'

Ben nodded. Then he told her that Freya had said that he'd be out of his mind to let Carey get away because she was clearly the woman for him; that she was sorry she hadn't realised it from the start herself; and that Sylvia and Maude also agreed that they were meant for each other and how they all believed that things could work out in the end because they truly thought that Carey loved him too.

'They're all completely insane,' said Carey. 'And so are you.'

'Maybe,' said Ben.

'So our families, who were against the whole thing at the start, now think we're a match made in heaven.'

'Yes.'

'And does my family know about the big break-up between you and Leah? Or did they expect you to sweep me off my feet and then come home and break up with her all over again?'

'Of course they know,' said Ben. 'Naturally Freya told them about my public mortification. Apparently your mother laughed.'

Carey rubbed her shoulders and sat down on one of the granite benches near the pool. 'What a mess.'

'Do you love him?' asked Ben suddenly. 'Peter?'

She hesitated. 'He once broke my heart,' she said. 'Mind you, so did you.'

'And now you're engaged to him,' said Ben. 'Do you really want to marry him?'

439

Carey gazed into the distance. 'He was good to me after I left you. I stayed with him, you know.'

'Did you sleep with him?'

'That's none of your business.'

'I'm sorry.' He sighed. 'This was a mistake, wasn't it?' He looked towards the hotel where a group of people were standing on the verandah, clinking glasses and laughing in celebration of something together. 'I shouldn't have come.'

'Probably not,' she said.

'I know we did it all the wrong way round,' he said urgently. 'Getting married first, not really knowing each other. But I did – *do* love you. What I felt for you was real, unlike anything I ever felt before. I just think we needed time to work at it. I'm sorry I made a complete cock-up of everything, not just tonight.'

She said nothing.

'I'm not a serial womaniser,' he said. 'You asked me that before and I told you I wasn't.'

'I only asked because you said that you were!'

'I'm not,' he repeated. 'But I know I've made mistakes. I'm the kind of bloke that women sit around and complain about. Emotionally stunted. Play football on Saturdays . . .' She laughed shortly. 'I just wanted you to give it one more go. That's why I'm here.'

'Actually you're here because your controlling sister and my manipulative mother and equally manipulative sister coerced you into it. And because you've finally split up with Leah. And you can't face being on your own.'

'That's not true,' he said. 'I'd rather be on my own than get it wrong again. But I don't think being with you would be wrong.'

'Too much unfinished business,' said Carey.

'I know.'

She looked down at the third finger of her left hand, where her engagement ring should have been. She wished she hadn't forgotten to take it out of the safe.

'If you love him then forget I came.' Ben sat beside her. 'I've messed things up too much for both of us. I don't want to mess it up for you any more, Carey. No matter what.'

She gazed at the reflection of the coloured lights in the pool.

'Don't you think we'd just mess it up ourselves anyway?' she asked without looking at him.

'Maybe,' he said. 'But at least we'd have given it a proper try.'

'We thought – you and me – that it must have been just the sex,' she told him.

'It was great sex,' he admitted. 'But you know what, Carey? When you moved out, it was you that I missed.'

'Really?'

'Well, I missed your shoe collection too. That goes without saying.'

Her smile was shaky.

'I missed talking to you,' he went on. 'Being with you. When I met you again – when I saw you in Habitat – I wanted to be with you. I remembered why I fell in love with you in the first place. And when you phoned me about Jeanne and Gary I was pleased that I could help. Pleased that you thought of me.'

'I thought of you because you were the only person I knew who might have his phone number,' said Carey crisply.

'That day,' he said, 'when I got dizzy, when you let me lie down on your sofa . . .'

'Yes?'

'I dreamed we were together again.' He looked at her sheepishly. 'Actually I had a very erotic dream about us being together again but that wasn't the point. When I woke up, when I realised that it was just a dream . . . Carey, I didn't want to leave you. But I didn't know what to say.'

She swallowed hard. 'My place,' she said. 'Brand new. And you live in Portobello.'

'That's not a problem.'

'You'd move across the river?' She laughed shortly.

'Yes,' he said.

'I was hurt,' she told him, her voice finally breaking. 'I thought we had something really good and then it turned into nothing.'

'Oh, Carey.' He put his arm round her. 'It didn't turn into nothing. We lost sight of it, that's all.'

'I don't want to make more mistakes.' She shrugged his arm from her shoulder. 'I should've learned from my mistakes by now.'

441

'I don't want to make mistakes either,' he said. 'We didn't give it a chance and I want to give it a chance. OK, if it still goes wrong it still goes wrong. But I really want to try.' He looked at her and made a face. 'I know that coming here, doing this – well, it was flamboyant and maybe as stupid and crazy as when I first met you. You have that mad effect on me.'

She looked up. 'It's not necessarily a good effect though.'

'It feels good when it's happening!'

She rubbed one of her faded mosquito bites. 'It would be really nice if everything worked out neatly, wouldn't it? If Leah became really successful and you and I got back together again and everyone lived happily ever after. But that doesn't happen, Ben. Not in real life.'

'Why?' he asked.

'Because people change.'

'I know,' he said. 'I've changed. I've changed a lot. That's why I think it will work this time.'

'Clever,' she said admiringly.

'Listen, I haven't been very clever about any of this so far. Allow me a moment!'

'Fair enough.' She laughed.

'I do love you,' he said. 'It was just my timing was wrong.'

'Timing is everything,' she told him as she picked up the Perspex shoes. 'Everyone knows that.'

She walked barefoot into the hotel. People were still gathered in the bar area in small groups, laughing and talking. Rita saw her and waved frantically at her.

'Carey,' she said, as she stared at the man who'd followed her into the hotel. 'Is this your fiancé at last? Has he come to stay?'

'No.' Carey smiled slowly as she turned to Ben. 'No, Rita. This is my husband. This is Ben. And, who knows, if we get it right this time – maybe he has.'

442